LUCA VITIELLO

Cora Reilly

Cover design by Romantic Book Affairs Designs

Book design by Inkstain Design Studio

LUCA VITIELLO

AUTHOR'S NOTE

This is *Bound by Honor* from Luca's point of view. While there are a few new scenes, it mainly reiterates the events from the book. If you want to find out what went on in Luca's head, this is for you!

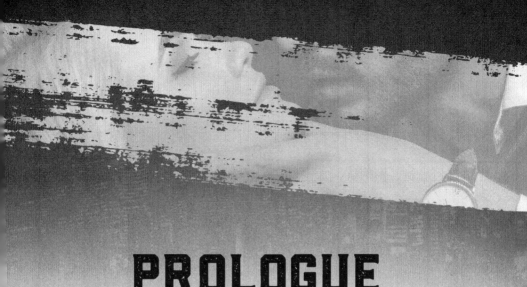

PROLOGUE

I was the boy who killed his first man at eleven.

I was the teenager who crushed his cousin's throat at seventeen.

I was the man who bathed in his enemies' blood without a flicker of remorse, who relished in their screams as if it was a fucking Mozart sonata.

Monsters are created, not born.

Bullshit.

I was born a monster. Cruelty ran in my veins like poison. It ran in the veins of every Vitiello man, passed on from father to son, an endless spiral of monstrosity.

I was a born monster shaped into an even worse monster by my father's blade and fists and harsh words.

I was raised to become Capo, to rule without mercy, to dish out brutality without a second thought.

I was raised to break others.

When Aria was given to me in marriage, everyone waited with baited breath to see how fast I'd break her like my father broke his women. How I'd crush her innocence and kindness with the force of my cruelty, with relentless brutality.

Breaking her would have taken little effort. It came naturally to me.

A man born a monster, raised to be a monster, bound to be a monster to become Capo.

I was gladly the monster everyone feared.

Until her. Until Aria.

With her, I didn't have to cover up my darkness.

Her light shone brighter than my darkness ever could.

With her, I didn't want to be the monster. I wanted to shield her from that part of my nature.

But I was born a monster. Raised to break others.

Not breaking her would come with a price.

A price a monster like myself shouldn't risk paying.

CHAPTER 1

Matteo and I sat at the dining table, our eyes trained on the door, waiting for Mother. The bell for dinner had rung a long time ago.

Our nanny Marianna stood against the wall, glancing toward the clock on the sideboard, then back to us. Father rarely ate with us, but Mother always did—at least dinner, even when she could hardly stand. She was always on time in case Father decided to show up.

Where was she?

Was she sick?

Yesterday she'd looked white, except for the blue and yellow blotches on her face and arms where Father had disciplined her. She often did things wrong. It was difficult not to do wrong with Father. A thing that was okay yesterday could be wrong today. Matteo and I often confused one with the other and got punished as well.

Matteo took his knife and stuck it into the bowl with mashed potato that had stopped steaming before slipping the mash-covered blade into his mouth.

Marianna clucked her tongue. "One day you'll cut yourself."

Matteo shoved the knife back into the mash and licked it off again, his chin jutting out stubbornly. "I won't."

I pushed my chair back and stood. It wasn't permitted to get up before dinner was eaten, but Father wasn't home, so I was the master of the house because Matteo was two years younger than me.

I walked around the table. Marianna made a step in my direction. "Luca, you shouldn't..." She trailed off as she looked at my face.

I looked like Father. That's why she was more scared of me than Matteo. That, and because I was going to be Capo. Soon, I'd be the one to punish everyone for doing wrong things.

She didn't follow me when I walked through the foyer and up the stairs. "Mother? Dinner's ready."

No answer. I stepped onto the landing, then approached Mother's bedroom. The door was ajar. The last time that had happened, I'd found her wailing on her bed, but it was quiet inside. I pushed the door open, swallowing. It was too quiet. Light spilled out of the open bathroom.

Downstairs, I heard Father's voice. He had arrived home from work. He was probably angry that I wasn't sitting at the dining room table. I should have gone downstairs and apologized, but my feet carried me toward the light source.

Our bathrooms were white Carrara marble but, for some reason, a pink glow reflected in the room. I stepped into the doorframe and froze. The floor was covered with blood. I'd seen it often enough to recognize it, and its smell, a hint of copper and something sweet, was even sweeter today as it mixed with Mother's perfume.

My eyes followed the river of blood, then the dried waterfall of red staining

4

the white tub up to a limp arm. The white flesh was parted, giving way to dark red below.

The arm belonged to Mother. It had to be her, even if she looked alien. Masklike and stiff, her eyes were dull brown. They were staring at me, sad and lonely.

I moved a few steps closer. "Mother?" Another step. "*Mom?*"

She didn't react. She was dead. Dead. My eyes registered the knife on the floor. It was one of Matteo's, a black Karambit knife. She didn't have her own weapons.

She had cut herself. It was her blood. I looked down at my feet. My socks were soaked with the red liquid. I stumbled away and slipped, falling back, crying out. My butt hit the floor hard and my clothes soaked up her blood, sticking to my skin.

I scrambled to my feet and stormed outside, my mouth open wide, my head throbbing, my eyes stinging. I collided with something. Looking up, I found Father's furious face glaring down at me. He hit me hard across the face. "Stop screaming!"

My lips snapped shut. I'd screamed? I blinked up at my father but he was blurry. He gripped me by the collar, shaking me. "Are you crying?"

I wasn't sure. I knew crying wasn't allowed. I never cried, not even when Father hurt me. He hit me even harder. "Speak up."

"Mother's dead," I croaked.

Father frowned, taking in the blood on my clothes. He moved past me toward the bedroom. "Come," he ordered. I noticed his two bodyguards in the hallway with us. They watched me with a look in their eyes I didn't understand.

I didn't move.

"Come, Luca," Father hissed.

"Please," I said. Another forbidden thing: begging. "I don't want to see her again."

Father's face twisted with rage, and I braced myself. He was upon me and gripped my arm. "Never again. You won't ever say that word again. And no tears, not another disgusting tear, or I'll burn out your left eye. You can still be a Made Man with one eye."

I gave a quick nod and wiped my eyes with the back of my hand. I didn't fight when Father wrenched me back into the bathroom and I didn't cry again, only stared at the body in the tub. Only a body. Slowly, the roar in my chest quieted. It was only a body.

"Pathetic," Father muttered. "Pathetic whore."

My brows drew together. The women Father met when he wasn't home were whores, but Mother wasn't. She was his wife. Whores took care of Father so he didn't hurt Mother as badly. That's what she explained to me. But it didn't work.

"One!" Father bellowed.

One of the bodyguards entered. His name wasn't One, but Father didn't bother learning the names of low soldiers and gave them numbers instead.

One stood close behind me, and when Father inspected Mother more closely with a cruel smile, he squeezed my shoulder. I peered up at him, wondering why he was doing it, what it meant, but his gaze was focused on Father, not me. "Get someone to clean up this mess and call for Bardoni. He needs to find me a new wife."

My brain stumbled over what he'd said. "New wife?"

Father narrowed his gray eyes. Gray like mine. "Change clothes and act like a goddamn man, not a boy." He paused. "And get Matteo. He needs to see what kind of cowardly whore his mother was."

"No," I said.

Father stared at me. "What did you say?"

"No," I repeated in a small voice. Matteo loved our Mother. It would hurt him.

Father glanced at the hand still on my shoulder, then up at his bodyguard. "One, beat some sense into him."

One pulled his hand away and, with a short glance at my face, he began beating me. I fell to my knees, back to crouching in Mother's blood. I barely felt the hits, only stared at the red on the white marble.

"Stop," Father ordered, and the blows did stop. I looked back up at him, my head ringing, my back and stomach burning. He looked into my eyes for a long time, and I stared back. No. No. No. I wouldn't get Matteo. I wouldn't whether One kept beating me or not. I was used to pain.

His mouth thinned. "Two!" Bodyguard Two came in. "Get Matteo. Luca will only get blood on the expensive Persian rugs."

I almost smiled because I had won. I tried to jump to my feet to stop Two, but One gripped my arm hard. I fought and almost freed myself, but then Matteo appeared in the doorway and I went slack.

Matteo's brown eyes became huge when he saw our mother and the blood, then his knife next to the tub. Father motioned at Mother. "Your mother abandoned you. She killed herself."

Matteo only looked.

"Get your knife," Father ordered.

Matteo stumbled inside, and One's grip on my arm tightened. Father glanced at me, then back at my brother, who picked up the knife with shaking hands.

I hated Father. I hated him so much.

And I hated Mother for doing this, for leaving us with him.

"Now clean up, the both of you."

Matteo stood stock-still, staring at his bloody knife. I gripped his arm and pulled him out, stumbling after me. I led him into my bedroom, then into the bathroom. He still looked at his knife. I ripped it from his hand and held it

7

under the faucet, cleaning it with hot water to get rid of the dried blood. My eyes prickled, but I swallowed.

No tears. Not ever again.

"Why did she use my knife?" Matteo asked quietly.

I turned off the water and dried it with a towel, then held it out to him. After a moment, he shook his head, backing away until he bumped against the wall, before he sank down on his butt. "Why?" he muttered, eyes filling with tears.

"Don't cry," I hissed, quickly closing the bathroom door in case Father came into my bedroom.

Matteo jutted his chin out, narrowing his eyes even as he began bawling. I tensed and gripped a clean towel before I knelt in front of my brother. "Stop crying, Matteo. Stop it," I said quietly. I shoved the towel into his face. "Dry your face. Father will punish you."

"I don't care," Matteo choked out. "I don't care what he does." His words were proven wrong by the shaky note of terror in his voice.

I glanced at the door, worried I'd heard footsteps. It was silent unless Father was spying on us, but he was probably busy taking care of Mother's body. Maybe he'd tell his Consigliere Bardoni to drop her in the Hudson River. I shuddered.

"Take the towel," I ordered.

Matteo finally did and wiped it roughly over his red eyes. I held the knife out to him. He eyed it critically. "Take it."

He pressed his lips together.

"Matteo, you have to take it." Father wouldn't allow him to get rid of it. My little brother finally reached for the knife and curled his fingers around the handle.

"It's only a knife," I said, but I, too, could only see the blood it had been covered with.

He nodded and pushed it into his pocket. We stared at each other. "Now we're alone."

"You have me," I said.

A knock sounded and I quickly pulled Matteo to his feet. The door swung open and Marianna stepped inside. Her eyes crinkled as she looked at us. Her brown hair, which she usually wore in a bun, was all over the place as if she'd ripped the hairnet out of it. "The Master sent me to see if you were getting ready. Soon his Consigliere will be here." Her voice held a strange note I didn't recognize, and her lips trembled as her eyes darted between Matteo and me.

I nodded. She came closer and touched my shoulder. "I'm so sorry." I stepped back, away from the touch. I glared, because it made not crying easier.

"I'm not," I muttered. "She was weak."

Marianna took a step back, glancing between Matteo and me, her expression falling. "Hurry," she said before she left.

Matteo slipped his hand in mine. "I'll miss her."

I looked down at my feet, at my blood-covered socks, not saying anything because it would have been weak to do so. I wasn't allowed to be weak. Not ever.

Cesare landed a hard hit in my stomach. Gasping, I dropped to my knees. Marianna put down her knitting needles with a sharp intake of breath. Before he could land a hit on my head, I rolled away and pushed to my feet, then raised my balled fists.

Cesare nodded. "Don't get distracted again."

I gritted my teeth and attacked, feigning an upper cut, then smashed my fist into his side. He grunted then jumped back. Cesare had been giving me fighting lessons since I was three years old.

Cesare stepped back from me. "You'll be unbeatable when you're older."

I wanted to be unbeatable now so I could stop Father from hurting us. I was already much taller and stronger than the other kids in school, but I needed to be even stronger. I began to pull off my gloves.

Cesare turned to Matteo, who sat on the edge of the boxing ring, his legs pulled up to his chest, a deep frown on his forehead. "It's your turn."

My brother didn't react, staring off into space. I threw my boxing glove at him. He gasped, rubbing the side of his head, messing up his brown hair, then scowled. "Your turn," I said.

He got to his feet, but I could tell that he was in a sour mood. I knew why, but I really hoped he would keep it to himself.

"Why aren't we at Mom's funeral?"

Marianna was heading our way. I threw my second glove at him. "Shut up."

He stomped his foot. "No!" He jumped off the boxing ring and stalked toward the door of the gym. What was he doing?

"Matteo!" I shouted, chasing after him.

"I want to say goodbye to her! It's not fair that she's alone."

No, no, no! Why did he have to say something like that when others were around? I didn't look back at Cesare and Marianna, but I knew they'd heard every word.

I grabbed Matteo's arm shortly before the exit and jerked him back. He tried to shake me off, but I was stronger than him. He glared up at me with teary eyes. "Stop crying," I whispered harshly.

"Don't you want to say goodbye?" he rasped.

My chest tightened. "She didn't say goodbye to us either." I released Matteo, and he began crying again.

Marianna put her hand on his shoulder but not on mine. She'd learned. Every time she'd tried to console me in the last few days, I'd shaken her off.

"It's okay to be sad."

"No, it's not," I said firmly. Didn't she understand? If Father found out that Matteo was crying after our mother, especially when Cesare was around, he'd punish him. Maybe he'd burn his eye out like he'd threatened to do to me. I couldn't let that happen. I glanced to Cesare who stood a few steps back, unwrapping his tape from his wrist.

"Our mother was a sinner. Suicide is sin. She doesn't deserve our sadness," I repeated what the pastor had told me when I'd visited church with Father. I didn't understand it. Killing was a sin too, but the pastor never said anything to Father about that.

Marianna shook her head and touched my shoulder with sad eyes. Why did she have to do it? "She shouldn't have left you boys alone."

"She was never really there for us before, either," I said firmly, balling my emotions inside of me.

Marianna nodded. "I know, I know. Your mother..."

"...was weak," I hissed, drawing back from her touch. I didn't want to talk about her. I just wanted to forget she'd ever existed, and I wanted Matteo to stop looking at the stupid knife as if it would kill him.

"Don't," Marianna whispered. "Don't become like your father, Luca."

That's what Grandma Marcella had said before she'd died.

Grandma looked thin and small. Her skin appeared too big for her body, as if she'd borrowed it from a person twice her size.

She smiled in a way no one ever smiled at me and stretched out her old hand. I took it. Her skin felt like paper, dry and cold.

"Don't leave," I demanded. Father said she would die soon. That's why he'd sent me into her room, to understand death but I already did.

Grandma squeezed my hand lightly. "I'll watch over you from heaven."

I shook my head. "You can't protect us when you're up there."

Her brown eyes were kind. "Soon you won't need protection anymore."

"I'll rule over everyone," I whispered. "Then I'll kill Father so he can't hurt Matteo and Mother anymore."

Grandma touched my cheek. "Your father killed his father so he could become Capo."

My eyes widened. "You hate him for it?"

"No," she said. "Your Grandfather was a cruel man. I couldn't protect Salvatore from him." Her voice got raspier and very quiet so I had to lean close to hear her. "That's why I tried to protect you from your father but I failed again."

Her eyelids fluttered and she released my hand but I clung to it. "Don't become like your grandfather and father, Luca."

She closed her eyes.

"Grandma?"

I scowled, then glanced back at Cesare who was watching with his arms crossed. Had he heard what Marianna had said? Father would be angry with her. Very angry.

I turned on my heel and walked toward him, stopping right in front of him and narrowing my eyes. "You didn't hear anything."

Cesare's eyebrows rose. Did he think I was kidding?

I didn't have much I could do. Father held all the power. "You won't tell anyone anything, or I'll tell my father that you talked shit about him. I'm his heir. He'll believe me."

Cesare dropped his arms. "You don't have to threaten me, Luca. I'm on your side."

With that, he turned on his heel and went into the locker room. Father always said we were surrounded by enemies. How was I supposed to know whom I could trust?

LUCA, 11 YEARS OLD

Screams tore through my nightmare, through the images of red rivulets on white marble. I sat up, disoriented, listening to shouting and gunfire. What was happening?

Light flared up in the hallway, probably the motion sensors. I rolled over to the edge of my bed when the door opened. A tall man I'd never seen before stood in the doorway, his gun trained on my head.

I froze.

He was going to kill me. I could see it in his expression. I stared into his eyes, wanting to die with my head held high like a real man. A small shadow dashed forward behind the man and, with a battle cry, Matteo jumped on his back. The gun fired and I jerked as hot pain sliced through my middle.

The bullet went a lot lower than it was supposed to. He would have killed me if it hadn't been for Matteo. Tears shot into my eyes, but I stumbled out of the bed and wrenched my gun out of the nightstand. The man lifted the barrel at Matteo. I raised my gun, pointed it at his head the way Cesare and One had taught me, then pulled the trigger. Blood splattered everywhere, even over Matteo's shock-widened face. For a moment, everything seemed to stand still—even my heartbeat—and then everything sped up.

The man tumbled forward and would have taken my brother with him had he not jumped back in the last moment, still looking stunned. He blinked at me, then peered down at the body. Slowly, he dragged his gaze back up, lingering on my belly. "You're bleeding."

I clutched the wound in my side, shaking from the force of the pain. My hand with the gun shook, but I didn't drop it. Shots and screams still rang out downstairs. I nodded toward my closet. "Hide in there."

Matteo frowned.

"Do it," I said sharply.

"No."

I staggered toward him, almost passing out from the sharp pain in my body. I gripped Matteo by the cuff of his pajama and pulled him toward the closet. He struggled, but I shoved him inside and turned the lock.

Matteo hammered against the door from inside. "Let me out!"

Trembling with anxiety and pain, I crept downstairs, toward the living room where the sounds were coming from. When I stepped in, I saw Father crouched behind a sofa in a shooting match with two other men. Both had their backs turned to me. Father's eyes flitted to me, and for a moment, I considered not doing anything. I hated him, hated how he hurt Matteo and me, and even his new wife Nina.

Still, I raised my hand and shot one of the men. Father took care of the other. The man fell to the floor clutching his shoulder. Father kicked the gun away then shot him in both feet. Somewhere in the house I heard more gunshots, then heavy steps. One stumbled inside, bleeding from a wound in his head.

Father frowned. "Did you kill everyone?"

One nodded. "Yes. They got Two."

"They shouldn't have come as far as they did," Father muttered. Without warning, he aimed his gun at One and pulled the trigger. I cried out in surprise as the man fell to the floor beside me. I'd known him all my life.

My legs gave away, my wound throbbing. Father regarded me as he lifted his phone and spoke into it. "Send for the Doc, and come over with Durant. No one else until I know who the rats are."

Father stalked toward me and pulled me roughly to my feet. Holding me upright, he shoved my hand away from my bleeding wound. He prodded at it, and my vision turned black as I jerked in agony. Father shook me. "Get a grip on yourself. Don't die on me."

My eyes peeled open. Father shook his head then released me, and I sank back down to the ground. I braced myself on my hands, wheezing.

Father moved out of the room, leaving me alone with the attacker who was moaning as he tried to crawl away. When Father returned, he carried rope. He tied up the man then pulled out his knife and touched it to the man's forearm. He screamed when Father began to cut his skin off his flesh. *It's like peeling an apple.* That's what Father always said but an apple didn't screech and beg.

Cradling my bleeding stomach, I watched even as bile crawled up my throat. Father kept glancing my way. I knew he'd punish me if I looked away. The screams rang in my ears, and I shivered. My arms gave way and my cheek collided with the hard floor. The static in my ears soon drowned out the screaming, and then all was black.

The Underbosses and Captains waited in the living room of our mansion. Father stood in the middle and beckoned me forward. Every eye in the room followed me as I headed toward him. I held my head high, trying to appear taller. I was tall for my age, but the men around me still towered over me. They looked at me like I was something they had never seen before.

I stopped right in front of my father. "The youngest initiate the Famiglia has ever seen," he announced, his voice booming in the room. "Eleven years and already so much stronger and crueler than any father could wish for."

Pride swelled in my chest. Father had never sounded proud of me, never shown the slightest hint that I or Matteo were more than a burden. I straightened my shoulders, trying to appear like a man in my black suit and wingtip shoes.

"Our enemies will whisper your name in fear, my son. My *blood*. My heir."

He withdrew a knife and I held out my hand, knowing what was to come. I didn't flinch when Father cut my palm. He'd cut me many times before to make me strong for this day. Every time I'd flinched, he'd cut me again and dripped lemon juice or salt into my wound until I hid the pain.

"Born in Blood, Sworn in Blood. I enter alive and I leave dead," I said firmly.

"You are a Made Man of the Famiglia, Luca. You will kill and maim in my name. You will break and burn."

A man was dragged into the room. I didn't know him or what he had done. He was covered in bruises and blood. His swollen eyes met mine and they begged me. No one had ever looked at me like that, like I held all the power.

Father gave a nod and held the knife out to me, the same knife my mother had killed herself with. I took it from him then stepped up to the man. He struggled against the hold of Father's new bodyguards, but they didn't release him. My fingers tightened around the handle. Everyone was watching me, waiting for a flicker of weakness, but I was my father's son and I would be Capo one day. I quickly slashed my hand sideways, drawing the knife along his throat. The cut was messy and blood spurted out, splattering my shoes and shirt. I took a step back as the man's eyes widened. He was dropped on the floor, horrified eyes staring up at me as he convulsed and choked.

I watched as the life drained out of him.

Two days later, the most important words of my life were inked onto my chest, making me a Made Man for life. Nothing would ever be more important than the Famiglia.

CHAPTER 2

LUCA, 13 YEARS OLD

Father's grip on my shoulder was tight when we entered the Foxy. I'd been inside the place a few times before when he had to talk to the manager. It was one of the most expensive whorehouses we owned.

The whores were lined up in front of the bar and the manager stood beside them. He nodded at Father then winked at me. Father motioned for him to leave.

"You're thirteen, Luca," Father said. Surprise washed through me that he'd remembered my birthday was today. He hadn't mentioned it before. "You've been a Made Man for eighteen months. You can't be a virgin and a killer."

I flushed, my eyes darting to the women, knowing they had heard my father's words. None of them laughed, probably too scared of him. I straightened my shoulders, wanting them to watch me with the same caution they watched him.

"Choose two of them," Father said with a nod toward the whores.

Shock shot through me when I understood why I was here. Slowly, I made my way toward the women, trying to look calm even as nerves twisted my stomach. At almost 5'7", I was already very tall for thirteen, so the women were eye-level with me in their high heels. They weren't wearing much, only short skirts and bras. My eyes lingered on their chests. All of them had big tits, and I couldn't stop staring. I'd seen a few naked girls in our strip clubs but always only in passing, never this close-up. They were all pretty. I pointed at a woman with brown hair and one with blond hair.

Father nodded. One woman grabbed my hand and led me through the back door. The other was close behind me. Eventually, I was alone with them in a big suite at the back of the Foxy. I swallowed, trying to look like I knew what was going to happen. I'd watched porn and listened to the stories the other Made Men told, but this felt very different.

The blond woman began to undress slowly, touching herself everywhere. I stared but tensed when I could feel my pants becoming tight. The brown-haired woman smiled a fake smile and moved toward me. I tensed even more, but I let her touch my chest. "You're a big boy already, oh my," she said.

I didn't say anything, watching her closely. Then my eyes darted to the blond woman again, who'd started touching her pussy. My mouth became dry. The brown-haired woman slid her hand into my boxers, and I released a shaky breath. "Oh, I think this will work out just fine, don't you agree?"

I gave a nod, then I let her drag me toward the huge round bed in the center.

LUCA, 17 YEARS OLD

"I'm fucking glad to be away from Father, but I wish we didn't have to go to Junior to celebrate my birthday," Matteo muttered, shoving his shirt into his pants and checking his reflection. It was the fourth one he'd tried on. Fuck, how did he become such a vain bastard? It seemed to become worse every year. Now at fifteen, he was pretty much insufferable.

Cesare shot me a look. He, Romero and I had been waiting for Matteo to get ready for the last thirty minutes.

"It would have been dishonorable to decline an invitation from your cousin when he organizes a party for you," Romero said, sounding twice his age. He'd turned fourteen a few days ago, and he had been a Made Man since his father died a few months ago. His family needed the money, but we'd known each other for many years.

"I don't trust him," Cesare muttered. "He and his family are too ambitious."

My uncle Gottardo and his eldest Gottardo Junior definitely weren't in favor of me becoming Capo after my father, but that could be said about all of my uncles. They thought they would be better Capos. "We'll stay a few hours and then we'll come back here and have our own party. Or we'll drive back to New York and go into one of our clubs."

"Do you really think we'll be sober enough to drive back to New York? It's a long drive from the Hamptons," Romero said, frowning.

Matteo chuckled. "How come you're so goddamn rule-abiding?"

Romero flushed.

"Come, Matteo. Nobody gives a fuck about your shirt," I growled when it looked as if he was considering trying on another.

Uncle Gottardo's mansion wasn't far from ours, so we walked over. A guard opened the gates for us and we headed up the long driveway to the entrance door where Gottardo Junior was waiting. He frowned when he saw us. "I didn't expect you to bring more people along."

"Romero and Cesare are always with us," I told him as I shook his hand before he turned to my brother and congratulated him. We all stepped into the entrance hall. Loud music and voices were coming from the living area. I stripped off my gun and knife holders and dropped them on the sideboard as was expected. Matteo, Romero, and Cesare did the same before we followed my cousin toward the party. I knew most of the men only distantly since they were friends of Junior and his brother Angelo from Washington.

"How come you're here?" I asked, as I headed for the array of alcoholic beverages while several half-naked girls danced around us. Junior had even set up poles for them.

"I needed a few days off. Business has been soul-sucking."

I nodded. The Bratva had given us all trouble recently.

Junior smiled widely. "Now, let's have fun!"

A couple of hours later, we were all trashed. Matteo and I danced with a group of four girls. It would be a long night. One of the whores started twerking right in front of us, her ass cheeks glittery, her thong a thin strip of nothing. Romero had disappeared with another whore in a backroom. Maybe he'd finally get fucked. Cesare slouched in his seat, eyes half-closed as a woman rode him like a pro.

Matteo clapped the dancer's ass and she squealed, then whirled around and ground against his groin. More girls swarmed around us. I plopped down on one of the armchairs, the alcohol taking its toll, and one of the girls sank down in front of me, massaging my cock through my pants. A second came up behind me and ran her hands down my chest. I was about to snarl at her for being at my back when she fell forward, her cut throat spilling blood down my shirt. "Fuck!"

The whore massaging my cock looked up with wide eyes. I shoved myself out of the armchair and turned at the same time, bringing my arm up just when Junior brought his knife down. The blade grazed my forearm, cutting it open. The whores began screaming around us. Where was Matteo?

Junior slashed the knife at me again and I rammed my shoulder into his chest, then grabbed his throat and shoved him into the wall. Grunts and screams rang out around us. Then, the first shot sounded.

I was focused only on Junior. I was going to crush him to fucking dust. I wrapped my second hand around his throat as well then squeezed as hard as I could. "You fucking traitor," I snarled. Did he think he could kill me?

His eyes began bulging, and I squeezed even harder until the veins in his fucking eyeballs began to pop and his bones crumpled under the force of my grip. He jerked one last time, and I dropped him to the ground. My fingers were covered in his blood.

Slowly, I turned to find Matteo atop another attacker about to cut his throat. "No," I ordered, but it was too late. Matteo had sliced open the fucker.

Breathing harshly, I took in the mess around us. Cesare leaned against a wall, looking slightly dazed. He had a cut on the side of his neck and was staring down at the dead body in front of him. Romero was breathing harshly, only in his boxer shorts and a gun in his hand. Two whores were dead, and the others were crying and staring at me like I was the devil.

I walked past them toward Romero and Cesare. Romero was bleeding from a wound in his shoulder. Matteo staggered to his feet, eyes wide, almost feverish. It was the thrill of the kill I knew only too well. "You crushed his fucking throat with your bare hands!"

"Father won't be happy," I said, then glanced down at my hands. I'd killed so many, but this felt different. It had been more personal, fucking thrilling. Feeling the life drain out of him, feeling his bones break under my palms… Fuck, I'd loved it.

Cesare regarded my face. "You all right?"

My mouth curled. Did he think crushing my cousin's throat had bothered me? "Call my father." I turned to Romero, who looked a bit shaken. "How bad is it?"

He shrugged. "It's nothing. The bullet went straight through. One of Junior's friends got his guns the same time I did."

I nodded, but my mind kept replaying my cousin's death. My eyes were drawn to the uninjured whores, wondering if any of them had been involved in this.

Matteo stepped up to me. "Fuck. I can't believe our own cousin tried to kill us."

"You had your knife," I said.

"You know I never go anywhere without it," Matteo said with an unsettling grin.

"I won't put my fucking guns down ever again."

Romero came closer, looking a little shaky. "Do you think your uncle and your other cousin were involved?"

"Probably," I muttered. I doubted that Junior had come up with the plan by himself. It fit Gottardo's character that he'd talk one of his sons into this instead of risking his own fucking life. Coward.

"Why did he risk it? Even if he'd managed to kill us, there would still be your father, and he'd avenge you," Romero said.

"No," I gritted out. "If Matteo and I had been stupid enough to get us killed by Junior, Father would have considered us weak links. He would have allowed Nina to have a child, and then he'd have had a new heir. End of story."

Matteo grimaced because it was the truth. We both knew it.

"I need a fucking drink," I growled in the direction of one of the whores. She rushed toward the bar and poured me a whisky before she brought it to me. I regarded her closely as I took a sip, and she lowered her eyes. "Did you know?"

She shook her head jerkily. "No. We were told this was a birthday party and we were supposed to dance. That's all."

I walked over to one of the armchairs with my drink and sank down. The whore whose throat Junior had cut lay beside it in a puddle of blood. Eventually, Matteo, Cesare, and Romero sat down across from me as we waited for Father and his men. There was nothing else to do. We'd killed Junior and his friends, so we couldn't question them, and Gottardo and Angelo were all the way in Washington. I caught the looks Romero and Cesare gave me, a mixture of respect and shock.

Matteo shook his head. "Fuck. That's not how I wanted to spend this day."

Father, his Consigliere Bardoni, and several soldiers arrived about one hour later.

Father barely glanced our way before he headed for my cousin. "You crushed his throat?" he asked, inspecting what remained of Gottardo Junior. I caught the hint of pride in his voice. I didn't want his fucking approval.

I nodded. "I didn't have any weapons because I assumed I was among family and not a fucking traitor. He choked on his traitorous blood."

"Like a Vise," Matteo commented.

"Luca, the Vise," Father said with a strange smile.

———————>———————

It had been a long fucking day, long fucking weeks, one ordeal followed by another. I wanted to kill every single one of my uncles. "I'm so over them treating me like a fucking kid," I said as Matteo and I headed for the entrance of the Sphere.

Matteo grinned and ran his hand through his hair for what seemed like the hundredth time. One day I was going to knock him out and shave his fucking hair off to stop his annoying preening. "You're seventeen, Luca. Not yet a man." He imitated Uncle Gottardo's voice in annoying perfection, including the nasal undertone that made me want to rip his vocal chords out of his throat.

I had seen the fear in his eyes—the same fear I saw in many people's eyes since I'd crushed Junior's throat. Gottardo was only able to spew this bullshit because he thought himself safe as my uncle. I couldn't believe my father had believed him and Angelo…Or maybe he didn't and enjoyed their groveling. He'd definitely upped his security and guards since that day, so he knew there were still traitors among us.

"I'm more man than all of them together. I've killed more men, have fucked more women, and I have bigger balls."

"Careful with the ego there," Matteo said, chuckling.

"You've got a zit on your forehead," I muttered. It was a lie, but given Matteo's vanity, I knew it was my best bet to pay him back for being an insufferable asshole most of these days.

As predicted, Matteo immediately felt his skin for the offending flaw, then narrowed his eyes and dropped his hand. I rolled my eyes with a chuckle. We arrived in front of the bouncer of the Sphere. He greeted us with a curt nod and stepped back to let us through when a guy at the front of the long queue waiting to be allowed inside shouted. "Hey, we were here first! And that guy's not old enough to be in a club."

Matteo and I both looked at the idiot. He had been referring to Matteo, and of course, he was right. At fifteen, Matteo was definitely not allowed to be in a night club like this, but neither was I—only with my size, everyone assumed I was older.

Matteo and I exchanged a look and walked over to Big Mouth. Some of his bravado slipped off when I stopped right in front of him. "Got a problem there?"

"There are laws," he said.

Matteo flashed his shark-grin he'd perfected recently after spending too many hours in front of a mirror. "Maybe for you."

"Since when are boys allowed in clubs? Is this prom or what?" Big Mouth said to our bouncer.

Matteo was about to draw his knife right in front of everyone, and I had half a mind to let him for the fun of it when a woman in the queue spoke up. "He doesn't look like a boy to me," she said flirtingly in Matteo's direction.

"And you look like my next conquest," added the girl beside her with a smile at me.

I cocked an eyebrow. Matteo with his sunny boy charm was always a girl magnet, but my rougher predator charm definitely had its perks as well. Both women were tall, blond, and sex on legs.

"Let them in," I told our bouncer. He opened the barrier so they could slip through. "And he and his friends are banned from the Sphere," I added.

The sound of their protests followed us into the club, but I didn't give a fuck. I wrapped my arm around the blond at my side, who squeezed my butt and gave me a seductive smile.

Matteo and his girl were already tongue wrestling for all its worth.

"Is there a place where we can fuck?" Blond asked me, pressing herself against me.

I smirked. That's how I liked it best. Women who weren't work, easy lays, no questions asked. "Sure," I told her, reaching for her own ass and squeezing it.

"Is your cock as big as the rest of you?" she asked as I led her through the back door into a storage room.

"Find out for yourself," I growled, and she did. The moment the door closed, she got down on her knees and sucked any sane thought out of my brain. Her lipstick stained my cock red as she blew me like a fucking pro. I leaned my head back and closed my eyes.

"Fuck," I hissed as she worked me deep into her mouth. She was better than most of the whores I'd been with, and those women had spent years perfecting their craft. I relaxed against the door, getting closer and closer to spill my cum down her throat.

She shifted and tensed in a way that raised my suspicions. Instinct made my eyes shoot open a moment before she jerked something toward my thigh. I lashed out, hitting her arm. She dropped a syringe and scrambled for it again. Grabbing her throat, I hurled her away from me. The back of her head collided with the storage shelves with a sickening crunch, and she slumped to the ground. Breathing harshly, I stared down at the syringe. What kind of shit did she try to inject me with?

I pulled up my pants and staggered over to her. I didn't bother feeling for her pulse; her neck was twisted at an angle that left no doubt about her death. I bent over her and tugged her pants down, revealing her hipbone. There was a scar where someone had burnt away a tattoo. I knew what kind of sign had been on her skin: the crossed Kalashinkovs of the fucking Bratva that they inked onto the skin of every single one of their whores.

"Fuck," I snarled. This had been a trap, and I'd walked straight into it, had let my dick rule over my thinking, had lowered my guards. Shouldn't the incident with my cousin have taught me better?

I jerked upright. Matteo. Fuck. I rushed out of the room and searched the other back rooms. No sign of him or the other no-doubt traitorous whore. I stormed across the dance floor, searching the crowd for a sign of my brother, but I didn't see him anywhere. Where was he?

I headed outside past the waiting crowd and around the corner until I reached the small back alley behind the Sphere. Matteo was busy getting head. His eyes, too, were closed. We were fucking stupid idiots. No goddamn blowjob was worth forgetting about the first rule in our world: don't trust anyone.

The whore reached for something in her bag.

"Matteo!" I shouted, pulling my gun. His eyes shot open, his expression a mix of annoyance and confusion before he registered what she was holding in her hand. He reached for his knife and she raised the syringe to strike. I pulled the trigger and the bullet tore straight through her head, throwing it back. She fell to her side, the syringe tumbling out of her palm.

Matteo stared down at the woman, knife in hand and his fucking boner still on display. I moved toward him and revealed the burnt skin over her hipbone.

"I really wish she would have waited for me to come before she tried to kill me," he muttered.

I straightened, then grimaced. "Why don't you pull up your pants? There's no reason to present your junk anymore."

He dragged his pants up his legs and fastened his belt, then he looked at me. "Thanks for saving my ass." He gave me a smirk, but it was off. "Did you at least have your happy ending before your conquest tried to end you for good?"

I shook my head. "The Bratva almost got us. We both acted like fucking fools, letting those stupid whores lead us around by our dicks like randy teenagers."

"We are randy teenagers," Matteo joked as he sheathed his knife.

I glared down at the dead women.

"The other whore's dead as well?" Matteo asked.

I nodded. "Broke her neck."

"Your first two women," he said with a hint of wariness, his eyes scanning my face, looking for God knew what. "You feel guilty?"

I regarded the blood staining the concrete and the lifeless eyes of the woman. Anger was the prevailing emotion in my body. Anger at myself for being an easy target, for thinking a pretty woman was no threat. And burning fury at the Bratva for trying to kill me—and worse, Matteo.

"No," I said. "The only thing I regret is that I killed them before they could answer a few questions. Now we'll have to hunt down a few Bratva assholes and get info out of them."

Matteo picked up the syringe and I tensed, worried he could get some of the poison on his skin by accident. I had no doubt that whatever was in there would lead to an excruciating death. "We need to find out what's in there."

"First, we need to get rid of the two bodies before guests or the police find them." I raised my phone to my ear, calling Cesare. "I need you at the Sphere. Fast."

"All right. Give me ten minutes," Cesare said, sounding as if I'd woken him.

Cesare was more my man than he was Father's soldier, and I trusted him to keep his mouth shut when required. "Father won't be happy about this," I said.

Matteo gave me a curious look. "About us walking into a trap or that the Bratva tried to kill us?"

"The first, and maybe the second."

"I'm growing tired of people trying to kill us," Matteo muttered, his tone serious for once.

I took a deep breath. "That's how it is. How it'll always be. We can't trust anyone but each other."

Matteo shook his head. "Look at Father. He trusts no one. Not even Nina."

He did well not to trust his wife considering the way he treated her. The marriages in our world rarely led to trust, much less love.

CHAPTER 3

LUCA, 20 YEARS OLD

The second we entered the elevator, the sound of music and laughter drifted down to us.

"Seems like this party might be worth our time," Matteo said, checking his looks in the reflection of the doors. Except for our general facial features, we didn't look alike. I was still the spitting image of my father, same cold gray eyes, same black hair, but I'd never wear it in that disgusting slicked-back way he did.

"That would be a plus, but the main reason we're here is for connections."

The apartment belonged to Senator Parker who was away on business with his wife. His son, Michael, used the chance to throw a party, inviting pretty much everyone who mattered in New York.

Michael waited in the open door when Matteo and I stepped out into the hallway. It was the first time I'd seen Parker Junior without a suit, since he was trying to follow in his father's footsteps. He waved at us with a crooked smile, already drunk.

I nodded at him. For a moment, he looked as if he wanted to hug me like so many people tended to do with everyone, but then he thought better of it. Good for him. "So glad you could make it," he slurred. "Grab a drink. I booked a few bartenders who can prepare any cocktail you want."

The penthouse was packed with guests and the beat throbbed in my temples. Matteo and I wouldn't drink much, if anything. We'd learned from our mistakes of the past, even if the present crowd didn't pose a danger. Most of them would piss their pants if they knew half the things Matteo and I had done since we'd become Made Men. As it was, they only knew rumors. Officially, we were the heirs of businessman, real estate mogul, and club owner, Salvatore Vitiello.

The moment we entered, people began to whisper. It was always the same. Michael pointed at the bar and buffet, but I barely listened. My eyes were drawn to the dance floor, which had been set up in the center of the large open space that must have been the living room before the furniture had been removed for the party. Several girls who had been dancing with sons of other politicians were throwing glances our way.

Matteo and I exchanged a look. The thrill-seekers were about to descend on us. These kinds of girls, from good families, pampered, and entirely boring, were our main prey. They wouldn't end up trying to kill us.

One of the girls, a tall blonde sex bomb with fake tits and an outfit that clung to her body like a second skin, began eye-fucking me immediately. She left her dance partner standing dumbfounded on the dance floor and shimmied over to me on high heels.

Michael groaned. I glanced his way.

"That's my younger sister, Grace."

I frowned. This could complicate my plans. Michael looked at my face, then at Grace. "I don't care if you make a move on her. She does what she wants anyway. She's always on the lookout for her next conquest, but lots of wieners have been dipped into the mustard jar, if you catch my drift."

My eyebrows rose. I didn't care if Grace had fucked half of New York's male population. She was for fucking and sucking, not anything else. But if I had a sister, I would definitely mind if she acted like that, unlike Michael.

Michael shook his head. "I'm off. I don't want to witness that."

He moved to the bar and Matteo followed him, but not before he sent me a wink.

Grace danced closer and closer, then touched my chest. "I hear you're involved in organized crime," she crooned into my ear. Her hand slipped lower, her eyes eager and flirting. She definitely went for it.

If she reached around, she'd feel the gun in the holster at my lower back hidden under my t-shirt. "Is that what you hear?" I asked with the smile that got girls like her going. Dark enough to call to her bored-as-fuck-pampered-rich-girl persona but nowhere near my true dark side which would scare her away.

She shivered against me. "Is it true?"

"What do you think?" I growled, pulling her against me, letting some of my harshness show. Her lips parted, her expression a mix of fear and lust.

She pressed her mouth to my ear. "I think I want to be fucked."

"Good," I said darkly, "because I'm going to fuck you now. Lead the way."

With an excited smile, she grabbed my hand and pulled me along. Matteo grinned at me but, a second later, he was back to shoving his tongue down a brunette's throat.

Grace and I entered what I assumed was her bedroom. I pushed her toward her vanity and hoisted her up, knocking half of her lipsticks off in the process. She pursed her lips. "You're making a mess."

I gave her a dark smile. "Do I look like I give a fuck? The rest of your fucking lipsticks will fall off when I fuck you."

Her lips parted. She was used to weak-ass rich boys who'd never swung a fist in their life. "Then you'll have to pick them up later."

Was she testing me? Trying to see if I was someone who could be pushed around like her preppy boyfriends of the past?

Tugging her skirt down, I checked the unblemished skin of her hipbones. It was more habit than necessity. Definitely not a Bratva assassin.

"I won't do a fucking thing, Grace, got it?" I growled as I slid my hand under her skirt then pushed her thong aside, finding her wet. "People do what I tell them, not the other way around. New York is my fucking city," I added as I pushed two fingers into her. Her eyes flashed with fascination.

She was fascinated by the danger, even when she didn't know the first thing about it.

I finger-fucked her hard. "Choke me," she whispered.

One of those.

I closed my fingers around her throat and pressed her down on the vanity, shoving the rest of her makeup to the floor. She shuddered with pleasure. I hardly put any pressure behind my grip; if she knew that this was how I'd killed a man, if she knew how many worse things I'd done with these hands, she wouldn't have asked me to do this, but for her this was a game, a thrilling kink. It was the same with all the girls. I was their darkest fantasy come true.

She didn't understand that I didn't play a dark role for her, that this wasn't my dark side, not even close, but the only side I was allowed to show in public.

Matteo and I had gotten less than two hours of sleep when our father rang us out of bed, ordering us to come over for breakfast. But first, he wanted a word alone with me. Never a good thing.

"What do you think he wants?" Matteo asked as we headed toward Father's office.

"Who knows?"

I knocked.

"Come in," Father said after he'd made me wait for almost five minutes.

"Good luck," Matteo said with a twisted grin. I ignored him and headed into the room. I hated that I had to come running whenever he called me. He was the only person who could order me around, and he fucking enjoyed it. He sat behind his desk with that narcissistic smile I loathed more than anything. "You called for me, Father," I said, trying to sound like I didn't give a damn.

His smile widened. "We found you a wife, Luca."

I raised one eyebrow. I knew he and the Chicago Outfit had been discussing a possible union for months, but Father had never been very forthcoming with information. He loved having that power over me. "From the Outfit?"

"Of course," he said, tapping his fingers against the desk and watching me. He wanted me to ask him who she was, wanted to draw this out, wanted to see me squirm. Screw him. I pushed my hands into my pockets, meeting his gaze straight on.

His expression darkened. "She's the most beautiful woman the Outfit has to offer. A real stunner. Golden hair, blue eyes, pale skin. An angel come down to earth, as Fiore put it." I'd fucked so many beautiful women. Only last night I'd fucked Grace on every surface in her room. Did he really think I'd be awestruck because he'd found me a pretty wife? If it were up to me, I wouldn't marry anytime soon.

"I hope you'll enjoy breaking her wings," Father added.

I waited for the 'but'. Father looked too pleased with himself, as if he were holding something back that he knew I would hate.

"Maybe you have heard of her. It's Aria Scuderi. She's the daughter of the Consigliere and she turned fifteen a few months ago."

I wasn't quick enough to hide my shock. *Fifteen?* Was he fucking kidding me? "I thought they wanted the wedding to take place soon," I said carefully.

Father leaned back, his eyes looking for a flicker of weakness. "They do. We all do."

"I won't marry a fucking child," I growled, done with playing nice. I was sick of his games.

"You will marry her, and you will fuck her, Luca."

I exhaled before I said or did something that I'd regret later. "Do you really think our men will look up to me if I act like a fucking pedophile?"

"Don't be ridiculous. They look up to us because they fear us. And Aria isn't that young. She's old enough to spread her legs and have you fuck her."

It wasn't the first time I'd considered putting a bullet in his head. He was my father, but he was also a sadistic bastard I hated more than anything else in the world. "What does the girl say to your plan?"

Father barked a laugh. "She doesn't know yet, and it's not like her feelings are important. She'll do what she's told, and so should you."

"Her father doesn't mind giving his daughter to me before she's of age?"

"He doesn't."

What kind of bastard was Scuderi? I could see how much Father enjoyed my fury.

"But Dante Cavallaro was averse to the idea and suggested to postpone the wedding."

I nodded. At least, one person wasn't out of their fucking mind.

"Of course, we haven't decided yet what to do. I'll let you know once the decision is made. I'll be in the dining room in fifteen minutes. Tell Nina I want a five-minute egg. Not a second longer."

I left, knowing I was dismissed. Matteo leaned against the wall across from Father's office. I strode past him, trying to get a handle on the rage burning through my body. I wanted to kill someone, preferably our father. I went straight toward the bar area in the living room of the house.

"What did our sadist of a father do now?" Matteo asked as he fell into step beside me.

I glared. "He wants me to marry a fucking child."

"What the fuck are you talking about? I thought he was trying to set you up with the most beautiful woman of the fucking Outfit," Matteo said mockingly.

"They must be out of pretty woman over there, because they want me to marry Aria Scuderi, who's fucking fifteen."

Matteo whistled. "Holy shit. Have they lost their fucking mind? What did the poor girl do to deserve such a fate?"

I wasn't in the mood for his jokes. I wanted to hit something—hard. "She's the oldest daughter of the Consigliere, and she looks like an angel come down to earth if you believe Fiore Cavallaro."

"So they marry her off to the devil. A match made in hell."

"You're starting to piss me off, Matteo." I reached over the counter of the bar and grasped the most expensive whiskey bottle, which our father kept for special occasions. I brought it to my lips and took a deep swig.

Matteo snatched the bottle out of my hand and tipped it back, downing a considerable amount of the amber liquid before sliding it back over to me. We went back and forth like that for a while before Matteo spoke again. "Are they really going to make you marry that girl? I mean, I'm all for the kinky stuff, but fucking a fifteen-year old is too freaky even for me."

"Her asshole of a father would hand her over to me tomorrow. That bastard doesn't seem to care."

"So what are you going to do?"

"I told Father I wouldn't marry a child."

"And he told you to grow a pair and to do what your Capo tells you."

"He can't see why the girl needs to be older for the wedding. All she has to do is spread her legs for me."

Matteo narrowed his eyes in that fucking annoying way he had when he was trying to figure something out. "And would you?"

"Would I what?" I knew what he meant, but it annoyed the living hell out of me that he had to ask. I expected that question from everyone else, but not him. He knew even I had certain lines I wasn't willing to cross. Yet. Life could be a bitch, especially if you were in the mob, so I'd learned that 'never say never' was a motto to live by.

"Would you fuck her?"

"I'm a killer, not a pedophile, you stupid asshole."

"Spoken like a true philanthropist."

"Fuck you, and stop reading the fucking dictionary."

Matteo grinned and I shook my head with a smirk. That fucker knew how to make me feel better.

Matteo had barely stopped talking since we'd gotten off the plane, and he obviously had no intention of doing so now that we were in the Scuderi mansion. I was seconds away from punching him in the throat. "Stop sulking, Luca. You should be happy. You'll meet your fiancée today. Aren't you curious how she looks? She could be butt-ugly."

She wasn't. Father wouldn't let the Outfit cheat us like that. But I hadn't found a photo of her on the internet. Scuderi seemed to keep his family out of the public eye.

"I'm surprised the maid didn't follow us. It seems like a risk to let potential enemies walk through the house without supervision. Makes me wonder if this is a trap," Cesare said as he kept looking over his shoulder.

"It's a power play. Scuderi wants to show us that he isn't worried about our presence," I said as we headed in the direction the maid had pointed us toward.

I could hear people running our way. My hand went to my gun. Cesare and Matteo did the same as we turned the corner. When I saw what caused the commotion, I relaxed. Children were chasing each other, hurtling straight toward us. The boy managed to stop, but a young girl rushed toward me, her arms flailing, and crashed into my body. My hands shot out to catch her. She stared up at me with wide eyes as I held her by the shoulders.

"Liliana," one of the other girls shrieked. My eyes snapped toward her, then her golden blond hair, and I knew who she was. Aria Scuderi, my future wife. She was the oldest of the bunch, but damn it, she looked so fucking young. I mean, it wasn't as if I'd expected a grown woman, but I'd hoped it wouldn't be so fucking obvious that she was only fifteen. When I was that age, I already felt and acted like a man. I wasn't sure what I'd have done if Cavallaro and my father hadn't agreed to wait until she was eighteen.

She was beautiful in a childish way, but there was the promise of breathtaking beauty under her young features. She was small but, with my size, most women were. In a few years when she'd become my wife, she'd be stunning. She'd better learn to hide her emotions better until then. She looked fucking terrified. I was used to people giving me that kind of look, but with women I preferred admiration and lust to terror any day.

"Liliana, come here," she said. It was pretty obvious that she was trying to look strong and grown-up. She would have been more convincing if her voice wasn't shaking and if there wasn't that petrified glint in her eyes. I loosened my grip on her sister, who bolted toward Aria as if the devil were at her heels. Had these girls never met other men? Scuderi probably kept them in a golden cage, which suited me just well.

"That's Luca Vitiello!" a redhead blurted and actually wrinkled her fucking nose at me. I wasn't used to so much rudeness. People knew better than to disrespect me. Not Scuderi's brats, however.

There was a hiss and the boy shot in my direction and actually attacked me. "Leave Aria alone! You don't get her!"

Cesare made a move to interject as if I needed help against a midget.

"No, Cesare." I stared down at the boy. His fervor was almost admirable if it wasn't so futile. I caught his hands.

Aria crept toward me as if she thought I might snap her brother's neck and then her own. Fuck, what had her family told her about me? They should have lied. I knew I had a reputation and I was fucking proud of it, but Aria didn't need to know about it—yet.

"What a warm welcome we get. That's the infamous hospitality of the Outfit," Matteo said, as usual letting his fat mouth run free.

"Matteo," I warned before he said more. These were children, even my future wife, and they didn't need to hear his colorful vocabulary.

The midget was squirming in my grip, snapping and growling like a wild dog.

"Fabiano," Aria said, her eyes darting up to me for a millisecond before she grabbed her brother's arm. "That's enough. It's not how we treat guests."

Despite her breakable appearance, Aria seemed to hold some power over her siblings. Her brother stopped struggling and looked at her as if she were the center of his world. "He's not a guest. He wants to steal you away, Aria."

Sorry, buddy, nothing about this fucking arrangement was my idea. And yet I had to admit that, after having seen Aria, I wouldn't let her slip out of my grip for anything in the world. She was mine now. I regarded her as she smiled down at her brother with so much kindness, stunning me.

Matteo chuckled. "This is too good. I'm glad Father convinced me to come."

"Ordered you." Our father never tried to convince anyone. He ordered, bribed or blackmailed.

Aria had a hard time meeting my gaze; she was obviously embarrassed by my attention. A deep flush had spread on her cheeks. I released her brother, and she clutched him against her body protectively. She was so shy and terrified that I wondered if she'd dare to oppose me if I actually made a move toward her brother. Not that I'd ever do that. There was no honor in attacking children and women.

"I'm sorry," Aria said feebly. "My brother didn't mean to be disrespectful."

"I did!" the boy shouted. Aria's hand shot out and clamped his mouth shut. I almost laughed. It had been a while since a woman had made me want to laugh, even by accident.

"Don't apologize," the redheaded girl hissed. "It's not our fault that he and his bodyguards take up so much room in the corridor. At least, Fabiano speaks the truth. Everyone else thinks they need to blow sugar up his ass because he's going to be

Capo—"

I sent Matteo a look. That girl had the same bad temper as him.

After more bickering, Aria finally got her siblings to leave. I was glad to see them gone. They grated on my nerves. It was no surprise that Scuderi wanted to marry his daughters off as quickly as possible.

Aria squirmed when she looked at me. "I apologize for my sisters and brother. They are—"

"Protective of you," I helped her out. "This is my brother, Matteo."

Aria barely glanced his way, but she wasn't really meeting my eyes, either.

I nodded to my side. "And this is my right hand, Cesare."

She blinked. She looked like she would bolt if I took a step in her direction.

"I should go to my siblings." She whirled around and hurried away until her blond head disappeared from view.

"You've still got it, Luca. Terrifying girls left and right with your rough charm," Matteo said.

"Let's get going. Scuderi will be wondering what's taking us so long." Scuderi was the last person I wanted to meet, unless said meeting involved knives and guns and a bloodbath. I hated him without ever having met him. What kind of father married a girl like Aria off to a guy like me? She looked like an angel, and she was as shy and innocent as one, and I had absolutely no illusions what I was: a cold bastard on the best of days, and a monster the rest of the time. At least, she had three more years before I got the chance to destroy her life with my darkness.

———————✕———————

There wasn't enough booze in the world to make Scuderi and Fiore Cavallaro's presence more bearable. I wanted nothing more than to slice their throats open and watch them bleed to death. Matteo shot me a sideways glance, probably knowing exactly what I was thinking. He wouldn't hesitate a second if I asked him to pull his knives. Matteo was always ready to stick his knife into the next person who annoyed him.

"She's a real beauty, Luca," Scuderi said proudly. "You won't regret your choice."

There hadn't really been a choice on my part, but I kept the words to myself. There was no use in starting an argument, especially with Father watching me like a hawk.

"She's completely pure. She's never allowed to go anywhere without her bodyguards. She's only yours."

I forced a smile. Not that I didn't appreciate it. The idea that someone might touch Aria made my blood throb furiously in my veins. I felt fucking possessive of her. I'd never cared if the girls I'd had affairs with fucked other men, but with Aria I'd kill anyone who dared to look at her the wrong way.

"There's nothing better than breaking them in," Aria's cousin Raffaele said. He was a head smaller than me. If tonight ended in a bloodbath, he'd be the one I'd kill last, so I could take my time with him. Let's see if he'd still manage that ugly grin with my knife sticking out of his eye socket. Dante sent his soldier a hard look and Raffaele quickly glanced back down to his drink. It was the first time Dante had shown any kind of emotional reaction at all. His wife had died not too long ago.

Fiore was officially still the Boss of the Outfit, but I couldn't help but wonder if Dante was the man who ran the show.

Someone knocked.

When the door opened and Aria slipped in, keeping her back to us, I stiffened. She didn't look like the girl I'd seen yesterday. She was wearing a skimpy dress, revealing long, lean legs, creamy skin, and a nice butt. Damn it. When she finally turned, I found that the front was just as nice to look at. Then my eyes traveled farther up. Aria kept her head down, her eyes cast on the ground, and I could see her shivering in fear and discomfort. Something protective and furious reared its head in my chest, startling me. She was mine. How could her mother have let her walk around in this outfit? I'd bet my left ball that Aria hadn't had a say in choosing that fucking joke of a dress. I'd fucked girls with skimpier dresses but this was my future wife, and she was only fifteen. Her parents should protect her, not treat her like this. She finally risked a peek up and met my gaze. For fuck's sake, she looked like she wanted to cry. If I ever got the chance, I'd kill Scuderi and I'd fucking enjoy it. I put my glass down before I could fling it at the wall.

Aria's eyes flitted around nervously. The other men in the room watched her with the necessary respect, but that fucker Raffaele was undressing her with his fucking eyes. If this were New York, I'd relieve him of the burden of ever seeing anything again. And maybe I'd do it anyway if he didn't stop the leering soon.

Oblivious to Raffaele's disrespect, Scuderi ushered Aria toward me. He looked at me as if he expected my jaw to drop to the floor because of Aria. She *was* gorgeous, and in three years I might appreciate her being dressed like this, but now it only pissed me off that Scuderi tried to make Aria look like some fucking sexbomb when she obviously hated it.

"This is my daughter, Aria," Scuderi said with an eager look like a German shepherd waiting for his master to throw a stick.

Fiore gave me a self-satisfied grin. "I didn't promise too much, did I?"

Fuck you. "You didn't."

Aria's little brother snuck up on her and slipped his hand into hers. My eyes went to her legs for a moment but I tore them away.

"Maybe the future bride and husband want to be alone for a few minutes?" Father said with a look I knew only too well. He probably thought he was doing me a fucking favor. I didn't miss Aria's panicked expression, or the way she practically begged her father with her eyes to forbid it.

Of course Scuderi didn't. He'd probably let me manhandle her right in front of him as long as I didn't steal her virginity before the wedding.

"Should I stay?" her bodyguard asked.

Relief flashed across Aria's face. I had no illusions as to what I was, but in this room I was the one Aria had to fear the least.

"Give them a few minutes alone," Scuderi said, and Aria froze. What did she think I was going to do to her? Ravish her on the sofa? Father winked at me. He obviously thought I was going to grope at my fifteen-year-old fiancée.

He probably would have. Everyone started to leave until only the little boy was left, clinging to his sister protectively. I had to give it to the midget, he was the only one from the Outfit with an ounce of courage.

"Fabiano. Get out of there *now*," Scuderi snapped, and the boy let go of Aria and sent me a scathing look before he left. I liked that insolent brat.

The door fell shut and Aria and I were alone. She peered up at me through her long lashes, biting her lip. Did she have to look so fucking terrified? I knew how I appeared to others, and for a petite girl like her, I probably looked like a menacing giant about to crush her, but I had absolutely no intention of hurting her, much less feel her up no matter how delicious she looked. I wasn't that depraved. I'd never forced myself on a woman, and Aria was only a girl. My fiancée. *Mine. Mine to protect.*

To distract her from her obvious terror, I asked, "Did you choose the dress?"

She jerked, her eyes growing wide. Huge blue eyes, so full of innocence I felt like they could wash even my sins away. And that golden hair…fuck me, I wanted to touch it to find out if it was as silky as it looked.

"No. My father did," she said in that soft, genteel voice.

Of course he did. I could see her shivering from cold and fear. I decided to cut this ridiculous meeting short before Aria passed out on me, and I reached for the ring I'd bought for her a couple of days ago. My little fiancée flinched, and my mood dropped even further. I showed her the velvet box, hoping it would set her at ease, but she only stared. I wanted to shake some sense into her but that would only have proven her fears right. I shoved the box at her and she finally reached for it. When her fingers brushed mine, she pulled away with a gasp. I had to stifle my annoyance—not at her, but at her parents, Cavallaro, and my father who'd brought this mess down upon us. She was too young. I could only hope she'd gain some confidence in the next three years. I didn't want a wife who cowered in front of me.

"Thank you," she said after she'd checked out the ring. Her eyes met mine. I held out my arm. She took it with barely any hesitation and I led her toward the living room to the people who'd betrayed her.

The moment I released her, she rushed off to her sisters and mother as if they could protect her from what was to come.

I went over to the men.

"And?" Father asked smugly.

I wasn't sure what he expected. A lewd comment about how I'd used my chance alone with Aria?

Matteo shot me a sideways glance.

"Aria accepted the ring," I said matter-of-factly.

Scuderi's face fell. "As she should. My daughter was brought up to be obedient. You'll see."

"Luca will make her obey him. He can bring the strongest men to their knees. A weak woman will bow to his will," Father said snidely.

Dinner was served that moment and saved us from a fight. It was a pity. I would have enjoyed it thoroughly.

I sat down beside Scuderi as tradition dictated. Matteo sat across from me, a flicker of boredom on his face. A bored Matteo was always a ticking bomb.

Fiore Cavallaro raised his glass. The way his eyes went out of focus, I'd say he should stop drinking. Old bastard. I would have preferred dealing with his son, the cold fish Dante, but as long as his father was still in command, I'd have to live with the demented old fool. "To a long and successful partnership."

I lifted my glass and downed the red wine. My eyes found Aria again. She was sitting at the other end of the table with the other women. She peered down at her ring as if it were something terrifying. Of course, it was. It bound her to me. It marked her as mine. When she looked up, our eyes met. She flushed and quickly turned away, red traveling up her delicate throat.

Matteo kicked me under the table, smirking. "Already lusting after your child bride?"

"I can wait," I said. "It's not like I can't keep myself entertained." But from this day, she was mine.

After dinner, we moved to the lounge to drink and smoke. Rocco Scuderi and Fiore Cavallaro were insufferable show-offs, and Father tried to overshadow them with his own bragging. I wanted to stuff my ears with hot wax to be spared their bullshit talk. Aria better be worth it, because peace sounded less enticing with every fucking second I had to spend with the Outfit bastards.

I was on my fourth glass of scotch when everyone had finally left the lounge except for Matteo, Romero and Cesare. Father had left to meet with a high class prostitute from the Outfit's best whorehouse, but I had no intention of risking a repeat performance of the Bratva whore incident.

I allowed myself to relax against the marble ledge of the fireplace. My eyes were heavy from being alert all day, and I couldn't risk letting my guard down as long as we were in Chicago. Matteo was sprawled out on an armchair as if he owned the place. His grin didn't bode well.

"It could have been worse," Matteo said, grinning even wider. "She could have been ugly. But, holy fuck, your little fiancée is an apparition. That dress. That body. That hair and face." Matteo whistled.

Anger surged through me. Matteo and I often talked about women like that, and even with less favorable words, but this was different.

"She's a child," I said dismissively, hiding my annoyance. Matteo would only irk me further if I gave him an opening.

"She didn't look like a child to me," he said, then clucked his tongue. He nudged Cesare. "What do you say? Is Luca blind?"

Cesare shrugged with a careful glance in my direction. "I didn't look at her closely."

"What about you, Romero? You got functioning eyes in your head?"

Romero looked up, then quickly looked back down to his drink. I stifled a smirk.

Matteo threw his head back and laughed. "Fuck, Luca, did you tell your men you'd cut their dicks off if they looked at that girl? You aren't even married to her."

"She's mine," I said quietly. I glared at Matteo. My men respected me, but Matteo was a losing battle. Not that I had to worry. He'd never lay hand on my woman.

Matteo shook his head. "For the next three years, you'll be in New York and she will be here. You can't always keep an eye on her, or do you intend to threaten every man in the Outfit? You can't cut off all of their dicks. Maybe Scuderi knows of a few eunuchs who can keep watch over her."

"I'll do what I have to," I said, swirling the drink in my glass. I had considered what Matteo had said before, and it didn't sit well with me. I didn't like the idea of being so far from Aria. Three years were a long time. She was beautiful and vulnerable, a dangerous combination in our world.

"Cesare, find the two idiots who are supposed to guard Aria," I ordered.

Cesare left immediately and returned ten minutes later with Umberto and Raffaele. Scuderi was a step behind them, looking pissed.

"What's the meaning of this?" he asked.

"I want to have a word with the men you chose to protect what's *mine*."

"They are good soldiers, both of them. Raffaele is Aria's cousin, and Umberto has worked for me for almost two decades."

I mustered them both. "I'd like to decide for myself if I trust them." I stepped up to Umberto. He was almost a head smaller than me. "I hear you're good with the knife."

"The best," Scuderi interjected. I wanted to silence him once and for all.

"Not as good as your brother, as rumor has it," Umberto said with a nod toward Matteo, who flashed him his shark grin. "But better than any other man in our territory," Umberto admitted eventually.

Matteo *was* the best with a knife. "Are you married?" I asked next. Not that marriage had ever stopped a man from having another woman.

Umberto nodded. "For twenty-one years."

"That's a long time," Matteo said. "Aria must look awfully delicious in comparison to your *old* wife."

I shot Matteo a look. Couldn't he keep his mouth shut for a second?

Umberto's hand twitched an inch toward the holster around his waist. My own hand was already resting on my gun. I met Umberto's gaze. He cleared his throat. "I've known Aria since her birth. She is a *child*."

He said it with a hint of reproach. If he thought that would make me feel guilty or anything close to it, he was a fool. "She won't be a child for much longer," I said.

"She will always be a child in my eyes. And I'm faithful to my wife." Umberto glared at Matteo. "If you insult my wife again, I'll ask your father for permission to challenge you in a knife fight to defend her honor, and I'll kill you."

That would make Matteo's day. There was nothing he enjoyed more than a bloody knife fight, probably not even a pussy. "You could try," Matteo said, baring his teeth, "but you would not succeed."

Umberto wasn't a threat. Neither for Matteo, nor for Aria. I could tell he was protective of her in a fatherly way. "I think you're a good choice, Umberto."

I turned to Raffaele. If we'd been in New York, I'd have already put a bullet in his head. Perhaps he thought I hadn't seen the looks he'd given Aria when he thought nobody was paying attention. I stepped right in front of him. He craned his neck to meet my gaze. He tried to look cool. He wasn't fooling me. There was fear. Good.

"He's family. Are you honestly going to accuse him of having an interest in my daughter?" Scuderi butted in from the side.

"I saw how you looked at Aria," I said to Raffaele. His eyes flickered nervously.

"Like a juicy peach you wanted to pluck," Matteo threw in, enjoying this entirely too much.

Raffaele's eyes darted to Scuderi like the spineless wimp he was. I knew guys like him. They got off on preying on the weak, especially women, because it was the only way they could feel strong.

"Don't deny it. I know want when I see it. And you want Aria," I growled. Raffaele didn't deny it. "If I find out you're looking at her like that again…If I find out you're in a room alone with her…If I find out you touch as much as her hand, I will kill you."

Raffaele flushed red. "You aren't a member of the Outfit. Nobody would tell you anything even if I *raped* her. I could break her in for you. Maybe I'll even film it for you."

I grabbed the bastard and threw him to the ground. His face hit the floor hard and I dug my knee into his back. I wanted to break his spine in two and rip off his fucking balls. Then he'd never even think about using the words 'rape' and 'Aria' in the same sentence again.

Raffaele struggled and cursed. He was like a bothersome fly: weak and disgusting. Worth less than the dirt on my shoes. That he even dared think about touching Aria, about breaking her in…I grabbed his wrist and pulled out my knife.

I should cut off his balls and dick. That was what he deserved. But this wasn't my territory. Even though it pissed me off, I looked at Scuderi for permission.

Scuderi nodded. I brought my knife down on Raffaele's pinky, cutting through bone and flesh and relishing in his pussy screams.

A female cry echoed through the walls.

I let go of Raffaele and stood. He cradled his hand like a baby, a blubbering mess. Disgusting. Romero and Cesare had drawn their weapons.

Scuderi went to open a secret door, revealing the redheaded sister and Aria.

"Of course," Scuderi hissed. "I should have known it was you causing trouble again." He wrenched the redhead away from Aria and into the lounge, raised his hand, and slapped her hard across the face. My fingers on the knife tightened.

And then the fucker stepped toward Aria, raising his arm again. Fury burned through me. *Mine.*

I caught his wrist, stopping him. It took all my willpower not to ram the bloody knife into his stomach and let him bleed out like a pig.

From the corner of my eye, I saw Umberto drawing his knife and Scuderi reaching for his gun. Matteo, Romero, and Cesare had drawn their own guns.

I hated the words I had to speak next. "I didn't mean disrespect, but Aria is no longer your responsibility. You lost your right to punish her when you made her my fiancée. She's mine to deal with now."

Scuderi glanced at the ring on Aria's finger, marking her as mine. He gave a nod and I released him.

"That's true." He stepped back from me and gestured at Aria. "Then would you like the honor of beating some sense into her?"

I turned my eyes on Aria. She was pale. Her fearful eyes darted to the knife in my blood-covered hand, then back up to my face. She froze. The idea of raising my hand against her was ludicrous. What kind of man hit a woman? And Aria? No, the mere idea set my teeth on edge. She weighed less than half of me. She was innocent and vulnerable. "She didn't disobey me."

Scuderi looked fucking unhappy. As if I gave a fuck. "You're right, but as I see it, Aria will be living under my roof until the wedding, and since honor forbids me to raise my hand against her, I'll have to find another way to make her obey *me*." He hit Aria's sister a second time, and I had half a mind to intervene again, but that was beyond my control.

"For every one of your wrongdoings, Aria, your sister will accept the punishment in your stead," Scuderi said. Aria looked as if she'd rather have him hit her than her sister. She was way too innocent and gentle for someone like me.

Scuderi turned to the bodyguard. "Umberto, take Gianna and Aria to their rooms and make sure they stay there." Umberto sheathed his knife and led them out. Aria avoided looking at me as she helped her sister.

Raffaele's whimper drew my attention back to him. He was still clutching his hand, crying like the fucking wimp he was. Matteo held out a tissue. I took it and cleaned my hand and knife roughly. I'd need water and soap to get rid of it completely.

"I trust you'll keep Aria safe from male attention," I said coldly, fixing Scuderi with a hard look. "I don't want him anywhere near her. If I hear that someone as much as looks at her the wrong way, nothing will stop me from dragging Chicago into the bloodiest war you can imagine. I don't share what's mine, and Aria is mine. Only mine. She's under my protection from this day on."

Scuderi's mouth thinned, but Fiore would lose his shit if peace broke because Scuderi couldn't protect his own daughter. "Don't worry. She will be protected. Like I said, she attends a Catholic school for girls and is never alone with men."

I knelt beside Raffaele and he shied back, terror flashing in his eyes. I leaned even closer. "This was nothing," I growled. "This pain is a fucking joke compared to the kind of agony you'll be in if you go near Aria ever again. If you ever touch as much as a hair on her body," my voice turned even deadlier, shaking with the force of my rage, "a single fucking hair, I'll shove my knife up your ass and fuck you with it slowly until you bleed out through your asshole. Got it?"

He gave a jerky nod.

"I want to hear it."

"I won't touch her," he pressed out, looking like he was going to puke onto my shoes at any moment.

I stood and stepped back, my lip curling in disgust at the coward in front of me. "We're done here," I said.

"I'll see you out," Scuderi said in a clipped voice.

Romero, Cesare, Matteo and I followed him. We didn't shake hands as we parted. Those kinds of fake pleasantries could wait until my wedding.

After returning to our hotel, we gathered in the bar for another drink. Romero was the only one who barely touched his, always dutiful. I regarded him. I knew him since we were kids. He was close to Matteo's age, and they'd gone to school together. He was a good soldier and a trustworthy man.

Noticing my attention, he frowned. "Is something the matter?"

"What do you think of Aria?"

Cesare and Matteo both fell silent.

Romero set down his glass, his body tightening. "She's going to be your wife."

"I don't want you to state the obvious. I want to hear your impression of her."

"She's shy and obedient. Well behaved. I don't think she'll cause trouble in the next three years." His words had been chosen carefully.

"She's beautiful now. She'll be out-of-this-world stunning in three years. I need someone to be her bodyguard, someone I can trust not to touch what's not his or anyone else's."

Romero's eyes widened, finally catching up. Matteo and Cesare looked surprised as well. "Luca," he said quietly, "if you choose me to guard Aria, I swear she'll be safe. And I won't ever even think about her in an inappropriate way."

Matteo snorted. "Don't swear on it. I have a feeling it'll be difficult not to have inappropriate thoughts about Aria."

I fixed Romero with a hard look. "You know I trust you, and you're one of my best soldiers, but what I just said to Raffaele holds true for *anyone* who touches her." My eyes slid over all three men before I smirked and raised my arm, asking the barkeeper for another round. They'd got the message.

CHAPTER 4

ALMOST THREE YEARS LATER

Matteo waved a newspaper in the air when he entered my penthouse. Setting my cup of coffee down, I raised my eyebrows. "Since when do you read the newspaper?" I asked. Of course we needed to stay up to date on political events, especially legislation, but that's what the internet was for. Did Matteo think it would make him look better? Like some fucking Brooklyn hipster?

I wouldn't put it past him to carry a newspaper with him for fashion purposes.

His answering grin raised my suspicions. "I saw an interesting article online when I checked the news in bed this morning and decided to get physical proof of it."

"Of what?"

Matteo stepped up to the kitchen bar and put the newspaper down in front of me. My eyebrows rose in surprise when I saw the headline and the photo.

This is the woman who snatched New York's most sought-after bachelor from the market!

Below the headline was a photo of me and beside it a photo of Aria. For a second, I froze. I hadn't seen Aria in the last three years since our engagement. There hadn't been any reason to do so. I'd sent her presents for Christmas, the anniversary of our engagement, Valentine's Day, and her birthday—the last one yesterday for her eighteenth birthday.

Aria was painfully beautiful. The photo wasn't an official one. It looked as if paparazzi had taken it without her knowledge, so her gaze was distant as she looked into the camera. She was walking the streets in Chicago, carrying a few shopping bags, and followed by Umberto and her second bodyguard. She was dressed in a short gray winter coat, an oversized white wool pullover, a heart-stoppingly short plaid skirt, and gray overknee suede boots that showed off her slim calves and legs. Her long blond hair trailed down her shoulders and good Lord, her face…I wasn't even sure if she wore make-up, but she was stunning.

"You're drooling," Matteo said as he leaned across from me.

My eyes snapped up to his.

"But so was he." Matteo pointed at a man in the photo who almost broke his neck to stare after Aria, checking her out. I felt the urge to find out who he was and kill him just for the thrill of it. But I had a feeling I wouldn't stop killing if I punished every guy who checked out my fiancée.

"I have to say I'm a bit offended that they didn't consider me the most sought-after bachelor in New York. I mean, look at me." Matteo stepped back so I could admire him in his outfit. Fucking biker boots, leather jacket and ripped jeans.

"You don't have to worry about it anymore. According to this, I'm now off the market," I said dryly.

"Did you know the news would be leaked to the press?"

I shook my head. Father hadn't told me when exactly the announcement would go out. I scanned the article to see what they'd written about Aria.

Luca Vitiello's long row of conquests will certainly shed a couple of tears finding out that the heir with an estimated net worth of 600 million dollars is no longer up for grabs.

"They even disinherited you in their article," I said to my brother. He and I would both inherit Father's fortunes, and it was closer to 700 million dollars, but what were one hundred million give or take for the press? They kept their fact-checking to a minimum as usual.

His future wife, Aria Scuderi, Italian-American as expected, is the oldest daughter of restaurant chain owner Rocco Scuderi.

I almost snorted. Rocco definitely had his hands in several restaurant chains, but that was definitely not his job description.

His connections to the Chicago underworld have been rumored but never confirmed. The same can be said for the Vitiellos, which leads to the question of how the connection came to be. Salvatore Vitiello and Rocco Scuderi declined any comment. One can't help but wonder how Aria Scuderi convinced the Vitiello heir to give up his bachelor ways.

I closed the newspaper. What bullshit.

My phone rang and Grace's name flashed across the screen. She usually knew better than to call me. I was the one who asked for a meeting, not the other way around.

"It's an angry ring," Matteo said with glee.

I picked up but, before I could say a word, Grace's voice shrilled in my ear.

"When were you intending on telling me?" Her voice was pissed and whiny.

Matteo chuckled and emptied the rest of my coffee.

"Telling you what?"

"That you're going to marry, of course!"

"It's none of your business."

"What?" she screeched. "We've been fucking each other for three years. I think I deserve—"

"You don't deserve shit, Grace. It's like you said. We *fucked*, and if I remember correctly, we both fucked others in that time as well."

Silence. "I would have agreed to being exclusive if you'd asked me."

"I didn't want to. I don't care whom you fuck."

Matteo was laughing quietly, making me want to chuck my phone at his pretty head.

"So you think I'll just let you keep fucking me when you're married as if nothing's changed?"

"First of all, I'm not married yet. Second, you've fucked married guys before. And third, you aren't anything special, so I don't give a fuck if you let me fuck you or not."

"Luca," her voice became even whinier. "You don't mean it. Why don't we meet later and have some fun?"

I hung up. That woman had no pride.

Matteo grinned. "Your Grace drama brightens my day once again."

"Let's head to the dojo. I want to rearrange your pretty face with my fists."

Matteo clapped his hands. "All right."

I shook my head and followed him toward the elevator. There were several reasons why I needed a good fight, and Grace was only a minor one. The major one was that I needed to release the pent-up desire stirring in my body since I'd seen Aria.

There were still six months until I could finally touch that body. Six fucking long months.

SIX MONTHS LATER

"So, are you nervous, Luca?" Matteo grinned.

"No. I'm never nervous."

"But you haven't seen Aria in three years. What if she doesn't look hot in person? Photos can be deceiving. Then you'll be stuck fucking an ugly woman for the rest of your life."

As usual, Matteo's favorite pastime was to annoy the crap out of me. "You're full of shit." She'd been pretty three years ago. I could only imagine how beautiful she'd be now. The photos of her had been the worst kind of torture I could imagine. When she'd been underage, I'd managed to stop myself from imagining fucking her but, for a while now, every look at the photo of her had turned my cock rock-hard.

We arrived at the door to Aria's suite. I paused, looking around for her bodyguard who was supposed to keep watch. He wasn't there. "I should have sent you to guard Aria years ago," I told Romero, then I knocked.

Light steps rushed toward us and the door was ripped open by a girl with dark blond hair. She was dressed like a cheap rocker girl. She was obviously trying to impress me with her barely-there hips and moderate chest. I had trouble remembering her name; she had to be the kid sister.

"Hi Luca," she said, actually smiling in a flirty way. I had to stifle a chuckle. Did she really think I didn't see how young she was? Then it finally clicked. "You're Liliana, the youngest sister."

"I'm not that young."

"Yes, you are," a familiar soft voice said. "Go to Gianna."

And there she was. Damn it. Three years ago she'd shown promise, but today she looked like a fucking wet dream come true. Long blond hair, smooth skin, lean legs and firm tits. I couldn't wait to see every fucking inch of her body.

"I didn't know we'd meet in my suite," she said with a hint of disapproval. What a warm welcome.

"Are you going to let me in?"

She stepped aside. I gave Cesare a sign to wait outside before the rest of us walked into the suite. Matteo headed straight toward the redhead. As usual, he was attracted to the troublemaker. My eyes were once again drawn to Aria's fucking hot body. Only a few more days and she'd be mine. I couldn't wait.

"You shouldn't be here alone with us. It's not appropriate," Gianna muttered.

Of course it wasn't. That's why there was supposed to be a guard in front of their door. "Where's Umberto?"

Aria shrugged. "He's probably on a toilet or cigarette break."

"Does he often leave you without protection?"

"Oh, all the time," Gianna said mockingly. "You see, Lily, Aria and I sneak out every weekend because we have a bet on who can pick up more guys."

Matteo shot me a grin. I wasn't sure how he could be in such a disgustingly good mood. If I had to spend any more time with the big-mouthed redhead, I'd lose my shit. "I want to have a word with you, Aria," I said.

Gianna had to butt in again, of course. "I was joking, for god's sake!" The brat actually tried to step between Aria and me. Thankfully, Matteo dragged her away. I really hoped the glint of fascination in his eyes was only that.

"Let go of me, or I'll break your fingers," Gianna growled. Matteo raised his hands with a wide grin. Those two were more than even the most patient saint could handle.

"Come on." I turned to Aria and barely touched her lower back. She swallowed and tensed. Had she still not gotten over her fear of me? "Where's your bedroom?"

No, she definitely hadn't. I usually only saw that kind of look on the faces of my enemies after I got my hands on them. Aria pointed toward a door to our right and I nudged her in that direction, trying to ignore the way she trembled under my touch. It was starting to seriously annoy me.

Of course the bigmouth had the last word. "I'll call our father! You can't do that." As if Scuderi would care.

We stepped into the bedroom and I closed the door before facing Aria, who was staring up at me with fear-widened eyes. "Gianna was joking. I haven't even kissed anyone yet, I swear." She blushed deliciously as she said it. That's why she was so scared? I had to admit that hearing her confirm what I'd known made a possessive beast in my chest rear its head. "I know."

Her fucking kissable lips parted in surprise. Damn it. I wanted to push her against the door and kiss her. "Oh. Then why are you angry?"

"Do I look angry to you?"

Her expression was like an open book. It would make things easier for me. "You don't know me very well."

She shot me an indignant look. "That's not my fault." This was the first real sign of defiance from her, and I was fucking glad about it. I really couldn't live with a terror-stricken wife. I wasn't the most sensitive guy and would lose my patience pretty quickly if I had to tiptoe around Aria like she was breakable.

I took her chin between my thumb and forefinger. She stiffened, and defiance was replaced by worry. "You're like a skittish doe in the clutches of a wolf. I'm not going to maul you." I'd do many other things to her, but she'd enjoy them all.

She pressed her lips together, obviously not believing me. She looked fucking beautiful, and her skin was like velvet under my fingertips. Would every inch of her feel so soft? I leaned down to kiss her, wanting to know if she'd let me. Women had rarely refused me, but Aria wasn't like them.

Her eyes grew wide. "What are you doing?"

Man, did she have to act as if I were a creep who'd trapped her in a dark alley? "I'm not going to take you, if that's what you're worried about. I can wait a few more days. I've waited three years, after all."

Fury flickered across her pretty face, and I fucking loved the sight of it. "You called me a child last time."

She remembered that? I let my eyes trail over her amazing body, then smirked. "But you aren't a child anymore." Damn it, I wanted her more than I'd ever wanted a woman, but the horrified glint in her eyes stopped my cock from getting any ideas. I moved even closer. "You're making this really hard. I can't kiss you if you look at me like that."

"Then maybe I should give you that look on our wedding night," the little vixen actually said. Two could play that game.

"Then maybe I'll have to take you from behind so I don't have to see it."

It was meant as a joke, even if the idea of having her perfect butt propped up in front of me was too good. Aria paled and flinched away from me before bumping into the fucking wall. For fuck's sake, did she really think I'd throw her on the bed and mount her from behind in our first night together? Not that I didn't have the intention to have her braced on all fours in front of me while I slammed into her, but that would have to wait until later. From her fearful expression, she really thought I'd take her virginity like a beast.

Stifling my annoyance, I said in as calm a voice as I was capable of, "Relax. I was joking. I'm not a monster."

"Aren't you?"

What the fuck? I hadn't come here to let her insult me. If she wanted to see me as a monster, then I could gladly act like one. I glared down at her. "I wanted to discuss the matter of your protection with you. Once you move into my penthouse after the wedding, Cesare and Romero will be responsible for your safety. But I want Romero at your side until then."

"I have Umberto," she said with a frown.

Right. That's why I could walk into their suite without anyone trying to stop me. "Apparently, he's taking too many toilet breaks. Romero won't leave your side from now on."

"Will he watch me when I shower, too?"

Not in a million years. "If I want him to."

Defiance returned with full force. "You would let another man see me naked? You must really trust Romero not to take advantage of the situation." She tried to make herself taller, which was still more than a head smaller than me.

"Romero is loyal," I said, then bent down until we were at eye level. "Don't worry, I'll be the only man to ever see you naked. I can't wait." I made a show of undressing her with my eyes, and of course she wrapped her arms around herself, looking as if she were about to cry. I couldn't deal with crying women.

"What about Lily?" she asked quietly. If she didn't stop looking so damn vulnerable, I might feel the need to console her, and that would be a fucking premiere for me. I wasn't the consoling type. "She and Gianna share this suite with me. You saw how Lily can be. She'll flirt with Romero. She'll do anything to get a rise out of him. She doesn't realize what she could get herself into. I need to know that she's safe."

"Romero won't touch your sister. Liliana is playing around. She's a little girl. Romero likes his women of age and willing," I told her. I trusted Romero. He took his job seriously, and no matter how much Aria's little sister flirted, it wouldn't change the fact that she was a kid. I knew there were Made Men that wouldn't hesitate to take advantage of a girl that age, and even some who preferred them that young, but those pieces of shit would never be in my inner circle.

Aria's eyes found the bed, and I wondered what she was thinking. Before my own dirty mind could start imagining all the things I wanted to do with her, I said, "There's something else. Are you taking the pill?"

"Of course not." It was almost cute how offended she was by my question.

"Your mother could have made you start it in preparation for the wedding." I had absolutely no intention of using a fucking condom with my wife. I wanted to bury my cock in Aria's pussy without anything between us. I was the only man who'd ever have her, and I had always made sure to use a condom with the women I'd fucked in the past.

Aria's lower lip trembled. "My mother would never do that. She won't even talk to me about these things."

I loved that Aria was only mine, but I wasn't used to this level of inexperience. Only half-joking, I asked, "But you do know what happens between a man and a woman on a wedding night?" If I had to give her the sex talk, I'd have to fucking kill someone, or I'd seriously lose my shit.

"I do know what happens between normal couples. In our case, I think the word you're looking for is rape."

Fury burst through my body, making me want to lash out at anything and anyone. I'd gotten better at controlling myself over the years, but I still had to wait a moment before I was sure I wouldn't snarl at her. "I want you to start taking the pill." I handed her the packet the Doc had given me.

"Don't I need to see a doctor before I start taking birth control?"

"We have a doctor who's been working for the Famiglia for decades. This is from him. You need to start taking the pill immediately. It takes 48 hours for them to start working."

"And what if I don't?" she challenged. Anger was still simmering under my skin, but when wasn't it? "Then I'll use a condom. Either way, on our wedding night, you're mine." I opened the door. Aria staggered out. I hadn't meant to terrify her, but she'd better get used to it. I wasn't a kind man.

CHAPTER 5

Father sat with a self-righteous expression in the pew at the front as if this wedding was his ultimate triumph. I didn't think a marriage to Aria would lead to indefinite peace with the Outfit. Maybe the euphoria of the union would carry us through a few more years, but that was it.

Matteo leaned closer when the string quartet and piano started to play, announcing Aria's entry.

"Nervous? These are your last moments as a free man."

I rolled my eyes at him. A marriage wouldn't bind me the same way it would bind Aria. And free? That's not something I'd ever been. From birth, I'd been bound to the Famiglia, and that wouldn't change until my death. The Famiglia was the only thing that mattered in my life.

Matteo let out a low whistle and I followed his gaze toward the back.

Aria stood at the end of the aisle, white and golden. My eyes drank in every inch of her body, but a veil covered her face. My stomach did tighten for only a moment before I reined myself in.

When she and her father arrived in the front, he finally lifted her veil and, for the briefest moment, before Aria could mask it, I could see utter fear in her eyes. Damn it. Damn them all for forcing her into a marriage with me. But most of all, damn myself, because nothing in the world would have stopped me from making her mine, not anymore, not ever.

I held out my hand and Scuderi gave her to me with almost the same self-righteous smile my father wore on his face. Aria didn't look at me. She was fighting for composure. Her hand was cold in mine, and a tremor went through her body.

I wasn't sure what she expected of me.

The priest in his white frock greeted us, then the guests, before he began his opening prayer. It was tradition to get the church's blessing, but I didn't believe in a god. I doubted we'd all be here if there was one.

"Luca and Aria," the priest addressed us. "Have you come here freely and without reservation to give yourselves to each other in marriage? Will you love and honor each other as man and wife for the rest of your lives?"

Love. As if this marriage was about love. I didn't love anyone and never would. Love was a weakness. Aria's hand stiffened, and I wondered if she was stupid enough to hope for something like that. I would treat her with respect and perhaps even come to tolerate her as a partner, but love her? I almost laughed. The Famiglia, that was the only love I had. "Yes," I said, because it was expected. Aria's own yes held no hesitation.

The priest nodded, satisfied. "Since it is your intention to enter into marriage, join your right hands and declare your consent before God and his Church."

I took Aria's hands in mine and turned toward her. For the first time since she'd lifted the veil, she met my eyes. Her face didn't betray anything, but her eyes couldn't hide her emotions. Fear. Despair. Hopelessness.

Anger filled my bones. "I, Luca Vitiello, take you, Aria Scuderi, to be my wife. I promise to be true to you in good times and in bad, in sickness and in health. I will love you and honor you all the days of my life."

I tried to ignore her shaking when I slipped the ring on her finger. "Aria, take this ring as a sign of my love and fidelity. In the name of the Father, and of the Son, and of the Holy Spirit."

She was mine now.

It was Aria's turn to put the ring on my finger, but she was trembling too fucking much. I steadied her hand. People didn't need to see how terrified she was of me. Matteo with his fucking hawk-eyes noticed, of course, and gave me a smirk. I wouldn't hear the end of it.

"You may kiss the bride," the priest said.

Aria's head shot up. She stiffened further and her eyes held trepidation and embarrassment. Fuck. I squeezed her hands. I wasn't even sure why.

I hated to share this moment with all the fuckers in the room. I'd kissed so many women, fucked just as many, but this first taste of my wife…that wasn't something I wanted to share. I knew Aria would have preferred more privacy—of course she would, this was her first kiss.

Her first fucking kiss.

I leaned down and brushed my lips over hers. It was nothing. More air than touch. Not worth a second thought, but damn, my body sprang to life anyway. Aria was mine.

A blush spread on her cheeks, and it took every ounce of self-control not to throw her over my shoulder and carry her up to our room right away. I couldn't wait to have her naked body under me, to bury my cock in her. As if she could read my mind, Aria shuddered violently, and my lust evaporated.

I didn't want to consider the possibility that she might react the same way to my touch tonight. Fuck.

I took her hand and led her down the aisle. The men of the family gave me nods as they clapped. A waiter headed our way at once, balancing a tray with champagne glasses on his palm. I took one for my and one for Aria, handing it to her.

Aria clutched the glass in her delicate fingers but didn't react otherwise, not even looking my way. Soon our guests crowded around us to offer us their blessings. It was a necessary tradition we couldn't avoid, even when all I wanted was to fast-forward to my first night with my wife.

Aria's gaze was distant, her lips a thin line in her pale face. I dipped my head down to her. "Smile. You're the happy bride, remember?"

As if a switch had been turned, Aria's face became a mask of happiness, all fake. I took a sip of the champagne, stifling my frustration over her apparent unhappiness. This marriage hadn't been my idea. I wouldn't have married at all. My life was devoted to the Famiglia, and a woman had no place in it.

The first guests appeared before us, my father and Nina. She stood a step behind him as he expected.

My father put a hand on my shoulder. He was my height, the only man at the party who was, and his eyes met mine. Gray eyes and dark hair like me. But that was the extent of our similarities, if you disregarded our streak of cruelty. "Luca, my eldest," he said in a booming voice, drawing the attention of the surrounding guests to us. "Today marks a special day for you and the Famiglia."

I gave him a tight smile. He leaned closer, lowering his voice so only I could hear him. "I envy you tonight. There's nothing better than looking into a woman's eyes when she realizes you can do to her whatever you want, to crush those silly hopes and break their spirit and body. And I must say, your wife has expressive eyes. It'll be thrilling to see terror in them."

Something dark and cruel roared in my chest, but it was definitely not directed at the vulnerable woman at my side. I gave my father another smile, not saying anything from fear of revealing my thoughts. Father stepped back, and his gaze settled on Aria as he moved to congratulate her. My entire body erupted with tension as he kissed her hand. Then, Nina appeared before me and leaned up to kiss my cheek, saying in a conspiratorial whisper, "Oh Luca, that girl is petite. Don't break her your first night together. There will be many more nights for you to savor."

She had to know. My father enjoyed breaking her almost daily. Nina's spitefulness made me hate her fiercely, but I knew it was the only armor she had. Finally, my father and his wife excused themselves and allowed other guests to step forward.

As honor dictated, it was Aria's family. Scuderi looked like he'd won the Nobel prize as he shook my hand then hugged Aria. Her mother Ludevica stepped up to me. She briefly glanced up into my eyes, then lowered her gaze submissively. That was why Aria was like that. For a moment, Ludevica looked as if she wanted to say something, her gaze flickering from Aria to me, her face filling with worry before she managed to mask it. She swallowed hard and surprised me by stepping closer and taking my hands. "Aria is a good girl. She won't give you any reason to hurt her. She'll comply with your wishes..." Her voice was barely audible.

"Ludevica, the other guests want their turn," Scuderi said sharply, and his wife drew back from me at once. With a last pleading glance at me, she stepped up to her husband. It didn't take a genius to realize what her veiled words had meant. She begged me not to brutalize her daughter tonight because that was what a man like me would do. I didn't offer her words of assurance. Aria was no longer her responsibility. She was mine. Father stood back like a benevolent patron, but his sharp eyes watched my every move.

He wouldn't see a sliver of weakness. Not today, not ever.

Dante Cavallaro and his parents were next. It surprised me that Dante was at the front. It was a clear sign that he would soon become the head of the Outfit even when his father was still officially the boss.

His expression was stoic when he kissed Aria's hand, breaking protocol by greeting her first and not me. I regarded him closely, my eyes narrowing. When he finally stepped up to me, our gazes locked, and the same wariness I felt reflected in his eyes. This marriage was supposed to ensure peace, but neither Dante nor I trusted this fragile truce. "Congratulations on your marriage," he said emotionlessly.

"Thank you for giving me the Outfit's most beautiful woman, considering you are in need of a wife as well." Something feral flashed in Dante's eyes, but it wasn't the only emotion my words had summoned. There had been a flicker of sorrow and pain in his expression before the cold mask had returned. Dante missed his dead wife. The realization surprised me. I filed it away for possible later use. My father hadn't waited long to marry Nina once my mother was dead. Women were replaceable pleasure objects for him.

"My son has peculiar tastes when it comes to his next wife," Fiore butted in, stepping up beside his son.

I didn't say anything. Dante's eyes were already murderous and, while I would have enjoyed killing him and every Outfit fucker in the room, a wedding wasn't the right place or time. Mrs. Cavallaro waited with a pinched expression beside her husband and son. She barely talked. Maybe Fiore forbade her.

My eyes darted to Aria who stood with her hands folded before her stomach. Her expression reflected polite interest and fake happiness, but I could see the myriad of darker emotions lurking beneath her outward mask. Would she be like her mother, Nina, or Mrs. Cavallaro soon? Would I break her?

She didn't glance my way, but I was sure she noticed my gaze.

After her cousin Bibiana had talked to Aria, and I to her old fat husband, my wife's demeanor changed. I couldn't pinpoint why, but she kept risking peeks at me. I was talking to one of my captains when Aria watched me again, and I finally turned to meet her gaze. In it I saw curiosity and a flicker of hope. The latter was even more deadly than the former in our world.

Then a bright red dress and patent red leather heels caught my attention. My eyes returned to the line of well-wishers, and a curse died on my tongue.

Senator Parker and his family. I barely paid attention to the man whose campaigns we paid or his equally ambitious son who was also on our payroll. Behind them stood the last person I wanted to see at my wedding: Grace.

I was pretty sure she had been sewn into her fucking dress. I shook her father's and brother's hands before she stepped up to me. Senator Parker sent her a warning look, which Grace ignored like she always ignored sensible advice.

"Congrats, Luca," she said, her eyes practically trying to fuck me. If she didn't stop it soon, I'd have to throw her out.

"Grace," I said in a bored voice.

She stepped very close, closer than was proper, and I would have shoved her away if it hadn't caused a big scene.

"I'm so fucking wet for your cock, Luca. I want to taste your cum in my mouth," she purred into my ear. "Perhaps you'll think of me tonight when you fuck your little boring wife. She won't be half as good as I am."

I kept my face neutral, even if my blood boiled with fury. I doubted that had been Grace's fucking intention. Did she really believe I'd think of her when I was with Aria?

Aria was gorgeous. She was honorable. She was my wife.

Grace was nothing.

Of course, Aria wouldn't blow my mind with her skills. She had never been with anyone, but I'd teach her. Fuck, I couldn't wait to do it.

Then Grace actually hugged Aria and, when she pulled back, Aria looked as if she was going to be sick. What the fuck had Grace told her? She was a fucking backstabbing creature.

I reached for Aria's hand and she flinched so violently that I knew Grace must have divulged one of our harder adventures. As if I'd treat Aria as I treated Grace. That whore should have never been invited. My fucking father had probably done it on purpose to mess with me.

When the ordeal was over and we finally moved toward the tables, I almost groaned in relief. I wished I knew what was going on in Aria's head, but she wasn't even looking my way, intent on pretending I wasn't there, even though I held her hand. "You can't ignore me forever, Aria. We're married now."

'Bacio, Bacio'-cries rose from the crowd when we were about to sit down. Aria was still frozen at my side. Stifling my annoyance, I pulled her against me and kissed her again. I wanted nothing more than to deepen the kiss, to claim that sweet mouth, but I knew she would have hated to experience a more intimate kiss in front of so many people. She was already fucking embarrassed by the kiss we'd just shared, and that was tame.

The moment we sat down, the redheaded troublemaker took her seat beside Aria. I hoped she wouldn't make a scene. On the other hand, perhaps it would distract from the scene Matteo would undoubtedly make.

My brother took a large sip of wine before he leaned over to me. "All through church, I couldn't think about anything but to stick my knife into a few Outfit fuckers. A bloody wedding would be so much more interesting than this farce. And I don't mean our fucking bloody sheets tradition. At least you get to spill some blood tonight."

Matteo laughed and I fell in but then sobered again. I had been at a few presentations of the sheets over the years. Matteo and I had always made fun of them. My eyes found Aria, who was listening to something her sister whispered in her ear. Aria was my wife now. She was mine to protect. I hated the idea of presenting sheets with her blood in the morning. She'd be fucking embarrassed, that was for sure.

"You got a strange look on your face, Luca. Worried she won't bleed?"

I narrowed my eyes at Matteo. "I hope you're not insinuating that Aria isn't honorable."

Matteo snorted. "Oh please, it's obvious she's never even been close to a man, the way she acts around them, and you." He grinned. "But perhaps you can't go through with it."

I gave him a disbelieving look. "Really? You think anything or anyone could stop me from taking my wife tonight?"

Matteo smirked. "No, not a single man in this room could stop you, and probably not even all of them. But perhaps she will." He nodded toward Aria, who was holding her sister's hand, looking pale and small.

"You've lost your fucking mind, Matteo. You should know me better than that. I will fuck her."

Matteo shrugged. "Perhaps."

Matteo rose from his chair after everyone had settled down and clinked his knife against the champagne glass to silence the crowd. I sent him a warning look, which only made him grin. I'd kill him one day. "Ladies and gentlemen, old and new friends, we've come here today to celebrate the wedding of my brother Luca and his stunningly beautiful wife, Aria..." Matteo made an exaggerated bow in her direction.

Aria smiled tensely and Gianna sent her best death glare my brother's way. As if that would discourage him. "To uncharted grounds. Nothing better than to tread on fresh snow, leaving the first marks." He winked at me, then Aria, before he turned to the crowd. "I'm sure everyone here agrees! To uncharted grounds!

The men laughed and threw his words back at me, lifting their glasses in my direction.

I shook my head with a smile. Matteo was a fucking nuisance. My smile died when I saw Aria. She'd put her brave face on, but her skin was bright red from embarrassment and her eyes reflected anxiety. Gianna was clutching one of her hands, but the other was curled into a fist on her pure white dress. For some reason, I wanted to reach out and unfurl her fingers, link them with my own. It was a ridiculous notion I would never follow, especially not in a room with my enemies and my soldiers.

I was glad when my father and Scuderi were done with their toasts and the food was finally served. Not only was I starving, but I was tired of their bullshit talk.

The servers began piling the tables with antipasti.

"I wanted to make a toast as your bridesmaid, but Father forbade it. He seemed worried I would say something to embarrass our family," Gianna said loudly.

I looked her way then rolled my eyes and filled my plate with antipasti. Aria took a big gulp from her wine and lifted the glass for another. I stopped her with my hand on hers.

"You should eat." Her plate was empty, and she hadn't touched any of the appetizers during the champagne reception. Her lips thinned, but she picked up a piece of bread and took a bite before she dropped it on her plate. She didn't eat much more when the main course was served, and I had to hold back my frustration, especially when she drank more wine. Maybe she thought I didn't notice because my father and the Cavallaros dragged me into a conversation about the Bratva, but I wasn't blind.

When it was time for our dance, I rose and held out my hand. Of course the crowd requested another kiss the second Aria stood beside me. I pulled her against me, tightening my grip when she swayed. Her gaze wasn't as focused as it should be. She'd definitely had too much alcohol.

I had to steer her over the dance floor in a tight grip to keep her upright and stop her from stumbling, all the while fighting my anger.

I was glad when the dance was finally over, but before I led Aria back to the table, I whispered in her ear, "Once we're back at the table, you'll eat. I don't want you to pass out during our celebration, much less during our wedding night."

If she was drunk, I definitely wouldn't fuck her, and that wasn't going to happen. Under my watchful eyes, Aria ate her main course and drank two glasses of water. When Father stepped up to Aria to ask her for a dance, I almost snarled at him, but I had to hide my feelings and gave him a tight smile.

As was tradition, I had to dance with Nina while my father danced with my wife. Nina was surprisingly quiet as I led her over the dance floor, but my full attention was directed at my father and Aria, anyway. I could tell she was uncomfortable in his hold—not that she'd been relaxed when we'd danced.

"Jealous?" Nina asked.

"No," I said coldly.

Matteo strode past the other dancers and tapped Father's shoulder, asking to dance with Aria. He sent me a quick smile the moment he whirled my wife over the dance floor. Nina finally moved on, and I danced with Ludevica and then Liliana. When I noticed Grace heading in my direction, I quickly excused myself and headed off the dance floor and toward the table. No way in hell would I dance with Grace. Her brother grabbed her arm and forced her into a dance with him, to Grace's obvious dismay.

"They would have made a good-looking couple," Matteo said as he stepped up beside me. I followed his gaze and tensed.

Dante was dancing with Aria.

"'The golden couple' is what some people nicknamed them in the Outfit.

There were even rumors that Fiore considered cancelling your engagement to Aria so his son could have her."

"That would have meant war. I would personally have walked straight into Chicago, crushed Dante's throat and taken Aria home with me."

Matteo chuckled. "That sounds like more fun than this."

I left him standing there and headed for Dante and my wife. They'd danced long enough. It was time Aria returned to my arms.

Dante noticed me first. "I think your husband is eager to have you back in his arms," he drawled in that annoying way. He stepped back with a calculating expression, and I quickly took Aria's hand and led her away before we began dancing.

"What did Cavallaro want?"

Aria hesitated the briefest moment before her reply. "To congratulate me on the festivities."

That definitely hadn't been all they'd talked about, but the music stopped at a sign from Matteo and he silenced our guests with loud clapping.

"Time to throw the garter!"

The crowd circled us immediately. I'd witnessed this tradition so often, I knew what was expected. I got down on my knee and cocked my eyebrows expectantly at Aria. I knew her mother had instructed her on our traditions. I wasn't sure if it was the same in the Outfit.

Aria lifted her gown, revealing white high heels, slender calves, then gorgeous knees. Fuck. I didn't even know gorgeous knees were a thing.

I cupped Aria's calves, stifling a groan at the feel of her warm skin. This was the first time I'd touched her legs, for god's sake. The first time any man touched those legs. I slid my palms up slowly until I reached her thighs. She froze and goose-bumps rose on her skin. I searched her eyes, trying to figure out the emotion behind her reaction, but she had her public happy bride face in place.

In this moment, I wanted nothing more than to be alone with her. The feel of Aria's thighs made me want to reach higher, to discover the rest of her curves, but my fingers brushed her garter on her right leg. I used one hand to push her dress up further to reveal the garter, even if I didn't like the idea of all the men in the room seeing her thighs.

Aria gripped her dress and I crossed my arms behind my back then leaned forward, bringing my face closer to her leg. I was supposed to grab the garter with my teeth, but before I did, I couldn't stop myself from kissing the skin right below it. Aria sucked in a startled breath and I stifled a groan when her sweet scent drifted into my nose. My eyes darted up, but unfortunately the bunched up fabric barred my view of her panties.

I finally closed my teeth around the garter and dragged it down Aria's leg until it fell to the floor. Aria lifted her foot and I grabbed the piece of clothing and stood with it clutched in my hand for everyone to see. Our guests applauded wildly.

"Bachelors," I shouted. "Gather around. Maybe you'll be the lucky one to marry next!"

It took a couple of minutes for everyone to come together, or for the mothers to drag their protesting teenage sons to the front.

Aria let out a bell-like laugh. Stunned by the first carefree sound I'd heard from her, I glanced her way. She was beaming at her younger brother Fabiano, who stood with his arms crossed among the men. Would she ever look that happy when she lived with me in New York?

Shoving the thought aside, I raised my arm and threw the garter at the men.

Of course my brother dove for it, shoving a few less motivated guys out of the way, and caught it.

"Any willing Outfit ladies out there that want to further the bond between our families?" he boomed, wiggling his eyebrows.

I chuckled. He knew as well as I did that it was difficult to find that kind of entertainment at our gathering. Most female guests were from our world and not outsiders, so they were firmly off-limits.

I wrapped my arm around Aria and she flinched. My good mood evaporated at once.

Forcing my face to stay calm, I watched as Matteo started dancing with Liliana, who looked ecstatic about being the center of attention. I pulled Aria against me since we were expected to have another dance. This time, she barely tensed. I glanced down at her blond head and the way her face was tilted toward my brother and her sister.

"If my brother married your sister, you'd have family in New York," I said.

"I won't let him have Lily," Aria muttered, surprising me with the protective note in her voice.

"It's not Lily he wants," I said, glancing toward Gianna who was skulking at the fringes of the dance floor. Aria seemed shocked by my comment. Hadn't she noticed the looks my brother had been giving her sister? Maybe she didn't recognize desire on a man's face. That would soon change.

———————✕———————

When the first shouts rang out that suggested I bed Aria, I had to stop myself from jumping up, throwing her over my shoulder and carrying her to our room.

"You wed her, now bed her!" Matteo shouted, throwing his arms up and bumping into a chair.

I laughed at my brother's antics and rose from my chair. Aria stood as well.

"Stain the sheets red!" Father shouted with a lewd grin. Ignoring him, I led Aria toward our bedroom under the applause and shouting of the other guests.

Some of their comments made me want to punch them in the face, even if I intended to do everything they suggested, eventually. I couldn't remember the last time I'd felt close to bursting from desire. I really hoped I could hold back like I'd promised myself.

Father and my uncles clapped my shoulder and back as I stopped with Aria in front of our bedroom door.

Aria was silent beside me, glancing down so I couldn't see her face. I'd show her how much I wanted her. I shoved the door open and she slipped in. Finally mine.

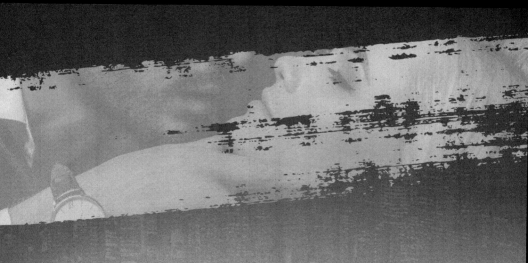

CHAPTER 6

I slammed the door shut in Matteo's face as he kept spewing suggestions of all the ways I could fuck Aria. If I didn't have better things to do, I'd go outside and kick Matteo's fucking ass. "Shut up, Matteo, and go find a whore to fuck," I shouted.

He finally shut his fat mouth, or maybe he'd passed out. From the amount of booze he'd downed, I wouldn't be surprised. Aria released a rushed breath behind me and I turned to her, my body already thrumming with desire. I'd had to watch her all evening in her sexy dress, not to mention the three years I'd spent waiting for her before. But tonight, the wait was finally over.

She was fucking gorgeous. Narrow waist, smooth skin, pink lips. I couldn't help but wonder if her nipples would be the same color. Fuck. I needed her. I threw my jacket over the armchair. I really hoped she would be up for more than one fuck tonight. I didn't think my cock would be satisfied after one round.

"When my father told me I was to marry you, he said you were the most beautiful woman the Chicago Outfit had to offer, even more beautiful than the woman in New York. I didn't believe him," I said. I hated that my father had been right, but damn it, in this case he'd been spot on. I walked toward Aria and grabbed her waist. She stilled completely, not meeting my gaze. I leaned down, inhaling her sweet scent. "But he told the truth. You are the most beautiful woman I've ever seen, and tonight you are mine." I bent low to kiss her throat, but she kept ignoring me. Was this some kind of game she was playing? She should know that the games I usually played were of a darker variety, and I always won.

"No!" she hissed and stumbled away from me, her eyes wide and horror-struck.

What the hell did she mean? "No?"

She glared, but behind her bravado was another emotion I was too angry to read. "What? Have you never heard the word 'no' before?"

"Oh, I hear it often. The guy whose throat I crushed said it over and over and over again until he couldn't say it anymore."

She backed away. "So you're going to crush my throat, too?"

She really knew how to push my fucking buttons. Did she really think that making me angry on our wedding night was the way to go? I'd sworn to myself that I would hold back for her. "No, that would defy the purpose of our marriage, don't you think?"

"I don't think my father would be happy if you hurt me," she said haughtily.

"Is that a threat?" I asked quietly, feeling my pulse pound in my veins. I had to fight the urge to throw her on the bed and show her what I really wanted to do to her. Maybe she was more like her insolent brat of a sister, Gianna, than she'd let on. Maybe the shy, innocent act had been for show.

But then she dropped her gaze and I could see her shivering as she whispered, "No."

Anger still simmered under my skin, and I wasn't in the mood to let her off easy. "But you deny me what's mine?"

"I can't deny you something that you don't have the right to take in the first place. My body doesn't belong to you. It's mine," she said fiercely, eyes shooting daggers my way. I couldn't believe her audacity.

I reached for her shoulder to pull her against my body and silence her with a kiss before she said anything else that drove me up the wall, but Aria flinched violently and clenched her eyes shut as if expecting a blow. I dropped my hand, stunned by her reaction. Did she think I'd hit her? I was a violent man with hardly any patience to spare, and my brutal reputation preceded me, but I'd sworn to myself that I'd never abuse my wife. I'd watched my father rape and beat my mother before she'd killed herself. I didn't want to become him in that regard at least. In all other areas of my life, I was already too much like him. "I could take what I want," I said, because I wasn't sure what else to do. Aria didn't need to know that it was an empty threat. While I could certainly follow through with it, I would never do it.

I hated my own confusion. I always knew what to do, but with Aria things were more complicated.

She peered up at me with her beautiful eyes. "You could. And I would hate you for it until the end of my days."

Hate was the prevailing emotion in most marriages in our world, from what I knew. "Do you think I care about that? This isn't a marriage of love. And you do already hate me. I can see it in your eyes."

This discussion was a waste of time, anyway. We had our traditions. Both Aria and I were bound by them. I pointed at the white sheets. "You heard what my father said about our tradition?" It was a ridiculous one. Not all women bled the first time, unless the man made sure to be rough, which some husbands actually did to guarantee the expected splotch of blood. I had absolutely no intention of being rough with her. I wouldn't hurt her more than absolutely necessary, but I was a big guy. It would hurt, and she would bleed.

Aria walked away from me and toward the bed, looking down at it as if it were her doom. Had she thought she could talk me out of consummating our marriage if it weren't for our tradition? Then she didn't know me very well.

I walked up to her. She looked like a goddess. I couldn't wait to get her out of her dress, to taste every inch of her. I put my hands on her naked shoulders. She was warm and soft, but she didn't turn. I stifled my annoyance at her refusal to acknowledge my presence. I would be patient, even if she provoked me. I brushed my hands over her collarbones to the soft rise of her breasts. I could feel my cock responding to the feel of her perfect skin, to her tantalizing scent. Fuck, I burned to bury myself in her.

Something wet dropped on my hand. I didn't have to see it to know it was a tear, a fucking tear. She was crying. I grabbed her shoulders and turned her around before I hooked my finger under her chin and tipped it up. Tears rolled down her cheeks. I knew some women could cry whenever they wanted, but the look in Aria's eyes told me all I needed to know. She was terrified and hopeless. I was a good judge of human character—I had to be to keep my men in check. Aria wouldn't fight me if I pushed her toward the bed, ripped her clothes off and took her. She'd lie back and let it happen. She would cry, but she wouldn't refuse me, not anymore. She was mine for the taking. It was expected of me to take her, to make her mine. Tears had never weakened my resolve. But before now, those tears had never belonged to my wife, to the woman I was supposed to spend the rest of my life with.

I couldn't fucking believe that the sight of my terrified wife got to me. I pulled away, cursing and so furious I could barely see straight. I punched the wall, glad for the blinding pain ripping through my knuckles that grounded me. I was going to be Capo in a few years. I had killed, blackmailed, tortured, but I couldn't take my wife's virginity against her will. What did that make me? Father would call me a pussy. Maybe he'd decide I wasn't fit to be his heir if I couldn't even fuck my wife. But I knew I wasn't growing soft, not in general. I could go out now and kill every fucking member of the Chicago Outfit without a flicker of remorse. Hell, I could go down now and slice my father's throat, and I'd fucking enjoy it.

Of course, we still needed to make sure everyone believed I had fucked Aria. There was only one way to do it. I turned back to my shaking wife and pulled out my knife. Not only was I denying myself the pleasure of being inside her tight pussy tonight, but I was also going to bleed for her.

The thought didn't sit well with me, and not because I cared about a cut. I'd suffered through much worse injuries, but I couldn't help but feel like my action would give Aria too much power over me. But I knew I'd already made up my mind.

She was watching me with barely hidden trepidation and, when I moved toward her, she flinched. Again. She expected the worst because I was a monster. I cut my arm, put my knife down on the table, and grabbed a glass to catch a few droplets of blood. Aria's surprise would have been amusing, if I wasn't still mad at myself. I headed into the bathroom to add a few drops of water to the blood, so it would look convincing. I hadn't been with a virgin before. My tastes had always run toward the rough, so experienced women had seemed the better choice, but I'd witnessed a few presentations of the sheets over the years, and I knew what was expected.

Aria hadn't moved from her spot when I headed back to the bedroom and toward the bed where I spread a few drops of the pink liquid. From the corner of my eye, I could see her approaching me carefully. She stopped a few feet from me, hope mingling with confusion on her pretty face. Some girls were ugly criers.

I didn't think Aria could ever look anything less than stunning. The deep blush on her cheeks made me hate myself even more for my weakness. I could have had her beautiful body beneath me tonight, but instead I was painting a fucking picture with my own blood for the fucking furies of my family.

"What are you doing?"

"They want blood. They get blood."

"Why the water?"

"Blood doesn't always look the same."

"Is it enough blood?"

What had the women of her family told her about first times? "Did you expect a blood bath? It's sex, not a knife fight."

She bit her lip again and an image of her doing that in the throes of passion slipped into my mind.

"Won't they know that it's your blood?" she asked quietly. She looked too damn gorgeous with that fucking blush and small, hopeful smile. I wanted to see if I could make her lovely blush spread all over her body.

I needed a fucking drink. If I didn't get laid today, I'd at least get drunk. Fucking waste of a night. "No."

I poured myself scotch into the glass with the blood-water mix. Aria didn't take her eyes off me as I threw my head back and downed my drink. She gave me a disgusted look.

"What about a DNA test?"

Was she serious? "They'll take me at my word. Nobody will doubt that I've taken your virginity the moment we were alone. They won't, because I am who I am." I had a reputation. I'd never shied back from doing something I was supposed to do. So why wasn't I getting Aria out of her dress to fuck her?

Fear filled her face and she took a step back as if she could read my mind and was thinking of running.

That was fucking why. While I enjoyed seeing fear on the faces of my enemies and occasionally my own soldiers, the idea of having Aria lie beneath me with a similar expression didn't turn me on at all. I didn't want her terrified of me.

"No," I said. "That's the fifth time you've shied back from me tonight." I put my glass down and grabbed my knife from the table before I walked toward her. She looked like she wanted to bolt. "Did your father never teach you to hide your fear from monsters? They give chase if you run."

She didn't say anything, but I could see her start shaking when she peered up at me. Did she think I'd fucking cut her? If I really was that kind of monster, we wouldn't be standing here. She'd be sprawled out on the bed, crying her eyes out because I'd fucked her.

"That blood on the sheets needs a story," I told her, hoping to fucking calm her, but she flinched *again*. "That's six times." I brought the knife down to the edge of her dress, making sure the blade didn't touch her unblemished skin. I sliced the fabric slowly until the dress finally fell apart and pooled around her heels. "It's tradition in our family to undress the bride like this." Aria was left in nothing but a tight corset and white lacy panties. Damn it. She was fucking sex on legs. And then she flinched *again.* "Seven," I said, wishing I could tear my eyes away from her gorgeous body. The rise of her perfect small breasts, her narrow waist, the thin fabric of her panties barely hiding her pussy.

"Turn around."

Fuck. Aria's back was even more tantalizing than her front. What was that thing she was wearing? She had a fucking bow over her perfectly round butt, practically inviting me to unpack her. It would be so easy to rip down her flimsy panties and bury myself in her. She smelled sweet and perfect, and she was mine, only mine. I tugged at the bow. It would be so easy.

"You already bled for me," she whispered in a small voice. "Please don't." My wife begged me not to hurt her. Maybe I was a monster. I ran my knuckles over the silky skin of her back, needing to touch her, before I cut through her corset.

She held onto it before I could catch a glimpse of her breasts. I wrapped my own arm around her, pulling her against me. She gasped and stiffened when my cock dug into her lower back, and the blush across her cheeks deepened further.

"Tonight you beg me to spare you, but one day you're going to beg me to fuck you. Don't think because I don't claim my rights tonight that you aren't mine, Aria. No other man will ever have what belongs to me. You are mine." She nodded quickly. "If I catch a man kissing you, I'll cut out his tongue. If I catch a man touching you, I'll cut off his fingers, one at a time. If I catch a guy fucking you, I'll cut off his dick and his balls, and I'll feed them to him. And I'll make you watch." She knew I wasn't kidding. She'd seen what I had done to her bastard of a cousin years ago. And that was nothing.

I let her go. Her proximity was giving me ideas I really didn't need right now. I walked toward the chair and got myself another drink as Aria disappeared into the bathroom. I heard the lock click into place and had to bite back a laugh. My wife was hiding from me behind a locked door. Everyone in this fucking mansion was probably getting more action than me tonight. Damn it.

I had downed three more glasses of scotch when Aria finally emerged. This was fucking torture. She was wearing a flimsy, see-through nightgown that didn't hide anything. Was she fucking kidding? "That's what you choose to wear when you don't want me to fuck you?"

Her eyes darted between the bed and me. I didn't need to read her mind to know that she still didn't trust me. In that outfit, she was probably right not to trust any man. "I didn't choose it."

Of course she hadn't. "My stepmother?" That woman was a meddlesome sadistic bitch.

She gave a quick nod. I was sick of her terrified expression. I set down my glass and stood. As usual, Aria flinched. I didn't even bother with a comment. I was too fucking annoyed. Without another word, I headed into the bathroom and let the door fall shut behind me. I got out of my clothes and stepped into the shower. Under the warm water, I jerked off to images of Aria's delicious body. I felt like a fucking teenage boy, and even back then I'd never had to use my hand when I shared the room with a gorgeous girl. Shooting my cum at the shower tiles didn't give me any kind of satisfaction, but at least my balls didn't feel like they were about to burst anymore.

When I stepped back into the bedroom fifteen minutes later, Aria was mostly hidden beneath the blankets, only her golden hair spread like a halo on the pillow. I turned off the light and got into bed. She was so still, she might as well not have been there at all. I knew she wasn't asleep. Her breathing was off. It screamed fear.

I crossed my arms behind my head and glared into the darkness, and then I heard it.

A *sob*.

Soon, more followed, and I could feel the mattress vibrate as Aria shook under the force of her crying. I was furious, but beyond that, there was an emotion I didn't think I was capable of: compassion. I wanted to console her. I hated that weak part of myself. A Vitiello never showed sympathy, and he certainly never bowed down to the ridiculous whims of a woman. That's what my father taught Matteo and me.

"Will you cry all night?" I asked sharply, letting my anger run free. It was the more familiar choice.

Aria didn't reply, but I could still hear her muffled sobs. "I can't see how you could possibly have cried any worse if I'd taken you. Maybe I should fuck you to give you a real reason." This was the man my father had raised me to be. Letting my fury out had always felt good, so why didn't it this time?

Aria shifted, but her cries got only worse. I switched the light on and sat up. For a moment, I was stunned by the sight of my wife curled up in a fetal position beside me, shoulders curled in protectively and body shaking with sobs. It was hard to hold on to my anger, seeing her like that. There were men who got a hard-on if a woman cried. I never understood them.

The problem was that I had no clue what to do with a crying woman. I'd never consoled anyone in my life. I touched her arm. That obviously wasn't the way to go, because she flinched and would have rolled off the fucking bed if I hadn't grabbed her by the hip and pulled her toward me.

"That's enough," I said, trying to keep my frustration in check. She was already scared out of her mind; if I let my anger out on her, things definitely wouldn't improve.

I rolled her onto her back. She lay unmoving, her eyes scrunched shut as if she were waiting for me to make a move on her.

"Look at me." Her eyes peeled open, big and blue, and filled with tears. "I want you to stop crying. I want you to stop flinching from my touch."

She blinked once, then nodded. She would have agreed to anything in that moment. I'd seen that look in other people's eyes before. "That nod means nothing. Don't you think I recognize fear when it stares back at me? The moment I turn out the light, you'll be back crying as if I'd fucking raped you." Rape was one of the very few despicable things I wasn't guilty of, and I had absolutely no intention to change that. "So to give you peace of mind and shut you up, I'm going to swear an oath."

Hope filled her face, making her look even more stunning. I wasn't sure why I even cared. I shouldn't. She licked her lips, and I almost groaned. "An oath?"

I took her small hand and pressed it against the tattoo over my heart. Her palm was warm and smooth, and it felt too good. I spoke part of the words I'd said many years ago during my initiation. "Born in blood, sworn in blood,

I swear that I won't try to steal your virginity or harm you in any way tonight." If Matteo could see me now, he wouldn't let me hear the end of it. I pointed at my cut. "I already bled for you, so that seals it. Born in blood. Sworn in blood." I covered her hand, then waited for her to say the words.

"Born in blood, sworn in blood," she said softly. There was the tiniest smile tugging at her lips, and the sight of it shouldn't have made me feel so...content. I let go of her and turned the lights off. She didn't cry again. Eventually, her breathing deepened. Of course I was wide-awake, but I couldn't even leave the room. If someone saw me running around when I should be banging my wife, that wouldn't go over well. Nobody could ever find out.

Listening to Aria's even breathing, I wondered if I'd get a sliver of sleep tonight. I hadn't ever slept when I had to share a room with anyone. I was a light sleeper, always vigilant, waiting for someone to stick a knife into my back or eyeball, and lowering my guard was out of the question when others were around. But Aria was my wife. And to be honest, she wasn't a threat in any regard. Not because she was weaker and untrained—that wouldn't matter if she poisoned me in secret—but because she didn't strike me as someone who could seriously injure, much less kill someone. It wasn't in her nature.

Slowly, my muscles slackened. Aria's breathing never hitched. It was calm, soft, her sleep unperturbed. No horrors in her past haunted her nights. Knowing what kind of man I was, I hoped her sleep would stay as innocent as it was.

CHAPTER 7

Something soft tickled my fucking nose. My eyes shot open, and I stared at hair the color of spun gold. I was spooning Aria's small body, my arm wrapped around her narrow waist, and she was completely relaxed in my embrace. I had slept with her body against mine. I'd never let a woman sleep in my bed. I'd thought it would take months before I'd get a decent night of sleep now that I was forced to share a bed with my wife.

Fuck. Aria was my wife.

And still a fucking virgin.

I propped myself up on my elbow. She didn't stir. Her pale eyelashes rested on her porcelain skin, lips slightly parted. Fucking perfection, that's what she was.

Her stomach lifted and fell under my palm as she breathed peacefully. I could feel her warmth through the little nothing she was wearing. I wanted to slide my hand down between her legs, wanted to feel the heat there. Wanted to bury my fingers in her—and my cock. Fuck. My cock sprang to life.

I wanted to claim her, because it was my right.

She was mine.

My wife. And because of that. I wanted to protect her, even from myself—the hardest task of all.

Aria's breathing changed, her stomach tightened under my palm, then her entire body stiffened. She was scared of me, of what I might do.

"Good, you're awake," I murmured.

She stiffened even further and, slowly, her eyes peeled open. Gripping her hip, I rolled her over so I could get a better look at her face. Even without a hint of makeup, with tousled hair and sleepy, Aria was stunning. Her eyes lingered on my chest, a blush spreading on her cheeks. While I'd never fallen asleep beside a woman, I'd spent more than enough time in bed with them, but for Aria, this was the first time she was so close to a man. The early morning sun let her hair glow in golden hues. I reached for a strand, marveling at the silkiness. Everything about her was soft, smooth, silky—beckoning to be touched, to be claimed.

"It won't be long until my stepmother, my aunts, and the other married women of my family knock at our door to gather up the sheets and carry them into the dining room where undoubtedly everyone else is already waiting for the fucking spectacle to begin."

Her blush deepened, acute embarrassment flickering in her eyes. The epitome of innocence, so different from me and yet at my mercy. She glanced down at the cut on my forearm.

I nodded. "My blood will give them what they want. It'll be the foundation of our story, but we'll be expected to fill in the details. I know I'm a convincing liar, but will you be able to lie to everyone's faces, even your mother's, when you tell them about our wedding night? Nobody can know what happened. It would make me look weak."

Weak. People said many things about me. Weak wasn't one of them. I had no trouble doing what was necessary, no trouble hurting and breaking others. I shouldn't have hesitated claiming Aria, shouldn't have been bothered by her terror and tears. I should have pushed her down on her knees so I didn't have to see her fear and fucked her from behind. That's what people expected from me.

"Weak because you didn't want to rape your wife?" she asked, her voice shaking.

My fingers tensed on Aria's waist. Rape— we both knew nobody in our world would see it that way. No matter how brutally I fucked Aria, they'd see it as my privilege, my right.

My lips pulled into a tight smile. "Weak for not taking what was mine for the taking. The tradition of bloody sheets in the Sicilian mafia is as much a proof of the bride's purity as of the husband's relentlessness. So what do you think it will say about me that I had you lying half-naked in my bed, vulnerable and *mine*, and yet here you are untouched as you were before our wedding?"

Fear simmered in Aria's eyes. "Nobody will know. I won't tell anyone."

"Why should I trust you? I don't make a habit of trusting people, especially people who hate me."

Aria touched the wound on my forearm, her eyes softer than before. "I don't hate you."

She had every reason to hate me because I owned her, because I would never release her now that she was mine. She'd be trapped in an expensive golden cage, safe from violence because I vowed it to myself, but condemned to live without love and tenderness.

"And you can trust me because I am your wife. I didn't choose this marriage, but I can at least choose to make the best out of our bond. I have nothing to gain from betraying your trust, but everything to gain by showing you that I'm loyal."

She was right. It was a matter of survival instinct that she'd try to gain my trust, even if it was a futile endeavor. She was at my mercy and needed to stay in my good graces. Aria was a clever woman, but she didn't know my treacherous uncles and cousins like I did.

"The men waiting in that living room are predators. They prey on the weak and they've been waiting for more than a decade for a sign of weakness from me. The moment they see one, they'll pounce."

My Uncle Gottardo had never forgiven me for crushing his son's throat. He was waiting for a chance to get rid of me.

Aria's brows puckered. "But your father—"

"If my father thinks I'm too weak to control the Famiglia, he'll gladly let them tear me apart." My father didn't care about me. I was his guarantee to uphold the bloodline. As long as he considered me his strongest, most brutal option, he'd keep me alive. If he thought I was getting weak, if he thought I wasn't fit to become Capo, he'd put me down like a fucking dog.

"What about Matteo?"

Father still believed Matteo would taste blood the second he saw his chance to become Capo instead of me. He would never understand that Matteo and I weren't enemies, that we weren't only bound by necessity and pragmatism. My brother and I would die for each other. Father hated his brothers as much as they hated him. He kept them alive because honor dictated it and because it gave him a fucking thrill to give them orders as their Capo, to have them grovel at his feet and try to stay in his good graces.

"I trust Matteo, but he's hot-headed. He'd get himself killed trying to defend me."

Aria nodded as if she understood. Maybe she did. She was a woman, shielded from most of the violence of our world, but that didn't mean she didn't hear about it.

"Nobody will doubt me," she said. "I'll give them what they want to see."

I didn't know Aria well enough to gauge her lying skills. Slowly, I pushed into a sitting position, which allowed me a better view of my wife. She lay on her back, her hair fanning out around her head, and the outline of her breasts teased me through the flimsy material of her nightgown. Aria's eyes trailed over my upper body curiously, and my groin tightened at her unpracticed appraisal. When her eyes finally met mine, her cheeks were flushed.

"You should be wearing more than this excuse for a nightgown when the harpies arrive. I don't want them to see your body, especially your hips and upper thighs. It's better they wonder if I left marks on you," I said, my eyes lingering on those pink lips. "But we can't hide your face from them."

I moved lower, reaching for Aria's cheek to kiss her when she closed her eyes and flinched as if she thought I'd hit her. Revulsion filled me at the mere idea of raising my hand against my wife.

"This is the second time you thought I was going to hit you," I said in a low voice.

She looked at me in confusion. "I thought you said..."

"What? That everyone expects you to have bruises on your face after a night with me? I don't hit women."

Even Grace, who had a talent to drive me to the brink, had never been on the receiving end of my violence. I'd spent my childhood and youth listening to my mother's broken crying, and, once she was dead, to Nina's. That wasn't what I wanted in a marriage. If I felt the need to break people, I had enough enemies to choose from. "How am I supposed to believe that you can convince everyone we've consummated our marriage when you keep flinching from my touch?"

"Believe me, the flinching will make everyone believe the lie even more because I definitely wouldn't have stopped flinching away from your touch if you'd *taken what's yours.* The more I flinch, the more they'll take you for the monster you want them to think you are."

I chuckled. "I think you might know more about playing the game of power than I expected."

"My father is Consigliere," she said. Aria wasn't only beautiful, she was also clever.

I pressed my palm against her cheek. This time, she managed not to flinch, but she still became tense. Before annoyance could claim me, I reminded myself that she wasn't used to a man's touch. That I was her husband wouldn't magically make her comfortable with the unfamiliar closeness. "What I meant earlier was that your face doesn't look like you've been kissed."

Aria's eyes grew wide. "I've never…"

Never been kissed. All mine. Always only mine.

I crashed my lips down on hers, and Aria's hand flew up to my chest as if she was going to push me away, but she didn't. Her palms shook against my skin. I tried to soften my kiss, not wanting to scare her, but it was a fucking struggle to be gentle and slow when all I wanted was to lay my claim on the woman beside me.

My tongue stroked her lips open, and Aria responded hesitantly. Her blue eyes flickered with insecurity, but I didn't allow her to worry. I took the lead, gave her no choice but to surrender to me. The feel and taste of her stirred the embers of my desire into a raging fire. I pressed harder into her, my kiss turning more forceful even as I tried to restrain myself. My fingers twitched against her cheek, wanting to travel south, wanting to stroke and discover every inch of her body. I pulled away before I could lose control. Aria blinked up at me, licking her lips, almost dazed. Her cheeks were flushed, her lips red.

I wanted her.

A knock burst through my lustful haze. I rolled over and got up, glad for the distraction. Aria gasped. I chanced a glance at her, catching her staring at my hard-on with widened eyes.

"A man is supposed to have a boner when he wakes up beside his bride, don't you think? They want a show, they'll get a show." My aunts, cousins, and especially Nina were eager for new tidbits of gossip that would make their dull lives a bit brighter. They'd descend like bloodthirsty hyenas on us if they suspected I hadn't claimed Aria. "Now go and grab a bathrobe," I ordered.

Aria obeyed at once, practically leaping out of bed and rushing into the bathroom. I had to admit her fighting spirit last night had pleased me more than her obedience.

My eyes strayed toward the fake blood stains on the bed sheet and a flicker of regret overtook me. There was a reason the Famiglia insisted on the bloody sheets tradition, particularly my father. I still remembered the sheets after his wedding night with Nina, and I had been only a child then.

Sighing, I headed toward the table and picked up my weapons. The knocking became more insistent, but I didn't give a fuck. Aria returned dressed in a long white satin bathrobe and holding her cut corset in one hand. She curiously watched me strap my knife and gun holsters onto my naked body, one of them covering the small cut on my forearm. Before I headed for the door, I shifted my boner so it would be even more prominent. That would give the furies of my family something to gossip about. Aria's gaze slid down to my groin once more, and the blush returned to her cheeks.

Aria moved toward the window, wrapping her arms around herself, looking breakable and perfectly beautiful.

Tearing my eyes from her, I opened the door to the eager faces of Nina, Cosima, and Egidia. Behind them, more women from mine and Aria's families had gathered.

Their eyes traveled the length of me. Some of them feigned shock even when it was obvious that they enjoyed the sight, considering the ugly old fools they were married to.

Only Nina pointedly ignored my undressed state, but I knew her and caught her nervous swallow. It was impossible not to know a person's mimic and gestures if you'd seen them at their lowest. Being married to my father, I'd seen more than enough of that side of her. "We've come to collect the sheets," she said, putting on her usual mask, smiling spitefully.

I allowed them to enter.

They practically shoved each other out of the way to reach the bed first. They whispered when they saw the stain, then looked toward Aria, who squirmed under their attention. She was already embarrassed as it was. I wondered how much worse it would have been if they would have actually been the proof of her lost virginity.

Nina and Cosima removed the bedsheets, giggling in that fake way that gave me a fucking headache. "Luca," Nina said with feigned indignation. "Did nobody tell you to be gentle to your virgin bride?"

More of those fucking giggles. I held Nina's gaze, my mouth pulling into a cold smile. "You are married to my father. Does he strike you as a man who teaches his sons to be gentle to *anyone*?"

Her smile became even less honest, and a flicker of pure animalistic fear flashed in her brown eyes. In this room, probably no one knew what she had to endure.

"Let me through!" Gianna screeched and stormed into the room. As an unmarried woman, she wasn't supposed to be here, but of course the girl didn't care. Her blue eyes landed on the sheets before they jerked toward Aria. Her face reflected worry and fear, and my annoyance with her decreased slightly. She was concerned for sister.

She turned to me with a look that was probably intended to intimidate.

I cocked my eyebrows at her and the little wench actually took a step in my direction to do god only knew what. Like her sister, she only reached my chest and weighed less than half of me, not to mention the only fight experience she probably had was with her tiny midget of a brother.

"Gianna," Aria said sharply, her eyes darting between her sister and me. "Will you help me get dressed?" Aria turned and walked toward the bath, her movements stiff as if she was sore. I was torn between admiration for her show and frustration over the fact that there was even a reason for her to pretend.

After she'd sent me another scathing look, Gianna followed after her sister and closed the door.

Nina shook her head, turning to Ludevica Scuderi. "Gianna doesn't know how to behave herself. I doubt her future husband will tolerate that kind of behavior."

Considering how little Rocco cared about the wellbeing of his daughters, he'd probably give her to a sadistic bastard who'd beat Gianna into shape, but that wasn't my concern.

Nina held the folded sheets in her palms, the blood stains on display.

Ludevica was pointedly not looking at them or me.

"I don't have all day," I said. "Why don't you head downstairs and prepare everything for the show?"

The women left and I closed the door, glad to have them gone. They hadn't been suspicious, that much was clear, and why would they be? I was Luca fucking Vitiello. Sparing my bride definitely didn't fit my reputation.

I headed for the bathroom. I needed a good shave and a fucking cold shower. I pushed the door open when I was met with resistance and Gianna's angry face came into view in the gap.

"You can't come in," she hissed, narrowing her eyes at me. She was a kitten trying to scare the tiger.

"I'm her husband, now step back," I said. I could have pushed the door open without trouble, but shoving a girl out of my way wasn't my favorite option.

"I don't care that you're her husband," she muttered.

Okay, I had given all of my meager patience to Aria last night. I pushed harder and Gianna stumbled backwards, her eyes flashing indignantly. The spitfire stepped in my way, trying to stop me, but my eyes were drawn to movement in the shower where Aria whirled around, turning her back to us. Sweet Jesus. That woman's back was already enough to give me another boner.

"Leave." Gianna's hiss brought my attention back to her.

"I need to get ready, and there's nothing here that I haven't already seen." A big fat lie, one I'd have to tell over and over again today when the sheets were presented.

I glared at Gianna. "Now leave, or you'll see your first cock, girl, because I'm going to undress now."

I reached for my boxers, but it was an empty threat, unfortunately. Scuderi would lose his shit if I showed my dick to his daughter—the one that wasn't married to me, at least. He probably didn't care what I did to Aria, considering he would have let me marry her when she was only fifteen. Not that I gave a fuck about Scuderi but it would have been dishonorable.

"You arrogant asshole, I—" Gianna began, and I was close to forget about doing the honorable thing when Aria told her sister to leave and finally the redhead moved toward the door. "You're a sadistic pig," she muttered before she closed the door. No one had ever insulted me like that and lived to see another day, but she was safe, because she was a girl and Aria's sister.

Stifling my anger, I moved toward the washstand, but my eyes remained on Aria. She tensed when the door shut and we were alone. She was still afraid of me, even though I'd bled and lied for her. I couldn't even blame her for her distrust. With a man like me, she had every reason to expect the worst. I took my brush and started spreading shaving cream on my face when she finally turned the shower off. Then she turned, and I halted in my movements. My eyes drank her in. She was perfection. Her skin glowed and looked like silk, even her pussy. She'd been waxed for her wedding night, only a small triangle of blond remaining, but nothing hid the delicious crease between her thighs, a place I could have sunk my cock into last night. Aria let me admire her, standing completely still, but a blush traveled over her throat and face.

I set my brush down and took one of the towels from the rack before I moved toward her. Aria's eyes held insecurity as she opened the shower stall and took the towel with a small thanks. I couldn't stop looking at her and, so close-up, her nakedness called even louder to the worst in me, the monster in me beckoning to be unleashed.

Aria wrapped herself in the towel and stepped out of the shower. She peered up at me. She was petite, vulnerable, breathtakingly beautiful and unconditionally mine.

"I bet you're already regretting your decision," she said, her eyes searching mine, looking for something all women hoped for: tenderness, affection, love. She wouldn't find any of those things in my eyes…or my heart.

I couldn't and wouldn't give her those things, but I could treat her with the respect she deserved as my wife, as the woman I swore to protect. I'd respect her body, would honor her 'no' as if it were my own. That was all I could give her.

I returned to the washstand and picked up my shaving brush. Aria slipped past me and was almost out of the door when I gave her an answer: "No."

She peered over her shoulder at me.

"When I claim your body, I want you writhing beneath me in pleasure, not fear."

Aria's eyes widened, lips parting, and then she quickly left.

I set the brush back down, grabbed the edge of the washstand and stared at my reflection. I had no trouble being a monster—it was in my nature and I enjoyed it—but the second I'd seen Aria, I'd made a vow to keep that part of myself away from her.

The women I'd fucked over the years had sought my closeness because they'd been looking for a thrill, had wanted to be dominated and to submit to someone dangerous. For them it had been a game, a sexual role play that got them wet, because those women didn't understand that it wasn't a role, not a fucking game. I was a monster. There wasn't a role I played when I was with them, and it definitely wasn't a role when I tortured and killed. Aria knew all those things. She knew the monster I harbored because she'd grown up in a world where men domineered women, where they owned them, where rape fantasies weren't just that. They were horror stories spoken in hushed whispers among the married women. They were the shapeless fears of girls before their wedding night.

With those clueless women, I'd enjoyed being rough, treating them like shit, because they got a thrill out of it and because it was the only way I could at least be partly myself, but with Aria, I didn't have to pretend I was someone else.

She knew what I was, and for some reason that made me want to be good to her, to show her that there was more than brutality. At least when she was concerned.

CHAPTER 8

I took a long time, showering and wanking like a goddamn teenage boy. With a gorgeous woman in my bed all night, I really shouldn't be suffering from blue balls, and yet here I was. Slinging a towel around my waist, I stepped out of the bathroom.

Aria perched on the stool in front of her vanity, blond hair trailing down her back and using whatever women used to accentuate their eyes—not that Aria needed it. Her eyes widened in shock when she saw me. They trailed the length of me, fascination reflecting on her face. Stifling a groan at her innocent appraisal, I stalked toward the wardrobe and grabbed a few clothes. Knowing she was still watching, I let my towel fall to the ground. She sucked in a breath and my cock gave a fucking twitch, imagining how she was blushing. When I'd put on briefs and pants, I turned. As expected, Aria's cheeks were flushed. She pretended to be busy inspecting her nails, but she wasn't fooling me. She was too embarrassed to face me.

It was something new for me. I didn't have experience with a girl like her. The women of my past had been straightforward with their demands and practiced in their advances. Aria wasn't, and I wasn't entirely sure how to handle her.

Taking the guns from the table, I began strapping them to my holsters as I did every day, as I'd done for as long as I could remember.

"Do you ever go anywhere without guns?" Aria asked quietly, turning around in her stool to face me. She was wearing some sort of long dress with a golden belt and golden sandals, reminding me of an Egyptian princess even if her hair didn't match the image. It was still strange to think that she was really mine, that she would be mine until the very end. This wasn't for one night or a few weeks of mindless pleasure. This wasn't no-strings-attached. This was forever, for both of us. She was my responsibility from this day on. Remembering how my father had failed his wives, both my mother and now Nina, it seemed like a fucking impossible challenge.

"Not if I can avoid it. Do you know how to shoot a gun or use a knife?"

"No. My father doesn't think women should get involved in fights."

"Sometimes fights come to you. The Bratva and the Triad don't distinguish between men and women." The Triad had laid low. Most of their territories had been claimed by the Bratva, so they were the ones we were worried about.

Aria tilted her head. "So you've never killed a woman?"

"I didn't say that." Aria didn't need to know how the Bratva had almost gotten me. It wasn't something I wanted people to know.

Aria rose from the chair, smoothing the long dress out. I was glad she'd chosen something floor-length. It made things easier. People might suspect I'd left my marks on her upper thighs. "Good choice. The dress covers your legs."

"Someone could lift the skirt and inspect my thighs."

I had seen the way many men had leered at her yesterday when they thought I wasn't paying attention. "Someone tries to touch you, they lose their hand."

Aria's eyes widened in shock. She'd have to get used to my possessiveness. "Come on." I led her out into the hallway and closer to the main hall. A few male guests were still in the lobby, but the majority of voices came from the dining room.

Aria stiffened. "Are they all waiting to see a bloody sheet?" Her skin turned red.

"Many of them, especially the women. The men might hope for dirty details; others might hope to talk about business, ask a favor, or get on my good side."

Aria made no move to descend the stairs, so I nudged her forward gently. We walked down close together and I had to slow my steps considerably to adapt to her shorter legs. I'd never walked hand-in-hand with a woman, so this was something new.

Romero greeted us with a smile. "How are you?" he asked Aria and then looked like he wanted to swallow his tongue.

Asking a bride that kind of question after her first night was definitely inappropriate. I chuckled, but my mood dropped when the gathered men sent me winks and grins. Everyone thought I'd spent the night banging my stunning wife. Aria surprised me when she pressed closer to me. It took me a second to realize she was seeking protection from their attention. I wrapped my arm around her waist and sent them a warning look. They averted their eyes.

"Matteo and the rest of your family are in the dining room," Romero said.

"Poring over the sheets?"

"As if they could read them like tea leaves," Romero confirmed, then gave Aria an apologetic look.

"Come." I led Aria toward the dining room despite her tension. The presentation of the sheets was something we couldn't evade. Everyone was waiting for us and fell silent when we entered. My father, the Famiglia Underbosses, the Cavallaros and Scuderi had gathered around the dining table. Most of the high-ranking Outfit men had already left with their families this morning to return to their respective territories.

Aria squirmed under the attention. Soon she'd have to face the women who looked like famished dogs with their sights set on a piece of meat. Father nodded toward me with a look in his eyes that made me want to push Aria behind me. Thankfully, Matteo chose that moment to walk up to us, looking a mess with bags under his eyes and stubble. For him, that was the equivalent of a stylish meltdown.

"You look like shit," I told him as he sipped on his espresso.

Matteo's eyes darted from me to Aria. "My tenth espresso and I'm still not awake. Drank too much last night."

"You were trashed. I'd have had your tongue cut out for some of the things you said to Aria if you weren't my brother."

Matteo gave Aria a grin. "I hope Luca didn't do half of the things I suggested."

Aria blushed furiously and leaned into me once more. I stroked her side in reassurance. She didn't have to be wary of my brother. She twitched, giving me a surprised look. To be honest, I wasn't sure why I'd felt the need to console her at all.

"Quite a work of art you presented us," Matteo said, nodding in the direction of the bloody sheets, causing Aria to stiffen in my embrace.

I searched Matteo's face, not sure if he suspected I had spared Aria. It couldn't be because of the sheets, because if something about them looked fake, he would have warned me.

Matteo's eyes held a knowing gleam. The asshole could read me too well. It

Father and Fiore waved at us to come over to them. Stifling a groan, I indicated Matteo that I'd have to move to the table. Matteo smiled but didn't move an inch, obviously not in the mood to talk to them.

Aria followed me toward the table. Her face reflected anxiety, and I could only hope that she'd be able to keep up the charade. The men rose. Father's leer made me want to drag Aria right back out, but that wasn't an option.

Scuderi spread his arms and I reluctantly released Aria so he could embrace her. I couldn't hear what he said, but Aria didn't look happy about it. Fiore smiled and shook my hand. "It seems you are still satisfied with our choice for you."

I nodded. I knew this was only the beginning. The moment Aria was out of earshot, the men would try to extract details of my night with her.

Father put a hand on my shoulder before he gave Aria and me his false benevolent smile. "I hope we can expect small Vitiellos soon."

Aria's eyes widened a tad before she could mask her shock. I had absolutely no intention of having kids anytime soon—not as long as my father was in power. He wasn't that old yet, only in his mid-fifties, but I hoped he'd find an end soon. "I want to enjoy Aria alone for a long while. And with the Bratva closing in, I wouldn't want to have children to worry over."

Father gave me a knowing smile, thinking I wanted to fuck my young wife in peace for a while. "Yes, yes, of course. Understandable."

"I hear the Bratva sent a new Pakhan into your territory," I said to Fiore, wanting the topic of my wife off the table.

Fiore nodded then looked at Dante who frowned. "Yes, Grigory Mikhailov. We're still trying to check his background. He used to work directly under the Pakhan in Yekaterinburg, and now he's taking over everything in Chicago. Unpredictable und brutal. They call him Stalin."

Aria peered up at me and I loosened my hold on her. This wasn't anything she needed to worry about. The women were throwing eager glances her way, anyway. She quickly walked away and toward them, stopping beside her mother and sister.

"Can't take your eyes off your wife?" Father asked with a chuckle.

I only smiled coldly. The less I said the better. Nina pointed at the sheets and giggling rose among the women. Only Aria looked like she wanted to be swallowed whole by the ground.

Scuderi turned to us. "I must say I find your tradition of the bloody sheets enlightening."

"Maybe it's a tradition you'd like to reintroduce once you're Capo," Father said to Dante who stood with his hands shoved into his pockets, looking completely uninterested. His cautious blue eyes settled on my father. "I prefer to focus on the future and not look for traditions of the past."

"That's good to hear," Fiore said pointedly to his son.

My father gave me a look. He, too, had noticed the tension between the Cavallaro men. Obviously Fiore was unhappy about Dante. I could only assume it had something to do with the fact that Dante still hadn't married even though his wife had been dead for years.

"What about you, Luca? Are you thinking of changing the old traditions once you're Capo?" Dante asked.

I smirked. "The Famiglia is built on tradition," I said, then nodded toward my father with faked respect. "I'm not going to be Capo for a long time. My father is strong and I trust in his leadership."

Father's answering smile made me want to take my words back and end him right here and there.

Dante nodded, but his eyes held calculation.

Peace between us had an expiry date.

"Don't hold back on us, Luca," Durant said. "Tell us more about your first night with your beautiful wife."

"I must say I would have expected more blood considering your size and hers," Uncle Gottardo said with a cackle and a wink. There was something in his eyes that made me consider crushing his throat like I had his son's. Dante's mouth curled in disgust. Scuderi, on the other hand, didn't seem to care that someone spoke like that about his daughter. If I ever had a daughter, I'd cut off anyone's head who dared to talk that way about her.

Every man looked toward Aria then at me. I didn't bother masking my anger and possessiveness. If my civil mask led to those kinds of questions, I'd rather drop it before my uncles got more blood than they bargained for. "I'm feared among my enemies and my soldiers. I don't need to claim my wife without preparation so she bleeds more to gain anyone's respect, *Uncle*."

These words were already more than I wanted to share even if nothing had happened between Aria and me. Father laughed, but his gaze was assessing. I'd have to be on my toes. Where had Matteo gone? Was he sleeping off his intoxication in a quiet room?

From the corner of my eye, I saw Liliana and Fabiano slip into the room. Neither was supposed to attend the gathering.

"Why's there blood on the sheets? Has someone been killed?" Fabiano bellowed, pointing at the sheets with wide eyes.

The men around me began laughing, except for Dante and me. We glanced at each other. We would never like each other, but maybe we could establish a base of respect to keep up the peace for a few years.

Suddenly, Aria rushed out of the room with her arm around her sister Liliana.

I excused myself to check on my wife, not liking her out of my sight. Romero leaned beside the closed door of the guest bathroom, and I relaxed. "Aria and Liliana are inside," he said.

"What's the matter?"

"Liliana looked sick."

The door swung open and Aria slipped out, quickly closing the door before we could catch a glimpse inside. "Is your sister okay?"

Aria tugged a strand of hair behind her ear, glancing between Romero and me with obvious nervousness. I had to remind myself again that this was new for Aria, that this was one of the first times she was alone in the presence of men that didn't belong to her family. "The sheets made her queasy," she said with a small shrug.

Romero's expression darkened. "They shouldn't allow young girls to witness something like that. It'll only scare them." Romero sent me an apologetic look, but I didn't care if he criticized that particular tradition. I didn't much care for it either, but it was one of the traditions that would be the hardest to abolish.

"You are right."

"Lily needs some tea," Aria said, glancing at me, and I realized she was unsure if she was allowed to go into the kitchen and prepare one.

"I can get it for her and stay with her so you can return to your guests," Romero said.

Aria's smile was hesitant. "That's nice, but Lily doesn't want you to see her."

I frowned, wondering what had happened. Romero really wasn't someone who scared females. He was one of the few soldiers with his talent who could hide his violence almost completely. "Is she scared of me?"

Aria laughed. "You sound like that isn't a possibility. You are a soldier of the mafia. What's not to be scared of?" She glanced toward the closed bathroom door before she continued in a whisper. "But that's not it. Lily has a major crush on you and doesn't want you to see her like that."

I gave Romero an amused look. "Romero, you still got it. Capturing the hearts of fourteen-year-old girls left and right." Romero shook his head, obviously uncomfortable with the whole thing. I turned to my wife who was still smiling, looking relaxed and almost happy. I knew my words would change that. "But we have to return. The women will be mortally offended if you don't give them all of your attention."

"I'll take care of Lily," Gianna said.

Looking over my shoulder, I found Aria's sister and brother heading our way. The redhead pointedly ignored me, but the midget gave me his best death glare.

I led Aria back into the dining room. The men had by then gathered around the sheets while the women flocked around the table. I reluctantly released Aria so she could head back to the harpies.

The men laughed at something Durant said. It was probably for the best that I hadn't heard it.

"There's the lucky bridegroom," Father intoned, holding out a glass of scotch to me. I took it reluctantly. Judging from the way he and his brothers smiled, they'd probably enjoyed more than one already. Only Scuderi, Dante and Fiore looked sober, which didn't come as a surprise considering they were in our territory.

Gottardo's beetle eyes held challenge when I stopped beside him. "So Luca, won't you at least tell us how many rounds you managed last night? Won't you share at least that piece of information with us?"

Durant smiled in a way that made me want to slice my blades from one fucking corner of his mouth to the other to see how much wider his fucking grin could get.

"I don't share, ever, not even the tiniest fucking bit of my wife," I snarled. My father and his brothers were disgusting pieces of shit. The same sadistic streak stained their blood. Sometimes I worried it ran in my veins as well and was only waiting to show its full potential. I was cruel and pitiless, but not like my father. Not yet.

Father shook his head with a bellowing laugh, but the laughter didn't extend to his eyes. They were vigilant and suspicious, and for a moment I worried he'd seen through the charade I was playing. But my father was always suspicious because he had reason to be. There was no one he trusted, and rightfully so. Everyone hated and feared him. That wasn't the base for trust. Not that I had many people I trusted, definitely not without reservations. Matteo had my trust and Romero to some degree, but everyone else could be an enemy disguised as an ally.

"Oh ho, quite possessive of your gorgeous young bride," Durant cackled. "Considering her beauty and your possessive streak, I'm surprised you agreed to wait three years before marrying her." His fucking beetle eyes latched onto Aria as she talked to the other women, and something in them made me want to stick my blade into his eyeball before shoving the fucking thing down his throat so he could choke on the slimy globe.

"I like my women of age," I gritted out. I could feel my blood pressure rising, my fury burning away at my self-control. I took a sip from the scotch even if it was too early for hard liquor and glanced toward my wife. She was smiling, but blatant embarrassment shone on her face and her cheeks were dusted pink. I could imagine too well what the women were talking about. Her eyes darted to me as if she noticed my attention and, for a brief moment, a small conspiratorial smile tugged at her lips, a moment without her usual wariness and submissive fear, a glimpse at her true persona when she was around people she trusted. It was a side of her I wanted to see more of.

"I still remember my first night with Criminella," Durant said with a twisted grin.

After that, they all launched into stories of their own wedding nights.

My mood was on the verge of homicidal when the ordeal was finally over and most of the guests had left. I touched Aria's back as I led her out of the dining room and up to our bedroom to pack. She was quiet and tense at my side, and I wasn't sure if it was because of the presentation of the sheets or because of something else.

We had almost reached our bedroom when my brother made an appearance. I scowled at him. I could have used his help at the presentation, though knowing his temper, especially when he had a headache from last night, it was probably for the best that he'd taken off.

"You two lovebirds will have to postpone your mating session. I need to have a word with you, Luca," he drawled, looking inexplicably cheery all of a sudden. Not a good sign. Aria cast her gaze up to me with obvious uncertainty, again asking me silently what to do. "Go ahead. Check if the maids packed all your stuff. I'll be back soon."

She didn't need to be told twice and rushed into our bedroom. She wasn't comfortable around my brother, or me for that matter, and I wasn't entirely sure it was only because we were men.

Matteo grinned like a wolf. "The sheets were fake, weren't they? My big bad brother spared his little virgin bride."

I got into his face, narrowing my eyes at him. "Keep your fucking voice down." We were alone in the corridor, but that could change at any point and then I'd have a lot of explaining to do.

Matteo cocked his head. "What happened? Did you have too much to drink and couldn't get it up?"

"Fuck off. As if alcohol ever stopped me," I muttered. When Matteo and I had partied the nights away, we'd always ended the evening banging a girl.

"Then what?" he asked, honestly curious as if it were incomprehensible that I could hold back.

The memory of Aria's blank fear of me and her hopeless tears flashed before my eyes. "She started crying," I admitted, my eyes darting to my forearm for a second. Matteo picked up on it of course and shoved the knife holder to the side, revealing my wound. I wrenched my arm out of his grip and repositioned the leather holder.

"You cut yourself," he said, searching my face. Matteo was the person who knew me best and yet he was surprised. His mouth twitched, then he shook his head with another chuckle.

"I knew it. I told Gianna last night that she didn't need to worry about Aria. You have a soft spot for damsels in distress."

That was bullshit. I'd never felt the urge to hold back for anyone. "I don't—" I began when his words registered fully. "You were alone with Gianna?"

Matteo nodded with a smile I didn't like one bit. He motioned for me to follow him away from the bedroom. I doubted Aria was behind the door spying on us.

"I kissed her, and she tastes even better than she looks."

"I can't fucking believe you got more action than me in my own fucking wedding night."

Matteo ran a hand through his hair. "The ladies can't resist my charm."

Did he really think this funny? I grabbed his shoulders. "This isn't a joking matter, Matteo. The Outfit won't find it funny if you go around deflowering their girls." Father would have to make amends to the Outfit if that happened, and I wasn't sure if these amends wouldn't include having Matteo handed over to Scuderi for disembodiment. Or maybe Father would order me to dish out the expected punishment and kill my brother. I'd kill Father and every fucker who wanted to kill Matteo, but it would lead to all of us losing our lives.

"I didn't deflower anyone. I kissed her," Matteo interrupted my thoughts.

"Yeah, as if that's ever the end of it." I had noticed the way Matteo watched the redhead, but I had hoped he'd be more sensible than actually pursuing her.

"I want to deflower her. But I'm not an idiot."

The facts were speaking a different language. Kissing a woman he wasn't married to, especially from the Outfit, was the biggest kind of idiocy imaginable. If Gianna told anyone, we'd be doomed. The only thing stopping her was probably that she'd be ruined as well.

"I want to marry her."

I froze. "Tell me you're kidding."

"I'm not. That's why I need your help. Father won't talk to Scuderi on my behalf if he thinks I want Gianna for any other reason than spite or revenge. You know him."

"So what do you want me to do?"

"Help me convince him that she hates me and insulted me and that I want to marry her to make her miserable."

"Isn't that the truth? The girl can't stand you, and you want her because of it. How is that any different from the story we're going to tell Father?"

"I don't want to make her miserable."

"The end result might be the same. That girl is going to drive you insane, you realize that, don't you? I'm really not sure if I want her in New York."

"You'll deal with it. And Aria will be happy to have her sister with her."

He had a point, but I wasn't sure if I wanted them to be together often. Gianna's influence wouldn't make my marriage to Aria less difficult. It would be hard enough to make it work. I didn't need additional complications. "You really think you thought that through, don't you?" I said.

"I did. And Father will choose some bitch that'll make me miserable for me soon enough."

"So you rather choose your own bitch who'll make you miserable."

He shoved my hand away, looking pissed. "Gianna isn't a bitch."

"You want to hit me because of her."

"I want to hit you for a lot of reasons."

Matteo was serious. I could tell how much this meant to him so, even if I considered it a bad idea, I knew I'd have to help him. As his first born, Father valued my word more than Matteo's. I could only hope this wouldn't come to bite Matteo and me in the ass.

———————✕———————

After Father promised to talk to Fiore and Rocco about Gianna, he asked me to stay for a private conversation. Matteo mouthed 'good luck' before he left Father's office.

I crossed my arms in front of my chest, waiting for my father to speak. He regarded me closely, and for a moment I wondered if he suspected the sheets were fake, but if this were that kind of conversation, he wouldn't have been alone with me. The surveillance cameras wouldn't save his life.

"Now that you're married, you might want to consider moving into the mansion with me and Nina. After all, it's our family's home."

"That's a gracious offer," I bit out, even when the words left a bitter taste in my mouth. "But like I said, this early in my marriage I want to enjoy my wife as much as possible, wherever I want, whenever I want."

Father nodded with a dark laugh, leaning forward. "I don't care if you do that in the mansion."

As if I didn't know that. But I would never live under the same roof as my father again, especially not with Aria.

Picking up on my reluctance, Father said, "I didn't expect you to be this possessive of your wife. It's a new side of you." He leaned back. "Very well. Stay in your penthouse for now." He tapped his fingers against the desk, making me wait to see if he was going to say anything else.

He nodded. "That's all."

I turned on my heel and stalked out, feeling my vein throb in my temple.

Every day it became harder to have my father tell me what to do, to bear his presence.

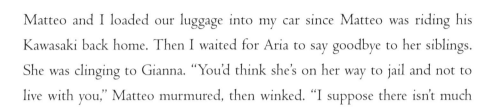

Matteo and I loaded our luggage into my car since Matteo was riding his Kawasaki back home. Then I waited for Aria to say goodbye to her siblings. She was clinging to Gianna. "You'd think she's on her way to jail and not to live with you," Matteo murmured, then winked. "I suppose there isn't much of a difference."

I ignored him and tried to stifle my impatience. I wanted to get back to New York. For one because I didn't want to spend any more time under the same roof as Father, and because I had a meeting to attend. Business had rested these last three days and, at the current time, that was too long.

Scuderi seemed to lose his patience at the same time as I did.

"Gianna, for Christ's sake! Do I have to come get you?"

Aria finally came toward me, looking like she'd been gutted. "Chicago isn't the end of the world," I told her. Her sisters could come visit occasionally.

Aria shook her head, biting her lip as if she were trying to force back tears. "It might as well be. I've never been separated from my sisters and brother. They were my whole world."

Matteo and I had never been separated for long either, but I still didn't get why she was so emotional over it. "We should leave. I have a meeting tonight."

I held the door open for Aria and she got in. Closing it, I jogged around the car.

"I'll be behind you," Matteo said, then headed for a motorcycle.

I slipped behind the steering wheel and revved the engine. Matteo was already racing down the driveway like a madman.

"No bodyguard?" Aria asked as she fastened her belt.

"I don't need bodyguards. Romero is for you. And this car doesn't exactly have room for additional passengers."

Aria didn't say anything, only stared out of the window. Looking at the miserable face of my wife, I wondered how life with her would be. I'd never shared my apartment. I had come and gone as I pleased, but now there would always be someone around.

It would be difficult to pretend 24/7. Aria would see my true self if she wanted to or not. I wondered if she'd be able to bear it. She seemed so fragile and innocent. What if my darkness was too much for her?

CHAPTER 9

We didn't speak during the drive to New York. I didn't really care. Talking to women had never been a top priority. The only topic I cared about was the mafia, and women had limited knowledge of the realities of mob life, if any. Without a word, I got out of the car and grabbed our luggage. Matteo could pick up his bag with his spare car key later. When I headed for the elevator, I realized that Aria was still beside the car, her arms wrapped around her middle, looking around in trepidation.

"Thinking about running?"

Shaking her head, she finally headed my way. "You would find me."

"I would." Now that she was mine, I'd search the entire world for her. The elevator glided open and I got in, followed shortly by Aria who glanced around curiously and scanned the number of floors.

"The elevator is private. It leads only to the last two floors of the building.

My penthouse is at the top, and Matteo has his apartment on the floor below."

Aria turned to me. "Can he come into our penthouse whenever he wants?"

I couldn't read the tone of her voice. "Are you scared of Matteo?"

"I'm scared of the both of you, but he seems more volatile, while I doubt you'd ever do anything you hadn't thought through. You seem like someone who's always firmly in control."

If she was already scared of me when I showed only my civil side, I didn't want to know what would happen if she ever saw me at my worst. "Sometimes I lose control."

Aria peered down at her wedding band and twisted it. I really wished she'd at least look at me so I could gauge her emotions.

"You have nothing to worry about when it comes to Matteo. He's used to coming over to my place whenever he wants, but things will change now that I'm married. Most of our business takes place somewhere else, anyway." Matteo and I hadn't discussed the matter so far, but considering that Aria might walk around the apartment naked at some point, I definitely didn't want my brother to show up unannounced.

The elevator beeped and came to a stop, then the doors slid apart. Aria became tense and took a deep breath as I motioned for her to enter my apartment...*our* apartment from now on.

It was strange to allow a woman into my domain. I didn't really count my housekeeper Marianna as a woman in this case. She worked for me, after all. I'd never had one of my affairs or one-night-stands over, and even Nina had only managed to weasel her way inside once when she accompanied my father. But this would be Aria's home now, not just mine.

As I watched her take in my penthouse, I realized that was probably why she looked so tense. She hadn't chosen this place like she hadn't chosen me, but she'd have to call it home from this day on.

I wondered if she liked it. There were no frills or soft colors, no plush throw pillows or fluffy rugs. I'd asked the interior designers to keep it functional and modern, with grays and whites and blacks. The only dashes of color were the modern art paintings that hung from walls—and now Aria.

She stepped up to the French windows. With her bright orange dress and her long blond hair, she was an absolute eye-catcher in my colorless apartment. I wasn't sure how long I'd stared at her when I finally snapped out of it.

"Your things are in the bedroom upstairs. Marianna wasn't sure if you wanted to put them away yourself, so she left them in your suitcases," I told her. Her family had sent most of her belongings to New York a couple of days ago.

"Who's Marianna?" Aria asked without turning. I walked up to her until I could see her face in the window.

For once her expression was blank, impossible for me to read. "She's my housekeeper. She's here a couple of days per week."

"How old is she?" Aria asked. She tried to sound casual, but the delicate blush traveling up her throat betrayed the reason for the question.

"Are you jealous?" I asked. I touched her hips and, as always, she froze for a split second before she caught herself. I'd been doing everything I could to treat her right, but she still acted as if I'd brutalized her. I'd never felt more like my goddamn father than in this moment.

Aria slipped away from me and moved toward the doors. When she faced me, her expression was perfectly controlled once more, and I hated it. "Can I go outside?" she asked.

"This is your home now, too," I gritted out, trying to hold back the darkness that threatened to claw its way out of my chest.

Aria stepped outside and headed directly for the banister. I followed her, suddenly suspicious of her motives.

"You're not thinking about jumping, are you?" I asked as I leaned beside her. The idea that Aria might choose death over me like my mother had chosen death over my father, and ultimately Matteo and me, felt like a punch to the stomach.

Aria looked up at me with a small frown. "Why would I kill myself?"

"Some women in our world see it as their only way to gain freedom. This marriage is your prison." She knew that as well as I did. There was no sense in lying to her.

"I wouldn't do that to my family. Lily, Fabi and Gianna would be heartbroken."

Of course they would, and of course Aria would think of them. I still remembered her anguish over having to leave them. "Let's go back inside," I said, wanting this conversation over. I led Aria into the apartment, my hand on her lower back. Despite her constant tension, I couldn't stop touching her. It annoyed the hell out of me. "I have a meeting in thirty minutes, but I'll be back in a few hours. I want to take you to my favorite restaurant for dinner."

"Oh," Aria said, eyes growing wide. "Like a date?"

I was surprised by my suggestion as well. It was a spur of the moment decision, wanting to show Aria that life in New York wouldn't be as bleak as she feared. "You could call it that. We haven't been on a real date yet," I said, wrapping my arms around her. Aria tensed as usual.

"When will you stop being afraid of me?" I asked quietly. People were always scared of me, but not the people who mattered: Matteo and Romero.

Aria bit her lower lip. "You don't want me to be afraid of you?"

Dark amusement rose in me but I shoved it down. "You are my wife. We'll spend our lives together. I don't want a cowering woman at my side."

Some of the tension disappeared from Aria's face and a small smile played around her lips. "Are there people out there who don't fear you?"

"A few," I said. With the way she smiled, I couldn't resist kissing her.

She froze briefly but I did my best to keep our kiss gentle, my lips tasting hers without demanding she open up for me. It was fucking hard, but Aria's softening body was my reward. She finally parted her lips for me and I dove in, teasing her tongue. She touched my neck, surprising me with the gesture. It was a soft touch as always. So soft and careful. When she put her palm up against my chest, right over my Famiglia tattoo, a surge of desire flooded me, but it wasn't the only sensation I felt. For the first time ever, a kiss gave me a foreign sense of…belonging. I drew back, staring into the hooded blue eyes of my wife.

I felt my phone vibrate in my pocket and almost groaned. "I have half a mind to cancel this fucking meeting," I murmured, stroking Aria's swollen lips, "but there's still more than enough time for this later." I glanced down at my watch. Only twenty minutes until the meeting with all of the Underbosses of the Famiglia. I'd suggested it myself, considering that they all were in the area because of the wedding, but now I really regretted my suggestion. "I really need to go now. Romero will be here when I'm gone. Take your time to look around and make yourself comfortable."

I quickly drew back from Aria before her soft body and enticing scent made me late. Without another glance at my wife, I headed for the elevator. It took me down to the garage, and I locked our floor with a code only Romero had. Checking my phone, I found a text from him telling me he'd be here in five minutes. That had been a couple of minutes ago. I headed for my car and got in. On my way outside, I passed Romero in his own. I gave him a quick nod before I sped up.

The meeting would take place in the Vitiello townhouse. I'd never understand why Father took business home. Matteo's bike was already parked in the front, right on the boardwalk, and he was perched on top of it, smoothing his hair back, and looking like he was waiting for a photographer to come along.

I parked, then joined him. "Not inside yet?"

"I was waiting for moral support."

"You mean someone who stops you from sticking your knife into one of our uncles?"

"I don't have a track record of killing family members, so if anyone ends up crushing our uncles' throats, it'll be you," he said with his shark grin.

Giving him the finger, I headed up the stairs. Matteo was close behind me.

I jabbed the code into the security panel then stepped inside. Male voices came from the back of the house where the meeting room was situated. When we entered the room, everyone had already taken their respective seats. Only the two chairs on Father's right side were still vacant, our seats.

Father scowled. "You're late."

My eyes darted to my watch. One minute late.

"I'm sure the boy got distracted by his stunning wife," Mansueto Moretti, Underboss of Philadelphia, said with a crooked smile. He was several years older than my father, which was why he dared to speak up at all, and his age was also why he was going to survive calling me boy.

"He should get his priorities straight. A whore can be replaced," Father drawled, turning around toward his liquor cabinet.

Matteo gripped my wrist hard, and my eyes jerked toward him. His warning gaze made me take a deep breath. I wasn't sure what he'd seen on my face, but it must have been bad. I turned back to the gathered men, most of them focused on my father who poured himself a scotch, but Mansueto and Uncle Gottardo had their eyes on me. The former didn't worry me as much as the latter.

I stalked toward my chair and sank down. Matteo took his seat beside me, still watching me warily. He could stop it. I wouldn't kill our father in a room full of Underbosses. I was fairly sure the Underbosses from Philadelphia, Boston, Charleston and Baltimore would be on my side, even if the last city was ruled by my Aunt Egidia's husband, Felix. She hated her brother and her husband definitely shared that sentiment. But the remaining men wouldn't be on my side. Father's Consigliere Bardoni because he knew I wouldn't keep him in that position the moment I was in power, and the other men because they were either loyal to my father or wanted to become Capo themselves.

My father took his seat at the head of the table and took a sip from his scotch. He didn't offer anything to us, but I hadn't expected him to. It was his way to show all of us that we were his subjects, which was also why he sat in a wide leather armchair while we perched on fucking wooden stools.

My father motioned with his glass toward his Consigliere, which was obviously his cue to report about the latest attacks from the Bratva in our territory. I knew of most of them already. I made sure to get updates from the Underbosses once a month at least, while my father never bothered to get involved. He preferred things being handled for him, especially in recent years. It led to some Underbosses, my uncles namely, doing whatever they pleased in their territories. That would change the moment I came into power, but knowing my father, he'd live forever out of spite.

The meeting dragged on for hours, and when we finally emerged from the house, it was getting dark.

Matteo blew out a breath. "I don't suppose you're up for a night in the Sphere?" he asked with lopsided grin, but his eyes were tired.

"You said it yourself, my days as a free man are over. I have a date with Aria."

Matteo shook his head. "Strange to think of you as a husband. Why don't you bring her along? I'm sure she can shake her booty to the beat."

"The only one she's going to shake her booty for is me," I muttered. The idea of Aria in a crowded club, even with me at her side, didn't sit well with me.

Matteo mounted his bike then put on his helmet. "Enjoy your wife, while I find a girl for a meaningless toilet stall fling." He laughed, then put down his visor and raced away.

Enjoying my wife was something I was fucking eager to do…if she'd let me.

It was strange returning home, knowing someone was waiting for me. Someone who'd be waiting for me all our lives.

But when I stepped into my penthouse, it wasn't Aria I saw. Romero sat on the sofa but got up when he saw me. "She's upstairs, getting ready," he said.

"How did it go?" I asked, regarding him closely. I trusted Romero, which was why he was allowed to be alone with Aria, but he was still a guy and she was a woman too beautiful for words.

"She was upstairs most of the time." He hesitated.

"What?"

"I think she cried, but I didn't check on her."

I gave a terse nod. "Matteo is on his way to the Sphere. Why don't you join him?"

Romero glanced at his watch. "My mother and sisters expect me for dinner. They'll be offended if I cancel."

When Romero had left, I made my way upstairs. The bedroom door was ajar, and I stepped inside. Aria came out of the bathroom, dressed in a white flowing skirt and a pink sleeveless blouse and pink high heels. A dash of color. Then my eyes registered her red eyes and the photo of her family on the nightstand farther away from the door.

"I wasn't sure which was your side. I can move it to the other nightstand if you want," she said, motioning at the bed.

I didn't really have a side I slept on, because I always slept alone. I had the entire bed.

"No, it's okay," I said. The side farthest from the door was a good choice since that meant I'd be between her and a possible attacker coming through a door, even if it was nearly impossible to get inside the penthouse without my permission. Even torture wouldn't make me give away the security code.

"Was the meeting okay?" Aria asked, hovering a few steps away from me.

"Let's not talk about it. I'm starving." I held out my hand, wanting the distance between us gone. Aria put her hand in mine, and I closed my fingers around hers loosely, marveling at how small it was in comparison to mine. I led her down into the underground garage silently. My mind kept drifting to Father and his lack of interest when it came to fighting the Bratva. He regarded the Famiglia and the Italian mob as superior and didn't even consider that the Bratva could beat us at our own game. He was blind, and one day it would cost us parts of our territory. Truce with the Outfit wouldn't change that.

I glanced toward Aria, the woman who was meant to bring peace. It seemed strange that she might have been my enemy if our fathers hadn't arranged our marriage.

Aria noticed my gaze and turned to face me.

"You look great," I said. Great didn't even begin to cover it. Aria was so breathtakingly beautiful.

She gave me a small smile. "Thanks."

I parked my car in a gated parking area that I always used when I was in the area. On our way to the Korean restaurant I'd chosen for the date, I caught the looks of the men, caught their admiration and awe when they saw Aria. My wife. Mine. The look I gave them made their eyes move on quickly.

Surprise flashed cross Aria's face when I led her into the restaurant. Matteo and I both enjoyed Asian food and had discovered the place due to business a couple of years ago.

One of the waiters came up to us at once and took us to a vacant table in the back. The place wasn't fancy. There were no white table cloth and fancy napkins. Instead, there were narrow tables and barely any space between them.

I ordered a lychee-martini, one of their signature drinks, while Aria scanned the drinks menu with furrowed brows. "I'll have the same," she said eventually, looking slightly overwhelmed and still stunned by my choice of restaurant.

"You look surprised," I said when the waiter had left.

"I didn't think you'd go for Asian food, considering *everything*."

"This is the best Asian restaurant in town, and it doesn't belong to an Asian *chain*. It's independent." The Triad hadn't been as strong in recent years. They had focused their forces on the West Coast, which suited me just fine.

"There are independent restaurants in New York?" Aria asked, surprised.

"A few, but we're in negotiations right now." Either they paid us for protection or the Russians. There really was no other option.

Aria huffed, her eyes still busily scanning the menu.

"Do you need help?" I asked when it became obvious that she was overwhelmed by the choices.

Aria gave an embarrassed smile. "Yeah, I've never tried Korean."

I'd suspected as much. Scuderi didn't strike me as a man who ventured out of his comfort zone very often. "The marinated silk tofu and the bulgogi beef are delicious."

Aria's eyes grew wide. "You eat *tofu?*"

"If it's prepared like this, then yes."

Aria regarded me like she saw me in a different light. Maybe she'd finally stop flinching whenever I was near.

"Just order what you think is best. I eat everything except liver," Aria said, closing her menu.

I was glad she wasn't one of those women whose list of the things they didn't eat was longer than the list of things they did. "I like women who eat more than salad."

When the waiter stopped at our table, I ordered for both of us while Aria battled the chopsticks.

"Have you never used sticks before?" I asked once the waiter was gone. I had to stifle laughter at the look of deep concentration on Aria's face.

"My parents only took us to their favorite Italian restaurant, and I wasn't really allowed to go anywhere alone."

Of course, she hadn't been. Rocco Scuderi had kept me updated on the state of things. "You can go anywhere you want now."

Aria raised her blond eyebrows. "Really? Alone?"

I leaned forward so the people at the neighboring table wouldn't overhear me. "With Romero or me, or Cesare when Romero isn't available."

I could tell that Aria wasn't happy about it, but she really couldn't have expected me to let her walk around without protection. Deciding to distract her, I picked up my own chopsticks. "Here, let me show you." I showed Aria how to open and close them.

Biting her lip in a very distracting way, she tried to imitate the motions, again with a look of utter concentration on her face. "No wonder New York girls are so thin if they eat like this all the time."

"You're more beautiful than all of them," I said without hesitation.

Aria peered up as if she wasn't sure I was being serious. It was the longest she had ever looked into my eyes, and I wondered what she was trying to see. I was toeing the line, trying to make her feel comfortable and being good to her without making her hope for something as ridiculous as love.

Aria had been completely sheltered; even if she knew the rules of our world and what kind of man I was. Her naïveté and innocence would still make her hope for something that would just never be.

I picked up a piece of the bulgogi beef and held it out to Aria. Surprise flashed across her face. I raised my eyebrows in challenge. She parted her lips, then closed them slowly around the sticks, and I almost groaned. Did she even realize what kind of images she created in my mind?

"Delicious," she said, smiling sweetly.

Watching her innocent joy over something as simple as eating Korean food filled me with a new appreciation.

Aria became tense the moment we returned to our apartment and quickly disappeared into the bathroom. I ran a hand through my hair as my eyes rested on the bed. This would be our first night in our apartment, in this bed.

Watching Aria enjoy herself during dinner had rekindled my desire for her. It was difficult to read her. Why was she so tense?

The door to the bathroom opened and Aria stepped out in a long dark blue nightgown that contrasted beautifully with her golden hair and pale skin. My eyes were drawn to the slit showing off a small sliver of her smooth thigh.

Unfortunately, Aria had the deer-in-the-headlights look going. I walked past her into the bathroom, needing to cool off. I splashed some cold water into my face. My body throbbed with the desire to lay claim on the woman in my bedroom. I'd never had to hold back, never wanted to, but Aria needed me to. Fuck. Staring down at the boner in my briefs, I pushed away from the sink.

Aria was my wife. She shouldn't still be a virgin. Maybe she was ready tonight. Maybe she'd only been terrified because of the pressure on our wedding night.

Wasn't she curious? I remembered how fucking eager I'd been before my first time despite my nerves.

When I stepped out of the bathroom, I found Aria in front of the panorama windows, her back turned to me, looking out toward the skyline.

I moved toward her, noticing the way her body tightened. It got only worse when I reached out for her. Her obvious nervousness set my teeth on edge, because I didn't know how to put her at ease. Words of consolation or reassurance weren't really my fucking strength. My first instinct was to give her an order to stop the tensing, but that wouldn't have gone over well.

I reached out for her and she stiffened even more as if she thought I'd grab her, push up her nightgown and fuck her right against that window—which was what I wanted to do but never would, unless she fucking wanted me to. I touched my knuckles to her soft skin and lightly ran them down her spine, trying to show her that I was going to hold back for her, that I'd be careful with her.

Apart from the goose bumps pimpling her skin, she didn't react. She obviously wouldn't act on her own accord. I had no trouble leading; the problem was that my style of leadership was usually not for sensitive women, and Aria was breakable.

I held out my hand to her, knowing that she would follow my silent order because she'd been brought up to obey. She finally turned around to me, but her gaze rested on the scar in my palm, which she traced with her fingertips. My skin tingled from the almost non-existent touch. It was strange being treated that carefully.

"Is that from the blood oath?" She looked up, finally meeting my gaze. She often averted her eyes, and I wasn't sure if it was because of my reputation or if her upbringing had taught her to cast down her gaze. It was something I wanted gone as soon as possible.

"No. This is," I said, showing her the scar on my other hand. It was much smaller than the one Aria was still touching. "That happened in a fight. I had to stave off a knife attack with my hand."

Aria's eyes widened, her lips parting in surprise. I needed to kiss that mouth. Wrapping my fingers around her wrist, I led her toward the bed. She followed obediently, even though I could feel her pulse pound in her veins in fear. I decided to ignore it for now, because I had a feeling she'd still be a virgin in a year if I waited for her to be relaxed around me.

I pulled her toward the bed where I sank down and positioned her between my legs. I kissed her, enjoying her taste, the way she adapted to my demands. I let myself fall back and took her with me, my kiss becoming harder, more demanding. The feel of Aria's body on top of mine awakened my cock. I traced her waist, her ribcage, and cupped her breast. Those clothes needed to go. I needed to feel her skin. Her heat, her scent, they were like a drug to me. I kissed her throat and ear.

"I've never wanted to fuck a woman as much as I want to fuck you right now," I rasped.

Aria stiffened and turned her face away when I tried to kiss her again. She tried to sit up. For a moment, I considered holding tight, but then I released her, confused by her change in mood. She'd been into our kiss. I bet she was wet for my touch. Why did she pull back?

"I don't want this," she said, sounding actually disgusted, and the look on her face made me feel like my fucking father.

Anger surged through me. If she thought this was a fucking game, she'd better think again. She slipped off me and crawled under the covers. I couldn't believe it. I'd never been turned down by a woman, much less twice, and definitely not by my own fucking wife.

Stifling my frustration, I turned the lights off. I wouldn't be made a fool of. If Aria had no intention to turn this into a real marriage, then so be it. I had never wanted to marry, and if she preferred to keep her distance, I could keep myself entertained. I didn't need this marriage to work. It was only for show, anyway.

I waited for her to fall asleep before I slid out of bed. It would have been disrespectful to leave while she was awake. It was a silent code of honor that husbands tried to keep that part away from their wives, even if their wives preferred them seeking out other women.

I grabbed my mobile and a few clothes before I headed downstairs. Aria's expression, full of disgust and anxiety, kept flashing in my mind, making me feel like my father. That was the last thing I wanted to be.

My days of seeking women in clubs were over, and I couldn't risk the press catching me. I sent Grace a text, even if I was starting to grow tired of her. "Apartment. Thirty minutes."

She'd have to hurry to make it there in time. I left the penthouse, locking it so Aria would be safe, and drove to the apartment where Grace and I often met to fuck. My anger at Aria's rebuke turned to anger toward Grace, because I knew she'd said something to Aria on our wedding day. Was that why she couldn't bear my fucking touch?

Grace stepped in almost on time, slightly breathless but as usual with a heavy layer of make-up. Either she slept with that shit on her face or she'd hurried to put it on so she could meet me. "You're two minutes late," I said coldly.

She flushed. "I'm so sorry, Luca. I came as quickly as I could." She removed her coat, revealing garters, a mini skirt, and a bra where her nipples peeked out. Usually that sight got me going, and I was getting hard, but for some reason it felt different, which annoyed the fuck out of me. If I couldn't enjoy my wife, I at least, wanted to enjoy other women, but even that seemed impossible now that I was with Aria. Fuck it.

I focused on my anger, on the monster inside of me. "I don't wait for anyone." I pushed away from the wall, but Grace quickly stepped in front of me, touching my chest. I narrowed my eyes at her.

"I'll make it up to you. I'll give you what you need. My pussy is dripping for your cock, Luca." She cupped me through my pants and squeezed hard. My cock jerked. I hadn't slept with a woman in two weeks. That was the longest dry spell I'd suffered through since I was thirteen. All for Aria. Damn it.

"I knew that virgin pussy couldn't keep you entertained."

I gripped Grace's neck hard and brought our faces close. "Don't mention my wife again, understood? And don't think I don't know you talked shit to her on our wedding day."

Grace winced, but my roughness turned her on. Her nipples puckered, and her lips parted. I just needed to get the fucking anger out of my system, the fucking desire for Aria.

"Get on your knees. I'm going to fuck your mouth."

Grace shivered and knelt before me. I opened my zipper, grabbed her hair, and guided her mouth to my cock. I fucked her lips hard and fast, deep throating her. She moaned around my cock a few times. I pulled back, suddenly unable to bear her moans, the wet sounds of lips smacking around my cock.

She got to her feet with a smile. "Condom," I told her. I didn't have any with me. I'd given them all to Matteo shortly before my wedding because I'd assumed I wouldn't need them again. Because I'd assumed my wife would want my touch and not look at me like Nina looked at my goddamn father. The mere idea that I could be like him, that Aria could think I was like that, it drove me insane.

Grace shook her head. "We don't need it," she said with a seductive smile.

"I'm taking the pill, and I never went bareback with any of the other guys I was with."

My lip curled. Did she really think I'd fuck her without a condom? I didn't trust her one fucking bit. In her twisted mind, she probably thought that if she got pregnant, I'd actually stay with her. "I don't go bareback, Grace."

She pouted. "I bet you do with your wife."

I stiffened. Shaking my head, I reached for my pants. "I warned you."

"Luca, wait!" she cried, grabbing my hand. "Come on. Don't be like that. Fuck me. I need you. I have a condom in my purse."

Shaking her off, I left her standing naked in the room. Fuck. Why did she have to keep bringing up Aria? And why the fuck did I care? Aria didn't want this to be a real marriage. She couldn't even stand my fucking closeness.

When I returned home, I went straight into the shower, not even glancing toward my sleeping wife, and cleaned myself under the hot spray. Returning to bed with Aria after what I'd done felt…wrong. I crept through the darkness, but even in the dim light I could make out the golden halo of her hair on the pillow. She was turned toward my side.

I carefully slid into bed. Aria didn't stir. As my eyes grew accustomed to the dark, I made out her face and her bare shoulder. Her sweet, flowery scent drifted into my nose and suddenly I felt the urge to shower again. Fuck. I never wanted to marry, never wanted a woman at my side, in my life. But now I had a wife, a wife who didn't want my touch when all I could do was think about touching her.

I rolled over, turning my back to her. I wasn't sure what Aria was hoping for, but I knew she wouldn't get it. And she was obviously determined not to give me what I wanted, either.

The next morning, I left bed early, not wanting to face my wife. I wasn't worried that she'd realize where I had been; Aria didn't have experience with men, so she wouldn't be able to link my behavior to my nightly visit, but I was wary of being in her presence because, even without having to look at her, my fucking conscience was already giving me trouble. Before Aria, I had been convinced I didn't have one to begin with.

I'd never felt like it, and it didn't even make sense. Aria didn't want this marriage. She'd been forced into this and made it plainly clear how unwilling she was.

CHAPTER 10

I felt like an intruder in my own penthouse. Trying to evade Aria was almost impossible. Wherever I went, her scent seemed to linger. I was growing tired of having to tiptoe around the fucking apartment, of not knowing how to handle the woman in front of me. My go-to reaction with anyone else would have been harshness, maybe even a threat or violence. My father had never walked on eggshells around his wives. He'd broken them until they anticipated his every demand before he ever uttered a word.

My eyes followed my wife as she sank down on the sofa with a book. She kept her distance from me, and so did I, but damn it, I couldn't stop looking at her. "I have work to do all day," I informed her. As if she gave a fuck.

"Okay," she said simply.

Stifling my frustration, I turned and headed for the elevator. Romero had sent me a message that he was almost there. The door opened on Matteo's floor and he joined me. "Still no luck?"

I glowered, knowing exactly what he meant. "No. She can't bear my touch."

Matteo regarded me curiously. "Maybe you're just trying the wrong approach."

"And what kind of approach do you suggest?" I gritted out.

He shrugged. "I don't know your wife well enough to tell you what kind of approach she requires. Maybe you should ask Romero—after all, he spends more time with her than you." Matteo grinned challengingly.

"Fuck you."

When we stepped into the underground garage, I almost bumped into Romero, who was about to take the elevator up to the penthouse.

"Luca, Matteo," he said with a small nod.

"I'll be gone all day to check on the drug lab that reported suspicious delivery trucks in their street and won't be back until midnight. Keep Aria busy."

"Yeah, keep her busy," Matteo said, wiggling his eyebrows.

I almost punched him. He was pushing all my buttons today.

Romero regarded us curiously. "You're gone a lot."

I was when I should be spending every second banging my beautiful wife.

"He's busy fucking his whore, Grace," Matteo said.

Disapproval flickered across Romero's face before he could hide it. "Aria is a good woman."

"She's my woman and none of your business, Romero," I snarled. "Make sure you guard her and keep her entertained." I stepped up to him. "And no word about Grace to her."

Romero gave a tight nod. He stepped inside the elevator without another word.

Matteo chuckled as he followed me toward my car. His bike parked right beside it. "You know how to make people hate you. Aria, Romero..."

"I don't give a fuck if they hate me, as long as they do as I say. Both of them are forever bound to me by their fucking vows."

Matteo mounted his bike. I got into my car before he could say anything else that would drive me up the wall.

Later that day I got a message from Father.

Matteo sent me a questioning look. "You look like you swallowed a bitter pill."

"Father wants to see us."

Matteo grimaced. "Again?"

"Come on. Let's head over there. I want to get this over with as soon as possible."

When we arrived in front of the mansion in the Upper West Side where Matteo and I had grown up, my insides tightened as they always did. I hated this fucking place, hated the memories connected to it. From the outside it was regally white, but it harbored only darkness. Light hadn't been part of our childhood, or our present.

Matteo was already waiting on the bottom of the stairs leading up to the double doors. He was always quicker on his bike. His expression held the same apprehension that I felt.

We didn't say anything as we headed up the stairs. The camera swiveled toward us. I keyed in the code that would switch off the alarm system and unlocked the door. The guards would already have seen our faces and stayed in their rooms in the back of the house. Matteo and I both froze in the entrance hall when Nina's cry rang out.

"I'm sorry, Salvatore. Please..." She cried out again.

My hand curled to a tight fist. "Father, we're here!"

Matteo shook his head, his mouth tight. "We should kill him," he whispered. "You're a better Capo. You're a better everything."

"Shhh," I growled. Matteo had spoken quietly, but Father was paranoid. I wouldn't put it past the old man to have micros hidden away somewhere so he could hear everything that went on in his home. There was nothing I wanted more than to kill my father, but the Famiglia would never accept patricide.

Father appeared on the landing, only in a bathrobe. He didn't even bother closing it, and I had to stop myself from grimacing in disgust. He was covered in blood and still sporting a fucking boner from whatever he'd been doing to Nina. His cold eyes settled on Matteo and me, and his mouth pulled into a creepy benevolent smile. "Sons, good to see you."

I knew he was trying to get a reaction out of us, daring us to look away from the sight of his disgusting old man dick. But Matteo and I were his sons. We had seen and done so many horrible things. No way in hell would we show weakness in front of that bastard.

"You called for us," I said simply. Matteo stayed silent, which was for the best.

Father regarded my brother, and I knew he was daring him to say something. My muscles tensed. He had at least six guards in the back of the house. If Matteo lost his shit and we had to kill our father and his men, it would get nasty. Thankfully, Matteo gave a tight smile. It was fucking fake, but Father wouldn't know that.

His self-satisfied smirk widened. "I have a few matters to discuss with you. I'm taking a shower and getting dressed. Check on Nina and see if she's still breathing."

I gave a terse nod. Satisfied with our obedience, Father turned and headed for his bedroom. Matteo met my gaze, and the look in his eyes worried me. "Let's check on Nina," I told him firmly.

Without a word, we headed upstairs and toward the bedroom Nina slept in. Father didn't share a bed with her; he only sought her out when he wanted to fuck or when they had social events to attend.

The door was ajar. Taking a deep breath, I pushed it open, hoping I wouldn't have to dispose of a body or make up an inane story about how Nina had died so we could publicly bury her.

Soft sobbing came from inside. My eyes landed on the bed where Nina was tied, spread-eagle. She was bruised, bloody, and naked.

"Fuck," Matteo muttered. It wasn't the first time that Father had done something like it. I pulled my knife, and so did Matteo. Nina whimpered when I cut through the binds around her ankles while Matteo freed her arms. She tried to sit up, but she must have been tied up for a while and couldn't manage.

I reached for the satin gown discarded on the ground and draped it over her before I pulled her into a sitting position. I bent low so I was eye level with her. "Why don't you run?"

Nina looked toward Matteo. "He would sent you after me." Matteo was the best hunter in the Famiglia. He'd hunted down a few traitors.

"Matteo wouldn't find you," I muttered.

"I can't," she said firmly. "Where would I go? What would I do? This is my world."

I straightened. Nina tolerated Father's sadism because she loved the luxury and the money he could offer her. I didn't understand it, and I didn't have the patience to try.

Steps rang out and I moved back. Father appeared in the doorway, dressed in a dark suit and a high collared shirt.

"Salvatore," Nina simpered submissively.

Father didn't look at her, only at me and Matteo. "Why don't you have a go at her? I don't mind sharing her with my sons."

He'd offered her to us before. I wasn't sure if it was another way to test us and if he'd really let us touch what was his. Hatred filled me. I couldn't understand my father's reasoning. He was a disgusting monster. Instead of protecting her, he treated her like shit. I'd never hurt Aria like that, much less allow anyone to see her naked, or, heaven forbid, touch her. I'd kill anyone who thought he had a right to my woman. She'd never have to submit to anyone but me.

"Luca's got his young, little wife. Why would he want me?" Nina said quickly as if she really thought I'd consider it. I hadn't last time, and I wouldn't. It was bad enough that she had to bear Father's touch; I wouldn't break her further.

"She's so shy and petite. I can only imagine how much fun it is to break her, right?" Nina said as if she needed other women to suffer so her own became easier.

I hated and pitied her equally.

"What about you, Matteo?" Father asked.

"I prefer my women young, and prettier," he got out. It was a lie. Nina wasn't that much older than the women we both took into our bed, and she was beautiful with her long brown hair and slender figure.

Father shrugged, then finally turned to his wife who'd managed to put on her bathrobe by now. "Take one of the guards and buy yourself a few new shoes and dresses."

She smiled and nodded.

"But put on make-up, you look like shit," he added.

I turned on my heel and left the room, not giving a fuck if Father still wanted me there. Matteo was close behind me, his eyes burning with rage. The same rage I felt. Maybe we should just kill him. Kill him today, and try to make it look as if someone else had. Nobody would be sad to see him gone. Not a fucking soul.

"In my office," Father ordered as he followed us.

He took his time to sit down and lean back in his office chair, regarding Matteo and me.

"Still satisfied with your bride?" Father asked with a curl of his mouth.

Satisfaction hadn't been part of my marriage so far, but that was something Father couldn't find out.

I smirked. "I am. As you said, Aria is more beautiful than any other woman I've ever seen."

"That she is," Father said in a strange voice, and my hackles rose.

Matteo looked from him to me and his eyes sent a clear message. He'd be with me. He'd cut the bastard down if I gave the sign. And I seriously considered it, because I hated him for what he'd done to Mother, for what he did to Nina and all the other women, hated him for how he'd ruined our childhood and still ruined our lives as much as he could, but right this second I hated him the most because of the fucking greedy note his voice had taken on when he spoke about Aria.

Father narrowed his eyes at me. I knew I hadn't been quick enough to hide my possessiveness, much less my murderous thoughts. My muscles tensed, trying to consider the best way to kill him…shoot the camera in the corner and then kill the guards before they could alert reinforcement. I knew Father was hated among our men, but even the respect they harbored for me wouldn't be enough to make me Capo, at least not of a united Famiglia. We would be torn in half between the men who were loyal to my father, or pretended to be because it suited them better, and my supporters. It would be the end of the Famiglia. The Outfit would use our moment of weakness to strike, truce or not. The Famiglia was my future, my fucking birthright.

I forced myself to relax. I'd kill him another day, when I'd figured out a way to do so without people finding out. Father smiled. "Do you enjoy breaking her?"

I stared into his eyes, my smile turning harsh. "I won't talk about my wife, Father. She's mine and whatever happens between her and me is only for me to know. I won't share a fucking memory with anyone. Mine alone."

Father chuckled, but then he sobered. "Good, good. As long as you don't mistake your ownership of her for something else. Don't let a cunt lead you around by your dick. Women are good for three things only." He waited for me to recite what they were.

My hands itched for my gun, or better yet my knife. This kill would have to be personal. I wanted his blood trickling over my fingers, wanted his last breath against my skin. I wanted to rip his bowels out one after the other as he watched. "Fucking, sucking, and showing off," I got out.

Father cackled.

"I assume you didn't call us over so we could untie Nina for you?" Matteo asked with cocked eyebrows.

I sent him a glare.

Father narrowed his eyes. "No. The Famiglia in Sicily is struggling. The Camorra over there is much stronger than they are in the States."

That was a safer topic than women, but my anger still simmered under my skin.

Aria was content ignoring me. She never sought my closeness and slept soundly beside me at night while I couldn't stop watching her and wondering why she looked at me as if I were my father when I'd sworn to myself to treat her right.

Fuck. I was turning into a fucking pussy.

Two days had passed since my last meeting with Grace, but today I met her again, and I didn't wait long. Grace didn't look at me with disgust. With her, I didn't feel like my sadistic bastard of a father, even when she wasn't the woman I wanted.

Within a few minutes of her arrival, I had shoved her on all fours on the bed and was fucking her from behind.

My mind kept drifting to Aria with every thrust. I pushed Grace further down so I only saw her hair—blonde but so very different from the spun gold of my wife. I tried to imagine it was Aria, tried to imagine her flowery scent, but Grace's sweet perfume clogged up my nose and her moans kept distracting me.

My grip on her hips tightened further and I thrust harder into her, but I could actually feel myself soften at her fucking view. That had never happened, not with anyone.

I closed my eyes so I wouldn't have to see the woman before me, and instead an image of the woman I really wanted formed before my inner eye.

"Yes! Harder!" Grace screamed, and I almost snarled at her to shut the fuck up. Instead, I tightened my hold on her hips and slammed into her, anger consuming my veins. What the fuck was I doing?

"God yes," she moaned.

A board creaked. Tension shot through me a second before I reached for my gun on the bed beside me and opened my eyes, expecting a Russian fucker trying to catch me by surprise. Fuck. Aria stared back at me with wide, horrified eyes. Shock washed over me and I stilled. What was she doing here? How had she found this place? I'd never wanted a Bratva ambush more than I did now. Anything was better than the hurt look on my wife's face.

"What's the matter, Luca?" Grace shoved her ass back, driving my cock deeper into her, but I was already going soft. Aria still hadn't moved, and nor had I. Her blue eyes filled with tears, and my chest tightened uncomfortably. She should never have seen this.

Before I could decide what to do or say, she whirled around and started running.

"Fuck!" I growled.

I pushed Grace away when she tried to reach for me. "Let her leave."

I pulled up my pants, fucking glad that I almost never undressed when I fucked Grace. I started chasing Aria with my shirt still unbuttoned and my fly open, not giving a fuck if someone saw. Aria disappeared in the elevator and, before I could reach it, the doors closed and it began its descent. Damn it. I took the stairs, trying to button up my shirt. I couldn't go out in public half-naked. That was a newspaper article I didn't want to have to explain to my fucking father.

I stormed out of the building, catching a glimpse of Romero running after Aria who hurried down the steps toward the Metro. I ran after them. Fuck. I needed to catch her, needed to stop her from doing something stupid, needed to explain. Fuck it all. People jumped out of my way in wide-eyed shock.

I jerked to a halt on the platform just when the doors closed. Romero was a few steps ahead, but he too hadn't managed to board the Metro.

I watched the Metro disappear with Aria in it. My heart pounded in my chest, not just from the sprint, but from worry over my wife. My crying, hurt wife.

"Fuck!" I snarled.

Romero turned to face me, panting. "I'm sorry, Luca. I don't know how she found out. She tricked me and slipped away."

I was too worried about Aria to be pissed at Romero for letting her run off.

I fumbled for my cell and lifted it to my ear, calling Matteo.

"I thought you were banging Grace," was the first thing out of his mouth. In the background, I could hear women laughing.

"I need your help. Aria caught me, and now she's disappeared. We have to catch her before something happens to her."

"Where are you?"

I told him where we'd be heading then hung up and called Cesare. Romero was already checking the stops of the Metro on his phone. "Where should we start?" he asked.

I took a deep breath, trying to anticipate Aria's next move, but I didn't know my wife well enough to guess where she'd be going, and she wasn't familiar enough with New York to have favorite spots. "I want you to return to the penthouse in case she goes back there."

Romero opened his mouth as if to protest, but I sent him a warning look. He'd messed up, not as bad as me, not nearly as bad as me, but still.

I went back to my car and drove to the first stop of the Metro. I doubted Aria had gotten off here, but I was at a loss as to where she could be.

Matteo pulled up next to me on his bike and opened his helmet. "Any clue where she could be heading?"

I shook my head.

"You realize your shirt is buttoned wrong?"

I ignored his comment. Where could Aria be? She was responsible and aware of the risks of our world. She would stay somewhere public, probably somewhere in Manhattan or maybe Brooklyn, but that still left about a million options. I closed my eyes briefly. If something happened to her…

"Luca?"

I looked at Matteo, who was frowning at me. "We'll find her. Aria won't run off. She'll come back eventually."

Eventually?

"Why don't you call Gianna?"

I nodded. That was a good idea, but I doubted Gianna would tell me the first thing. Grabbing my phone, I realized I didn't have the redhead's number.

"Do you have her number?" I asked my brother. After all, he'd kissed her, so who knew if they'd exchanged more than spittle.

Matteo shook his head.

"Calling Scuderi is out of the question," I muttered. Aria's father would call my father, and then things would get nasty.

Cesare pulled up in his car and got out. We were only three men who needed to search New York.

We had to find Aria. There was no other option.

We'd been searching for Aria for almost two hours, but there was still no sign of her. My temple was throbbing, and I actually considered calling Scuderi after all. Screw the consequences. The only thing that mattered was getting back Aria.

My phone rang, and I picked up immediately.

"Aria just came home," Romero said.

I sagged with relief. "Is she all right?"

"Yes," Romero said without hesitation.

"Keep watch on her. I'll be there as fast as I can."

Matteo, Cesare and I arrived less than fifteen minutes later at my penthouse. Romero perched on the barstool but jumped off the moment we entered. "She's upstairs, showering."

His face reflected the same relief that I felt.

I walked past him, then continued upstairs. I pressed down the door handle but it was locked. I knocked. "Aria?"

No response.

I knocked harder. Still nothing. I could hear movement behind the door.

"Aria, let me in!" I hammered my fist against the door once more. I needed to see her with my own eyes, needed to make sure she was okay, unharmed.

"I'm going to kick in the door if you don't let me in."

Matteo and Cesare slowly came up the stairs, watching me with worry. I didn't give a fuck.

"Aria, open the fucking door!"

Finally, the lock was turned and I shoved open the door and stalked inside. Aria stood in the center of the room, dressed in a silk nightgown, her eyes swollen and red. I moved toward her and grabbed her arm, needing to know where she'd been, needing to explain what she'd seen.

"Don't touch me!" she shrieked, wrenching out of my grip.

"Where have you been?" I rasped. I wanted to touch her arm again. I fucking needed to touch her, as if merely seeing her wasn't enough to confirm she was unharmed. Aria jumped back, her eyes flashing with anger. "No! Don't ever touch me again. Not when you use those same hands to touch your *whore*."

"Out, everyone. Now," I growled.

Steps rang out and then there was the familiar sound of the elevator.

"Where have you been?" My pulse was pounding wildly. Didn't Aria understand how much danger she'd been in?

Aria glared at me, but behind the anger lingered deep hurt, and I didn't get it. "I wasn't cheating on you if that's what you're worried about. I would never do that. I think faithfulness is the most important thing in a marriage, so you can calm yourself now—my body is still only yours. I only walked around the city."

If she knew how eager the Bratva probably was to get her hands on my wife, then she wouldn't have done it. "You walked around New York at night? *Alone?*"

"You have no right to be angry with me, Luca. Not after what I saw today. You cheated on me."

Guilt flared up in my chest, but I shoved it down. I was never guilty about anything. "How can I be cheating when we don't have a real marriage? I can't even fuck my own wife. Do you think I'll live like a monk until you decide you

147

can stand my closeness?"

Aria swallowed hard. "God forbid. How dare I expect my husband to be faithful to me? How dare I hope for this small decency in a monster?"

Faithful? Was this even a real marriage? Aria might have said yes, but she didn't act like she wanted to be my wife. She'd looked at me like I was my father. "I'm not a monster. I've treated you with respect."

"Respect? I caught you with another woman! Maybe I should go out, bring a random guy back with me and let him fuck me in front of your eyes. How would that make you feel?" Aria hissed, and something snapped inside me.

I grabbed her by the hips and hoisted her on the bed, pressing her down with my weight as I held her wrists above her head. Nobody would ever touch her. Nobody but me.

"Do it. Take me, so I can really hate you," Aria whispered harshly, tears glistening in her eyes. She closed them and turned her face away. My gaze traced her flushed skin, her trembling lower lip, the tears that clung to her lashes. Scared. Scared of me. Fuck. Aria. My wife. Mine to protect and honor. I needed to control myself better. I lowered my head and pressed it to her shoulder, breathing in her flowery scent. I exhaled, getting a grip on my anger. "God, Aria."

I released her wrists and raised my head. Aria didn't move, her arms still stretched out above her head submissively. The sight of her surrender left a fucking bitter taste in my mouth. I tried to touch her cheek, but she drew back. "Don't touch me with *her* on you."

She was right. She didn't deserve this.

I got up. "I'm going to take a shower now, and we will both calm down, and then I want us to talk."

Aria peered up at me. "What's there left to talk about?"

"Us. This marriage."

Slowly, she brought her arms down from where I'd pushed her into the bed. "You fucked a woman in front of my eyes today. Do you think there's still a chance for this marriage?"

"I didn't want you to see that," I murmured. Fuck, the look in her eyes when she'd caught me would haunt me for a long time, which was ridiculous considering how much I'd done and seen.

"Why? So you could cheat in peace and quiet behind my back?"

Aria was right, but she'd never showed any hint that she cared about this marriage. "Let me take a shower. You were right. I shouldn't disrespect you further by touching you like this."

She didn't say anything, only regarded me with those sad eyes that felt like a blade in my chest. I turned and headed for the bathroom. I wasn't sure how long I stood under the stream of hot water until I felt like I could return to my wife, like I'd washed every trace of Grace's perfume and touch away. I didn't like the heavy feeling Aria's tears had left in my body. It was a sensation I had no experience with and wasn't keen on experiencing more often.

After I'd wrapped a towel around my waist, I returned to the bedroom where Aria sat against the headboard. Her hands were folded in her lap, those blonde tresses cascading down her elegant shoulders.

I felt like even more of an idiot for going to Grace when I had someone like Aria in my bed, but she still didn't want me which became apparent once more when I dropped my towel and she quickly looked away as if she couldn't bear the sight of me. I wasn't vain like Matteo, far from it, but I knew how women checked me out. I worked hard for my body. After pulling on boxers, I sank down on the bed beside Aria. My gaze rested on her puffy eyes. It still caught me off-guard. "Did you cry?" The better question was why?

I'd have thought she would be happy if I left her alone and looked for another woman, like so many wives in our circles were.

She tilted her head toward me with a small frown. "Did you think I wouldn't care?"

"Many women in our world are glad when their husbands use whores or take on a mistress. As you said, there are few marriages based on love. If a woman can't stand her husband's touch, she won't mind him having affairs to satisfy his needs."

Her mouth thinned. "His *needs.*"

"I'm not a good man, Aria. I never pretended otherwise. There are no good men in the mafia." I'd been trying to be good to her even when I knew I'd fail eventually, but I'd hoped it wouldn't happen so soon.

Her gaze dipped to my chest, the spot over my heart. "I know, but you made me think that I could trust you and that you wouldn't hurt me."

"I never hurt you." Didn't she realize how hard I was trying?

"It hurt seeing you with *her*," Aria admitted in a whisper, looking away and swallowing once more as if she had to fight back more tears.

The urge to touch her was impossibly strong, but I held back. "Aria, I didn't get the feeling that you wanted to sleep with me. I thought you'd be glad if I didn't touch you."

Aria shook her head. "When did I say that?"

"When I told you I wanted you, you pulled back. You looked disgusted." Her expression had haunted me those last few days; how could she not remember?

"We were kissing, and you said you wanted to fuck me more than any other woman. Of course, I pulled back. I'm not some whore you can use when you feel like it. You're never home. How am I supposed to get to know you?"

She knew everything about me that mattered, and the things she didn't know were for the best.

Aria sighed. "What did you think? I've never done anything. You are the only man I've kissed. You knew that when we married. You and my father

150

made sure it was the case, and despite that you expect me to go from never having kissed a guy to spreading my legs for you. I wanted to take it slow. I wanted to get to know you so I could relax; I wanted to kiss you and *do other things* first before we slept together."

Fuck, my mind went into overdrive. "Other things? What kinds of other things?"

Aria scowled and turned away. "This is useless."

"No, don't," I murmured, touching her cheek and gently turning it back to me. Reluctantly, I dropped my hand. "I get it. For men, the first time isn't a big deal, or at least it wasn't for the men I know." I hadn't considered that Aria would need time to get used to a man's touch, to my touch. I'd hoped she'd be eager and curious.

"When was your first time?" Aria asked immediately.

"I was thirteen and my father thought it was time for me to become a real man, since I'd already been initiated. 'You can't be a virgin and a killer.' That's what he said. He paid two prostitutes to spend a weekend with me and teach me everything they knew." I still remembered the two days I'd spent in the Foxy.

Aria grimaced. "That's horrible."

"Yeah, I suppose it is," I said. For me, it had been what was expected. "But I was a thirteen-year-old boy who wanted to prove himself. I was the youngest member in the New York Famiglia. I didn't want the older men to think of me as a boy, and I felt like a big deal when the weekend was over. I doubt the prostitutes were overly impressed with my performance, but they pretended that I was the best lover they'd ever had. My father probably paid them extra for it. It took me a bit to figure out that not all women like it if you come all over their face when they give you a blow job."

Disgust flashed across Aria's face, and I couldn't help but laugh, even when I hoped that she wouldn't show the same reaction when I came in her mouth.

"Yeah…" I let a strand of her hair trail over my finger, enjoying the silky feel of it. Aria watched me with curiosity, but she didn't pull back. "I was really worried tonight," I admitted.

"Worried that I'd let someone have what's yours," Aria said. I didn't miss the hint of vulnerability in her tone.

Had I been worried that Aria would seek out other men? Never. Aria wasn't the type. "No, I knew, I *know* you are loyal. Things with the Bratva are escalating. If they got their hands on you…"

They'd hurt her. Me taking her on our wedding night, even against her will, would have been nothing compared to what they'd put her through. My stomach clenched in a mix of fury and worry.

"They didn't."

"They *won't*," I growled. I'd protect Aria no matter what it would take me. I trailed my fingers over Aria's throat, but she leaned back.

"You're going to make this really difficult, aren't you?"

She gave me an indignant look.

"I'm sorry for what you saw today," I said. Apologizing was something I didn't do. Father had beaten it out of me, but here I was doing just that.

"But not sorry for what you did."

"I rarely say I'm sorry. When I say it, I mean it." And I did. Aria shouldn't have seen what she did, and I shouldn't have gone to Grace. If I didn't want to be like my father, I couldn't act like him, not even in that regard.

"Maybe you should say it more often."

"There's no way out of this marriage for you, nor for me. Do you really want to be miserable?"

After a moment of consideration that almost made me lose my patience, Aria gave a small shake of her head. "No. But I can't pretend I never saw you with her."

I could only imagine what kind of images played out before her inner eye. Aria had never seen anything like it, and then she had to see me fucking Grace. "I don't expect you to, but let's just pretend that our marriage begins today. A clean start."

Longing flashed across her face but still she looked doubtful. "It's not that easy. What about her? Tonight wasn't the first time you were with her. Do you love her?" She looked so goddamn vulnerable.

"Love? No. I don't have feelings for Grace." I'd never had feelings for any of the women in my life, or anyone really, except for Matteo perhaps.

"Then why do you keep seeing her? The truth."

I hoped she could take the truth. "Because she knows how to suck a cock and because she's a good fuck. Truthful enough?"

Aria's cheeks turned red, and again I had to touch the heated skin, needed to feel her. "I love how you blush whenever I say something dirty. I can't wait to see your blush when I *do* something dirty to you."

"If you really want to make this marriage work, if you *ever* want the chance to do something dirty to me, then you'll have to stop seeing other women. Maybe other wives don't care, but I won't have you touching me as long as there's anyone else."

She was right, and it wasn't as if any woman could hold my interest. I had only thought about Aria since I'd seen her photo in the newspaper, even when I was with Grace. "I promise. I'll touch only you from now on."

Aria regarded me with narrowed eyes. "Grace won't like it."

Grace definitely wouldn't. "Who gives a fuck what she thinks?"

"Won't her father give you trouble?"

"We pay for his campaigns, and he has a son following in his footsteps who needs our money soon as well. What does he care about a daughter who isn't good for anything but shopping and eventually marrying a rich man?"

"She probably hoped you'd be that man."

Of course she did. "We don't marry outsiders. Never. She knew that, and it wasn't like she was the only woman I fucked."

Aria blinked, obviously stunned by my admittance. "You said it yourself. You have your needs. So how can you tell me you won't cheat on me again soon if you get tired of waiting for me to sleep with you?"

"Do you intend to make me wait long?" I asked.

"I think we have very different concepts of the words 'long wait.'"

"I'm not a patient man. If long means a year..." These last few days were already hell. The idea of sleeping in a bed with Aria for months without sleeping *with* her...That wasn't something I wanted to consider.

Aria glared.

"What do you want me to say, Aria? I kill and blackmail and torture people. I'm the boss of men who do the same when I order them to, and soon I'll be the Capo dei Capi, the leader of the most powerful crime organization on the East Coast, and probably the US. You thought I'd take you against your will on our wedding night, and now you're angry because I don't want to wait months to sleep with you?"

Resignation crossed Aria's face as she closed her eyes and scooted down on the bed. "I'm tired. It's late."

I leaned toward her and touched her waist lightly. "No. I want to understand. I'm your husband. You aren't like other girls who can choose the man they're going to lose it to. Are you scared that I'm going to be rough with you because of what you saw today?"

Aria gave the smallest shiver, confirming my suspicion, but by God, she didn't need to be scared. "I won't be. I told you I want you to writhe beneath me in pleasure, and while that probably won't happen the first time I take you, I'll make you come as often as you want with my tongue and my fingers until you can come when I'm inside you. I don't mind going slow, but what do you want to wait for?"

Aria's eyes fluttered open and the look in them sucked the breath cleanly out of my lungs. I wasn't sure why, but I didn't like it. This time, I managed not to run my fingers through the golden halo on the pillow.

"I won't make you wait for months," Aria whispered, sounding exhausted. She closed her eyes again, looking like a sleeping queen as she did. I swallowed, unsure what to do to make her happy in this marriage, unsure if I should try.

I lay down beside her, listening to her breathing that had already evened out in sleep.

I knew I wouldn't fall asleep anytime soon.

CHAPTER II

I woke before sunrise after less than two hours of sleep with my arm around Aria. For a few moments, I stayed like that, enjoying that she was relaxed in my embrace in sleep. Finally, I pulled back and reached for my cell on the nightstand. I quickly typed a message to Matteo, telling him that he'd have to talk to the manager of one of our whorehouses alone, then I wrote Romero. He wouldn't have to guard Aria today.

"Business?" Aria asked in a sleepy voice.

I glanced toward her and shook my head. "I cancelled my plans for the day so we can spend some time together and get to know each other."

Aria blinked, becoming more alert at once. "Really?"

"Really," I said. Resisting the urge to kiss her, I swung my legs out of bed. "I'll get ready, and then I'll think of something we can do today."

"Okay," Aria said with a small smile.

———✕———

Thirty minutes later, I was looking into the fridge, trying to figure out what we could make for breakfast.

Marianna had stocked the fridge well, but she wouldn't come over to cook today. Aria came down the staircase in shorts, showing off those legs. "Can you cook?"

Aria huffed as she headed toward me. "Don't tell me you've never made breakfast for yourself?"

"I usually grab something on my way to work, except on the days when Marianna is here and prepares something for me." I couldn't stop checking her out. "I love your legs."

Aria ignored my comment and peered into the fridge. Her arm touched mine and I had to stare down at her, at the golden crown of her head and the way her nose crinkled in thought.

Aria reached into the fridge, taking out eggs and red peppers. She looked like she knew what she was doing. That made one of us. I stepped back and leaned against the counter to watch her cook, but Aria wouldn't have it. She raised her eyebrows.

"Won't you help me? You can chop the peppers. You know how to handle a knife, from what I hear," she said teasingly.

I snatched a knife and stepped up beside her. Aria gazed up at me. She reached my chest and again a wave of protectiveness washed over me. Aria handed me the pepper and motioned at a wooden board. I'd seen Marianna use it for chopping before. While I cut the peppers, Aria scrambled the eggs, then poured them into a hot pan.

"What happens to these?" I showed her the peppers I'd chopped.

"Shit," Aria said with a grimace, glancing between the sizzling eggs and the peppers.

"Have you ever cooked?" I asked.

Aria grabbed the peppers and thrust them into the cooking eggs. I doubted they'd get done before the eggs. Leaning against the counter once more, I enjoyed watching Aria trying to unstick the eggs from the pan. Her expression became increasingly frustrated.

"Why don't you make coffee for us?" she asked with a pointed look.

She was really cute when she was trying to look angry.

I humored her and went over to the coffee maker while Aria muttered curses under her breath, trying to save the eggs.

When I finally put two cups of coffee down on the bar, Aria spooned the burnt mess of eggs down on two plates. I could stomach a lot, but this would be a new challenge. I sank down on a barstool and Aria climbed on the one beside me, watching me expectantly. Despite the burnt smell wafting up to my nose, I picked up the fork and shoved a piece of the eggs into my mouth. It was by far the worst omelet I'd ever had. Aria took a bite as well and scrunched up her face, then spit the eggs out immediately before drinking a large gulp of the coffee. She looked at me with watery eyes. "Oh my god, that's disgusting."

"Maybe we should go out for breakfast," I suggested. I had a feeling that if Aria tried to cook us something else, we'd either get food poisoning or she'd burn down the penthouse.

Embarrassment flashed across Aria's face as she glared down at her coffee. "How hard can it be to make an omelet?"

My chest vibrated with suppressed laughter, but it died when my eyes dipped down to Aria's bare legs. We were sitting close enough to touch and, gauging her reaction, I put my palm down on her knee. Aria paused with her cup against her lips. She didn't push me away or flinch, which I took as a good sign. I ran my thumb gently over her skin. "What would you like to do today?"

Aria's brows drew together as she glanced between my hand on her knee and my face. Did she enjoy the touch? "The morning after our wedding night, you asked me if I knew how to fight, so maybe you can teach me how to use a knife or a gun, and maybe some self-defense," she said.

That wasn't what I'd expected. Shopping or something like that, yes, but fighting?

"Thinking about using them against me?"

Aria rolled her eyes. "As if I could ever beat you in a fair fight."

"I don't fight fair," I teased.

"So will you teach me?"

"I want to teach you a lot of things," I murmured as I cupped her knee.

"Luca, I'm serious. I know I have Romero and you, but I want to be able to defend myself if something happens. You said it yourself: the Bratva won't care that I'm a woman."

Aria didn't know the Bratva. Even if she could defend herself, these fuckers would still be able to hurt her, if they ever got close. "Okay. We have a gym where we work out and do train. We could go there."

Aria smiled widely and hopped off the stool. "I'll grab my workout clothes."

I hadn't expected her to be this excited about the prospect of fighting.

———————><———————

The second Aria and I entered the Famiglia gym, every man in the room stopped what they'd been doing to stare at my wife. A glower from me quickly made them look away.

"Our changing rooms are men only. We don't usually have female visitors."

Aria grinned. "I know you'll make sure nobody sees me naked."

"You bet I will." Not that any of my men would dare to look at her. They

159

knew I'd crush them if they did.

Aria laughed, looking happy.

I led her toward the changing room. "Let me check if someone's in there," I said. The only dick Aria was going to see would be mine. I pushed inside. Three men were in different stages of undress. They turned to me and gave respectful nods.

"I'm here with my wife, and she needs to get changed," I said, giving them a cold smile.

They exchanged surprised looks then quickly put on their gym clothes. After they'd left, I led Aria inside.

Her face pulled into a grimace at the stench.

Such a girl. "We're not catering to sensitive female noses," I said with a smirk.

Aria tugged her bag out of my hand and headed for one of the lockers. I followed close behind, then dropped my own bag on a bench.

Aria grabbed the hem of her shirt, then stopped. "Aren't you going to give me some privacy?"

Was she being serious? I opened my gun holster and put it down, then pulled my shirt over my head.

Aria's eyes took in my upper body, indignation flashing in her eyes.

She turned her back to me before she pulled her t-shirt over her head. Aria reached for her bra, but I beat her to it and unhooked the clasp with one finger, brushing her skin. I wanted nothing more than to turn her around and kiss her, but I took a step back and changed into my gym shorts all the while watching in rapt attention as Aria pushed down her pants. Two perfect ass cheeks came into view. She was wearing a fucking thong and then she pulled that down as well before she bent down to pick up her shorts and the sight almost undid me. Didn't she realize what kind of view she just gave me? I exhaled. The small glimpse of her pussy sent blood into my cock.

I was almost relieved when she got dressed in tiny running shorts. When Aria turned around to face me, her eyes darted to the bulge in my pants and her eyebrows skyrocketed as her cheeks turned red once more.

"That's what you're wearing for self-defense lessons?" The shorts barely covered her upper thighs and were skin-tight, as was her tank top.

"I don't have anything else. This is what I wear when I go jogging."

"You realize I'll have to kick every guy's ass who looks at you the wrong way, right? And looking like that, my men will have a hard time *not* looking at you the wrong way."

"It's not my job to make them control themselves. Just because I'm wearing revealing clothes doesn't mean I'm inviting them to look. If they can't behave themselves, that's their problem."

Oh, they would behave themselves…

I nodded toward the door and led Aria outside, my hand in the small of her back. A few men looked up, then quickly down. I steered Aria toward the sparring mats, which two soldiers vacated with respectful nods the moment we approached. From the array of knives hanging at the wall, I picked one that was good for beginners and not too heavy, then held it out to Aria who took it with a look of confusion.

We faced each other on the mat. "Attack me, but try not to cut yourself."

"Won't you get a knife too?"

"I don't need one. I'll have yours in a minute." My biggest challenge would be to fight Aria without hurting her. I'd never had to be careful in a fight before, but she was tiny in comparison to me.

Aria was obviously annoyed by my comment, but it was the truth.

"So what am I supposed to do?" she asked, eyeing the knife uncertainly. It was obvious from the way she held it that she'd never fought with one before.

"Try to land a hit. If you manage to cut me, you win. I want to see how you move."

Aria glanced around us for a moment before she straightened her shoulders. She lunged forward, and I was surprised by how fast she could move, but I sidestepped her unpracticed attack easily. It was harder to grip her wrist without crushing it, and then I whirled her around until her back was pressed enticingly against my front.

"You don't have my knife yet," Aria said breathlessly.

I tightened my hold on her wrist ever so slightly then lowered my head to her ear. "I would have to hurt you to get it. I could break your wrist, for example, or just bruise it." Aria held her breath, her pulse thudding under my fingers. I released her and she quickly dashed out of my reach, whirling around to face me once more.

"Again," I said.

Fighting Aria was fun, and I could tell that she was growing annoyed by her inability to hit me. I'd never been beaten in a fight, and those men had been Made Men with years of experience and twice Aria's weight.

When she tried to kick my balls, I snatched up her foot and tugged. I underestimated her momentum and she landed hard on her back, gasping and dropping the knife.

I knelt beside her, touching her belly. "Are you okay?" I murmured, trying to look calm because my soldiers were watching.

Aria's eyes fluttered open. "Yeah. Just trying to catch my breath." She glanced behind me toward my men. "Don't you have a soldier who's only five foot something and terrified of his own shadow who would be willing to fight me?"

There were definitely a few men around who would be easier opponents for Aria, but I'd never let anyone fight her, not even in jest. "My men aren't terrified of anything," I said loudly as I helped Aria to her feet before I faced them. "Anyone willing to fight my wife?"

A few of them laughed, and others quickly shook their head.

"You'll have to fight me," I told Aria.

Aria definitely didn't want to give up, but I could tell that she was tiring. I was holding her against my body once again when a sharp pain in my bicep startled me. I loosened my hold and Aria managed to slip away, but before she could bring the knife down, I grabbed her wrist. My eyes darted to the spot on my upper arm where she had left teeth marks. "Did you bite me?"

"Not hard enough. There isn't even blood," she said, her lips twisting with amusement.

My stomach shook, but I held the laughter back. Aria's eyes shone with pride as she peered up at me. Fuck. I wanted to laugh, but with my men watching, I couldn't. A few low chuckles escaped anyway. Aria grinned.

I shook my head. "I think you've done enough damage for one day."

———————>✕———————

Aria had never been more relaxed around me than after our training. It had allowed us to be close physically without her having time to worry about where it might lead. "Let's get takeout," I said on our way home. "What are you in the mood for?"

Aria pursed her lips. "I've never tried sushi."

My eyebrows shot up. "Never?"

She shook her head. "But I'd like to give it a try. Maybe I'll like it."

There were so many other things she'd definitely like if she gave them a try, but I swallowed the words, not wanting her to get tense again.

I drove past my favorite sushi place and picked a selection of everything so Aria would find something she'd like, before we headed back home and settled outside on the roof terrace with our food and a bottle of wine. Aria tried every piece of sushi eagerly, nodding and humming her approval. I loved watching her.

"I'm surprised," Aria said as she settled against the backrest. I had my arm thrown over it, close to her bare shoulders. I wasn't sure what she was referring to. "I didn't think you'd really try."

"I told you I would. I keep my word," I said. I wanted this marriage to work.

"I bet this is hard for you." Aria motioned at the space between us.

"You have no idea. I want to kiss you really fucking bad."

Aria's eyes flitted to my lips. I put my glass back down on the table and leaned closer, touching her waist. "Tell me you don't want me to kiss you."

Aria opened her mouth, but she didn't say anything. Slowly, I leaned forward, giving her time to pull back, but she didn't. I kissed her, forcing myself to go slow, but soon our kiss became more heated. It was a struggle to keep my hand on her waist and not explore the rest of her body. I pushed my thumb under her shirt and rubbed her bare skin. Aria moaned softly into my mouth. I wasn't sure if she even noticed. I guided her back gently until she was stretched out on the lounge and I was half bent over her.

Aria tasted so fucking sweet as my tongue claimed her mouth. I could tell she was growing more and more aroused by the way she rubbed her thighs together.

I raised my head to gaze at her flushed face.

"I could make you feel good, Aria," I said, my fingers twitching eagerly on her hip, wanting to head south. "You want to come, don't you?"

Conflict danced in Aria's eyes, but then a determined glint took over. "I'm fine. Thank you."

My stomach twitched with suppressed laughter. "You are so stubborn." I knew she was wet. The way she'd pressed herself into me, the way she'd moaned...Fuck.

I claimed her lips once more, my tongue teasing hers as I wanted to do with her pussy, my finger rubbing circles right above her waistband, knowing she'd feel it between her legs too, but Aria stayed true to her words, even as she panted and moaned and shivered under my kiss. Eventually I had to stop, because my dick was so fucking hard in my pants, it got too uncomfortable.

Aria blinked up at me dazedly.

"We'd better stop now," I groaned. "My pants are getting tight."

Aria looked smug and embarrassed at the same time. I chuckled, pressed another kiss to her mouth, then pushed to my feet and pulled Aria with me. She held on to my hand for once, surprising me, and fuck if that didn't feel like a major victory. It was even worth the blue balls I suffered through all night as Aria slept in my arms.

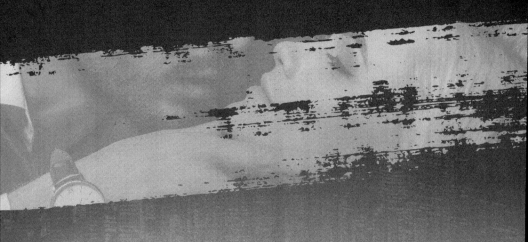

CHAPTER 12

My phone buzzed on the nightstand, startling me awake. I carefully untangled Aria from me and she rolled over. Grabbing the phone, I stood. It was Cesare. I quickly took the call.

"What's the matter?"

"The Bratva chopped up one of our chemists and spread his remains around the Sphere."

"Is someone taking care of it?"

"The cleaning squad is already there."

"All right, I'll be there as quickly as I can. Did you call Matteo already?"

"No."

"I'll do it then."

I called my brother, agreeing to meet in fifteen minutes before I returned to the bedroom and quickly picked out clothes and grabbed my guns.

When I was dressed, I headed into the hallway once more, telling Romero that he needed to come over sooner, then I went into the bedroom to wake Aria.

But she was already sitting up. "Are you leaving already?"

She actually looked disappointed. "The Bratva got one of ours. They left him in tiny pieces around one of our clubs."

"Somebody I know?" Aria asked. "Will the police get involved?"

I went over to her. She looked adorable with her tousled blond hair. "Not if I can help it," I murmured, cupping her face. "I'll try to be home early, okay?"

Aria gave a small nod and I dipped my head down to kiss her. She didn't flinch or draw back when our lips touched. Instead, she parted for me. I took her up on the invitation, eagerly deepening the kiss, but eventually duty called. I pulled back and left quickly.

The Bratva had graffitied their fucking Kalashinikovs onto the entrance of the Sphere, and the dead chemist wasn't the only one they'd killed. One of our most successful dealers had also been dismembered and left in his backyard with the same goddamn graffiti on his house front.

"Fucking Russians," Matteo muttered.

"It's another warning. They want their drugs back," Cesare said with a frown.

A group of Famiglia soldiers had stolen the Russian's last drug delivery in retribution for their attack on one of our drug labs.

"We need to send them a response," Matteo said.

The Famiglia cleaning squad, a group of initiates mostly, tried to remove the Kalashnikov graffiti. They'd already got rid of the blood stains on the walls and pavements, but the graffiti was harder to wash off.

I called my father again, hating that I needed to get his okay for possible actions. He picked up after ten rings, as usual making me wait. "I'm busy."

Not with business, that was clear. "We need to send the Bratva a clear warning. They're becoming too daring."

Father was silent. His disinterest in the Russians would cost us everything at some point. "I'll call Fiore."

"Fiore isn't here. He doesn't know what's going on in New York, and he probably doesn't give a fuck. The Outfit won't help us. They have their own problems. We need to act now. We can't wait for you and Fiore to discuss every fucking thing in detail. The Russians are turning us into fools."

Cesare stared at me as if I'd lost my mind for talking to my Capo like that, but I didn't give a fuck. I cared about the Famiglia, and if my father posed a risk to it, he needed to realize it.

"You aren't Capo yet, Luca. You won't be Capo for a long time, and you might not become Capo at all if I declare you as unworthy, don't forget it."

Most of the soldiers in New York already trusted my judgment more than his. I didn't say anything.

"Do what must be done so the Russians know their place," he said eventually.

"Will do," I got out, then hung up.

"I like the look on your face," Matteo said with his shark-grin.

"We'll attack one of their labs. They want their fucking drugs back? We'll steal more of it and crush a few Bratva assholes."

Matteo clapped his hand, grinning. "That sounds like my kind of entertainment."

I turned to Cesare. "Choose ten men to join us."

We couldn't allow the Bratva to destroy our drug trade. New York was our city. It was *my* city, and no one would take it from me.

The attack was bloody, brutal, and exhilarating, but it was a success, even if the Bratva almost caught us by surprise by the end. After hours of killing and torturing Russian bastards for information on possible future attacks, a veil of darkness seemed to cloak my mind, a need for more violence, more blood. I didn't bother getting out of my blood-soaked clothes before heading home. I just wanted to see Aria, wanted to feel that calm and belonging her closeness miraculously brought me.

But I was barely myself, or maybe I was my true self in those moments of mindless bloodshed, of unrestrained cruelty. It was difficult to say. More monster or man? Before Aria, the answer would have been easy...

Romero eyed me worriedly when I entered the apartment. "Are you okay? Or do you want me to stay?"

"Leave," I growled, my eyes latching onto Aria, who lay on the couch.

"She couldn't sleep because she was worried about you, and then she fell asleep on the couch and I didn't want to carry her upstairs."

I gave him a harsh look and he finally stepped into the elevator and disappeared. Slowly, I stalked closer to my beautiful wife. She was in her satin nightgown, revealing her slender legs and the enticing swell of her breasts.

Mine. Only mine. So fucking beautiful.

A dark hunger unfurled in my body, a need to finally claim the woman before me. I slid my hands under her back and legs, then lifted her into my arms. She smelled sweet and innocent. I wanted to corrupt her, to taste her, to fuck her. I wanted to make her mine.

"Luca?" Aria's soft voice echoed through the pounding in my ears, through the fog that always clung to me after hours of screams and shooting.

I carried Aria into our room and lay her down on our bed. My eyes traced her body in the dark. She was like a beacon of light in the black of the room.

She moved, and the room was flooded with light.

Aria's eyes met mine. Wide, fearful.

My gaze dipped to the swell of her breasts once more, then continued to her narrow waist and down to the valley between her thighs.

"Luca?"

I could have died today. I could die tomorrow.

I could die without having tasted every inch of my wife, without having claimed her.

I got out of my blood-soaked shirt then unbuckled my belt. My hands were steady, always steady, no matter what they did. They didn't shake when I pulled the trigger, when I cut a throat or when I skinned a fucker.

"Luca, you're scaring me. What happened?"

I shoved down my pants and knelt on the bed before wedging one of my knees between Aria's legs. I leaned over my wife, my eyes taking in the way her breasts rose and fell with every breath. Mine to claim.

Aria lifted her hands and touched my cheek, warm and soft and careful.

I blinked, my focus shifting to her face, to her fear-widened eyes, the barely contained terror in her expression. Man or monster?

I dipped my face down into the crook of her neck and breathed in her flowery scent, feeling her pulse throbbing against my lips. I concentrated on the feel of Aria's palm against my cheek.

Aria was my wife. Mine to protect.

"Luca?"

I peered at her face. I wouldn't be a monster with her. I shoved off her and quickly moved into the bathroom. Turning the shower to ice cold, I slipped under the stream, watching as it took away the blood and some of the darkness, but the rest clung to me as it did so often after days like these.

After I'd wrapped a towel around my waist, I strode into the bedroom. Aria watched me warily. I needed to be close to her, needed her to get rid of this fucking darkness for me. I dropped the towel, but Aria quickly rolled over so she wouldn't see me naked. I slipped under the covers and moved close to her until her warmth seeped into me. Wanting to see her face, I grabbed her hip and rolled her over.

She didn't resist. I peered down at her as she lay on her back in front of me, her eyes searching my face. I needed her even closer. Closer. Always closer. I reached for her nightgown, wanting that barrier gone, needing to feel her, skin on skin.

Aria touched my hand, stopping me. "Luca." Her voice held worry, and when I met her gaze, the same worry was reflected in her eyes.

She didn't have to be scared, not anymore. "I want to feel your body against mine tonight. I want to hold you."

It was a weak thing to admit, but I didn't care.

"Only hold me?" she asked, her blue eyes questioning.

"I swear."

Aria finally allowed me to pull her nightgown over her head, leaving her in only white panties. My eyes raked over her beautiful breasts, the way her pink nipples puckered. I ran my finger along the waistband of her panties, but she froze, and she was probably right. It was better if that small barrier remained between us. I rolled over on my back and took Aria with me so she laid on top of me, her knees beside my waist.

Our chests brushed, but she kept herself suspended as if she worried she could hurt me with her weight. I tightened my hold around her back, pressing her tightly against me. I trailed my palm along Aria's spine to the curve of her ass and began stroking her lightly. She was tense at first but slowly relaxed when it became clear that I wouldn't push her.

"Doesn't your cut need stitches?" Aria asked, her voice drenched with worry. Worried about me.

I pressed a soft kiss to her mouth, feeling more of the violence drain from my body. "Tomorrow." These wounds didn't matter, not at all. Tasting my wife did. Those perfect lips. I caressed her ass, my fingertips tracing her panty line, occasionally slipping beneath. So fucking soft.

Aria held my gaze with half-lidded eyes. She brushed her fingertips over my throat, a spot I'd never let anyone touch. Too vulnerable, but with Aria I enjoyed the touch, and then she pressed a kiss to a small wound there. So caring. Aria raised her head and gave me the smallest smile.

I wanted her closer, still closer. My hand cupped her ass cheek and squeezed lightly. My finger grazed her folds though the fabric of her panties.

Aria gasped, tensing on top of me. I watched her closely as I lightly traced her. Soon, her panties were drenched. My cock stirred, but the dark hunger from before had been replaced by a more restrained need.

So wet.

She lowered her eyes in obvious embarrassment and I halted my movements, needing to see her eyes.

"Look at me, Aria," I ordered, my voice harsher than I wanted. Aria's eyes darted up, swimming with mortification. How could she be embarrassed when I wanted to scream in triumph over her body's reaction to my touch?

"Are you embarrassed because of this?" I stroked my fingers along her crease and Aria bucked her hips, her lips falling open in a breathless moan. She was so responsive.

I caressed her carefully, allowing her to get used to my touch, to see that I'd hold back. Her grip on my shoulders tightened and her lips parted as she made small rocking motions. Watching her beautiful face as I guided her closer and closer to her first orgasm, as her juices soaked her panties, it was the best thing

I could imagine.

When my fingers slid over her clit, Aria started to tremble, her breathing ragged, and I didn't take my eyes off her, not for a single second as she came on top of me.

I kept my fingers on her pussy, feeling possessive and wishing she wasn't wearing panties so I could feel her folds slick with her arousal.

Aria pressed her face into my throat, holding on to me tightly as she tried to catch her breath.

Her pussy was so hot and wet. The thought of burying my cock in her was almost overwhelming. I sunk my nose into her hair, pushing my needs back. If I gave in to them now, things would get out of hand. Too much of the darkness, of the violent energy, still swam close to the surface. "God, you're so wet, Aria. If you knew how much I want you right now, you'd run away." A harsh laugh burst out of me. Part of me wanted her to run so I could chase and catch her. The thrill of the hunt, the need to claim. "I can almost feel your wetness on my cock."

My cock brushed Aria's thigh and a groan lodged itself in my throat.

"Do you want me to touch you?" Aria asked quietly.

I wanted more than that, and that was the problem.

"No," I got out, even if it cost me a lot. Aria raised her head, looking hurt.

She didn't understand my reasoning. She *couldn't* understand. "I'm not quite myself yet, Aria. There's too much darkness on the surface, too much blood and anger. Today was bad. When I came home today and found you lying on the sofa, so innocent and vulnerable and mine..." My desire flared once more, the need to claim what was mine. "I'm glad you don't know the thoughts that ran through my head then. You are my wife, and I swore to protect you, if necessary even from myself."

"You think you'd lose control?"

"I know it."

"Maybe you underestimate yourself." She stroked my shoulders, that careful touch I was starting to crave like a drug. I wasn't sure what Aria was doing to me, what was happening to me, but it was dangerous for both of us.

"Maybe you trust me too much," I murmured, trailing my finger along her spine, feeling her shiver—not with fear. "When I laid you down on the bed like a sacrificial lamb, you should have run."

Aria's mouth pulled into *that* smile. "Someone once told me not to run from monsters because they give chase."

"Next time, you run. Or if you can't, you ram your knee into my balls." I had a feeling that if I ever hurt Aria the way I was capable of, it would mess with me in ways I never thought possible.

Aria shook her head. "If I'd done that today, you would have lost control. The only reason you didn't was because I treated you like my husband, not a monster."

I caressed her lips and cheek, my heart seemingly clenching and unclenching at the same time. "You are far too beautiful and innocent to be married to someone like me, but I'm too much of a selfish bastard to ever let you go. You are mine. Forever."

"I know," Aria said, for once not sounding resigned. Fuck, Aria, you were meant to be our guarantee for truce, not more.

She put her head down on my chest. For some reason, it felt as if it were meant to be like this, as if Aria had always and would always belong right there—close to my cold, cruel heart.

I turned off the lights, staring into the dark, listening to Aria's rhythmic breathing as she fell asleep on top of me. The dark had always called to me because it was something I was familiar with, a place I'd grown up in. I didn't think there would ever be light in my life, that it could pierce the blackness that was my life. My eyes dipped to the golden crown of Aria's head—a beacon of light even in the dark of the room.

CHAPTER 13

I was blanketed in heat, but my limbs were still too heavy and sore to move. It took me a moment to realize the nature of the heat source: Aria. She was lying on top of me. The low buzz of my phone burst through my sleepy bubble. I jerked upright, my pulse rate spiking and my arm coming around my wife. I fucking hoped that Matteo didn't have more bad news for me. Yesterday had been enough of a train wreck.

I grabbed my phone from the nightstand but, before I could press it to my ear and take the call, I released a harsh breath. My cock was wedged between Aria's thighs, its length enticingly lined up against her pussy. Her heat seeped through her thin panties, giving me all the ideas I didn't need. I took the call, staring at my wife who clung to me with surprise-widened eyes.

Aria moved and my tip nudged her ass cheeks. Pleasure shot through me. I groaned, my body tightening.

"You looked like shit last night. An update would have been appreciated," Matteo muttered. "How bad is it?"

"I'm fine, Matteo," I said. My wounds were the least of my problems now. Blue balls was the only thing that would kill me.

"You don't sound it."

Because Aria is pressing her fucking pussy against my dick. "I'm *fucking* fine."

"I could send the Doc to check on you."

"No. I can handle this. I don't need to see the Doc. Now let me sleep."

I ended the call before Matteo could say another word and set the phone back down. Aria peered up at me, tension radiating off her body in waves. Her fingers dug into my shoulders. The nerves in her expression calmed some of my desire, and I laid back down to bring some distance between us and get a grip on my overeager cock.

Aria still straddled me but quickly covered her beautiful tits with her arm, her cheeks starting to fill with pink. She shifted, trying to get off me, and her thigh brushed my cock, sending another shockwave of need through me.

"Fuck," I hissed. Then I saw Aria's expression. She was looking down at my dick with wide, curious eyes. It was so fucking obvious that she had never seen a cock. It took all of my self-control not to tangle my fingers in her hair and guide her head down to sink myself into her enticing mouth.

"You're going to be the death of me, Aria," I murmured.

Aria quickly looked up, practically squirming from embarrassment. Her blue eyes met mine and I just wanted to kiss her senseless, press her into the mattress and show her how good I could make her feel. I'd desired women before, but it had been a brief burst of interest, a flicker that had been snuffed out as quickly as it had come, but my need for Aria burnt deeper, fiercer. Aria's gaze dipped down to my chest then slid lower once more.

"If you keep looking at my cock with that stunned expression, I'm going to combust."

"I'm sorry if my expression bothers you, but this is new for me. I've never seen a naked man. Every first I'll experience will be with you, so..." Aria said defensively.

I wanted to laugh at how oblivious she was to the reality of the situation. She didn't realize how much I burnt up for her, how fucking hard the thought of being her first made me.

I straightened, bringing our faces close. "It doesn't bother me. It's fucking hot, and I'll enjoy every first you'll share with me," I said, dragging my thumb over Aria's heated cheek. Her eyes flitted up to me and that irresistible mouth tipped up into the small smile that always got me. "You don't even realize how much you turn me on."

I kissed her, needing to taste her sweetness. Aria stroked my chest, fueling the desire already burning in my body. I pulled back. "Last night, you asked me if I wanted you to touch me."

Aria's lips parted. "Yeah." She licked her lips, making my insides tight with even more need. "Do you want me to touch you now?"

I wanted everything she was willing to give and more. "Fuck yes. More than anything." Aria was still covering herself. I grasped her wrist but didn't pull, wanting her to do this on her own terms. Another first. "Let me see you."

Insecurity flashed across her face. I didn't understand how a girl as beautiful as her could be shy about presenting herself. Her body was destined to bring men to their knees, even when she was only mine to see. She finally lowered her hand to her lap. My eyes took her in and my desire burned even hotter.

"I know they're not big," Aria said, bringing my attention back to her insecure face.

"You're fucking beautiful, Aria," I said, but my mind kept straying to her previous question. "Do you want to touch me now?"

Aria gave a quick nod, licking those irresistible lips, before she brushed her fingertips along my cock. The touch was barely existent, but fuck, it zipped through every muscle in my body, and my chest constricted in a sharp exhale. My gaze lifted to Aria's face, the way her lips were parted and her eyes shone with fascination. Fuck. No one had ever looked at my dick like that. She was so goddamn innocent, so beautifully mine. Her fingertips touched my tip and I jerked, barely holding back an upwards thrust. Fucking Aria's hand would have only disturbed her. Her innocence was torture and pleasure combined.

I allowed her to explore me for as long as I could stand it before gritting out, "Take me in your hand."

Aria's grip on my dick was as non-existent as her touch had been. She pumped her hand up and down, too gently, too slowly. I reclined on the pillow. Her cheek turned pink under my unwavering attention. Maybe it would have been easier for her if I'd looked away, but I simply couldn't.

"You can grip harder."

Aria's fingers became firmer around my dick but still nowhere as hard as I wanted or needed it. This was sweet torture.

"Harder. It won't fall off."

Shame flashed across Aria's face and she wrenched her hand away, averting her eyes. "I didn't want to hurt you," she whispered, sounding ashamed and on the verge of crying. Fuck. I was torn between laughter because she actually thought she could hurt me, and frustration because of my blue balls, but I pushed both down.

Grabbing Aria's arms, I pulled her on top of me, forcing her to meet my gaze. "Hey," I murmured, surprised by the calm note of my voice when inside I was close to combusting. "I was teasing you. It's okay." I kissed her, my lips stroking hers open, tasting her, forcing her to relax into the kiss, and soon she did. I stroked her body, my hand slowly making its way over the enticing swell of her ass. My fingers dove between her thighs. Aria halted when I traced my fingertips over her crotch. I kept my touch light, reminding myself over and over again that this was new for her. When she relaxed and the fabric of her panties was soaked, I ventured under the material. A growl lodged itself in my throat at the silky feel of Aria. Her blue eyes locked on mine with need and curiosity as I brushed my fingers along her tender flesh up to her clit. Aria released the most torturous moan before she leaned in for another kiss, surprising me when she deepened it on her own while she rocked lightly against my fingers as I stroked her.

I pulled back, my breathing ragged. "Want to try again?"

I kept teasing her nub, knowing it would lower her inhibitions, and I was right. As I brought Aria closer to release, her own hand slid down my body until she finally arrived at my dick. She gripped it harder than before but still too gently. While my fingers kept working Aria's pussy, I wrapped my other hand around those clutching my dick and squeezed hard. Surprise flickered across Aria's face at the force of my grip. Then I showed her how to stroke me. I watched her as she watched our hands work my cock. I was already leaking pre-cum like a pubescent boy.

Aria panted, pressing her pussy against my fingers almost desperately, chasing her orgasm as our hands pumped me hard and fast.

Aria's eyes widened. "Luca." The exclamation went straight to my dick, which swelled even more. I flicked her clit and she exploded, jutting her butt back, shoving against my hand. The sight sent me over the edge and cum shot out of my dick like a goddamn New Year's Eve firework. I jerked and groaned as if I'd just had the fuck of my life, when it had only been a hand job. Damn. Aria slumped against my side, staring at the mess I'd made on my stomach. I reluctantly withdrew my fingers from her swollen pussy and stroked her ass.

Aria looked happy as she closed her eyes and rested her cheek against my chest. I pressed a soft kiss to the crown of her head. Why? I'd never done this before, never felt the urge to do it. The idea of having someone's hair all over my face and lips had definitely never called to me.

Annoyed by my own confusion, I reached for a few tissues and cleaned my cum off. I didn't even remember the last time I hadn't come in or on a woman. I gave Aria a bunch of tissues and she wiped her hand clean without meeting my gaze. I searched her face as her brows furrowed. She looked as confused as I felt, but I wasn't sure why.

I stroked her arm, trying to distract her, another goddamn new thing. Why the fuck was I feeling the urge to do all this shit?

Aria jerked into a sitting position. "You're bleeding." Her fingers hovered over a cut on my ribs. "Does it hurt?"

I glanced down. I'd completely forgotten about it. My body throbbed with a dull ache, but it was nothing I couldn't deal with, and this cut served me right for letting the fucker get too close to me. "Not much. It's nothing. I'm used to it."

Aria's brows tugged together as she caressed the skin below the wound. "It needs stitches. What if it gets infected?" Her lashes fluttered as she looked at me. Was she concerned for me?

"Maybe you'll get lucky and become a young widow." It was the dream of many wives, and I didn't kid myself into thinking that Aria had been happy about our union. Being shackled to a man like me was a fate many women would do anything to escape.

She narrowed her eyes at me. "That's not funny."

I regarded her, trying to detect deceit in her expression or tone, but I couldn't find any. She seemed serious. Her reasoning was difficult to grasp. Maybe she feared she'd be married off to the next monster if I died, though she could hardly think there were worse monsters out there than me. But there were monsters who didn't hide their monstrous side.

I could have taken her worry by telling her that she wouldn't remarry even if I died. If Matteo was Capo then, he wouldn't force her, that much was clear. But my father? I wouldn't put it past him to dispose of Nina and marry Aria himself.

"If it bothers you so much, why don't you grab the first-aid kit from the bathroom and bring it to me," I said, breaking my disturbing strand of thoughts.

Aria didn't hesitate to jump out of bed. "Where is it?"

"In the drawer below the sink." My gaze followed her beautiful ass and slender waist as she strode into the bathroom. Fuck. I didn't fear death, but I really loathed the idea of dying before I got the chance to have Aria at least once. And even one time seemed entirely inadequate to sate my desire for my young wife.

Aria returned with the first-aid kid. To my disappointment, she put on her nightgown before she climbed on the bed. She avoided looking anywhere near my half-erect cock.

I ran my thumb over her heated cheek. "Still too shy to look at me after what happened." I touched her satin nightgown. "I liked you better without it."

Aria ignored my comment. "What do you want me to do?"

The way the pursed her lips, one thing immediately came to my mind. "Many things."

She rolled her eyes, but I caught the pleased shiver that passed through her body. Aria was getting more comfortable around me. "With your cut."

"There are disinfectant wipes. Clean my wound, and I'll prepare the needle."

Aria wiped my wound clean while I unpacked the needle. The sharp stench of the disinfectant tingled in my nose and the familiar sting of it numbed my wound. "Does it burn?"

"I'm fine. Wipe harder." Usually Matteo or Cesare took care of my wounds, if I didn't handle them myself, and they definitely weren't as careful as Aria.

I stitched myself up under her watchful gaze, wondering what she was thinking. I threw the needle away when I was done.

"We need to cover it," Aria said, searching the kit for bandages.

I stopped her. "It'll heal faster if it's allowed to breathe."

"Really? Are you sure? What if dirt gets in?"

If I told her often I'd been wounded in the last decade, she would trust my word. "You don't need to worry. This won't be the last time I'll come home injured."

I opened my arms, not in the mood to get up yet. "Come."

"Don't you have to leave?" Aria's eyes darted to the clock. We hadn't spent many mornings in bed together so far, but I really wanted to change that.

"Not today. The Bratva is dealt with for the moment. I'll have to be in one of the Famiglia's clubs in the afternoon."

Aria's answering smile was dazzling and knocked the breath right out of my lungs. She pressed close to me, one arm slung over my stomach, and I held her tightly, stunned by the burst of emotion I felt.

"I didn't expect you to look so happy," I admitted, even if I regretted it right after. I needed to be more careful what I let slip. Emotions could be used as a weapon, and even if I didn't think Aria would do something like that, I should be careful.

"I'm lonely," Aria whispered. Life at my side would always be a golden cage, and making friends as the future Capo's wife was as good as impossible. The majority of people would only seek Aria's closeness because they hoped to gain something from it. Her sisters would probably always remain her only true friends. Maybe Matteo's obsession with Gianna would be good for something, after all. Aria would have one of her sisters in New York. That would make her happy, even if the annoying redhead would probably bring me nothing but trouble. Unfortunately, I couldn't tell her about Gianna yet, not until things were ready to be announced.

"I have a few cousins you could hang out with. I'm sure they'd enjoy going shopping with you," I said instead.

"Why does everyone think I want to go shopping?"

"Then do something else. Have a coffee, or go to a spa, or I don't know."

"I still have a spa certificate that I got at my bridal shower."

"See? If you want, I can ask a few of my cousins."

She shook her head quickly. "I'm not too keen on meeting another one of your cousins after what Cosima did."

Cosima was one of my least favorite cousins. She was good friends with Grace and both lived for bitching. "What did she do?"

Aria lifted her head, eyes widened in what looked like realization. A fucking bad feeling overcame me.

"She gave me the letter that led me to you and Grace," Aria whispered, her voice catching. She withdrew from me and hugged her legs to her body, looking small and hurt. The sight, the fucking sight felt like a sucker punch. I pushed upright, bringing us closer, wanting to console her and assure her but, as so often. at a loss at how to do it, especially now when my concern for my wife battled with fury with my cousin in my mind. Following my instinct, I kissed her shoulder. "Cosima gave you a letter that told you to go the apartment?" She wouldn't have done it by herself. Grace and her had come up with the plan.

I was going to kill the bitch.

Aria shivered, and I touched her waist, sliding my thumb along her soft skin. "And a key. It's still in my bag," she said quietly.

"That fucking bitch." Grace was pissed about my marriage with Aria. The brainless twit had probably hoped to become the next Mrs. Vitiello. As if

I'd ever marry an outsider, especially one of the fucking thrill-seekers who'd always only be with me to be in the spotlight and add a kick to their pathetic lives. A woman like that would never understand what it meant to be bound to the mafia, what kind of sacrifices were required to be part of our world. Sacrifices were a foreign concept to a creature like Grace.

"Who?" Aria asked.

"Both of them. Grace and Cosima. They're friends. Grace must have put her up to this. That cunt."

Aria jerked away from my anger, eyes wide and shocked. Fuck. I wrapped an arm around her and pulled her close. My nose in her hair, I breathed in her scent. At once, my anger dimmed. Aria wasn't supposed to witness my brutal, vengeful side.

Aria softened in my hold. "Grace wanted to humiliate me. She looked really happy when I found you."

"I bet," I muttered. Grace and Cosima had probably met right after the incident and laughed their fucking heads off. They wouldn't laugh for much longer. "She's a fucking rat trying to humiliate a queen. She's nothing."

Aria was a queen, and nobody would treat her as anything less than that.

"How did she react when you told her that you couldn't see her anymore?" Aria asked curiously.

I hadn't seen or talked to Grace since our last fuck, and I had no intention of doing so. I'd never even considered telling her that we were over. Why? We'd never been a couple or even an affair. I'd messaged her when I'd wanted to fuck, and she'd always come running. We hadn't gone on dates or even been exclusive. Far from it.

"You promised you wouldn't see her or other women again," Aria whispered, and I realized my fucking mistake. She tried to escape my embrace, body trembling, but I didn't allow her to pull away.

"I did, and I won't. But I didn't talk to Grace. Why should I? I don't owe her an explanation, just like I don't owe a fucking explanation to the other sluts I fucked." Aria was stiff in my hold, not believing me. I tilted her face up so she had no choice but to meet my gaze. She needed to get my next words into her head. "You are the only one I want. I'll keep my promise, Aria." It was the goddamn truth. I desired Aria like I'd never desired a woman—in the obvious way, but also in a deeper way that didn't even make sense to me.

Aria searched my eyes. "So you won't see her again."

"Oh, I will see her again to tell her what I think about her little stunt." I'd probably end up killing her. I'd never been more furious in my life. Grace tried to mess with my marriage, and I knew she wasn't done yet—if I didn't put a stop to it once and for all.

Aria touched my arm. "Don't."

I stared at her incredulously. I thought she wanted me to end it verbally.

"I don't want you to talk to her again. Let's just forget her."

Forget how Grace had not only tricked me but also tried to humiliate my wife? "Please," Aria begged, her fingers digging into my biceps.

Fuck. How was I supposed to deny her when she looked at me like that? Begging didn't work with me, but Aria...

I nodded, even if I knew I couldn't do nothing. I'd keep my word and not contact Grace, but I sure as hell wouldn't forget what happened. Next time I saw her father to give him money for his campaign, I'd tell him exactly what was on my mind. He knew that Grace was good for nothing. "I don't like it, but if that's what you want..."

"It is," she said quickly. "Let's not even talk about her anymore. Pretend she doesn't exist." Aria gave me a small smile. I touched her parted lips, loving their softness.

"Your lips are too fucking kissable."

Aria averted her eyes in embarrassment. Shy and sweet. That men like Fiore Cavallaro and my father had chosen this kind of woman for me was a miracle, but one I was definitely grateful for.

"There's something I wanted to talk to you about," she mumbled.

"More bad news?" I asked carefully. The Grace thing was already souring my morning.

Aria shrugged. "Well, I guess that depends on your viewpoint. I want Gianna to visit me. Her school doesn't begin for another two weeks, and I miss her."

I stifled a groan. "It's been only a few days since you saw her."

"I know." Aria's expression became pleading once more, and I knew I was screwed. If Matteo found out that Gianna was coming to visit, he'd be ecstatic.

"Where would she stay?"

I immediately knew what she was up to.

"I don't know. Maybe in our guest room?" She bit her lower lip with that smile, her eyes so fucking hopeful that I knew there was no way I could say no to her, but she didn't need to know that.

"Your sister is a major pain in the ass," I muttered.

Aria leaned closer, her expression pleading.

My eyes dipped down her nightgown to her beautiful tits. "How about a deal?"

Aria's smile fell, anxiety taking over. "A deal?"

She sounded as if I was going to force her to let me fuck her. I wanted nothing more than finally being with her, claiming her, but not if she was so fucking terrified. "Don't look so nervous. I'm not going to ask you to sleep with me so you can see your sister. I'm not that big of an asshole."

"No?" Aria grinned, her entire face transforming, and I just couldn't resist. I kissed her hard, needing to taste those lips.

"No. But I'd like to explore your body," I said, my hand trailing over her waist and hip, imagining how it would be to taste her beautiful tits and pussy, to bury myself between her legs. Fuck, I was getting hard again.

"What do you mean?" Aria asked, her voice low.

"Tonight, I'll try to be home early from the meeting at the club, and I want us to soak in the Jacuzzi for a bit, and then I want you to lie back and let me touch you and kiss you wherever I want." I ran the tip of my tongue along her ear, showing her what I'd do to her lovely pussy. "You'll love it."

Aria exhaled, her body tensing under my touch. Her eyes reflected her conflict, torn between curiosity and anxiety.

I slid my hand between her thighs, putting pressure against her clit. Aria's resulting moan and the twitch of her hips made me smile. Her mind was anxious, but her body definitely wasn't. Her panties were wet with her need for more. She was so wonderfully responsive. The idea of how slick she'd be around my cock almost drove me to insanity.

"You like this, Aria. I know you do. Admit it." There really was no doubt about it. Her body sent a clear message, and the soaked lace was all the answer I needed. I pressed the heel of my palm against her clit again, earning another gasp.

Aria's face was flushed, her eyes hooded. "Yes." Watching her, I rubbed my palm over her slowly, enjoying her amazed pants. "Don't stop."

"I won't," I rasped against her throat. I wouldn't stop at all if she allowed it. I wished she'd allow herself to turn off her brain and let her body take over control. "So, will you let me have my way with you tonight? I won't do anything you don't want."

"Yes."

I kissed and nibbled her throat as I stroked her pussy through her panties, faster and harder, matching the rhythm of her desperate rocking. She arched and cried out as she came under my touch.

I regarded her closed eyes, parted lips, pink-tinged cheeks. Breathtakingly gorgeous.

I left another lingering kiss on the tip of her chin before I met her gaze. It was obvious that Aria's mind was a whirlwind of thoughts again, worrying, wondering.

She pressed her head against my shoulder, gripping my biceps.

"So, can I call Gianna and tell her to buy plane tickets?" she whispered against my skin.

Back to business, the little minx. "Sure, but remember our deal." The buzzing of my phone ruined the moment again, and any chance of me getting another hand job or, better yet, a blowjob. I didn't even look at the screen before growling, "For fuck's sake, Matteo, what now?"

"We got another message from the Russians," he said. "They left pig heads in front of Ferris' best restaurant."

I shoved down the string of curses lingering on the tip of my tongue. Business wasn't something we should discuss in detail over the phone. I gently untangled myself from Aria and stood. "We've got his back. I won't let another fucking restaurant go to the Russians."

"Father wants us to have a word with him."

"Yeah," I gritted out. I'd assumed that much. Ferris' restaurant chain paid a shitload of money for our protection. We definitely didn't want to lose him to the Russians because their threats got to him.

"ASAP," Matteo added.

"Yeah. I'll be ready in thirty minutes."

So much for enjoying a nice, calm morning with my wife. I dropped my cell on the nightstand. At least my annoyance over the Bratva had gotten rid of my boner.

"I have to talk to the owner of a restaurant chain," I told Aria.

She was propped up on her elbows, her hair spread out behind her. There were a million things I'd rather do than convince Ferris that being on our bad side was worse than having the Bratva as his enemy.

Aria's face fell. "Okay." She looked honestly sad about my leaving. The realization gave me a strange sense of satisfaction.

I moved back to her and bent over her. "Call your sister and tell her she can come. And I'll be back in time for dinner, okay? I have a few take-out menus in the kitchen. Order whatever you want." I kissed her, realizing with a start that I, too, was disappointed about not getting the chance to spend more time with her. I enjoyed being around Aria, and not only because I couldn't keep my hands off her. "Let Romero take you to a museum or something like that."

Aria nodded. I kissed her again then headed into the bathroom for a quick shower. When I emerged, Aria was typing on her phone with a small smile, probably telling the bitchy redhead that she was allowed to visit. Seeing Aria's happiness, I couldn't even be pissed over having to endure Gianna for a few days.

Pressing a quick kiss to her forehead, I mumbled, "Can't wait for tonight."

"Be careful," Aria whispered.

I pulled away, then turned and left, feeling slightly stunned by her words. Nobody had ever said something like that to me.

Matteo waited for me in the underground garage and we took my car to Ferris' place. He was a sleek business type who owned close to thirty restaurants in New York and New Jersey. The Russians were trying to convince him to switch to them. That wasn't going to happen.

"You look better than I thought after last night," Matteo commented, scanning me.

"I've had worse."

"Did Aria help you recover?" His lips pulled into a suggestive grin.

"Do you have the video of me torturing that Bratva bastard on your phone?"

"So no sharing naughty details?"

"Matteo," I growled.

"Of course. It was one of your brightest hours, torture-wise. All that pent-up sexual frustration is good for something, after all. If I wasn't already such a master torturer, I'd consider a few celibate days."

I rolled my eyes.

When we pulled up in front of the restaurant in Brooklyn, I spotted Ferris pacing the boardwalk, speaking into his phone. We got out and headed for him. His agitated expression turned to anger when he saw us. A few of his employees were scrubbing the once white front, trying to get rid of the blood splatters. The pig heads were already gone. "I have a business to run and a reputation to uphold. This is unacceptable. If you don't put a stop to it, I'll have to consider a new cooperation."

Cooperation? Did he think we were some kind of business venture he could decide to work with? I smiled coldly. "Why don't we head inside to discuss this away from the public eye. You don't want to attract the wrong attention," I said in forced calm.

He scowled and moved into his restaurant, actually believing me. Fucking idiot.

Matteo and I stalked inside after him. The moment we reached his office, my pleasant mask slipped right off.

I grabbed him by the collar and raised him up, shoving him against the door. "Have you lost your mind? I'll call…"

"Call the police?" I finished in a deadly murmur. "We pay more than half of them. We pay the people who matter in this city, too. And let's not forget the things you don't want to get out in the open, Ferris. Like the pretty little bellboy you're banging behind your wife's back."

I set him down slowly and waved Matteo forward.

"Now listen up, Ferris, and listen well, because I'll say this exactly once. Our *cooperation* ends when we end it, not one fucking day sooner, and if it ends, trust me, you won't like it."

Matteo held his cell in front of Ferris' face, then played the video of me slicing the Russian into tiny pieces. His screams blared from the speakers. Ferris squirmed, trying to get away. When I didn't let him, he closed his eyes.

"Either you open your eyes or I'll remove your fucking eyelids."

His eyes flew open and his face began to perspire as he watched the video. He retched and I quickly shoved him away from me so he threw up on his shoes and not mine.

Matteo flashed me his shark grin and put his cell back into his back pocket.

"We'll handle the Russians," I said. "You only need to worry about paying us in time."

Matteo clapped the man's back hard. "Good talking to you."

We left.

"Why do they always throw up?" Matteo asked as we headed for my car.

"I need to pay Cosima a visit," I said.

Matteo sent me a curious look. I'd never talked to Cosimo by choice. "I have a feeling it's got something to do with your Grace debacle."

"It does. She told Aria where to find me."

Matteo whistled. "Bitch." He regarded closely me as we settled in the car. "But Aria forgave you?"

I frowned. I'd avoided talking to him about this topic. "She doesn't really have a choice. This marriage binds us both." It was the half-truth, but I wasn't willing to discuss Aria in detail, especially not my feelings or hers. I wasn't sure if she'd forgiven me, and she probably shouldn't, but Aria wanted this marriage to work, and I was grateful for it.

We pulled up in front of Cosima and Giovanni's house. She'd been married to him for four years now. His father was one of our Captains.

"Want me to come along?"

I shook my head. "I'll handle this alone. It won't take long."

I walked up to the townhouse and rang the bell. A maid opened the door, her eyes widening in alarm upon spotting me. "The master isn't home."

"I need to see his wife," I said, stepping forward, forcing her to open the door wider and allowing me entry.

"Who is it? I told you not to let anyone in, you useless cow!" Cosima screamed, appearing in the hallway. She froze. She was still in her bathrobe. "Giovanni is not here," she said quickly.

I closed the entrance door, meeting her gaze. "I'm not here for him." I turned to the maid. "Leave us alone."

She quickly hurried off. Cosima crossed her arms in front of her chest, but worry shone in her dark eyes. "You can't be alone with me. It's not proper."

I gave her a cold smile and advanced on her. "I know you sent my wife to my fuck date with Grace."

Cosima's expression slipped for a moment, then she quickly masked it with feigned shock. "I didn't do anything. How can you accuse me of something like that?"

"Do not lie to me," I growled, and she backed away but bumped into the wall.

"I'll call Giovanni," she said, reaching for her phone in the pocket of her robe before she raised it.

I grabbed her arm. "This is between you and me."

With her free hand, she clutched her robe closed, lowering her eyes. "Giovanni and my father won't be happy if you dishonor me."

I released her as if I'd been burnt. "Fuck, Cosima, I'm not going to touch you like that."

"Everyone knows the stories of your father. Don't pretend you're not like him. Even he didn't crush a family member's throat."

I leaned down, scowling. "I can promise you I'll crush your throat before ever fucking you."

I nodded toward her phone. "Call Giovanni. Then I can have a word with him as well. He should keep a closer eye on you."

She didn't call him. Instead, she looked up at me with badly played guilt. "It wasn't my idea. Grace came up with the plan. She wanted to win you back and destroy your marriage."

I laughed darkly. "My wife is my possession, Cosima. You know that as well as I do. This marriage will last until the bitter end." Nobody would ever find out how desperate I'd been when Aria had run off. "The only thing your insane plan did was make me furious, and trust me when I tell you that it's never a good thing to be on my bad side, dear cousin. So the next time Grace asks you for a favor, you'll say no, or your husband won't become Captain."

She paled. Cosima was ambitious. She'd dreamed of marrying an Underboss, but she hadn't been graced with the beauty required to lure a man in that position. If Giovanni remained a mere soldier, that would be a humiliation she wouldn't survive.

I left her standing there. She'd think twice before going against me again.

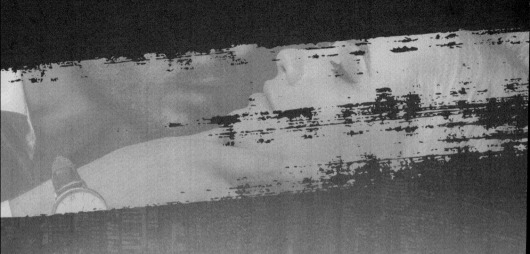

CHAPTER 14

Matteo leaned against the hood of my car, taking a fucking sunbath from the look of it. "And?" he asked, face still tilted up to the sky. "Get into the car," I said.

The moment he was in the passenger seat, he cocked an eyebrow. "I hope you didn't make a mess."

"She's our cousin."

"That didn't stop you with Junior."

"She's a woman."

"That didn't stop you with the Bratva whores."

I sent him a scowl. "She didn't try to kill me, happy?"

"Maybe next time Grace will try to poison your wife," Matteo joked, but I almost steered us into oncoming traffic because I jerked.

"I was joking," Matteo said, surprised.

I swallowed, trying to mask the turmoil his words had cause. "Let's head to the Sphere now. We still have to meet our bookkeeper."

Several hours later, I was on my way back home while Matteo headed out to party with Romero.

My phone rang, and Father's name flashed on my dashboard.

I took the call and Father's voice boomed in the car. "How did it go? Did you convince Ferris of the perks of working with us?"

"Matteo and I made our point very clear to him, yes," I said.

I wasn't in the mood to talk to my father now. I just wanted to return home to my beautiful wife and discover her body with my hands and lips. It was what had kept me going throughout the day.

"Very well," he drawled. "I think we should attack a few more of the Bratva establishments in retaliation. What's their most popular club?"

"The Pergola. Most of the high ranking Bratva members frequent it. Unfortunately the half of New York society that doesn't come to the Sphere is there as well. An attack might draw lots of unnecessary media attention to us." Attacks on labs or whorehouses were the safer option, since both were out of the public eye.

"Figure something out. I want them to bleed," Father clipped. I wondered if he'd talked to Fiore...or why did he suddenly give a fuck about the Bratva?

"They will," I promised as I steered my car into the underground garage. "Is there anything else you want?"

"On your way to your wife, or why are you eager to shake me off?"

Because I hate your goddamn guts. "It's been a long, fucked up day."

"I want you, Matteo and Aria to come over to dinner as soon as possible. Talk to Nina to arrange a date and time."

He hung up, not waiting for a reply because it was an order, not a request. I really didn't want to be around my father more often than absolutely necessary, but, most importantly, I didn't like him anywhere near Aria.

My muscles brimmed with tension when I stepped into the elevator. Another fucking mess of a day. Despite all the shit thrown our way today, I made good to my promise to Aria and was home earlier than usual. When I entered our apartment, Romero was perched on a barstool, working on his tablet. I'd sent him photos of a surveillance camera from the restaurant because he was the best when it came to detecting suspicious behavior. Maybe he'd be able to figure out who'd left the fucking message, so I could kill them personally. Carrying pigs' head through Brooklyn couldn't have gone unnoticed.

He stood, grabbed the tablet, and stepped into the elevator. "I'll work on this tonight."

"Aria's still your top priority, so don't pull an all-nighter."

Romero smiled. "You know me. I'll be as vigilant as always for work tomorrow."

I nodded. He was one of my best men.

"Aria's on the roof terrace," he said before the doors closed.

I put my phone down on the kitchen counter. Matteo would be able to deal with shit if something came up tonight. I wanted to enjoy this evening with Aria without interruption.

Outside, Aria had set up the table with candles, white cloth and fresh flowers. She was dressed in an elegant flowing yellow dress. With the last rays of the setting sun, she was like a golden apparition. The most beautiful woman the Outfit had to offer. My father's words. He'd been wrong, so fucking wrong.

Aria was the most beautiful woman I'd ever seen. There couldn't possibly be a woman more beautiful than her on this planet.

Aria noticed me and gave me a small smile.

"I thought we could eat here?" She gestured at the table.

I wasn't all that hungry for food, but Aria had already put an array of dips, breads and samosas as well as a steaming curry on the table. I wrapped my arm around her and kissed her lightly. Her lashes fluttered and her smile became less tense. "I ordered Indian."

"I'm hungry for only one thing," I said in a low voice, feeling my groin tighten at the idea of getting Aria out of this dress.

Aria looked away. "Let's eat." She drew away from my embrace and sank down. Maybe food would help her calm her nerves. I really didn't understand what she was so nervous about. I'd told her I'd touch and kiss, not fuck her. My lack of practice handling female emotions was definitely a problem when it came to treating Aria right. I sat down across from her. A few strands of hair whirled around her head and the setting sun made Aria's cheekbones glow.

"You look fucking sexy." My brain and body were on a one-way street. I just couldn't think straight today. I wanted to lose myself in Aria, in her gorgeous body, in lust, and forget the Bratva.

Aria ripped off a piece of naan bread and ate it with a bit of dip. "Romero took me to the Metropolitan today. It was amazing."

I ate a bite myself, stifling a laugh at Aria's feeble attempt to distract me. "Good."

"What about the restaurant owner? Did you convince him that the Famiglia will protect him from the Russians?"

It wasn't really a topic I wanted to discuss, especially with Aria. Business was something I wanted to shield her from. "Of course. He's been under our protection for more than a decade. There's no reason to change that now."

"Sure." Aria picked up her wine glass and nipped at it, not meeting my eyes. She seemed far away, but it didn't take a genius to guess what was bothering her.

"Aria?"

"Hmm?" She still didn't look up.

"Aria," I said, putting more force into my tone and, as expected, her head jerked up. Her blue eyes swam with anxiety. It was a new experience to have a woman scared of being with me. I leaned back in the chair, wondering how I should handle the situation. "You're scared."

"I'm not," she said quickly, but her cheeks reddened at her lie. She was such a bad liar. I fixed her with a stare, wanting her to tell me the truth. Lying wasn't something I'd tolerate. "Maybe a bit, but mostly I'm nervous."

Nervous. I could work with nervous. It was so much better than fear. I stood and walked toward her, holding out my hand. "Come on."

Aria raised her eyes to mine, searching like so often and whatever it was she seemed to find it because she took my hand and I pulled her up. She was still looking up at me. "Let's get into the Jacuzzi, okay? That'll relax you," I said quietly, softening my voice to set her at ease. "Why don't you grab your bikini and I'll set it up?" I would have preferred to soak in the tub with a naked Aria, but I doubted that would help her relax.

Aria gave a quick nod before she disappeared inside. Sighing, I took a sip of wine. Patience had never been my strength, and I was surprised at how much of it I actually possessed, at least around Aria.

After I'd turned on the Jacuzzi, I followed my wife. When I arrived in the bedroom, I could hear her in the bathroom. I got out of my clothes and slipped on my black swim shorts. For a moment, I wondered if Aria was hiding from me inside the bathroom, but then the door swung open and she stepped out in a white bikini with dots. I almost groaned because she somehow managed to look sexy and innocent at once, bringing out my protective as well as my predatory side. Fuck it.

I touched Aria's hip. "You are perfect." I was rewarded with a small smile and led her out of our bedroom and back out onto our roof terrace.

Goose bumps covered Aria's skin and her nipples strained against her thin bikini top. I lifted her into my arms and she pressed against me, seeking protection from the wind that had picked up. Her palm rested lightly against my chest, right over my heart, as if she needed to reassure herself that I did, indeed, have one. Sometimes even I wasn't sure that was the case.

I stepped into the hot water with her and lowered us so we were both covered up to our shoulder blades. Aria clung to my neck, her lips against my skin. I stroked her back, feeling the tension rippling in her body. "There's no reason for you to be scared."

"Says the man who crushed a man's throat with his bare hands."

"That's got nothing to do with us, Aria. That's business." I wasn't a good man, and I wasn't kidding myself into thinking I could be, nor did I want to. I was the man I needed to be to become who I wanted to be: Capo.

Aria sighed. "I know. I shouldn't have brought it up."

I peered down at my wife but only saw Aria's hair. She was hiding her face from me. "What's really the problem?"

"I'm nervous because I feel vulnerable, like I'm at your mercy because of the deal."

I managed to swallow the first reply that shot through my head: that Aria had been at my mercy from the moment she'd become my fiancée. If I'd insisted, her father would have given me his fifteen-year-old daughter, and, since she'd become my wife, everyone in our world considered her my property. "Aria, forget about the deal. Why don't you try to relax and enjoy this?" I lifted her face so she had to look at me.

Aria licked her lips nervously. "Promise you won't force me to do something I don't want to do," she whispered, then continued in an even softer voice, her gaze cast down once more. "Promise me that you won't hurt me."

For a second, I wasn't sure what to say. I'd thought these last few days had showed Aria that I was trying to be good to her—as good as a man like me could be. Maybe that was the problem. Aria knew what kind of man I was, and she was waiting for me to reveal my true nature to her. Maybe she had reason to be wary. Maybe this side of me was bound to fail. Maybe I was a monster trying to be more. Was the gentle side something I had in me, or only something I forced on myself?

"Why would I hurt you?" I said quietly, keeping my thoughts to myself. "I told you I won't sleep with you unless you want me to."

Aria's eyes widened in alarm. "So you will hurt me when we sleep together?"

Her innocent shock almost made me laugh. "Not on purpose, no, but I don't think there's a way around it," I murmured, kissing the soft skin below her ear. "But tonight I want to make you writhe in pleasure. Trust me."

I wanted her trust not because she gave it freely, but because I deserved it. I wanted to earn it.

Shoving those thoughts aside, I ran my tongue along her pulse point and inhaled Aria's sweet scent. My grip on her tightened as I suckled her skin. She felt and tasted so good, and my body reacted to her closeness. I trailed my kisses back up until I reached Aria's sweet mouth, which I claimed for a hard kiss as I pressed my erection against her butt. Fuck, I wished we were naked.

Aria drew back and I let out a groan in frustration. I wanted to lose myself in her taste. "Can we talk for a bit?" she asked softly.

Trying to hide my impatience, I sat back. "What do you want to talk about?"

My hands had a mind of their own, stroking along Aria's naked back and waist, then lower to her bikini bottoms. Her breath caught when my fingers slid along her ass.

"What happened to your mother?" she asked, completely catching me by surprise.

My hands froze and my chest squeezed into a tight ball. "She died," I clipped. I turned away from Aria's compassionate face, annoyed that she'd bring something like that up. "That's not the kind of thing I want to talk about tonight."

I didn't want to talk about her at all. She was the fucking past. Her death had messed up enough of my past; it wouldn't mess up my future as well.

Aria gave a nod. I slid my hand along her thigh, wanting to distract myself and her. I pushed my fingers beneath her bikini bottoms, brushing over her pussy lips. So velvety. Fuck. I used my other hand to free her breasts from her top. Her nipples puckered deliciously in the cold. Good Lord. I lowered my head and drew a hard pebble into my mouth, sucking it softly at first, then harder. I flicked my thumb over her clit, making her arch and gasp. She pressed herself into me as I swirled my tongue around her nipple. I couldn't take my eyes off Aria's face as she surrendered to pleasure. Her cheeks heated under my unwavering attention, and she looked away.

"No. Look at me," I commanded, and her eyes darted back down to me. I wanted her to see what I was doing, wanted her to remember that she was mine, that every beautiful inch of her was mine.

Fixing her with my eyes, I sucked her nipple into my mouth while my fingers worked her pussy, teasing her nub and folds. I grazed Aria's nipple with my teeth, testing if she'd enjoy a bit of pain. Aria bucked her hips with a cry, her body becoming tight as she came. The sight was marvelous, but I didn't allow myself to bask in it. I quickly hoisted Aria onto the edge of the Jacuzzi, spreading her legs.

Aria's eyes widened in shock. "Luca, what—"

I ripped her bikini bottoms away, shoving my way between her legs. My eyes dipped down to her pink pussy lips and my cock jerked. I bowed down my head, needing to get a taste. I dragged my tongue along her glistening folds. Fuck, I'd waited way too long for the first taste of my wife. Aria let out an astonished cry. Her legs were starting to soften against my biceps as she surrendered to the new sensations.

I licked Aria long and deep, my tip sliding along her slit, tasting that torturous sweetness.

"Fuck, yes." I could feel myself leaking at the first taste of her. A new wave of possessiveness hit me as I regarded her pink pussy. Only for me to savor. I sucked one soft fold into my mouth, teasing it with my lips and tongue. Aria gasped, half-lidded eyes checking our surroundings.

"Look at me," I demanded, pulling back a bit from her. After a moment of hesitation, she met my gaze despite her obvious embarrassment. Her cheeks were flushed, her lips parted. I wanted Aria to watch when I ate her out, wanted to see her beautiful face when she came in my mouth for the first time.

Slowly, I leaned forward and raked my tongue along her crease, lightly nudging her lovely nub.

"You are mine," I rasped, as her taste swirled on my tongue, fueling my own arousal. I took another lick. "Say it."

Aria's eyes flashed with need. "I'm yours."

Mine. I stroked those puffy lips apart, baring her clit, knowing she'd come if I sucked that little button. Fixing my eyes on her needy face, I fluttered my tongue over her clit. Aria's eyes opened wide, lips falling apart in a moan as she yanked at my hair, pressing her pussy against my face. She clenched against me, those lovely folds twitching under the force of her orgasm. So unbelievably responsive. Aria threw her head back as she writhed against my mouth, and I took everything she offered, licking up her arousal, getting so turned on by her obvious pleasure that I could hardly hold back. I plunged my tongue into her, groaning against her at how tight those walls clamped around the digit.

I suckled her, making sure she could hear how much I enjoyed this, and it didn't take long for her body to respond to my loud appreciation. Aria was turned on by the sounds, and fuck if that didn't turn me on even more. I lapped at her with more fervor, and then my lovely wife arched again and rewarded me with another beautiful orgasm.

I drew back, my breathing ragged, my dick throbbing so furiously I was sure I'd lose my goddamn mind any second. I needed to be inside her, needed to claim every little part of her. I burnt up with the need to do it. Bringing a finger up to her pussy, I entered her in a swift move.

Aria cried out, her walls clamping down on my finger. For a moment, I considered shoving down my pants and finally taking what I wanted, but the impulse lasted less than a second.

"Fuck, you're so fucking tight, Aria," I rasped. Her channel gripped me tightly, and I could feel more resistance against my fingertip. Fuck. Soon I'd be claiming that part of her, making her mine once and for all.

Aria didn't say anything, didn't move. I glanced up, snapping out of my lust haze. She lay flat on her back, arms pressed against her sides, and was staring up at the sky with furrowed brows. That wasn't what I'd expected. Slowly, I shifted up and leaned over her.

"Hey," I murmured, trying to get her attention. The distant look needed to go. Aria finally dragged her eyes down to mine. Her mouth was set tight, her brows still puckered, and I felt like an asshole, realizing I'd hurt her.

"I should have entered more slowly, but you were so wet," I said, getting as close to an apology as I ever allowed myself.

Aria tilted her head, then nothing. A strange sensation squeezed my chest. Maybe it was guilt. I had trouble putting my finger on it. I kissed her, but I still hadn't pulled my finger out of her. She felt too damn good. I wanted all of her. I'd never had to wait for something I wanted.

"Does it still hurt?" I asked. Aria moved, making my finger shift in her pussy, and I stifled a groan.

"It's uncomfortable, and it burns a bit," she admitted.

I traced my tongue over the seam of her lips. "I know I'm an asshole for saying it, but the thought of my cock inside your tight pussy makes me so hard."

Aria stiffened, the douse of cold water for my overeager cock. "Don't look so terrified. I told you I wouldn't try it tonight," I said, even as I wished she'd let me.

"You also told me you wouldn't hurt me," Aria said, voice small and vulnerable.

Fuck. It was definitely guilt squeezing my chest into a bloody pulp.

"I didn't think it would, Aria," I murmured. It hadn't even crossed my mind that my finger would cause her the slightest bit of discomfort. I'd never been with a virgin, never considered how different it would make things. "You were so wet and willing. I thought my finger would go in without trouble. I wanted to finger you for your fourth orgasm."

A shudder went through her. I lightly stroked her inner thigh, my silent apology.

"Did it hurt because you took my, you know. . ." Aria squirmed, her cheeks turning red.

Holy shit. "Your virginity?" I said roughly. "No, *principessa*. I'm not that deep in, and I want to claim that part of you with my cock, not my finger."

Had I just called her *principessa*? I wasn't even sure why. I'd never heard anyone call a woman that. Hope flared in Aria's eyes, hope that shouldn't be there because what she was hoping for wasn't going to happen.

I withdrew my finger and brought it up to her parted lips, tracing it over them before I dipped it inside. I wanted her to taste herself, and Aria caught me by surprise when she licked the digit as if it were a lollipop, or better yet, my cock.

My dick jerked in my pants. I'd definitely die of blue balls. I kissed her harshly, tasting her but still needing more. Always more with Aria. I wasn't sure what was wrong with me. Maybe it was the thrill of having to wait, first three years until she was of age and now for her to be ready. Maybe that was why I was so fucking obsessed with my wife. I'd never felt like this before, and it was starting worry me. Maybe once I claimed her, that burning need would finally subside and I could return to being my normal self. No tight chest or strange sensations anymore.

I straightened. "Let's go inside. I want to lick you again." Aria blinked up at me. "Will you let me put my finger in you again? This time I'll go really slow."

The second she said yes, I got out of the pool and lifted her into my arms. Aria slung her legs around my middle, pressing that wet pussy against my abs.

I hurried inside, my fingers digging into her ass cheeks. After I'd set her down in our bedroom, I went into the bathroom to grab a towel. I took my time rubbing her dry. Her lashes fluttered shut as I massaged her shoulders and arms, then moved onto her back and stomach. Goose bumps pimpled Aria's skin when I slid the towel over her breasts.

"Are you cold?"

Aria opened her eyes, peering up at me in a way no one ever had. I wasn't sure what it meant. I released the towel and caressed her bare arms.

"A bit," she said.

"Lie down. I'll warm you up." Aria climbed on the bed, giving me a prime view of her ass before she stretched out on her back. I reached for my wet shorts and shoved them down, not wanting to get the bed wet, but even more than that: wanting to feel Aria as close as possible. My erection bounced and Aria's eyes were drawn to it.

Her expression shifted, turned anxious then wary. She pushed back against the headboard and tugged her legs against her chest protectively. What the hell?

"Aria?" I said carefully, unsure how to react to her obvious fear. I reached for her leg but she jerked and pressed it even tighter against herself.

Seeing Aria like this brought up emotions I wasn't familiar with, emotions

I didn't want to deal with. Emotions were weakness, and a Capo couldn't be weak. "What now?" I muttered, annoyed at myself and at Aria because she evoked those sensations in me.

I sank down beside her, trying to be patient and keep my frustration at bay. "Say something."

Aria shook her head. "This is too fast."

Too fast? I hadn't fucked her in our wedding night like everyone expected, still hadn't fucked her or gotten more than a hand job. That wasn't fast in my world. The frustration of the day, the confusion over my emotions began to catch up with me, and I knew I couldn't let it. "Because I got naked?" I asked in a moderately calm voice. "You've seen my cock before. You even jerked me off."

Aria flushed. "I think you're trying to manipulate me. If I gave you the chance, you'd go all the way today."

"You bet I would, but I can't see what manipulation has to do with it," I gritted out. Didn't she understand what kind of man I was and what men like me usually did when they had a beautiful woman, their wife, at their disposal? "I want you. I never lied to you about that. I'm going to take whatever you're willing to give, and you were willing in the Jacuzzi."

Aria's eyes flashed with anger. "Not about the finger. Maybe you'll try the same with sex."

I laughed at her cluelessness. "That won't work. My cock won't slide in that easily, believe me, and it will hurt a lot more."

Aria blanched. I could have kicked myself for my words. It was the truth, but she didn't need to know it. Gathering what remained of my patience, I continued in a softer voice, "I shouldn't have said that. I didn't mean to scare you."

But I had. It was plain as day on Aria's face. I caressed her side, showing her that I still had every intention of being gentle with her. "Tell me that you enjoyed what I did to you on the roof."

"Yes."

Thank god. I leaned down to her. "What did you enjoy the most? My tongue fucking you? Or when I ran my tongue all the way over your pussy? Or when I sucked your clit?"

Desire replaced the apprehension on Aria's face. "I don't know."

"Maybe I need to show you again?" I said, then slid my hand between her legs and covered her pussy with my palm. Aria moved to lie down, but I shook my head. This position was perfect. "No. Stay like that." I began to stroke her as I held her in my arms. The way her legs were still pressed against her chest, additional pressure was added to her pussy and she loosened up in no time.

"Relax," I encouraged her before I dipped one finger against her opening. I took my time entering her this time, allowing her to grow used to the intrusion. The sight of my finger sliding into her pussy was the best.

I dragged my eyes up, catching Aria watching my hand. "Look at me."

Aria cast her eyes up.

"You are so wet and soft and tight. You can't imagine how fucking good this feels," I told her. The tip of my cock dug into her thigh, leaking pre-cum all over her smooth skin. I kissed her, tangling my tongue with hers as I kept finger-fucking her gently. This time, when I pulled my finger out, Aria let out a huff.

Chuckling, I knelt between her legs and entered her with my middle finger. It slid in as easily as my little finger had done. I watched Aria's face as her walls encased it. When I began swirling my tongue around her clit, Aria threw her legs open, giving me better access. Smiling against her pussy, I licked and sucked her as I slid in and out of her. Aria's thighs began quivering and then she jerked under me, rewarding me with her release. Would the sight of her coming apart ever not lodge my breath in my throat?

Fuck me.

Wiping my mouth, I climbed back up, kissed her cute belly button and stretched out beside her. Aria ran her fingertips over my slick tip.

I thrust up with a groan. "I want your mouth on me."

Aria gave me a look as if I'd asked her to chew on broken glass. I almost laughed again, but I could tell that her mind was already going a hundred miles an hour worrying about my request.

"Is this because you don't want to, or because you don't know how?" I asked. "You can jerk me off like last time." I stroked her hair, searching her eyes for a clue about her feelings. I really wanted to come in her mouth, but not if she gave me this panicked look. I'd feel as if I were molesting her.

"No, I mean, I think I want to do it."

"You think? But?"

Aria tilted her head to the side in contemplation. "What if I don't like it?"

I really hoped that wouldn't be the case. "Then you don't. I won't force you."

Aria leaned down, bringing her mouth closer to my cock. My fingers in her hair tightened, and it took me all my willpower not to guide her head down. Aria paused with a small laugh, casting those baby blues up in embarrassment. "I don't know what to do."

Fuck. My cock twitched. Aria laughed again, this time without restraint, and I couldn't help but grin. "You like to torture me with your innocence, don't you?"

Aria blew against my cock, causing me to twitch again. I felt like a goddamn teenager. "I don't think that's why it's called blow job, right?" Aria asked, biting her lower lip playfully, her eyes full of mischief.

A laugh burst out of me. I couldn't even remember the last time I'd felt this…at peace. "You're going to be the death of me, *principessa*."

Again, *principessa*. Fuck if I cared that sweet talking to Aria made me look weak. Anyone who thought I wasn't still the same brutal asshole than before would get a taste of my monstrous side.

"Don't laugh. I don't want to do something wrong."

"Do you want me to tell you what to do?" I asked.

Aria nodded.

"Okay," I said, trying to relax against the pillows. "Close your lips around the tip and be careful with your teeth. I don't mind it a bit rougher, but don't chew on it."

Aria snorted in the most undignified way ever, but then she became very quiet. I could tell that she was nervous, which she really didn't have to be. I knew she didn't have any experience and didn't expect her to blow my mind with her skills. The way my balls were already throbbing, I'd probably shoot my load the second her lips touched my fucking dick.

When Aria didn't budge, I stroked her scalp until I cupped the back of her head. Again I had to fight the urge to push her down like I would have done with my past fuck buddies. Finally, Aria closed her lips around my tip. The sight of my cock in her mouth was the best thing I'd ever seen. All I wanted was to thrust upwards and bury myself in her.

"Now swirl your tongue around it." Aria's brows furrowed as she tried to move around my thick head. "Yes, just like that." She slowly got the hang of it, and I gave her the time she needed, wanting her to learn enjoying this. "Take a bit more of me into your mouth and move your head up and down. Now suck as you move. Yes, fuck." This felt amazing, because seeing Aria turned me on like nothing ever had. I thrust up without thinking about it. Aria flinched away when I hit the back of her throat. She coughed, eyes watering.

"Fuck, sorry," I rasped. I stroked Aria's lips before I settled back once more. "I'll try to stay still."

Aria surprised me by licking my entire length, base to tip. She paused. "Is that okay?"

"Fuck yes."

She began licking my dick as if it were a popsicle, and fuck it felt good. My balls tightened. "This feels really fucking good, but I really want to come."

Aria peered up at me. "What do you need me to do?"

"Suck me harder, and keep looking at me with your fucking beautiful eyes."

Aria began working my cock in earnest now, her cheeks hollowing as she sucked me harder while her fingers tightened around my base. Pleasure built in my balls. Fuck, so good. I wouldn't last much longer. "If you don't want to swallow, you need to get away," I got out.

Aria pulled away, and I came all over my stomach and thighs. My eyes fell shut as I drew in a ragged breath, my cock still twitching. I rubbed my fingertips along Aria's scalp then began to pull away to reach for a tissue. Aria grabbed my hand and leaned into the touch.

I opened my eyes in surprise. Having her cheek pressed against my palm felt good. Her eyes searched my face nervously, as if she worried that I would refuse her. I stroked her cheekbone and, slowly, her lips pulled into a grateful smile. My stomach filled with warmth. I tore my gaze away from my lovely wife and took in the sticky mess I'd made. "I need a fucking shower." I wiped away the worst of it with a tissue before I slid out of bed before I could get my cum all over the sheets.

Aria rolled over to her side, positioning her arms and legs so she was covered.

Did she think I'd leave her lying there? "Come on. I don't want to shower alone." Aria quickly took my hand and I pulled her with me into the bathroom.

I turned on the water, then stepped under the hot stream. I tugged Aria against my body and pressed a kiss to the top of her head. She beamed up at me like I'd given her an expensive gift. I began washing her, enjoying the feel of her skin under my hands. Aria relaxed, her eyes closing. I'd never washed another person, never felt the urge to do it. I embraced her from behind, then bent low until my mouth was close to her ear.

"So was it okay for you?"

Aria nodded with a sheepish smile. "Yeah."

I pressed a kiss to her throat, my arms tightening around her middle. "I'm glad, because I really enjoy being in your mouth."

Aria turned red but I could tell that she was pleased. Had she been worried I wouldn't enjoy it?

She tilted her head to glance up at me. "Are you angry that I didn't, you know, swallow? I bet the women you've been with so far always did."

She was right, but I'd never warned a woman before. They'd been able to tell the signs of my orgasm and could have pulled back if they'd wanted. They never did though. "No, I'm not angry," I said honestly. "I won't lie, I'd love to come in your mouth, but if you don't want that, it's okay."

I really hoped Aria would give it a try and enjoy it.

Ten minutes later, we returned to bed. It was close to midnight and I had an early day ahead of me, but sleep deprivation was definitely worth it. Aria snuggled up to me and put her cheek against my chest. I turned off the light then wrapped my arm around her. How could this feel so right? As if it had never been different?

I wasn't even sure where exactly I'd dropped my gun. I always knew where I had my weapons when I was around other people, but with Aria...I just didn't feel the need.

"When your father told you to marry me, what was your reaction?" Aria's voice drew me out of my thoughts.

I wondered what she expected me to say. "I'd expected it. I knew I'd have to marry for tactical reasons. As future Capo, you can't let emotions or desires rule any part of your life."

Aria didn't say anything. I was glad for the dark, because I knew she would have looked for something in my eyes again, something that would never be there. "And what about you?"

Aria exhaled. "I was terrified."

"You were only fifteen. Of course you were terrified." She'd been so young and innocent. She was still too innocent for me.

"I was still terrified on the day of our marriage. I'm still not entirely sure you don't terrify me."

This side of me, the side Aria got to see, it was one no one got to see. It was as gentle as I could ever be and she was still scared of me? "I told you, you have no reason to fear me. I'll protect and take care of you. I'll give you anything you want and need."

She only had to ask. Father didn't give a fuck how much money I spent. We had more than enough, and soon everything would be mine anyway.

"But the Famiglia always comes first. If you had to kill me to protect the business, you would."

My fingers on her waist clamped up in shock.

Born in Blood. Sworn in Blood.

I could practically feel the sting of the tattoo needle when the motto of the Famiglia had been inked into my chest.

I'd sworn my life to the Famiglia. Becoming their Capo, leading my men, was the future I'd been raised for, the future I lived for. Every breath I'd taken so far, every life I'd ended, every wound I'd suffered had brought me closer to my goal. There had been nothing else in my life. Before Aria, my first thought when I got up in the morning had been about business, and so had been my last before I'd fallen asleep.

I'd never considered that something or someone could ever share the spotlight with the Famiglia, that anything could ever matter at all in comparison to my life as a Made Man.

Love is a weakness a Capo can't afford. My father's words rang loud and clear in my head. I'd always rolled my eyes when he'd uttered them, convinced that they were a waste of time and effort considering that I was incapable of giving the slightest shit about a woman.

Yet, the woman in my arms had wormed her way into my thoughts—and worse, my heart. More than once I'd caught myself thinking of her while being away for business.

This wasn't love. I wasn't capable of love. This was...I wasn't sure. I cared about Aria. I wanted to protect her, wanted to keep one woman in my life safe.

It wasn't love, but it was more than my father would ever tolerate. If he found out my wife wasn't just a fuck thing for me, a beautiful trophy I paraded around, then he'd make sure to erase what he considered a risk from my life.

Aria's body had softened in my hold, and her breathing evened out. I buried my nose in her hair, breathing in her vanilla scent. She'd be safer if I treated her with cold detachment, if I made her hate me. It would be so easy to get her hate. Nothing was easier. I'd only have to take what was mine without consideration, without care. But the idea of doing so, of having Aria watch me the way my mother and Nina watched my father, it turned my stomach to ice.

Fuck.

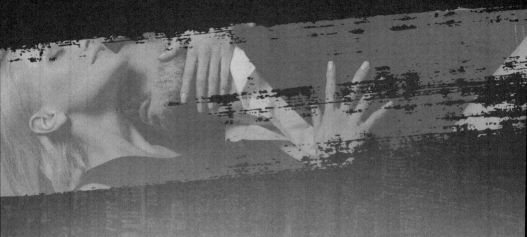

CHAPTER 15

My ringtone tore me from sleep. I opened dreary eyes, fumbling for my phone on the nightstand. When I finally had a hold of it, I pressed it to my ear without looking at the screen. "Can't you deal with whatever shit came up alone? I have a fucking boner to take care of, Matteo."

"Good Morning, Luca," Nina said.

I groaned. Aria lifted her head, looking thoroughly disheveled, and fucking kissable.

"Nina, what do you want?"

"Salvatore asked me to invite you to dinner."

Fuck. He was way too eager to have Aria and me over. I hated the old bastard. "In case you didn't notice, Matteo and I are busy dealing with the Russians."

"I'll have the cooks prepare a feast for tonight. Be here at seven."

"I don't have time, Nina," I gritted out. Hearing my stepmother's high-pitched voice this early in the morning gave me a fucking migraine.

"Luca, your father was very adamant about having you over," she said. There was a moment of silence. "You will come?"

Her voice shook, but she quickly masked it with a cough then cleared her throat. "He won't be happy with you if you refuse his invitation."

He wouldn't be happy with her. He'd blame her, telling her she was incapable of getting even the easiest tasks right. "We'll be there," I muttered and hung up. "Fuck it."

Aria's eyes widened. "What's wrong?" She touched my chest. Why did she always have to be so concerned? There was no reason to be worried about me. She was the one I needed to protect.

"Nina invited us to dinner for tonight."

"Oh," Aria said, frowning. "So we'll eat with your father and his wife?"

I nodded. "Matteo will be there as well." He wouldn't like it one bit, but he'd better move his fucking ass over there if he knew what was good for him.

"You don't sound happy," she said carefully.

Sighing, I untangled myself from her embrace and perched on the edge of the bed. That put it mildly. "My father...he's..." A sadistic rapist. A fucking psychopath. A murderous asshole who deserved to die. "...a difficult man."

Aria nodded as if she understood.

She couldn't, and she wouldn't, if I had a say in the matter. She pushed herself to a sitting position and touched my shoulder. "It's just dinner. Everything will be all right."

She was right. It would be all right because I wouldn't let my father ruin the one good thing in my life.

Aria's phone beeped. I chuckled darkly. "It seems we both won't get our peace of mind this morning."

Aria reached over, grabbing her phone and quickly scanning the message.

Her entire face transformed into a smile.

"Your sister?" I guessed, brushing a strand away from her glowing face.

She nodded. "She got a flight in two days!"

Aria's grin lit up everything, and my own lips wanted to pull into a smile, even if I felt like smashing something to pieces, but I held back. I stood, needing to bring some distance between my wife and me, not just physically but especially mentally if I wanted to get through tonight without my father getting suspicious.

Aria glanced up from her phone, but I walked into the bathroom without another word and closed the door.

I left shortly after breakfast to meet the manager of several of our whorehouses. The only thing Father did anymore was play golf with politicians or test the whores.

We were a bit early in the Foxy and took a seat in two plush armchairs. One of the whores came over with our drinks. She put them down on the low table, giving us a prime view of her ass, then she straightened and touched my shoulder with a flirtatious hand.

"Did I give you permission to touch me?" My eyes flashed up to hers and she quickly dropped her hand before she rushed back to the bar. I wouldn't break the promise I'd given to Aria, not even in that small way.

"What's crawled up your ass?" Matteo asked after he'd taken a sip from his Negroni.

"Do you think I'm growing soft?"

I leaned back and watched through narrowed eyes as my fucking brother almost pissed himself from laughing.

"Gi---give me a moment," Matteo bit out.

"Know what?" I muttered. "Maybe I should beat some sense into you to test my theory."

Matteo grinned, eyes teary. "Oh, Luca. This was good." He shook his head with another fucking chuckle. "You're many things, but soft? Come on, what's wrong with you?"

I considered not saying anything. Making myself vulnerable in front of others, even my brother, wasn't something I ever did.

Matteo's smile slipped off. "It's because of Aria?"

Fuck, I trusted the asshole, so fuck it all. "I still haven't fucked her, and I promised her never to touch another woman either. What does that make me?"

Matteo shrugged. "A good husband by normal standards, I suppose."

"As if we give a fuck about normal standards. Those aren't the rules we play by."

"You will be Capo as soon as our father dies. You'll make the rules soon enough."

"Some traditions can't be shaken, and our father is still Capo. If he knew that I haven't fucked my wife yet..." I trailed off.

"He'd probably do it himself," Matteo said. And I lost it.

"He touches a fucking hair on her body, and I'll end him, that's a fucking promise," I growled.

Matteo nodded. "One word from you, and I'm in on it. You know that, right?"

"I know," I said quietly. Matteo and I had been entertaining thoughts of how to kill our father for years. "But the Famiglia won't accept a Capo who killed his father."

Matteo sighed. "Why can't the old sadist just die?"

"Maybe Nina finds the courage to slip poison in his food at some point. How much longer can she or anyone bear the humiliation and beatings he gives her?"

"Maybe she'll kill herself instead of him," Matteo muttered. Not voicing the "like our mother" that we were both thinking. "And you'd have to kill her if she killed our father."

"She'd run off to Europe, and I won't have time to hunt down a woman," I said. If Nina ended our father, I definitely wouldn't punish her for it. I hated her but, compared to my father, she was a victim.

"You know," Matteo said in a low voice, "I knew you wouldn't force Aria."

I regarded him, not liking the heavy note underplaying his words.

"You still hear our mother's begging in your nightmares?" he continued in a whisper.

My stomach twisted. "Too often."

Matteo took out his knife, his eyes focusing on the gleaming blade as he turned it slowly. It was his favorite. The knife our mother had used to cut her wrists with. "A woman shouldn't have to beg her husband not to rape, beat and humiliate her. I'm a cruel fucker, but even I know that."

I nodded. I remembered only too well how our mother had looked in the mornings after those nights. Bruised, with a look in her eyes like a beaten dog. The idea that Aria could ever look like that made me want to kill everyone around me. Aria would never look like that. She'd never suffer violence through mine or anyone else's hands. I'd cut my fucking fingers off before I'd hit her, and I'd chop my dick into pieces before I'd ever rape my wife. She would be safe with me, in bed and anywhere else.

"You've got your Aria expression on again."

I frowned. "What the hell is that supposed to be?"

Matteo smirked. "It's a mix of protectively murderous and dreamily reverent."

I pushed into a standing position. "Fuck you, Matteo."

His smile widened. "I have enough women to fuck, but thank you."

I gave him the finger and turned on my heel, heading for the bathroom to take a piss.

———✕———

A few minutes before seven, we pulled up in front of the Vitiello townhouse. The drive had passed in silence; neither Matteo nor I felt like chatting before a dinner with our father and Nina, and Aria hadn't tried to make conversation either.

Nina opened the door before we could even ring the bell. Seeing her so eager to have us over wasn't a good sign. My hand on Aria's hip tightened, and she gave me a curious look, but then she greeted my stepmother with an awkward hug. Aria's eyes lingered on Nina's face, which was covered in a thick layer of makeup, but it didn't hide her swollen lip despite the dark lipstick she wore. Aria's expression remained perfectly polite. She'd probably seen more than enough bruises in her life.

Nina smiled her fake smile. "Good to have you over. Dinner's about to be served."

She led us into the dining room where Father waited in his usual chair at the head of the table. He didn't stand, only nodded, but his eyes latched onto Aria.

I took the seat beside him before he could offer it to her and gave him a tight smile.

Nina sat on Father's other side and Matteo across from Aria. My stepmother snapped her fingers and, at once, the maid rushed in with the starters. Father's favorite: liver paté.

I ate a bite while Aria peered down at her food then at me. It took me a moment to realize why. She didn't like liver. She'd mentioned it to me on our first date.

"Don't you like your food?" Nina asked with pursed lips, her gaze darting from Father to Aria.

He regarded Aria in a way I didn't like one bit.

Aria gave an embarrassed smile. "I'm not very fond of liver. It looks delicious, though."

"Luca eats liver," Father said disapprovingly.

Aria glanced at me, obviously not sure where my father was going with his comment. She couldn't know that Nina had to like what my father liked or face the consequences. I opened my mouth to tell him that I didn't give a fuck if Aria ate liver or not, but Matteo was quicker.

"Luca also likes torturing and killing, that doesn't mean his wife has to like it." He sent our father his fake smile.

A muscle in Father's cheek twitched. "I don't appreciate good food going to waste, Aria," he said to my wife.

"I'll eat it," I gritted out, reaching for the plate.

"Your wife will eat it," Father ordered.

Aria froze.

"She won't," I growled. "Aria's my wife. She won't answer to your demands, *Father.*"

Nina had become perfectly still in her seat, clutching her knife.

Matteo's hand had slipped off the table. I didn't reach for my own gun and gave him a warning glance.

Not like this. Not today.

"So possessive!" Father laughed, throwing his head back as if I'd told a fucking joke, as if the whole situation was funny. Nina fell in at once.

I forced a smile and so did Matteo. Aria laughed uncertainly. She didn't know my father well enough. Maybe she really thought it had been his twisted way of making a joke. I hoped it for her sake.

The second we were back in the car, away from my father, Matteo leaned forward with a grin, but it was off. "I hear your sister comes to visit us."

At once, the tension slipped out of Aria and she nodded with a smile. "Yes." She narrowed her eyes after a moment. "Why do you care?"

The protective note in her voice was unmistakable and might have made me laugh if I wasn't still so fucking tense from the dinner with Father. It was a good thing that Matteo managed to distract her from it. Aria didn't need to know that today could very well mark the date when I gave up my life, and any chance at a united Famiglia. Even without saying a word to him, Matteo *knew*, and he'd be at my side, no questions asked.

———✄———

The moment Aria joined me in bed, I pushed her on her back and moved down her body, dragging her panties down her legs before I settled between her parted thighs. Aria was still mine, would always be mine. I made her come twice with my tongue before I laid down beside her. She kissed me softly, her fingers caressing my chest. It felt good on so many levels. She always got through my walls. I wasn't even sure how she did it. I pulled out of the kiss. "I want your mouth."

Aria paused. Even without seeing her expression, I knew she was confused by my harsh tone. She moved down and then I felt her lips around my tip. I relaxed, letting my father's words drift away, enjoying the moment, my wife, the only way that was safe.

I came on my stomach like last time, then cleaned myself roughly before I settled on my back with Aria pressed up against my side. "Is everything okay?" she whispered.

"Yes." She stiffened at my clipped reply but nodded after a moment. It took a long time before she fell asleep. I knew I wouldn't get any sleep tonight, not when I kept thinking of ways to dispose of my father without anyone finding out.

CHAPTER 16

Aria kept throwing glances my way as we pulled up in front of JFK Airport. I'd barely talked to her all day, and it was obviously bothering her. But this was for the best. Despite my resolve to keep a safe distance from Aria, my hand found its way to her back as we walked into the arrivals hall of the airport. I couldn't stop touching her. It was maddening.

"Are you sure you'll be okay with Gianna staying with us for the next few days?" she asked.

"Yes. And I promised your father to protect her. It's easier when she's living in our apartment." Scuderi had made it clear that Gianna needed close supervision, and I didn't doubt it. The girl was trouble.

Aria smiled apologetically. "She will provoke you."

"I can handle a little girl."

"She's not that little. She's barely younger than me."

I regarded my wife. Sometimes I forgot how young she was. When I'd been her age, I'd already been a Made Man for seven years, had slept with countless women, had done and seen so much shit, but Aria was young and sheltered, and so was her sister. "I can handle her."

"Luca, Gianna knows how to push people's buttons. If you aren't absolutely sure that you can control yourself, I won't let her near you."

What did she think I'd do? Gianna was a seventeen-year-old girl. "Don't worry. I won't kill her *or you* in the next few days."

"Aria!" Gianna's screech rang through the hall.

The redhead stormed in our direction and collided with Aria. They hugged each other as if they hadn't seen each other in months.

When they finally pulled away from each other, Gianna made a show out of checking Aria's body. "No visible bruises. You only hit places that are covered by clothes?" She narrowed her eyes at me and I gave her a cold smile. I didn't give the slightest fuck what she thought. Aria, on the other hand, looked worried.

"Get your luggage. I don't want to stand here all night," I said.

Gianna turned around and grabbed her suitcase from where she'd dropped it. "A gentleman would have got it for me."

"A gentleman, yes." Gianna definitely didn't bring out anything gentle in me. It was a good thing that my father hadn't chosen her for me.

I turned and began walking back to the car, only occasionally making sure that Aria and Gianna were close behind in case something happened.

Aria and Gianna actually both wanted to sit in the backseat.

I gave my wife a scowl. "I'm not your driver. Get in the front with me."

She flinched at my tone, and again I wanted to find a way to get rid of my father. I hated keeping Aria at arm's length until he was out of the way.

"You shouldn't talk to her like that," Gianna butted in.

Aria slid into the seat beside me. "She's my wife. I can do and say to her what I want," I told Gianna.

Aria regarded me with furrowed brows, hurt and confusion swirling in her eyes. I almost reached out to stroke her cheek. Fuck, keeping my distance was impossible.

Turning my attention back to the street and away from Aria's reproachful expression, I started the car and pulled away from the airport.

"How are Lily and Fabi?" Aria asked, turning around in her seat to look at her sister.

"Annoying as hell. Especially Lily. She doesn't stop talking about Romero. She's in love with him."

Aria let out her bell-like laugh, carefree and unguarded. I felt the treacherous twitching of my own stomach, then mouth, but I held back.

Aria put her hand on my thigh with a soft smile. My eyes darted to hers and, without thinking about it, I covered her small hand with my big one. Keeping my distance was a losing game.

When we stepped into the apartment, the smell of roasted lamb and rosemary wafted over to us.

"I told Marianna to prepare a nice dinner," I said casually. If I really wanted to succeed in pushing my young wife away, I was definitely using the wrong approach. Fuck it.

Aria gave me that smile, that goddamn smile. "Thank you."

I resisted the urge to dip my head to kiss that sweet mouth. "Show your sister to her room, and then we can eat." I didn't wait for her reaction. Instead, I moved into the kitchen area where Marianna was wielding her cooking magic.

"Luca," she said with a brisk smile, then checked on the lamb.

I reached for one of the roasted potato halves swimming in a sea of olive oil and rosemary. Marianna swatted my hand away, clucking her tongue. "*Not before dinner,*" she chided in Italian.

My eyebrows rose and, holding her gaze, I took a potato and put it in my mouth. She shook her head. The fucking thing burnt my tongue, but the delicious taste was worth the pain.

"*How's your girl?*"

"*Good,*" I said.

She shook her head. "*She's too beautiful to be alone so often.*"

"Marianna," I warned. I liked Marianna, and I'd known her all my life, but I wouldn't let her meddle.

She sighed and turned back to the lamb.

The elevator began its ascent, then paused on this floor. I hit the button that unlocked the door and they slid open a moment later. Matteo strode out like a fucking runway model. His eyes scanned the penthouse and, when he didn't spot his new obsession, his annoying smile dropped. He came toward me and snatched a rosemary potato in passing. Marianna tried hitting him with the wooden spoon, something she didn't try with me, but Matteo spun around and out of her reach.

"I don't know why I'm putting up with you two insolent boys."

"Because you can't resist our charm like the rest of the ladies," Matteo said with a cocky grin. "Though Luca's rough charm really leaves something to be desired."

Marianna muttered something under her breath. She had been grateful when I'd asked my father that she be mine and Matteo's maid. Marianna had always been terrified of Father, but she could never have stopped working for him. He wouldn't have let her.

"Why don't you sit down at the table and not stand in my way?"

Marianna said.

Matteo and I moved toward the dining area. "And?"

"And what?"

"How does she look?"

I raised my eyebrows at him when we arrived at the table. "She's got her bitch face in place."

Matteo chuckled, as if that were the best news he could imagine.

"You really think marrying her is a good idea?" I tried again. I couldn't stop hoping Matteo would come to his senses.

Steps rang out, then Aria and Gianna entered the room.

Gianna spotted my brother and made a face as if she smelled something rotten. "What's he doing here?"

Like a masochistic moth, he was drawn to her fiery bitchiness. He sauntered over to her and kissed her hand. "Nice to see you again, Gianna."

I rolled my eyes at his antics.

Gianna wrenched her hand away. "Don't touch me."

Matteo's eyes flashed with eagerness. I knew that look. I'd have to keep a close eye on those two. They had already kissed. I didn't need another exchange of bodily fluids while the girl was under my protection. We all took our seats, Matteo across from me and beside his future wife.

Aria watched them with a small frown, obviously as worried as me, and she didn't even know about their impending nuptials yet.

Marianna bustled in, serving roast lamb, rosemary potatoes and green beans. Her face softened when she patted Aria's shoulder. What was it about Aria that made people go all soft?

"Why did you crush that guy's throat?" Gianna asked when we were done eating.

Aria froze before she turned to me. I leaned back in the chair. This was a story I'd recounted countless times in my life.

"Come on. It can't be that big a secret. You got your nickname for it," Gianna taunted me, her eyes holding obvious challenge, but I wasn't Matteo and not as easily baited.

Matteo grinned. "The Vise is a nice name."

"I hate it," I said. As if that one moment defined me. I'd killed more brutally, and yet everyone only remembered that one fucking day.

"You earned it," Matteo said. "Now tell them the story, or I will."

"I was seventeen. Our father has many brothers and sisters, and one of my cousins climbed the ranks in the mafia alongside me. He was several years older and wanted to become Capo. He knew my father would choose me, so he invited me to his house and tried to stab me in the back. The knife only grazed my arm and, when I got the chance, I wrapped my hands around his throat and choked him."

"Why didn't you shoot him?" Gianna asked.

"He was family, and it used to be tradition that we put down our weapons when we entered the home of a family member. Not anymore, of course."

Family. That word was a joke. My uncles and aunts didn't give a shit about Matteo or me; nor did our father. For the former, we were competitors for the position of Capo, for the latter a means to an end. If Father figured out a way to clone himself or live forever, he'd kill my brother and me without hesitation. A family based on trust and love that was something I'd never experienced, nor did I hope for it. Some things were out of reach, and I'd learned not to waste energy on longing for them when I had something I could fight for: the Famiglia.

"The betrayal made Luca so angry, he completely crushed our cousin's throat. He choked on his blood because the bones in his neck cut through his artery. It was a mess. I'd never seen anything like it." Matteo flashed me a grin. He'd always been more eager to tell my story than me. He found it amusing, while it only made me angry. I'd been foolish in the past, had put my trust in people who didn't deserve it, and it had almost killed me. I wouldn't make that mistake again. Trust was stupidity. Love was weakness. My eyes found Aria, who watched me with compassion.

"That's why Luca always sleeps with an eye open. He never even spends the night with a woman without a gun under the pillow or somewhere at his body," Matteo's voice cut through my thoughts, and I realized he was right. Since that day, I'd never been without a gun around other people—until Aria. I glared at my brother. Couldn't he just shut up?

Matteo raised his hands. "It's not like Aria doesn't know you screwed around with other women."

Did he think that was why I was pissed? He blurted out facts I had no intention of sharing. Aria knew I was unarmed around her. I didn't want her to read too much into it. Gianna leaned forward on her elbows, eyebrows cocked. "So are you wearing a gun now? We're all family, after all."

"Luca always wears a gun." Matteo leaned toward Gianna. "Don't take it personally. I don't think even I have seen him without a gun since that day. It's Luca's tic."

I could feel Aria's eyes on me, could see her thoughts whirring behind those baby blues. She *knew*. I sent her a harsh look, trying to dissuade her from making a big deal of my actions. So what? I didn't wear a gun around her because she wasn't an opponent to fear. That was all.

After dinner, I helped Aria move the plates into the dishwater while Matteo and Gianna kept on their arguments in the living room.

Aria yawned again, blinking slowly. "Let's go to bed."

Her eyes darted to my brother and her sister sitting across from each other on the sofas. "Not before Matteo leaves. I won't leave him and my sister alone."

She had a point. I didn't trust Matteo to honor the rules of our world when it came to Gianna, and I doubted she gave a flying fuck about losing her v-card on her wedding night. "You're right. She shouldn't be alone with him."

I walked over to my brother, who tore his gaze away from Gianna with a grin. I bent down. "That's your panty-dropper grin. Bag it and get down to your fucking apartment. You won't go anywhere near Gianna's panties before she's your wife."

"Says who?" Matteo challenged.

I gave him a warning look and he pushed to his feet with a scowl. What had he thought? That's I'd allow him to spend the night with the girl? That was a war declaration in the making. Father would lose his shit and make us both pay for losing face. I had a feeling he'd finally found a way to make me pay in ways that would have a lingering effect. My eyes found Aria who leaned against the kitchen counter. It would take time to come up with a foolproof plan to get rid of the bastard; until then, I needed to make sure Father had no reason to target my wife.

With a last grin at Gianna, Matteo left the apartment.

Ignoring me, Gianna moved over to her sister. "He's obsessed with me."

She was right.

"Then stop teasing him. He likes it," Aria said as I walked over to her and leaned beside her.

"I don't care what he likes."

I wrapped an arm around Aria's waist, remembering a moment too late that I was trying to be less affectionate toward her. "Matteo is a hunter. He loves the chase. You'd better not make him want to chase you," I told Gianna.

Gianna rolled her eyes. "He can hunt me all he wants. He won't get me." That's where she was wrong. Matteo already owned her, and soon she'd find out.

"You don't intend to go to bed now, right?" Gianna asked Aria.

"I'm really tired."

Gianna's shoulders slumped. "Yeah, me too. But tomorrow I want you all to myself." She sent me a scathing look, as if that had an effect on me, before she headed for the guest bedroom. "If I hear screams, no gun under a pillow will save you, Luca." She closed the door with a bang.

Aria's cheeks were flushed. I dipped my head. "Will you scream for me tonight?" I trailed my tongue over her throat.

"Not with my sister under the same roof," Aria said in embarrassment.

"We'll see about that," I murmured, nibbling her throat the way she loved it, and was rewarded with a breathy moan. I'd get Aria's screams tonight. Without another word, I led her into our bedroom. Shutting the door, I tugged Aria toward me then slipped her dress off. My eyes trailed over her white lace underwear in appreciation before I lifted her off the ground and carried her over to the bed where I put her down. I didn't waste any time before I bowed my head over her parted legs and kissed her pussy through her panties. The material was already soaked, and Aria's sweet scent tightened my groin with arousal. I kissed my way up to her chest.

"Mine," I murmured against her breast before I opened her bra and removed it. "I fucking love your nipples. They're pink and small and perfect."

I pulled her panties down next and stroked her swollen pussy lips, already eager for attention, but I focused on her nipples until Aria was writhing under me. Then I moved lower and dipped my tongue between her folds. Soon she was panting. When I suckled her harder again, she clapped her hand over her mouth, stifling her moans.

"No," I ordered, grabbing her hands and holding them down against her stomach.

"Gianna will hear."

I hope she did. It would probably drive her up the wall. Keeping my eyes on Aria's needy face, I began teasing her clit with my lips until she couldn't hold back her sounds anymore. She was so fucking wet that my finger slipped in easily. "Oh god," Aria gasped.

I fingerfucked her gently as I sucked her clit, and then she came hard. She pushed her face into the pillow, but a few moans rang out loud and clear. The sight of Aria losing control alone made me want to eat her out every day.

I crawled back up her, kneeling between her legs.

"When will you let me take you?" I asked in a low voice as I pressed a kiss to her pulse point.

Aria stiffened. I looked at her. "Fuck. Why do you have to look so fucking scared when I ask you that question?"

"I'm sorry. I just need more time."

More time, when I wasn't sure how much time we had. I gave a terse nod.

Aria stroked my chest through my clothes, smiling apologetically. I leaned back and took off my shirt. She helped me out of my gun and knife holsters before she kissed my tattoo, then the wound over my ribs. Suddenly her expression turned daring, and she raked her fingers over my nipples. I groaned then quickly got naked and settled on my back.

Aria leaned over my erection and stopped with her lips only an inch from my tip. "If you're not quiet, I'll stop."

I touched the back of her head, loving this teasing side of Aria. "Maybe I won't allow you to stop."

"Maybe I'll bite."

I crossed my arms behind my head. "Have your way with me, I won't make a sound. Don't want to offend your sister's virgin ears."

"What about my virgin ears?" She kissed my cock, making me twitch.

Still a virgin. "You shouldn't still be one," I got out, but then Aria started sucking me and I focused on the feel of her hot mouth and staying quiet. Like last time, I warned her before I came and she quickly pulled back.

Afterwards, I spooned her and turned off the lights.

"I'm sorry for what your cousin did," Aria said suddenly.

It took me a moment to understand whom she was referring to: Junior, my traitorous cousin. The worst thing was that I hardly ever thought about his betrayal anymore because there were so many new threats in my life, not all of them Russian. "I should have known better than to trust anyone. Trust is a luxury people in my position can't afford."

"Life without trust is lonely."

"Yes, it is," I agreed, kissing her neck. Part of me wanted to risk trusting Aria. It was a part I thought long dead.

I woke after Aria for once. When she returned from her shower, I was already sporting a morning rod. Aria gave me a disbelieving smile, but I didn't wait long. I got out of bed and pressed her to my chest, facing the floor-length mirror. I made her watch as I teased her nipples, even as her cheeks turned red in shame.

Of course, her sister was an early riser as well, and soon called for Aria right in front of our door, but I didn't release her. I wasn't done with her yet. Far from it.

"Your sister is a fucking nuisance," I whispered in her ear as I eased my finger between her folds then pushed into her. "But you're so fucking wet, *principessa*." Aria rewarded me with more arousal.

"Yes," I groaned as I thrust my finger into her slowly, watching her as she watched everything.

"Aria?" Gianna hammered against the door.

I stroked her clit and kissed her harshly, swallowing her cries as she came hard under my fingers. I pushed her forward and knelt behind her. Fuck, the sight of her ass and pussy on display was almost too much. I dragged my tongue along her crease then dove back in until Aria's second orgasm caused her legs to give away.

Panting, she knelt beside me. I straightened, bringing my dick close to her face.

After a moment of hesitation, Aria took me into her mouth. Having her on her knees sucking my cock was the hottest sight I could imagine.

"You're so beautiful, Aria," I murmured as I started thrusting gently, trying to see if she could take me like that.

Gianna finally gave up as well, but I could only watch Aria as she blew me slowly. I began guiding her head into a faster rhythm. "Cup my balls."

Fuck, this felt amazing. I rocked my hips as Aria sucked me. "I want to come in your mouth, *principessa*."

When Aria nodded, I almost came right then, but I held off until it just got too much. My hips jerked as I came hard, all the while watching my wife. I stroked her cheek as she tried to swallow everything. I pulled Aria up to me, not wanting her to get insecure, and kissed her harshly.

"I hope you remember this all day." I definitely would.

After a quick breakfast, I left for a day in the Sphere. Matteo and I had our drug sale numbers to go over and to finally discuss our father's end.

We settled across from each other in the office.

"So you finally want to give the sadistic asshole what he deserves?"

"He's barely doing what needs to be done so the Famiglia stays at the top."

Matteo grinned. "As if that's why you want to kill him. You don't like how he treated your wife."

"I don't like how he treats a lot of people."

Matteo's expression made it clear that he wanted me to cut the bullshit.

I leaned forward, lowering my voice. "He ruins everything. He thrives on misery. I just want him gone. You with me?"

"Do you really have to ask? I've wanted to kill him for as long as I can remember."

I nodded, then leaned back. "We have to be careful. We can't risk anything being traced back to us."

Matteo considered that. "Father is paranoid. The only time he isn't heavily guarded and doesn't have his bodyguards sitting right beside him is when he meets with his mistress."

"We can't kill him ourselves."

Matteo's mouth tightened. "I really want to be the one to do it, but I get your point."

"We'll figure something out. Father's got a long row of enemies. There has to be a way to get one of them to kill him."

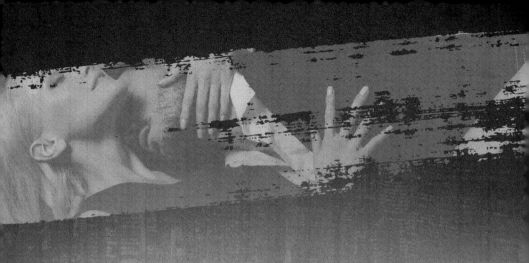

CHAPTER 17

Matteo and I were checking our sales numbers for cocaine and synthetic drugs when my phone beeped.

It was a message from Romero's cell.

A wants to hit a club. Permission?

"I hope no more bad news," Matteo muttered as I typed **"No"** and sent it off.

"Aria and Gianna want to go dancing."

"I assume you said no."

"If Aria wants to hit a club, she'll have to do it with me."

We returned to business. Going through the sales figures sorted by cities in our territory always took forever, but I wanted to know what was going on in our territory.

Another hour passed before a knock made me look up from the laptop.

"Come in," I said.

Our barkeeper, Tony, poked his head in. I frowned. Usually he stayed behind the bar. This was close to peak time, so I doubted the bar could do without him.

"No drinks for us?" Matteo said with a grin.

Tony smiled, but I could tell that he was nervous. I narrowed my eyes. That meant I wouldn't like what he had to say.

"Romero sent me," he said carefully. "Your wife and her sister are here, dancing."

I shoved the laptop to the side and got up, as did Matteo. Fury shot through me. I had given Romero a clear order. Of course I doubted he'd gone against it without good reason, and I had a feeling Aria and her sister had found a way to force him here. I motioned for him to leave, and he did quickly. "Damn it," I growled, then staggered out of the office. Matteo was close behind me. "Seems like Aria isn't as well trained as you thought."

I shot him a glare. "That's Gianna's doing, no doubt. That girl's a trouble maker."

We entered the dance floor and it didn't take long for me to spot Aria. It was impossible to miss her. Her long blond hair glowed under the lights, and a gathering of men danced around her and Gianna, admiring them.

Fuck. I'd never seen Aria dressed like this. I walked closer, taking in every inch of her tight leather pants, the way they accentuated her perfect butt. She swayed her hips to the rhythm, rotating and twisting, making me wonder how it would be once she rode me. I sent death glares toward the fuckers who'd dared to dance near my wife, and they backed off. One fucker hadn't noticed me yet, too focused on Aria and actually motioning for her to dance with him. I met his gaze with the full force of my fury, and he looked away and turned. Good for him.

CORA REILLY

I stopped right behind Aria. She swung her hips to the rhythm, then arched her back, presenting that perfect, peach-shaped ass. I grabbed her hips, feeling her heat. Aria tensed then relaxed. She surprised me by jutting her ass against me. With her heels, her cheek pressed enticingly against my cock. I jerked her against me, then bent down to her ear. "Who are you dancing for?" I asked, my voice shaking with possessiveness.

Aria leaned back, her blue eyes meeting mine. "You. Only you."

Only me. Always. "What are you doing here?"

"Dancing."

"I told Romero 'no.'"

"I'm not your possession, Luca. Don't treat me like one."

Aria didn't understand how far I'd go to make sure she was only mine, to guarantee her safety. "You are mine, Aria, and I protect what's mine."

"I don't mind being protected, but I do mind being imprisoned," Aria shouted as she turned to face me, allowing me a glance down her see-through shirt to a glittery bra beneath that accentuated her breasts. Another wave of possessiveness hit me. "Dance with me," she pleaded with a soft smile.

Fuck. That smile. Gripping her hips tighter, I started to move to the music. It had been a while since I'd enjoyed time in a club, but for Aria, this was the first time. Another first she shared with me. I dipped my head to her ear. "You look fucking hot, Aria. Every man in the club wants you, and I want to kill them all."

"I'm only yours," she said without hesitation. I kissed her, wanting to taste her and show everyone that she was mine.

"I'm so fucking hard," I groaned. "Fuck. I have a call set up with one of our distributors in five minutes." He made sure that we had enough acid, ecstasy and all of the other shit we sold to the crowds in our clubs.

Aria touched my chest. "It's okay. Come back when you have time. I'm going to grab a drink."

"Go to the VIP area." It would make Romero's job much easier.

"I want to pretend I'm an ordinary girl tonight."

Did she really think that would work? Aria was the center of attention wherever she went. "Nobody who looks at you will think you're ordinary." I glanced at my watch. Fuck. I needed to get back into the office. "Cesare and Romero will keep an eye on you."

Aria paled when she looked toward the VIP area.

I followed her gaze. "Fuck it," I muttered when I saw Grace doing a lap dance for a guy. "She's not here because of me."

Aria gave me a sad smile. "Yes, she is."

Grace looked up briefly, catching my eyes. Aria was probably right. I had to put a fucking stop to Grace's obsession. "I can't throw her out. She comes here all the time to party. I haven't seen her since that night. I usually stay in the back."

Aria didn't say anything and I cupped her cheek, forcing her to meet my gaze.. "There's only you, Aria." I risked another glance at my watch. Damn it. "I really need to go now. I'll be back as soon as I can." With a last glance at my wife, I quickly stalked back to my office, followed by Matteo.

The second I stepped into the room, I lifted my cell to my ear before I continued to the back office where I had more quiet. Matteo stayed in the front, checking the rest of our numbers.

———————✕———————

Matteo pushed into the room with a dead serious face. "Someone put roofies in Aria's drink."

I jerked upright, hanging up without a word. The fucking drugs could wait.

"He didn't do anything. Romero and Cesare were there," Matteo added hastily, but I barely listened as I stormed past him into the front office. Aria clung to Cesare, her face ashen, legs barely supporting her. Fury burnt through me when I glanced from my drugged wife to Rick, one of our drug dealers. The fucker would soon wish he had never been born.

"What happened?" I got out past the burning fury throbbing in my throat, in my veins, in every fucking inch of my body. I crossed the room and took Aria from Cesare, who released her at once. I lifted her into my arms and her head dropped against my chest, dazed eyes peering up at me. Fuck it. That's why I didn't want Aria in places like this. With so many people around, protecting her was close to impossible, and I needed to protect her no matter the cost. A brief burst of anger toward her for disobeying flickered in my body, but it slipped away as I peered down at my helpless wife.

Gianna kept bitching in her high-pitched voice, but my focus tunneled in on Aria. Her blue eyes clung to my face, her fingers crinkling my shirt.

Romero explained some shit about roofies to Gianna as I put Aria down on the sofa. She looked small and vulnerable. I turned toward Rick and stalked to him. I wanted to smash his skull against the wall, leave a goddamn dent in the plaster from the force of it. But a quick end like that? No, that wasn't going to happen.

"You put roofies in my wife's drink, Rick?" I asked, my voice vibrating with my barely contained anger. Without Aria and Gianna in the room, I would already have started slicing him into bite-sized pieces.

Rick's beady eyes shot open, mouth gaping. "Wife? I didn't know she was yours. I didn't. I swear!"

I shoved Romero aside to get into Rick's ugly face, then gripped the knife still sticking out of his thigh and turned it sharply. Rick roared in agony, eyes rolling back, but Romero kept the fucker on his feet.

"What did you plan to do to her once you had her outside?" Fuckers like Rick used roofies for a chance to get their dick wet, and they sold roofies to assholes who wanted to do the same because no women would ever give them the time of day.

"Nothing!"

"Nothing? So if my men hadn't stopped you, you would have just dropped her off at a hospital?" The mere idea that his piece of shit could have touched Aria drove a burning ball of fire into my chest.

Aria murmured a few incoherent words. I moved to her side and got down on my haunches to be eye level with her.

"What did you say, Aria?"

"'I'll fuck your tight ass. I'll make you scream, bitch. I'll fuck you bloody, cunt.' That's what he said to me," Aria dragged the words out of her mouth, her eyelids fluttering. Gianna lost her shit before I could, raging and screaming.

"You will die!" she screamed at Rick.

He wouldn't only die. Death was for a simple transgression. This was the ultimate crime, the fucking ultimate sin.

I stood, feeling my pulse slow as it always did before the kill, before the torture. Matteo was holding Gianna back from scratching Rick's eyes out.

"They will make you bleed, and I hope they'll rape your ugly ass with that broomstick over there."

"Gianna," Aria whimpered, and briefly my pulse spiked, then my eyes settled on Rick, assessing him, trying to decide how to cause him the most agony possible in as short a time as possible. Aria needed to go home, to sleep off the drugs.

"I'll make him pay, Gianna," Matteo promised to his red obsession.

I shook my head. "No. He's my responsibility." Matteo glanced toward me, scanned my face. He knew me, and he knew that I needed to crush the fucking bastard in front of me.

I stepped up to Rick. His chin wobbled, his eyes twitching with fucking terror. Oh, he knew the stories of what I did to people who fucked with me. Drug dealers who kept a higher percentage than was agreed on, the goddamn Bratva assholes who tried to ruin everything with their low-quality drugs…He knew those stories, and that had been business. This was fucking personal. It couldn't *get* any more personal.

I leaned down, even if the stench of smoke and cheap aftershave made my lip curl. "You wanted to fuck my wife? Wanted to make her scream?"

He wasn't worth breathing the same air as Aria. He should never have even dared to look at her.

Rick began crying. "No, please."

I gripped his throat and jerked him up, choking him, but this wouldn't be his end. Too easy, too painless. I shoved him away from me so he smashed against the wall then dropped to the ground. His gaze briefly flitted toward Aria as if he hoped for her help, and I fucking snapped.

"I hope you're hungry, because I'm going to feed you your cock." I staggered toward him, static rushing in my ears, poisonous fury sloshing in my veins as I withdrew my knife.

I registered Matteo ushering the girls out. Good. I knelt beside Rick. A moment later Matteo was beside me, holding down the thrashing bastard. I jerked down his pants and he screamed. "No, no, please!"

Begging didn't work with me. I brought the knife down—not on his cock, though. Not yet. First, I wanted answers.

Soon, Rick revealed that a blond woman had given him money so he'd put roofies in Aria's drink. It must have been Grace. I should have known the bitch wouldn't give up easily. The only other option was a Russian spy, like the killers who'd been sent out to kill Matteo and me. Or maybe even a woman sent by my father, in case he feared Aria could turn me soft. But Rick was a blubbering mess and his brain too frayed from years of taking shit himself. I wouldn't get more information out of him.

Rick hadn't known Aria was my wife. It didn't matter. "Please," he begged again. "I told you everything. It won't happen again."

I brought my face close, smiling harshly. "You're right. It won't happen again." Then I brought my knife down on his cock, and his screams pitched higher until they turned in a choked gurgle. When I was done, I stood and so did Matteo. Rick still occasionally twitched in the sea of blood around him. I went over to the sink, washed his filthy blood off my hands and face and knife. Then, I left without a word. Matteo would find someone to clean up the shit.

I went through the back entrance toward the waiting car. Romero stood beside it. The moment Gianna spotted me, her bitch-face dropped, turning to shock.

"Holy fuck. You're covered in blood."

"Only my shirt," I told her. Romero grabbed a fresh shirt from the trunk as I slipped out of the ruined one.

"You have no shame," Gianna said as she watched me. She didn't take her eyes off my upper body though.

"I'm taking off my shirt, not my fucking pants. Do you ever shut your mouth?" I growled, my darkness still simmering under my skin, the call for more blood still singing its siren's song in my goddamn veins.

Romero held out the clean shirt to me. "Here, Boss."

I put it on and handed Romero the bloody one. "Burn that one and take care of everything, Romero. I'll drive." Romero hesitated, his eyes flickering toward Gianna and Aria, and I realized he was reluctant to leave them alone with me. My first impulse was to smash him against the wall for even considering to defy me, but then I decided he probably had reason to be wary of me. But it wasn't his call to make. After a moment, he turned and left. I leaned inside the back of the car where Aria was sprawled out, looking pasty and shaking. I touched her cheek and her eyes briefly focused on my face.

Some of my fury slithered away. I drew back and got behind the steering wheel. I wanted to get us home, where I could hold Aria in my fucking arms until the last of my bloodlust had died down.

Red locks took shape in my peripheral vision. "You are quite a hunk, you know that? If you weren't married to my sister and not such an asshole, I might consider giving you a go."

I slanted her a quick glance, a nasty reply on my tongue.

"Gianna," Aria half-begged her sister. Was she worried I'd lose my shit on the bitchy redhead? I didn't like Gianna, but she was a seventeen-year-old-girl.

"What, cat got your tongue? I hear you usually jump everything that doesn't have a dick."

She finally shut up when I didn't take the bait. We pulled into the parking garage and I got out of the car.

I lifted Aria into my arms and carried her into the elevator. Gianna leaned across from me, and I didn't like her expression one bit. I lowered my gaze to Aria, knowing she'd speak to the calm in me, a place few people knew existed. "Have you ever had a threesome?"

Did the bitch really expect any answers?

"How many women have you raped before my sister?"

My head jerked up. I wasn't sure how much Aria shared with her sister. I wanted to crush Gianna and knew I could have done it by dishing out the simple truth that Matteo owned her pussy, but Aria touched my chest, and the anger drained out of me as I met her gaze. She was begging me to stay calm. "Can't you do something else with your mouth than yap?" I muttered.

"Like what? Give you a blow job?"

I glanced up. That would be Matteo's privilege. "Girl, you've never even seen a dick. Just keep your lips shut."

"Gianna," Aria whispered.

I strode quickly toward the stairs to take Aria to our bedroom, but Gianna barred my way. "Where are you taking her?"

"To bed," I told her, trying to move past her, but she got in the way.

"She's high on roofies. That's probably the chance you've been waiting for. I won't let her be alone with you."

Was she suggesting I'd fuck Aria while she was helpless like this? "I'm going to say it only once, and you'd better obey: get out of my way, and go to bed."

"Or what?"

That was the fucking problem. There was little I could do. For one because she was a girl, and for two because she was *Matteo's* girl.

"Gianna, please," Aria pleaded.

Gianna finally stopped the bullshit. "Get better."

Without another glance at the bitch, I carried Aria into our bedroom. She squirmed in my hold, shivering. "I'm going to be sick."

The moment I held her over the toilet, Aria threw up, still shaking. "I'm sorry," she whispered, sounding embarrassed and miserable.

"What for?" I asked as I wrapped my arm around her and helped her up.

"For throwing up."

I soaked a towel and held it out to her. Aria took it with a weak smile and cleaned her face, shaking in my hold.

"It's good that you got some of that shit out of your system. Fucking roofies. It's the only way for ugly fucks like Rick to get their dicks into a pussy," I growled, my anger rekindling. If I didn't already have so much on my plate, I'd have drawn his torture out over a few days.

I helped Aria into the bedroom. She leaned heavily on me. Glancing down at her, I asked, "Can you undress?"

She gave a small nod. "Yeah."

I released her and she lost her balance. She landed on the bed and began laughing before she grimaced, holding her head. She definitely wouldn't be able to undress herself. I leaned over her, trying to catch her attention. It took a moment before her eyes focused on me.

"I'm going to get you out of your clothes. They stink of smoke and vomit," I explained slowly. For some reason it felt wrong to undress her in her state. She was drugged and obviously not in a state of mind to refuse advances. There was a good reason why roofies were the drug of choice for rapists.

I hooked my fingers under Aria's shirt and gently slid it up. She giggled again, but I ignored it and her wiggling. Despite my best intentions, I couldn't help but check her out when I pushed down her leather pants. Goosebumps covered her gorgeous lean legs right up until her tiny lace panties. I reached under her back, causing her to arch with another giggle as if I'd tickled her. I doubted she realized what she was doing. Her unfocused eyes were playful as she looked up at me. I unhooked her bra and pulled it off, then tossed it carelessly away.

Good Lord, even drugged Aria stole my breath. She was sprawled out before me in nothing but a tiny piece of lace covering her pussy, her nipples erect in the cool room, and smiling up at me. There was no anxiety, no fear. I quickly turned away before my thoughts could wander down a dark path. I got out of my clothes before I grabbed a shirt from my drawer then helped Aria to a sitting position. It took several tries to get her into the shirt, but it would have taken even more tries to get her into one of her flimsy nightgowns. I lifted Aria once more and laid her down with her head on the pillow. She didn't move, only peered up at me with the same dreamy smile. I stretched out beside her.

"You're impressive, you know?" she said, her eyes trailing over my chest, going in and out of focus.

I touched her forehead. She was overly warm. Aria giggled and touched my lower abs before she slid even lower. I quickly stopped her wandering hand and held it fast. "Aria, you're drugged. Try to sleep."

She gave me a droopy smile that was probably meant to be seductive. "Maybe I don't want to sleep."

I stroked her hair from her forehead. "Yes, you do."

Aria blinked then yawned. "Will you hold me?"

I turned off the lights and cradled her in my arms. "You'd better lie on your side in case you feel sick again," I murmured against her neck.

"Did you kill him?" she mumbled.

I considered how much to tell her, but Aria knew the rules of our world. She knew the man I was. "Yes."

"Now there's blood on my hands."

"You didn't kill him."

"But you killed him because of me."

"I'm a killer, Aria. It had nothing to do with you." I didn't want her to feel guilty for something like that. This death was on me, like every death in my past, like every death in my future. They would never tarnish Aria, because I wouldn't let them. I wanted her life to be free of the horrors of my existence. I wouldn't let the darkness consume her like it had my mother, like it did so many women in our circles because their husbands didn't give a fuck about them.

Aria's soft voice tore through the dark once more. "You know, sometimes I wish I could hate you, but I can't. I think I love you. I never thought I could."

My heart stuttered in a way it never had, and heat flooded my chest. Love? Fuck. Aria couldn't love me. She didn't know what she was talking about. She was drugged. The roofies had messed with her brain.

After a long exhale, Aria continued, her voice becoming drowsier. "And sometimes I wonder how it would be if you made love to me."

I wanted to claim Aria, to own her, to fuck her...to make love to her? I'd never made love, and I didn't think I was capable of it. "Sleep."

"But you don't love me," Aria continued, her words a slur filled with misery. "You don't want to make love to me. You want to fuck me because you own me."

She was right, and yet her words didn't ring true. I wanted more than that. With Aria, I simply wanted. I wanted all of her, every little thing, not just her body, also her smiles and her closeness and her astonished gasps and breathless moans. I tightened my arm around her. Love.

How did you know if you loved someone?

"Sometimes I wish you had taken me on our wedding night; then at least I wouldn't still wish for something that will never be. You want to fuck me like you fucked Grace, like an animal. That's why she told me you would fuck me bloody, right?"

It took my mind a moment to fully process her words. Grace had told Aria I would fuck her bloody? "When did she say that? Aria, when?"

I gripped Aria's upper arm. "When?" I growled, but she had passed out.

I'd suspected it was Grace behind the attack, and now Aria's words confirmed my suspicion. My body was bursting with tension and with the need to seek retribution. Rick had already gotten what he deserved, but there was still Grace. I wanted to kill her. She was a woman, but she was a despicable human being most of all. Could I dispose of her? She wasn't her father's favorite child, far from it, but there was a difference between not liking your daughter and wanting her to be killed. We needed his cooperation if we wanted to gain influence. Father definitely wouldn't allow me to risk it by killing Grace in blind rage. It would only make him question my feelings for Aria, another thing I couldn't risk.

CHAPTER 18

Aria's sleep was fitful, which in turn led to me being awake most of the night. I couldn't stop checking on her breathing, worried the roofies would lead to her losing consciousness or worse. The idea of losing Aria, of almost having lost her last night, it left me restless...and furious.

She lay curled up on her side, eyelids fluttering, body trembling. I brushed a strand of hair from her sweaty forehead. A small moan passed her lips—not the beautiful sounds she made when I gave her pleasure but a shuddering sound of discomfort.

Her eyes opened and, for a moment, she blinked up at me before she jerked up, cupping a hand over her mouth and rushing toward the bathroom.

I untangled myself from the blankets and followed her. She was clutching the toilet, breathing harshly.

I flushed the toilet because it was obvious that she was too shaky to do it, then brushed more wayward strands from her forehead.

Aria let out a mirthless laugh, peering up at me with teary eyes. "Not that hot anymore, am I?"

Aria was mine to protect. She was my responsibility and yet someone had dared attack her in my own club. "That shouldn't have happened. I should have kept you safe."

"You did," Aria said feebly, pushing to her feet. I steadied her, worried she'd pass out.

"Maybe a bath will help," I said. My mind was still trying to come up with ways to pay Grace back.

Aria shook her head. "I think I'll drown if I lie in the bathtub now."

I opened the faucet but didn't let go of Aria in case she passed out. I had no intention of letting her go into the water alone in the state she was in. "We can take a bath together."

The right corner of Aria's mouth tipped up. "You just want to grab a feel."

I stroked her wrist with my thumb. "I won't touch you while you're still vulnerable." When I'd imagined our first bath in the tub together, there had definitely been hot sex involved, but that was out of the question for several reasons. One of them being that my wife was still a virgin...I couldn't stop thinking about what would have happened if Rick had made it out of the club with Aria, if that had been her first experience. Unreasonable fury burnt through my veins once more, and only Aria's presence stopped me from going on a rampage.

"A Capo with morals?" she teased.

"I'm not Capo yet," I objected. But if everything went as I hoped, Father wouldn't be Capo much longer, definitely not beyond this year. "And I have morals. Not many, but a couple." And one of them would always be not to hurt Aria.

Aria pressed her forehead against my chest. Her skin was burning up. "I'm only teasing." Running my hand along her spine, I kissed the crown of her head. Aria relaxed under the touch and released a small breath. Eventually she walked over to the sink to brush her teeth. My eyes followed her every move. She looked tiny in my shirt. Vulnerable.

I turned off the faucet before I tugged the shirt over her head. She held onto my arms to steady herself. Hooking my fingers in her panties, I dragged them down her lean legs, unable not to take in her beautiful body as I did so.

Despite everything, I could feel blood shooting into my dick when I pulled down my shorts. I helped Aria into the tub then got in behind her, pulling her flush against me. My cock slid along her outer thigh. Definitely not a good man. Aria surprised me when she turned around to face me, straddling my legs. The position made her pussy glide over my dick. She grew tense at the feel of me against her. Fuck, the feel of her opening against my tip was the sweetest torture I could imagine.

I shoved my dick back then slid in deeper into the water so Aria lay sprawled out on my chest, no longer pressed up to my erection.

Aria gave me that trusting look I didn't deserve. "Some men would have taken advantage of the situation."

"I'm that kind of man, Aria. Don't kid yourself into believing I'm a good man. I'm neither noble nor a gentleman. I'm a cruel bastard."

"Not to me," Aria said softly and buried her nose against my throat, holding on to me tightly.

My heart sped up, remembering her words from last night, and I kissed her head again. "It's better if you hate me. There's less chance of you getting hurt that way."

"But I don't hate you."

Emotions had never been part of the deal. This was for peace, for power and money. Aria had been my way to ensure the Famiglia's success, to make sure I'd rule over a stronger Famiglia than my father had.

"You mentioned something Grace said to you," I said, not wanting to consider Aria's feelings for me, or mine. "Something about fucking you bloody." The familiar fury resurfaced, an emotion I could deal with.

"Oh, yeah. She said you'd hurt me, fuck me like an animal, fuck me bloody when she talked to me during our wedding reception. Scared me out of my mind."

No wonder Aria had looked like she'd seen a ghost. I wondered if Grace's words were the main reason why she was so terrified of sleeping with me. Hadn't I shown her that I was going to be gentle with her?

"I think that guy last night almost said the same thing," she added after a moment.

"Before I killed him, he said one of the women who bought dope from him told him you were a skank who needed to be taught a lesson. She gave him cash." I didn't mention the sordid details of his last minutes.

Aria raised her head. "Do you think it was Grace?"

"I'm sure it was her. The description fits, and who else would have an interest in attacking you." I'd have never thought that Grace would go as far, but I'd obviously underestimated her obsession with me.

"What are you going to do?"

"I can't kill her, even if I want to cut her fucking throat—that would cause too much trouble with her father and brother. I'll have to talk to them, though. Tell them they need to put her on a fucking leash or there won't be any more money from us."

"What if they refuse?"

I stroked Aria's spine. She didn't know how much money we shoved into Senator Parker's ass. "They won't. Grace has been fucking things up for a long time. They'll probably ship her off to Europe or Asia for rehab or some shit like that."

Aria leaned up and left a sweet kiss on my mouth. I'd never been kissed like that, never thought it was something I'd like. She was pure sweetness, and she was mine. Again, the image of Rick's filthy hands on her and how he'd have hurt her flashed through my mind, and I almost lost my shit. Aria deserved to be treated like a queen. "I can't stop thinking about what would have happened if Romero and Cesare hadn't been there, if that fucker had gotten you out of the club. The thought of his dirty hands on you makes me want to kill him again. The thought that he might have..."

Aria nodded, but I couldn't read the look in her eyes and then she ducked her head and made it completely impossible. "When Gianna leaves in a few days, you can have me."

Surprise washed over me. Maybe I should have told her that she didn't have to promise me something like that, but I burnt up with the desire to be as close to her as possible, to make her mine.

———————>———————

The second Aria and I emerged from our room around noon, Gianna rushed toward her sister. "Are you okay? I was so worried because you didn't come out of your bedroom." She sent me a quick disapproving glance as if I cared. I kept my hand on Aria's lower back as I led her toward the kitchen. She needed to eat something.

"Can you cook?" I asked the redhead.

Gianna glowered. "Because I'm a woman?"

I cocked an eyebrow. "Your sister is living proof that not all women can cook," I said, stroking Aria's back to soften my words.

Aria glanced up at me with a small laugh, and I knew I'd burn down the world to protect this woman. I'd start with killing my father, even if it meant ruling over a torn Famiglia until I'd removed every single one of my enemies.

Gianna watched us for a moment before she shrugged. "I can try to make pancakes or something like that, but I can't promise anything."

Gianna wasn't a much better cook, but it was edible. Afterwards, I gave Aria and her sister some privacy and went down to Matteo's apartment while Romero guarded the penthouse.

"How's Aria?" Matteo asked when I sank down on his couch.

"Better," I said. "I need to talk to Senator Parker. He needs to send Grace away. If she stays in New York, I'll kill her."

"Father won't like it. You know how much he cares about schmoozing the politicians."

That was the only thing he still did.

Matteo propped his elbows up on his thighs. "Have you thought about how to solve the problem? The Bratva is always an option."

I shook my head. "It would make them too confident. Killing a Capo is a big deal. The Famiglia would appear weak."

Matteo nodded but I could tell that he considered the Bratva our best bet, and he was probably right, but I preferred a less obvious solution. "I think we should go the poison route. Many men in Father's family have suffered from strokes or heart attacks. There are poisons that have the same effect."

"Very few of them are untraceable."

"Most of our options are only traceable if you look for them specifically. Neither Nina nor we will ask for a thorough exam."

"Our uncles might," Matteo said with a twisted grin.

"Then we'll handle them."

"When?"

I'd considered our options. I wanted him gone as fast as possible, but we needed to figure out the perfect timing, not to mention that I still wasn't sure who should put the poison in his drink. "Father's suspicious. We should wait a few days at least. Maybe we can wait until Gottardo or Ermano come for a visit. We can blame them if the poison is detected."

"I assume you don't want to involve Nina."

"I don't trust her. She hates Father and wants him gone, but once he's dead, she might put the blame on us."

Matteo and I discussed a few more details before I grabbed my phone to talk to Father about Grace. As expected, he wasn't fond of the idea of me asking the Senator to banish his daughter. I couldn't wait to kill him.

Matteo came over for dinner that day, to Gianna's dismay, but she was mostly busy keeping a close eye on her sister. I had to give it to the redhead: she was fiercely protective of Aria. It was one of her few character traits I liked.

After dinner, Aria and Gianna disappeared upstairs only to return a few minutes later in bikinis.

Matteo followed his future wife with keen eyes, but I, too, had trouble looking anywhere but at Aria in her tiny pink bikini.

"I really hope you have your eyes firmly focused on your future wife," I muttered. I knew Matteo would never hit on my wife, but I still hated that he saw her this scantily dressed.

"I can't process your words, the blood has left my brain," Matteo said with a chuckle.

Aria sent me a quick smile before she and Gianna walked out onto the roof terrace and stepped into the Jacuzzi.

"We could join them," Matteo said eagerly.

"Yeah, right. You and Gianna in a Jacuzzi half-naked together. That's not going to happen." I motioned toward the kitchen. "Let's grab an espresso."

Matteo reluctantly followed me. I prepared us espresso but my eyes kept returning to Aria, remembering when we'd been in the Jacuzzi.

"You watch her as if you want to devour her," Matteo said.

"You're one to talk. You're eye-fucking Gianna all day, when she isn't even your wife yet."

"Aria *is* your wife and you still don't get more action than me," Matteo taunted.

"Trust me, I'm getting more than you can dream of, and soon…" I stopped myself, realizing I was talking about sex with Aria with my brother. In the past we'd always shared our sexual adventures with each other, but Aria was my wife and I respected her too much to divulge that kind of information.

Matteo chuckled. "Come on, Luca. You've never been like this. I'm your brother. Tell me, how is it to be with one of our girls? Are they too stuck up for blowjobs? I can't imagine Aria loosening up. She doesn't seem like a woman who'd ever suck a dick unless you forced her, and we both know you can't hurt a single golden hair of hers."

Anger shot through me, and I raised a hand in warning. "Don't talk about Aria like that. Ever."

Matteo tilted his head, regarding me curiously. Scowling, I averted my eyes. Fuck it.

"You're very protective of her, and it's definitely not just possessiveness."

My eyes were drawn to my wife once more as she and Gianna chatted and laughed in the Jacuzzi. I felt possessive of Aria, there was no denying it, but it definitely wasn't the extent of my feelings, not even close.

CHAPTER 19

I was fucking ecstatic when Gianna finally disappeared from view on her way to her plane back to Chicago. Aria looked heartbroken. It gave me a strange sense of…unease, because I realized she felt lonely in New York. Aria whirled around and threw herself into my arms, sniffling. I caressed her back, my mind drifting to my plans for the night. They'd hopefully distract Aria from her sadness. "I thought we could grab dinner and then have a relaxing evening."

"Sounds good," she said quietly, but her expression flickered with anxiety. I wasn't sure how to relieve her of her fear. All my life my purpose had been to terrify others. Soothing someone's fear was completely out of my comfort zone.

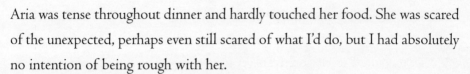

Aria was tense throughout dinner and hardly touched her food. She was scared of the unexpected, perhaps even still scared of what I'd do, but I had absolutely no intention of being rough with her.

"Why don't we head inside?" I suggested.

She gave a small nod.

I wasn't a patient man. I'd never had to wait for anything in my life. I knew she was nervous, but I wanted her tonight; my cock was fucking eager to claim her. We stepped inside and Aria moved toward the liquor cabinet, reaching for the brandy. I grabbed her wrist and pulled her against me. Her eyes widened. "Don't," I said quietly. I didn't want her to be drunk when I claimed her. I needed her 'yes' to be real.

I lifted her into my arms and carried her upstairs, hardly able to wait. I put her down on the bed, my cock straining against my pants as I climbed on top of her, claiming her lips. She tasted like fucking perfection, and I was the only one who'd ever got to taste her. That knowledge filled me with the desperate need to own her completely. I kissed her harder before I drew back and sucked one perfect, firm nipple into my mouth. Fuck. I was so hard. I helped Aria out of her dress then moved lower. I let my eyes trail over her body. She was stunning. She was only mine.

I lowered my face to her panties and pushed a tongue between her perfect pussy lips. Fuck. Perfection. My cock twitched. I drew back, gripped her flimsy panties and ripped them away before I tasted her pussy again. But my need was too fucking huge. I needed to make her mine. Mine alone. I pushed a finger into her and the thought of how it would feel to have her tight walls squeeze my cock almost sent me over the edge. I stood and got out of my clothes.

Aria lay on the bed, blonde hair spread around her, legs parted, revealing her perfect pink pussy. "You're mine," I growled. I'd waited so fucking long for this.

I moved between her legs and parted them, spreading her open for me and lining my cock up with her hot entrance. The sensation of her pussy against my cock was like a revelation. I'd never had sex without a condom before.

Aria's nails sunk into my shoulders, pulling me out of my fog of desire. I glanced down. Her eyes were squeezed shut, her lips pressed together, as she waited for pain. I could feel how tense she was against my cock.

Aria leaned up and pressed her face into my neck, shaking, taking deep breaths.

Her heat beckoned me to bury my cock inside of her, but her trembling body and her tension stopped me. "Aria," I murmured. "Look at me."

She pulled back and opened her eyes, and fear stared back at me. She was completely terrified, and I pounced on her as if she were some whore. I lowered myself until our bodies were pressed up against each other. "I'm an asshole," I rasped as I kissed her temple and cheek.

Those beautiful lips parted in surprise. "Why?" Her voice was a broken whisper.

I'd sworn to be gentle with her, sworn I'd protect her, and now when she needed me to be gentle the most, I acted like a fucking caveman. "You're scared, and I almost lost control. I should know better. I should prepare you properly, and instead I almost shoved my cock into you."

Aria moved under me and let my tip glide over her opening. She gasped fearfully and I exhaled sharply because a dark part of me wanted to shift my hips forward and finish what I'd begun. She was mine for the taking, had been for weeks. I closed my eyes, trying to get a grip on myself. That part of me, the monster, wasn't meant for her. This was Aria, my wife, mine to protect. I would treat her like a queen. I opened my eyes and found her watching me with a mix of fear and confusion. I shifted until my head hovered over her perfect breasts and her pussy was pressed up against my abs.

"You are my wife," I said.

Aria held me gaze and trust shone in her eyes. My fingers closed around her nipples and I tugged lightly the way she liked it. A moan was my reward, but Aria arched at the same time and made her pussy rub against my abs. Too fucking tempting.

"Stop squirming," I said roughly. I was teetering on the edge, my darkness so damn close under my skin that it wouldn't take much to unleash it, and that's not something I'd ever do to Aria. I tugged at her nipple, relishing in Aria's moans as I teased her breasts without the previous hurry. Soon she was breathless and shifting beneath me. I trailed my hand down her ribs and waist, worshipping her with my fingertips before my lips did the same. I bit the soft skin over her hipbone possessively as I kneaded her thighs.

Aria was starting to relax. I parted her legs, laying her open for me. She was glistening, and I pressed a soft kiss against her folds. She let out a small sigh, quivering. I lightly bit her inner thigh. Aria arched up, gasping, and I wedged my palms under her firm ass. Keeping my eyes on her face, I lifted her pussy to my mouth and planted another kiss to the soft flesh.

Aria whimpered, and I repeated the motion. Her eyes opened and they were filled with need. She enjoyed having her pussy kissed like this. My eyes locked on hers. I parted her a bit more and kissed her tight opening, my lips brushing her soft inner folds. Aria's lips parted in a soft moan. Her heady scent reached my nose and I spread her open with my thumbs, revealing her juices. I lapped them up, and she trembled with need and rewarded me with another wave of her sweetness. I loved her taste, and I fucking loved that she responded so eagerly. She grew wetter and wetter as I sucked at her lips lightly. I couldn't take my eyes off her as she moaned and whimpered, as she squeezed her eyes shut and jerked her pussy against me. I circled her opening lightly and her walls clenched. My cock jerked against the mattress, but I needed to be patient, and so I trailed my tongue up, never to her clit.

"Luca, please," she begged, lifting her hips, and fuck, I almost lost it.

"You want this?" I brushed her clit and she moaned.

"Yes."

"Soon," I growled and eased a finger into her slowly. So damn tight. I ran my tongue around my finger and Aria's entrance, then trailed it up to her nub. Aria moaned as I closed my lips gently around her clit and began to suck.

"Tell me when you come," I murmured before I continued my suckling. My finger slid easier in and out of Aria's channel as she grew wetter.

"I'm com—"

I quickly retracted my finger and pushed two fingers in. Fuck, she was tight. Her face flashed with pain and pleasure as her walls clenched around my fingers. I kissed her thigh then groaned from the grip of her walls on my fingers. "You're so fucking tight, Aria. Your muscles are squeezing the life out of my fingers."

Fuck, this shouldn't have excited me as much as it did.

Aria peered down at me, face flushed. I slowly pulled my fingers out a bit but she tensed even more and winced. I slid back in and established a slow, gentle rhythm of my fingers fucking her.

"Relax," I said, but she didn't. "I need to widen you, *principessa.*"

If she was already this tense with only two fingers, getting my cock inside her would be a fucking disaster. I circled her clit with my tongue lightly until she let out a soft sigh, her walls easing their grip around my fingers as she grew even more aroused.

When she relaxed, I pulled my fingers out and moved up, hovering over her. I gently pushed her legs farther apart and lined my cock up with her entrance. My cock looked fucking huge against her pink pussy, and it gave me a thrill, knowing how tightly she'd grip me. She tensed when my tip brushed her opening. I lowered myself and left gentle kisses on her face, hoping it would take some of her fear. "Aria," I rasped. She raised her gaze to mine, blue eyes swirling with anxiety. She wrapped her arms around me, shaking fingers touching my back. She gave me a tense smile. Fuck. I wanted to protect and care for this woman.

I increased the pressure on Aria's entrance, trying to get past her clenched walls, but she was tense. I could have broken through her tension with more force, but that was the last thing I wanted to do. "Relax," I said, cupping her cheek and kissing her lips. "I'm not even in yet."

I ran my fingertips down her side before I gripped her thigh and parted her further for me, hoping it would allow me to enter her more easily. Shifting my hips and gritting my teeth, I slid into her about an inch. She dug her nails into my skin, her face flashing with pain, her body tensing even further in expectation of more pain. The grip of her walls brought a blinding wave of pleasure. Only the look at her pain-stricken face allowed me to stay in control and not seek more of the pleasure her tightness could offer me. Aria whimpered, a sound that sliced cleanly through me. I'd heard cries of agony that had bothered me not a fucking bit, but this. . .

I stopped and started stroking Aria's breasts, hoping it would allow her body to adapt to the penetration.

"You are so beautiful," I whispered into her ear, not even sure where those words came from. I'd never sweet-talked a woman. If anything, I told them how I wanted to fuck them. "So perfect, *principessa*."

My words finally made Aria relax and her eyes shone with gratefulness. She shouldn't have felt that way about me, not when it was me who hurt her, who pushed her past her boundaries because I didn't want to wait any longer to lay claim on her. I knew all that and still I didn't stop, couldn't fucking stop. The need to finally have this woman was too strong, and I was a bastard.

I eased my cock deeper into her and she tensed again. Kissing her, I rasped, "Almost there." It was a fucking lie. I wasn't even halfway in. I moved a hand between us and rubbed her clit, hoping to get her to relax with pleasure.

Aria released a small huff, her lips parting, and hesitant flickers of pleasure showed on her face. Soon Aria softened around me and let out hesitant moans.

I didn't warn her before I thrust the rest of the way into her, breaking through her body's resistance with more force than I'd planned. Aria arched under me, gasping, her eyes closing under the force of the pain. I stilled, overwhelmed by the sensations of her tightness and the look of pain on her face. She pressed up to me, her breathing harsh against my throat, her body trembling.

I slid out slowly, but she choked, "Please don't move."

I froze at the begging note in my wife's voice. I pushed up and nudged her face up. It took a moment before she met my gaze. Her eyes were teary and filled with acute embarrassment. She swallowed hard.

"Does it hurt that much?"

"No, not that much." She winced, tensing even further around my cock, sending a jolt of pleasure through my body. "It's okay, Luca. Just move. I won't be mad at you. You don't have to hold back for me. Just get it over with."

I stared at my wife, realizing how strongly I hated the idea of hurting her. "Do you think I want to use you like that? I can see how fucking painful this is. I've done many horrible things in my life, but I won't add this to my list."

"Why? You hurt people all the time. You don't have to pretend to care for my feelings only because we're married."

How could she think I didn't care about her? I'd never treated anyone like I treated her, never felt this strong protectiveness toward another person. "What makes you think I have to pretend?"

Aria's expression flickered with hope as her eyes searched mine, and the look in them tightened my chest. Fuck, she shouldn't be looking at me like that.

"Tell me what to do."

Her fingers stroked my shoulder blade gently. "Can you hold me close for a while? But don't move." Again the acute embarrassment mingled with a hint of begging as if she still wasn't sure I would ignore her request. I wasn't going to be that kind of monster with her, not today, not ever.

"I won't." I kissed her lips then lowered myself completely. The movement caused her walls to cling tightly to my cock and, for a second, I was sure I'd go insane from the force of the sensations. Instead I focused on Aria and carefully wrapped her in my arms, holding her tightly. I kissed her again, slowly, gently, so unlike any kiss I'd ever had before. Aria's closeness, the feel of her body softening under my gentleness, the tender trust in her expression…it filled my chest with a strange sense of peace and warmth. I trailed my palm down her side and hip then back up. Shifting, I brought my hand between us to tease her breasts, hoping it would relax her. She was beautifully responsive as usual, and I felt her body's gradual softening, growing used to the intrusion. Despite my need to move, to feel Aria's walls sliding around me, I stayed still. Aria arched when I flicked her nipple and she pulled away from my lips. Her breathing was ragged and her lips were swollen from our kiss. She was so fucking sexy.

Aria smiled softly. "Can you still…?"

I almost laughed but stifled the reaction. Instead, I carefully moved my hips, allowing Aria to feel my boner shift inside of her. Surprise crossed her face.

"I told you I'm not a good man. Even though I know you're hurting, I still have a boner because I'm inside you," I told her because it was the truth. If I were a good man, I wouldn't have pushed her, would have given her all the time she needed, but I was a goddamn bastard, even when I tried not to be one with her.

Aria stroked my back. "Because you want me," she whispered. There was a hint of uncertainty in her voice. How could she have any doubt about it?

"I've never wanted anything more in my life." Again the truth. A truth that I shouldn't have voiced aloud because it gave Aria power, because it showed her how much I burnt up for her closeness, and not just the sex. Fuck, not just the sex.

"Can we go slow?" Aria asked, a small, apologetic smile tugging at her lips. As if she had reason to apologize for that.

"Of course, *principessa*," I said firmly. I regarded her expression closely as I began to move, making sure to keep my motion as controlled and gentle as possible. My muscles quivered from the effort it took. It was something alien to me, something I'd never done before.

Aria released a small breath, her brows drawing together. Discomfort, but not as bad as before.

I never took my eyes off her as I slid in and out slowly. My pleasure coiled tighter and tighter, causing my leg muscles to quiver. My body screamed at me to go faster, but I shoved down my own need. Another first. Aria wasn't the only one who shared her firsts with me. Only mine were a bit different. I repositioned my knees and shifted the angle. She jerked with a gasp.

I fell out of rhythm. "Did that hurt?"

Aria gave a small shake of her head. "No, it felt good."

Finally. I angled my thrust the same way, then kissed Aria's parted lips, tasting her, needing her even closer when we were already closer than I'd ever been with someone before. The pulsating need in my balls, in my entire body, turned into a low burn of desire. Aria shifted slightly under me and I could feel her body becoming a bit tenser, and definitely not because she was going to come. "Are you okay?" I asked.

Embarrassment crossed her flushed face. "How long until you...?"

"Not long, if I go a bit faster."

I wasn't sure if Aria's body would be able to handle it. Not that I would slam into her like a fucking animal, but this level of gentle sex wasn't going to make me come. Aria nodded, giving me the permission I needed.

I pushed up onto my elbows and sped up, hitting deeper and harder. My balls soon began to clench, the familiar pulse of desire returning. Aria clung to me, her body coiling even tighter, squeezing my cock. Fuck, this felt like paradise. "Aria?" I ground out when she flinched after another thrust.

"Keep going. Please. I want you to come."

A goddamn bastard, that's what I was, but I was beyond stopping now. My balls tightened, waves of pleasure radiating out from my cock, and I snapped, groaning, my thrusts becoming jerky as I shot my cum into her. My cock twitched and twitched as if I hadn't had sex in years. A strong wave of possessiveness burnt through me, but beneath it was a warmer emotion that was entirely foreign. I kissed Aria's throat, feeling her pulse race under my lips. Her warm breath fanned over my skin, ragged like mine. Her palms stroked my back, fingers soft and trembling. My wife. The woman I'd protect at any cost, even if it meant killing my father.

I closed my eyes for a moment, relishing in the feel of her pliable body under mine, in her sweet scent now mingling with mine, and a darker note of sex. Mine. Goddamn mine.

I carefully slid out of her and stretched out on the bed, then tugged her toward me, wrapping my arms around her. I did it without thinking, wanting her close. I knew she would need my closeness now, but when I stroked her flushed face, I realized it wasn't the only reason why I held her in my arms. She wanted to see the good in me when no one had ever bothered, and I wasn't entirely sure there was something inside of me worthy of the label 'good.'

Aria's eyes widened then darted down. In my after-sex stupor, it took me a second to realize why. My cum. Kissing her temple, I slid out of bed. "I'll get a washcloth."

I moved into the bathroom and my eyes landed on my cock. It was covered in blood. Aria had been so damn tight. It had been thrilling and torturous at once. I cleaned myself and soaked a washcloth with warm water before I returned to the bedroom, finding her staring at the bloodstains on the sheets. "There's much more blood than the fake scene you created during our wedding night," she whispered.

I sank down beside my wife and gently parted her legs. Her pussy was swollen and smeared with blood. The sight tightened my chest because it was another reminder of how painful it had been for her. Giving pain was something I'd always been good at. I pressed the cloth to her sore flesh, earning a gasp.

I kissed her knee, fucking relieved that this wasn't our wedding night, that I wouldn't have to present these sheets. "You were a lot tighter than I thought," I said quietly. The red in Aria's cheeks became more pronounced. I threw away the washcloth before I pressed my palm against her lower belly. Her muscles contracted under the touch and I had to resist the urge to slide lower again. Aria wouldn't be ready for sex in a while. "How bad is it?" I asked.

Aria stretched out on the mattress before me. "Not that bad. How can I complain when you're covered in scars from knife and bullet wounds?"

I shook my head. That wasn't the point. She wasn't meant to ever experience pain. I wouldn't fucking allow it. "We're not talking about me. I want to know how you feel, Aria. On a scale of one to ten, how much does it hurt?"

"Now? Five?"

Fuck. Five now? I'd hoped for five during. I laid down beside her and wrapped an arm around her. She regarded me with that hint of shyness and a flicker of relief. Relief because she got her first time over and done with. Not the most ego-boosting thought. "And during?"

Aria looked away, licking her lips. "If ten is for the worst pain I've ever felt, then eight." There was a note to her voice that told me she was still not telling the truth. Damn it.

"The truth."

"Ten."

I stroked her belly. Aria's admittance didn't sit well with me, even if I reminded myself that she had a different pain level than I did. I never wanted to be the one who caused her that much pain. "Next time will be better." I hoped it would be. I wasn't sure how to make this easier for her. She was petite and nervous, and I was an asshole that burned with the need to have her.

Aria gave me an apologetic look. "I don't think I can again so soon."

"I didn't mean now. You'll be sore for a while." I still wanted her, maybe more than ever. Claiming her definitely hadn't sated my desire for her, or the need to have her as close as possible. It was unnerving.

"On a scale of one to ten, how fast and hard did you go? The truth," Aria asked in a teasing voice.

I considered lying, but for some reason I didn't want to. I wanted Aria to know the truth about every aspect of me, the bad, the worst. I wasn't even sure why. I'd never bothered sharing anything with anyone except for Matteo.

"Two," I said, watching her closely as I did. She tensed, shock flashing across her face. I'd gone as gentle with her as I was capable of. I'd never been this close to someone while sex, never gone as slow, or tried to pay attention to a woman's facial expressions to make sure she was okay.

"Two?"

"We have time. I'll go as gentle as you need me to." Fuck, and it was the honest to God truth. If Aria needed me to, I'd go the vanilla route for months.

Aria smiled in a way that went straight through me. It was a look I wanted to see as often as possible. "I can't believe Luca—The Vise—Vitiello said 'gentle.'"

My men wouldn't believe it if anyone told them I could be gentle. And my father, my fucking father, he'd lose his shit. He'd demand I fucking grow a pair and beat my wife into submission. He'd never understand that it didn't show strength to abuse someone who couldn't protect themselves, someone meant to be under your protection. A man should know whom to treat with care and whom to crush. I touched Aria's cheek and leaned in, murmuring, "It'll be our secret." It had to be. Nobody could know. If my father considered Aria a risk to my ruthlessness, he'd kill her immediately. I'd end his miserable life, would show him that the same sadistic streak he had ran deeply in my veins, but it wouldn't save Aria.

Nothing would ever happen to her. Not as long as I was alive. I'd kill anyone who dared to consider hurting her.

Aria nodded, her expression softening. "Thanks for being gentle. I never thought you would be."

"Believe me, nobody's more surprised about this than me," I said. Gentleness wasn't in my nature, never had been, and I doubted it would ever be something anyone else but Aria would get to experience.

Aria turned to me and pressed against my side, her head on my shoulder. I tightened my hold on her. She let out a small sigh as if I'd given her a fucking gift for allowing closeness. I lightly stroked the soft skin of her waist, feeling a sense of calm.

"You've never been gentle to someone?"

I wrecked my brain for a moment in my life when I'd shown a softer side of me, but the only memory I came up with was when I was a boy of five. I'd found my mother crying in her bed and had walked over to her even though I wasn't allowed in her bedroom. I had been scared by her wailing and had touched her hand to stop her. My mother had jerked her hand away and

Father had come in a moment later. He'd dragged me out and beaten me for trying to cater to the silly whims of a woman. "No. Our father taught Matteo and me that any kind of gentleness was a weakness. And there was never any room in my life for it," I said. All the sentimental baggage from my past wasn't something I wanted to lay in the open, not even to my wife.

"What about the girls you were with?" Aria asked. Her voice shook with a hint of worry and jealousy. I peered down at her blond crown, her naked body stretched out beside mine, elegant, breathtakingly gorgeous, *mine*. It was understandable that she worried about other women after the Grace incident, but I didn't have the slightest intention to ever touch another women again, and all the women of my past had meant nothing. I didn't even remember most of their names or faces.

"They were a means to an end. I wanted to fuck, so I looked for a girl and fucked her. It was hard and fast, definitely not gentle. I mostly fucked them from behind so I didn't have to look them in the eyes and pretend I gave a shit about them."

Aria surprised me by kissing my Famiglia tattoo, her lips soft. I held her even tighter, not sure how to react to her loveliness, her innocent tenderness. It wasn't something I'd ever been on the receiving end of. I wanted to give her something as meaningful in return, and there was only one way I could do it. "The only person who could have taught me how to be gentle was my mother," I said, even as the words felt like shrapnel in my throat. I didn't like talking about her, or even remembering her. "But she killed herself when I was nine."

"I'm sorry," Aria whispered, tilting her head back to meet my gaze. She pressed her soft palm against my cheek. No one had ever done something like that before Aria, and whenever I'd witnessed that sort of affectionate gesture with other people, I'd wondered why the hell anyone would touch a cheek or would want their cheek touched when they could have their cock sucked. A fucking cheek. But this felt good. Not as good as the other, but damn good anyway. Aria's eyes held compassion, but I didn't want to dwell in the past.

"Does it still hurt?" I asked, and when it became clear that she wasn't sure what I was talking about, I brushed my fingertips over her abdomen.

Aria blushed, golden lashes fluttering in embarrassment. "Yeah, but talking helps."

"How does it help?" It seemed impossible for mere words to do that. When I was in agony, I definitely didn't want to talk to anyone, much less listen to anyone's rambling, even though Matteo mostly ignored my wishes.

"It distracts me," Aria admitted, her eyes still on mine. It was the longest she'd ever held my gaze, and I had to admit I enjoyed it. "Can you tell me more about your mother?"

There were so many things I remembered as if they'd happened yesterday, but none of them were happy. I wasn't sure if my mother and I had shared a single happy memory, if anything hadn't been tainted by my father's brutal shadow. "My father hit her. He raped her. I was young, but I understood what was going on. She couldn't bear my father anymore, so she decided to slice her wrists and overdose on dope."

Aria shivered. I wasn't sure if it was because she imagined what my mother had gone through. I was fairly sure Aria had worried it would be her fate as well. The mere idea that I could do to Aria what my father had done to my mother, that Aria would lie under me broken and terrified, made me want to take a shower.

"She shouldn't have left you and Matteo alone."

This was what got to her? Aria was too kind, too good for me, and as usual she barreled straight through another one of my walls. I'd spent all my life building them, strong as steal, and here she was taking them down without realizing it. "I found her."

Aria sucked in her breath and those blue eyes filled with tears. Tears for me. "You found your mother after she'd cut her wrists?"

Emotions squeezed my chest, but I shoved them down, deep deep down where they belonged. "That was actually the first body I saw. Of course it wasn't the last," I said, glad that my voice was firm and hard.

"This is horrible. You must have been terrified. You were only a boy."

I had been a child and I hadn't been. My life had always been filled with blood and violence, with the cries of my mother at night. "It made me tough. At some point, every boy has to lose his innocence. The mafia isn't a place for the weak."

"Emotions aren't a weakness."

I searched Aria's eyes. The softness and compassion in them were already a risk. Those were emotions I couldn't risk, definitely not in public, and even behind closed doors they weren't wise. I needed to be tough as steal, feared and brutal, if I wanted to rule over the Familgia one day, and until then I had to keep my bastard of a father off my back. "Yes, they are. Enemies always aim where they can hurt you most."

Father would use Aria against me in his fucking mind games if he thought she was more to me than a pretty fuck thing I could dominate and brutalize. He posed as much of a risk for my wife as the Bratva, maybe more because my options to protect her from him were limited for now.

"And where would the Bratva aim if they wanted to hurt you?" Aria asked softly, sounding hopeful and curious at once. My gaze traced the tender lines of her face.

Since Matteo was strong enough to defend himself, there had been no one my enemies could have used as leverage against me. They knew I didn't give a fuck about anyone, only the Famiglia. My life was devoted to the mafia, my only goal in life to become Capo. I had been raised with only this purpose.

Everything else was supposed to be irrelevant, especially a woman. Women could be replaced. That's what Father had taught Matteo and me, and it was something he'd lived by. It hadn't taken him long to replace Mother with Nina.

The look in Aria's eyes hammered away at another of my walls, but I couldn't let her. I turned off the lights, needing the dark to hide the emotion in her face. "They won't ever find out," I said.

Aria released a small breath, deflating against me. She needed to stop wishing for something I couldn't give her, wouldn't give her for both our sakes. It would have been easy to crush her hopes, to nip her emotions in the bud. A few cruel words that always came so easily for me. *I got what I wanted, stop the fucking emotional bullshit. All I give a fuck about is your tight pussy milking my cock. You're nothing to me but spread legs to relieve tension.* Those words would have cut Aria to the bone, they would have stopped her from prying past my walls ever again. She would have believed them to be true, no doubt, because they were words more fitting to the man I was than the sweet nothings I'd murmured while taking her virginity. Everyone would believe them to reflect the true nature of my feelings for the woman beside me. The words lingered on my tongue, needed to be said to protect Aria and my claim to power, but I couldn't get them past my lips. I couldn't fucking lie to Aria like that, couldn't crush her like that.

But most of all, I couldn't bear the thought of how she'd look at me afterwards, of how she'd never give me that small, trusting smile again.

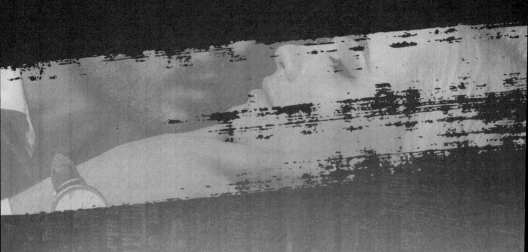

CHAPTER 20

I woke with Aria pressed up against me, her forehead leaning against my chest, our legs scissoring. Her stirring had woken me. She tried to untangle herself from my hold without waking me, which was a futile endeavor. My sleep was light, and I woke at the smallest sound or movement. "What's wrong?" I rumbled.

"Need to go to the bathroom," Aria said in a sleepy voice.

I loosened my iron grip around her and she pulled back, peering up at me. I watched her through half-closed eyes. Aria bit her lip, smiling uncertainly. She was shy because of what we'd done last night.

I rubbed my thumb over her swollen lips, watching the blush bloom on her cheeks. Slowly she climbed out of bed, her movements stiff. My eyes followed her beautiful ass as she walked toward the bathroom. Her gait was slightly off from discomfort. I was glad for the reminder because my cock was already erecting a tent with the covers. Groaning, I reached for my phone on the nightstand. It was only eight, and Romero was supposed to arrive at nine to guard Aria.

I sent him a short text, telling him to be there at twelve, then another text to Matteo informing him that business would have to wait until later. Then I shut off my phone, not in the mood for my brother's annoying questions just yet.

Aria returned ten minutes later, her face twisting occasionally.

"Sore?" I asked, even if it was a rhetorical question. Even someone less familiar with the signs of pain would have seen that she was in discomfort.

Aria stopped in front of the bed, nose crinkling in shame. "Yeah. I'm sorry."

"Why are you sorry?"

Aria stretched out beside me, her eyes briefly darting down to my groin then back to my face. There was no way I could have hidden my desire for her, but that didn't mean I'd disregard her body's needs.

"I thought you might want to do it again, but I don't think I can."

I caressed her ribs and side. "I know. I didn't expect you to be ready so soon." Aria's skin pimpled under my ministrations. I stroked her belly then the edge of her lovely blond triangle. She held her breath. "I could lick you if you're up for it." Desire consumed my insides at the idea of burying myself between her thighs.

Aria swallowed. "I don't think that's a good idea."

I leaned back, but I didn't take my eyes off her. Her nipples puckered under my attention.

Aria leaned over me, her gaze lingering on my chest and abdomen. Her expression wasn't sexual, so she wasn't admiring my muscles, but I knew they turned her on, just like Aria's body drove me raving mad with desire. I reached up and stroked the pad of my thumb over her pink nipple. Every inch of Aria was perfection, not just the outside but also her sweet persona. I'd been with so many beautiful women who'd fulfilled my every fucking desire. Women who had never known a single truth about me, women who had never wanted to know more than what I could give them.

I had taken everything I desired without a fucking care for their emotions, had chosen them by their looks, the size of their tits or shape of their lips, by the skill of their tongue or willingness to take it up their ass.

Aria was the first woman I hadn't chosen for myself, and I probably wouldn't have ever chosen. If Father had left the choice up to me to pick an Outfit girl, I'd have chosen someone else because, from the first moment I'd seen Aria, I'd wanted to protect her. Even back then I'd known deep down that marrying her posed a fucking risk to everything I'd built. Marrying Gianna would have been the safe choice because, with her personality, I wouldn't have had trouble to be an asshole, to keep up my monstrous mask. With Aria it was a losing game. The most dangerous game I'd ever played.

What the fuck was she doing to me? "Your breasts are fucking perfect," I said into the silence, needing to break this insane moment.

Aria brushed her fingertips over a scar on my stomach. "Where did you get this scar?"

Safer terrain. "I was eleven." The memories slithered up, clawing their way through all the other, many worse memories.

Shock flashed across Aria's face. She knew what story was coming. Everyone knew the story. The boy who killed his first man at eleven, even then a monster. His father's son. Maybe people had been scared of me even before then, but the first time I noticed how other people regarded me like someone to be wary of was after that first kill.

"The Famiglia wasn't as united as it is now," I began and told her how everything had started, how I'd become a Made Man, a killer. Even back then I hadn't felt guilt over killing another human being. Killing my father could rip the Famiglia apart again if I wasn't careful.

Aria watched me with an intent expression, lacking the sick fascination or reverent fear usually directed my way when this story was told.

"That was your first murder, right?"

"Yeah. The first of many." I wasn't exactly sure how many people I'd killed, not just because it wasn't always clear if Matteo's or my bullet ended someone in the chaos of a mass shooting, but also because at some point I'd stopped counting. What did it matter if I'd killed twenty, fifty or one-hundred?

Aria's fingers still stroked my scar, but I doubted she noticed. She was completely focused on my face. "When did you kill again?"

"That same night. After that first man, I told Matteo to hide in my closet. He protested, but I was bigger and locked him in. By then I'd lost quite a bit of blood, but I was high on adrenaline and could still hear shooting downstairs, so I headed for the noise with my gun. My father was in a shooting match with two attackers. I came down the stairs but nobody paid me any attention, and then I shot one of them from behind. My father took the other down with a shot in the shoulder."

"Why didn't he kill him?"

Oh, Aria, so innocent. "He wanted to question him to find out if there were other traitors in the Famiglia."

"So what did he do with the guy while he took you to the hospital?"

As if my father would have ever stopped torturing someone to get me medical help, much less take me to a hospital.

"Don't tell me he didn't take you."

"He called the Doc of the Famiglia, told me to put pressure on the wound and went ahead and started torturing the guy for information."

Aria shook her head slowly. "You could have died. Some things need to be treated in a hospital. How could he do that?"

"The Famiglia comes first," I said. It was a truth I lived by. It was something we demanded of our soldiers and something Matteo and I had to live by as well. "We never take our injured to a hospital. They ask too many questions and the police get involved, and it's an admittance of weakness. And my father had to make sure the traitor spoke before he got a chance to kill himself."

"So you agree with what he did? You would have watched someone you love bleed to death so you could protect the Famiglia and your power."

Love.

Someone you love.

Did Aria really think I was capable of love? That men like my father or I had it in us to harbor that kind of pure emotion? Maybe every child was born with the need to love and be loved, but I'd been raised without that notion and eventually it had been burnt out of me with violence, betrayal and cruelty.

"My father doesn't love me. Matteo and I are his guarantee for power and a way to keep the family name alive. Love has nothing to do with it."

Aria's face scrunched up, despair flashing in those baby blues. "I hate this life. I hate the mafia. Sometimes I wish there was a way to escape."

My body grew tense at her admittance. "From me?" I asked, holding back the fury as well as pain the idea brought me.

"No. From this world. Have you never wanted to live a normal life?" She tilted her head and again searched my eyes, looking for a flicker of good or hope. She needed to understand who I was, who I'd always be.

"No. This is who I am, who I was born to be, Aria. It's the only life I know, the only life I want. For me to commit to a normal life would be like an eagle living in a small cage in a zoo." Fuck, I'd never even considered a normal life an option. I'd never dreamed of going to college, of having a normal job. I wasn't even sure what I could have become if I wasn't a Made Man. For as long as I could remember, becoming a Made Man, becoming Capo had been my goal. Nothing else had ever mattered. I'd finished high school, more for appearances than anything else, and only because Father's influence and money had made the school board ignore my absence rate. "Your marriage to me shackles you to the mafia. Blood and death will be your life as long as I live," I said at last, hating having to crush Aria's wishes and hopes but knowing it was better early on.

She'd always be mine, had no choice in the matter because I wouldn't give her one. If she settled for what she had instead of hoping for more, if she resigned herself to a marriage of respect instead of love, then maybe she could survive this life and her bond to me.

The thought didn't sit well with me, but entertaining silly emotional fantasies had been beaten out of me as a kid.

Aria nodded, but she didn't look crushed. She actually looked determined. "Then so be it. I'll go where you go, no matter how dark the path."

And, in true Aria style, all innocent and caring, she blasted through another wall I had absolutely no intention of lowering, taking with her my goddamn determination to make her settle for a bond of respect and convenience. I kissed her harshly, burning up with a myriad of conflicting emotions, most of them entirely foreign and utterly insane.

Aria wanted a fucking fairy-tale, a love story worthy of a goddamn Hollywood blockbuster. She was determined to get it, and I wasn't sure if I was strong enough to deny her.

———————>✕———————

Aria and I went down into the kitchen together. It was a few minutes before noon, and I had to meet Matteo and drive to the Sphere afterward. I hadn't intended to stay in bed for so long, but after last night I felt the urge to keep

Aria close for as long as possible.

Romero wasn't there yet when Aria searched the fridge for something we could manage to turn into something edible and I prepared coffee. My eyes kept returning to her. She was dressed in a white summer dress with colorful dots, her hair still damp from our shower, her feet bare, and humming a soft tune I didn't recognize. She looked as if a weight had been lifted off her shoulders.

When the cups were filled with coffee, I set one down beside Aria, who'd assembled two bowls with fruit and cereal. Taking a sip from my coffee, I slid my arm around her waist from behind. Aria leaned back at once, the back of her head resting on my sternum as she peered up at me.

"You look happy and relieved," I said quietly.

She bit her lip with a small laugh. "I am."

"Why?" I asked in a low voice. I couldn't stop touching her and only barely stopped myself from burying my nose in her blond hair.

She sighed. "Promise not to be angry?"

I frowned. "That's not something I can promise, but trust me when I say I have a hard time being angry with you."

Aria smiled. "I'm just relieved that it's over."

My eyebrows climbed my forehead. "You realize we'll have sex again."

Aria giggled, nudging me with her elbow. "I know. But I'm relieved that you finally made me yours..." Her voice dipped, her eyes flitting down to my nose in embarrassment.

That made two of us, but coming from Aria it sounded as if she'd survived a painful medical treatment, not sex. My confusion must have been plain as day, because Aria continued without prompting. "I was so scared because I wasn't sure what to expect, scared of the unknown, especially because I wasn't sure if you'd be gentle with me...but now I know I don't have to be scared of being with you."

I cupped her face and kissed her. "You won't ever have to be scared of me, Aria, not in bed and not outside of it. I'll always be gentle with you."

I was utterly fucked.

The elevator binged. My eyes darted to the clock in the fridge. Point noon. Romero was on time as always. I stepped back from Aria, straightened and took another sip from my coffee. When the doors to the elevator slipped open and Romero stepped out followed by my pain in the ass brother, my face was back to my emotionless mask. Aria watched me, then took her own coffee and walked over to the barstool. Her gait was slightly off and, of course, both Romero and Matteo noticed. We had been taught by years as Made Men to notice the slightest shift in demeanor of others because it usually meant danger.

Aria noticed their attention and turned bright red, her eyes darting to me, then quickly down to her hands clutching the cup. A smirk curled my lips. She was too fucking cute when she was embarrassed. Romero narrowed his eyes in confusion, but Matteo gave me his fucking shark grin. "I see you finally took a stroll through undiscovered land," he said.

Aria set her cup down with a clang, her expression falling in open horror.

I was going to kill Matteo. "Why don't you keep your fucking mouth shut?" I growled. Seething, I regarded Romero, trying to gauge if he'd understood Matteo's stupid comment. Romero's expression was carefully blank, but he wasn't fooling me. He knew exactly what Matteo meant, especially considering Aria's behavior. Damn it.

"Will you have breakfast?" Aria asked into the tense silence, nodding towards the bowl with cereal.

"No time," I snapped, regretting the sharpness in my tone when Aria jumped. My anger wasn't directed at her. Fuck. And in front of Romero and Matteo, I couldn't even make it up to her. I walked over to her, barring her from view with my body, then bent down. Matteo and Romero would only see me acting all possessive and kissing my young wife after I'd claimed her. "We'll have dinner tonight," I murmured in her ear, lightly rubbing her lips with my thumb before I pulled back.

Aria gave a small nod. My expression was stone when I turned back to Romero and my brother. Matteo looked like he was close to bursting out laughing. One day I was going to drown him in the Hudson river.

With a last glance at Romero, knowing I'd have to confront him later, I stalked into the elevator. Matteo leaned beside me and, the second the door closed us in, his mouth pulled wide. "Aria finally allowed you to pop her cherry?"

I glowered.

He shrugged. "Come on. The way she acted it was so obvious you'd dipped your cock into virgin waters."

"Careful," I warned.

He shook his head with a disbelieving laugh. "No sharing naughty tidbits. Protective husband mode. And waiting for your virgin bride to be ready before you claim her. If I didn't know you, I'd say you have a soft spot for your little wife."

"Why don't you scream it from the fucking rooftops or, better yet, announce it to our goddamn father so he can use Aria to keep me in check? He'll think I'm growing soft, or that I care about her, and we both know he'll make sure that doesn't happen."

"And do you?" Matteo asked carefully.

"Do I what?" I growled, all my defenses shooting up into place.

"Care for her. We both know there's no way you're going soft. You're a brutal fucker."

Staring Matteo down was futile. Everyone else would have cowered under the force of my anger, but he held my gaze. The elevator doors slid open and I staggered into the parking garage. Fuck this shit. This marriage was supposed to bring peace and keep the fucking Outfit off our backs, not turn me into a fool.

"I take it that's a yes," Matteo said from close behind me.

I turned and gripped his shoulder in a hard grip. "This isn't a fucking game, Matteo. I don't want people to think they could use Aria against me, so keep your mouth shut for once."

"Fuck," he muttered. "You do care about the girl. Do you—"

"Just shut up, all right?" I said, losing my patience.

Matteo gave a sharp nod, surprising me. "You know I won't tell anyone you're being a decent human being to your little wife."

I narrowed my eyes at him. "You as good as told Romero that I haven't fucked my wife until last night."

"You know Romero, he won't tell a living soul, probably not even the ghost of his father."

Trusting people with my secrets, especially if they held the potential to destroy everything, wasn't something I liked to do, but now I had to rely on Aria, Romero and Matteo to keep their silence.

Matteo hit my shoulder. "Stop being a pussy. Everything's going to work out. People fear you too much to even consider the possibility that those sheets were faked. You are the Vise." His grin made me sigh, but the knot in my chest loosened. "And now tell me, how was it?"

I gave him a look. "I'll pretend you didn't ask that."

"I can ask again."

I went around my car and got in.

"Give me at least some pointers for when I'll have to deflower Gianna!" Matteo bellowed then laughed.

I gave him the finger then revved the engine and drove off. He could take his fucking bike.

———✕———

Matteo kept trying to extract information from me about my night with Aria all day, but he eventually gave up when I ignored him. Threats and anger only spurred him on. When I returned home that night, Aria and Romero were sitting outside on the roof terrace, playing cards.

I motioned at Romero to come inside and he did so at once. "I want a word with you."

Romero nodded, his expression carefully blank. I was fairly sure he knew why I cornered him.

"It's about what Matteo said this morning. You know me, but some people might not understand that I'll kill every fucker who takes me for weak."

Romero shook his head. "I didn't hear anything."

I narrowed my eyes. "Cut the bullshit. You're one of my best men. You know exactly what Matteo meant."

"I've never been a fan of the bloody sheets tradition. A man shouldn't have the goal to make his wife bleed."

"But it's our tradition and you know why."

Romero inclined his head, then he met my gaze. "I always respected you, Luca, and for treating your wife the way a woman should be treated, I respect you even more. You'll be the best Capo the Famiglia has ever seen."

I didn't say anything. Romero had always been the man I trusted most beside Matteo and Cesare, and one day I'd give him the recognition he deserved and make him Captain. Fuck tradition in that regard.

———————✕———————

I waited two days even though it almost killed me not to touch Aria, but I could tell how tender she still felt after her first time, and I didn't want to make it worse acting like a fucking horny bastard. That evening, we sat outside on the terrace and enjoyed the warm summer air.

I absent-mindedly stroked Aria's side, my thumb grazing her rib, feeling calm and at peace, and trying to remember if I'd ever felt anything close to it.

"I never thought I would like New York."

I peered down at her in surprise. "You like it?"

She gave a nod. "It's almost peaceful up here."

"If you ignore the honking," I said.

She laughed. "It's not that bad. I really love the view, and it's not like I ever lived in the countryside. Chicago is busy as well."

"I'm glad you're coming to terms with my city."

"Your city," Aria said, a smile in her voice, looking up at me. "It's strange to think that you'll be ruling over the East Coast, that I'll be the wife of a Capo."

I found it far stranger that I was sitting on my terrace with my wife as if it were meant to be like this. "With your beauty, you must have known from an early age that you'd be given to a man of power."

Aria pursed her lips. "I knew. People never stopped telling me so, but I never thought I'd be given to a future Capo. An Underboss, yes."

"I hear a few Outfit members would have preferred you at Dante's side," I said, my voice tense with possessiveness.

Aria laughed. "The Golden Couple rumor." She shook her head. "You and I were already engaged when he was looking for a new wife."

"Would you have preferred marrying him?" I couldn't keep the jealousy from my voice.

Aria blinked and then she burst out laughing in earnest. My own mouth pulled into a smile watching her. "No," she got out. "He always terrified me with his coldness."

"Good," I murmured as I pressed a kiss to Aria's temple. She lowered her head to my shoulder.

"Did you have anyone in mind for marriage before me?"

"No," I said without hesitation. "I never cared about marriage. I knew I'd be given someone from a high-ranking family."

"Not very romantic, is it?" she whispered.

"Mafia isn't really a place for romantic notions."

Aria was silent for a moment. "But this feels romantic."

She was right. I didn't have any experience with romance, but this moment felt right.

I kept stroking Aria's side. Her breathing deepened slowly and, for a moment, I thought she'd fallen asleep, but then she shifted and peered up at me. She leaned forward, kissing me gently. I cupped her cheek and sought her mouth, tasting her. Our kiss was slow and deep, our tongues sliding over each other without hurry. Soon Aria began rocking her hips almost imperceptibly, and my cock stood to attention. "Let's go inside," I rasped. Aria nodded, biting her lip. I caught the hint of anxiety behind the apparent need.

"No sex," I promised.

I lifted her into my arms and carried her inside then upstairs into our bedroom, where I lowered her on the mattress and covered her with my body. My lips found hers once more and I kissed her until she rocked her hips up against my leg. Slowly, savoring every second of uncovering inch over inch of her skin, I pulled down her pants then lifted her shirt over her head. The lacy underwear allowed me to see her pink nipples and the enticing golden triangle between her thighs. "Fucking gorgeous," I groaned before I lowered my head and sucked her breast into my mouth.

Aria gasped, squeezing her legs together. I took my time with her breasts, sucking and nibbling before I helped her out of her bra. Then I bent over her panties and parted her legs. I pressed a kiss to the delicate fabric over her folds. Aria moaned softly. I kissed the same spot then a bit lower. Soon Aria's panties stuck to her pussy with her arousal. I hooked my index finger in the garment and tugged it aside, revealing her pink lips. They were still slightly red, tender and sore. I sucked one lip into my mouth, earning a delicious gasp.

Dragging the panties down her legs, I trailed kisses over her skin. Then I pushed to my feet and got out of my own clothes. Aria watched me with hooded eyes, her legs closed, still shy about presenting herself to me. "Let's try something new," I told her.

I stretched out on my back and Aria frowned. "Kneel over me. Then I can lick you and you can blow me."

A fierce blush stained Aria's cheeks at my words, but she knelt and straddled my chest. Gripping her hips, I hoisted her closer to me so that her pussy was spread out before me like a delicious treat. Aria was a bit stiff, probably from self-consciousness about being exposed like this to me. But good lord, she didn't need to be. The sight of her pink lips and her perfectly shaped butt was like a fucking shot of pleasure straight into my veins.

Aria giggled. "You twitched."

"Because my mouth waters just imagining tasting your glistening lips, *principessa.*"

Her pussy clenched and I couldn't help but smile smugly, knowing that my words had turned her on. Aria loved it when I talked to her even when she was still very quiet.

I cupped her ass cheeks then leaned forward to feast on her, dragging my tongue over her slit, parting those pink lips. Aria moaned then lowered her head and took my tip into her mouth, sucking lightly. I groaned against her.

"Your stubble scratches," she whispered, then moaned again when I took a long lick.

"You want me to stop?"

"No," she gasped. I used the friction of my beard to tease her clit and Aria gasped again. Soon she arched back, presenting her pussy to me. I parted her and stroked my tongue lightly over her tender opening until she softened. Then I gently eased my tongue into her. I began to fuck her with my tongue as my thumb rubbed her clit. Fuck, I couldn't wait to sheath my cock inside her again. I thrust my hips upwards lightly into Aria's warm mouth. She was already so much better at this, trying to match my thrusts, and squeezing my cock with her fingers.

Aria tensed when she finally came, thrusting her pussy into my face, and I squeezed her ass encouragingly, loving to see her loosen up. She stopped sucking my cock as she moaned and helplessly shivered on top of me. Rubbing her back and ass, I rasped, "Turn around, *principessa*. I want to look at you when I come in your mouth."

Aria climbed off me then knelt between my legs, her cheeks flushed, both from her orgasm and my words. She gripped me then lowered her mouth back to my throbbing dick. I groaned when I watched my thick tip slip past her pink lips. Aria's hair curtained half of her face, and I pushed it aside to see her. "Look at me," I ordered.

Aria's eyes flashed up, her cheeks turning pink. I guided her head gently to show her the angle and pace I wanted. She averted her eyes again and I didn't push her, knowing it would take time for her to grow bolder. Soon my thrusts became jerky until I came with a groan. Aria's moves became uncoordinated as she tried to swallow around my tip. She pulled back and hesitantly licked her lips. I was still cupping her head and, like she'd done before Aria tilted her head, pressing it against my palm. She crawled up to me and I pulled her against my chest. "Am I getting better?" Aria asked with a small laugh.

My brows drawing together, I peered down at her, but she wasn't looking at me, instead at the hand tracing my stomach.

"Better at giving me head?" I asked with a chuckle.

Aria nodded. "I know I wasn't any good the first few times, and I'm probably still not very good, but I want to get better..."

"You're perfect," I said, sliding my hand along the curve of her body.

Aria gave me an indignant look. "I'm nowhere near perfect."

"Aria, I didn't expect you to be some kind of sex goddess when I married you."

"You resigned yourself to a life of mediocre sex," she said with raised eyebrows.

I chuckled again. "That's not what I said. I knew you'd have to learn, and you do. I'm fucking glad that you're not a prude who doesn't want to try new things."

"Okay," she said, growing soft in my embrace once more. I stroked her arm until her breathing evened out, her body falling into sleep with a small twitch. Falling asleep in someone else's arms or just in their company required a level of trust I could hardly grasp. Aria had no trouble making herself vulnerable in my company. Then again, it wasn't as if she was any less vulnerable when she was awake. She was at my mercy asleep or awake, and she knew it. I trailed my thumb down her arm then over her hips and the soft skin of her belly. With a small sigh, she pressed even closer to me, her fingers curling over my hip and holding onto me.

In moments like this, it seemed a lifetime ago that I'd slept without Aria at my side.

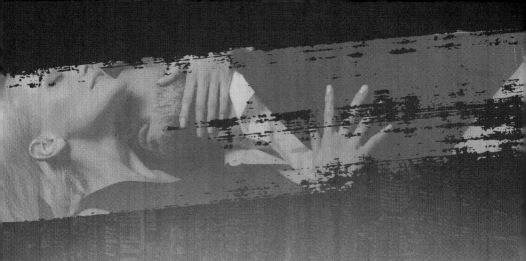

CHAPTER 21

Cesare waited for Matteo and me in front of our warehouse. He'd called me ten minutes ago to tell me that the Russians had attacked the building.

"The Doc's still trying to patch one of them together," Cesare said, his dark eyes bloodshot as he led me inside the gym. The smell of blood and vomit drenched the air.

My eyes took in the scene before me. Blood covered the floor and the walls. It looked as if the Russians had sprayed it all over the place on purpose. I stalked past the dismembered bodies and toward Doc and his assistant, a young woman from a soldier family. I counted two dead men but, when I arrived beside the Doc, I was surprised that it weren't three. I got down on my knees beside my soldier. He was a recent initiate, not even of age yet. I still remembered his induction about two years ago. I wasn't sure what the Doc was trying to do, because little of his body was intact. The Russians had broken every single bone in his legs and arms from the look of it before they'd skinned his limbs and cut open his belly. "Nico," I said firmly.

The boy's swollen eyes focused on me briefly before they fluttered shut again. I glanced at Doc, who shook his head. "It hurts…" he cried.

"I know," I said, touching his shoulder lightly. He shuddered, blood trickling out of his mouth.

Doc showed me five fingers. Five minutes of agony.

I pulled my knife, then leaned down. "I'll tell your family how bravely you fought. They will be proud of you, Nico."

He gave a small nod. I put my hand down on his ribcage and rested the tip of my knife below it. Then, with one hard shove, I drove my blade into his heart. Slowly, I pulled my knife out and stood, drenched in the blood of my soldier. A wave of anger crashed down on me. Too young to die.

Matteo stepped up beside me, shaking his head. "The Bratva will bleed for this."

They would bleed and suffer like my men had.

"Give me the addresses of the families," I told Cesare. I tried to tell the families of my soldiers personally when one of ours died. They deserved to be told by their Capo, the man they fought and died for, but my father didn't give a flying fuck about any of them, so I went in his stead.

The boy's family was last. The door to their apartment opened before I got the chance to knock. A woman in her late thirties stood in the doorway and, beside her, a younger girl. Her husband had died two years ago, I remembered her now, and her son Nico had taken the oath shortly after.

She let out a cry upon seeing me. She knew why I was here. She remembered the last time I'd come to visit.

I moved closer and she shook her head desperately, wailing. Another child, a boy, appeared behind her. He was thirteen or fourteen, not older. When he saw me, his eyes widened and then his face, too, transformed with horrified realization.

His mother rushed toward me, her face twisted with despair as she began pummeling me with her fists. "No! Not Nico. Not him too."

Her two children were frozen. I allowed her to hit me, but soon her son grabbed her arms and pulled her away. "Mom, calm down. Please."

She didn't. Words of consolation weren't in my nature. "Your son fought bravely."

She gave a weak nod. The boy looked at me, trying to appear like a man even with tears in his eyes. "I'll take the oath to provide for my family."

I pulled my wallet and handed him ten thousand dollars for the funeral and the next few weeks. "In two years. Until then, the Famiglia will provide for you."

If my father disapproved of my decisions, he should act like a Capo. Until then, I'd handle things the way I wanted. The boy led his mother back into their apartment, and I turned around and left. Afterward, I returned to the warehouse to help my men wash off the blood.

I felt like I'd been run over by a truck. Anger and frustration crowded my chest when I stepped into the penthouse. Romero got up from where he sat on the bar stool, the only source of light his phone screen. "How many?" he asked.

"Three," I said, already walking past him. I wasn't in the mood to talk. I wanted to wash off the grime and blood and get some sleep. If my body allowed me to find sleep at all tonight.

The bling of the elevator told me that Romero had left, and I made my way up the stairs. It was past midnight, so I was surprised to find Aria still up, reading a book.

Her eyes filled with worry when I continued into the bathroom without another word. I closed the door and showered for a long time, hoping to feel more like the man I wanted to be around Aria afterwards but, when I stepped out, an undercurrent of violence and anger still had a hold of my body.

I walked out, still not saying anything, and half fell into bed. Aria's gaze rested on my face as I glared up at the ceiling. I'd lost good men tonight, and their families had lost their fathers and sons. Money wouldn't be a problem, the Famiglia took care of their own, but that didn't provide solace for everyone.

"Bad day?" Aria asked softly.

She had propped herself up and, from the corner of my eye, I saw the way her nipples peaked. I was torn between wanting to claim her again, harder than last time, to find an outlet for my tension, and holding her in my arms to remind myself that a few good things remained in this life.

"Luca?"

"I lost three of my men today," I rasped. It wasn't the first time, but today had been brutal. The Bratva was getting too fucking confident, and they'd started working with local MCs who thrived on chaos and anarchy. In the past, after days like this, I'd gone to one of the Famiglia's clubs and found a woman for a hard fuck or given Grace a call, because she got wet on my violent side. That wasn't an option anymore. The woman beside me, my wife, wasn't someone I could take my anger out on.

Aria touched my bicep, trying to catch my eyes, but I didn't want to look into her innocent face, and even less for her to see the fucking darkness in mine. "What happened?"

"The Bratva attacked one of our warehouses." It didn't even begin to describe the fucking mess I'd witnessed, but it was too much for Aria to stomach. "We'll make them pay. Our retribution will make them bleed." They'd sent my men through hell. I would show them why some people feared me like the devil.

"What can I do?" Aria asked, stroking my chest lightly. I finally turned to her, realizing that she was trying to console me with her touch, with the gentleness of it. In the past, I'd fucked the anger out of my system, had burnt down the fire in my veins with more fire. I'd never considered another option, never wanted one, until Aria.

"I need you," I pressed out. Fuck, I needed her, but a war was still raging in my body.

"Okay." There was no hesitation in the word. She undressed, then waited beside me. My eyes trailed over her body and a roar of desire drowned out all else. I shoved down my boxers, already painfully hard. I reached for Aria and hoisted her on top of me, feeling her pussy against my skin. The idea of Aria riding me was enticing, but I caught the hint of apprehension in her eyes, the way her body tensed up. It was only her second time, and the last time had been painful for her. No angry fucking.

I grabbed Aria and lifted her onto my face. Her cry of shock turned into a cry of pleasure when I sucked her lips into my mouth. She rocked forward, hands clamping down on the headboard as my tongue darted out to lick every inch of her pussy before diving into her opening. I'd eaten Aria many times before, but this time I didn't hold back. I devoured her, leaving her no choice but to surrender. I ate her like I wanted to fuck her, without restraint, merciless and hard.

Aria's widened eyes peered down at me as I suckled her. She was so fucking wet, and the way she rocked her hips, mimicking the way I'd soon slam into her, drove me insane. I growled, and my hips began twitching with my fucking need to be inside of her. Aria pressed her pussy harder against my face as her head fell back and I tongue-fucked her.

She moaned louder than ever before, her body beginning to spasm. With a cry, she clamped up. "Luca, oh god!" I dug my fingers into her ass cheeks, shoving her pussy against my face as my tongue dove into her over and over again.

Aria straightened on top of me and tried to get away from my mouth, but I wanted to get her even wetter before I claimed her again. I held her firmly in place despite her whimper and took my time tasting her. Some of the burning anger had seeped from my pores, and I took my time enjoying Aria's arousal and building her pleasure once more.

Aria's moans rose once more, her hips jerking, but, before she could find her release, I flung her onto the bed and climbed between her legs, needing to fuck her. My cock brushed her opening, but I stopped myself from plunging into her in one hard stroke. She was clamped up in expectation of pain.

I bent my head so I could reach her pink nipple and suckled it as I slid my tip over her wet pussy. Soon my cock was slick with her arousal and Aria was making small rocking motions, her body seeking my cock despite its fear of pain.

I wanted Aria to come with my cock inside her. *Patience.*

I slid my tip into her, stifling a groan from the way her walls gripped my cock. I took a long time teasing her with only my tip until she stopped tensing. Her nipples were red and hard from my ministrations when I finally released them.

I looked into Aria's face when I pushed my tip into her once more, but this time I didn't stop. I pushed deeper into her tightness. It was as much to gauge her reaction as to satisfy the possessive side of me that needed to see me claim her.

Aria held her breath when I filled her completely, my balls resting against her firm ass cheeks. I cradled her head, holding her soft gaze as I began to thrust into her at a slow, careful pace. Her body still tensed with discomfort, but I could feel her walls loosening around me slowly. I slammed a bit harder into her, but Aria's immediate wince and the way her fingers dug into my biceps made me slow once more.

Tonight wasn't about angry, hard fucking. I pressed my mouth to her ear. "I loved the taste of you, *principessa*. I loved how you rode my fucking mouth. I loved my tongue in you. I love your pussy and your tits, and I love that you're all mine." I kept thrusting slowly, steadily, as I whispered into her ear, telling her exactly how much I loved eating her. And fuck did it work. Aria's channel became slicker and my cock moved more easily in and out.

My finger found her clit and I started teasing it. Aria moaned, pleasure reflecting on her face.

I fucked her faster, not harder though, and kept up the pace even when she whimpered. By the way her hips rocked upwards to meet my thrusts, by the wet sounds of our bodies, by Aria's astonished moans, I knew she was close.

"Come for me, Aria," I said, flicking her clit again as I slammed into her and Aria arched up, crying out, her walls clutching my dick like a vise. The mix of pain and intense pleasure pushed me over the edge. My thrusts became harder and uncoordinated as I released into her.

I pulled out of Aria, groaning at the tight grip her walls still had on me. She gasped. I relaxed between her legs, supporting my weight so I didn't crush her. "Was I too rough?" I'd thrust harder than intended when my orgasm had taken control.

"No, it was okay."

I kissed the corner of her mouth and her lower lip, showing her that she was safe in my arms and in bed with me. Kissing Aria always gave me a strange sense of calm, of belonging. It didn't take long for my cock to grow hard again. I wanted this woman so much.

Aria drew back with wide eyes. "So soon? I thought men needed time to rest."

Time to rest. I chuckled, loving her endearing innocence, and even more the knowledge that I'd be the one to rid her of it. I'd corrupt Aria, show her all the forms of pleasure. I couldn't fucking wait. "Not with your naked body beneath me." I slid my palm up her outer thigh before gripping her ass cheek. "How sore are you?"

"Not too sore," Aria said. but she was a horrible liar.

I rolled us over so she sat atop my abdomen. That way she could decide how much her body could take so soon.

I caressed Aria's legs, trying to take her anxiety. "Take your time. You're in control."

I lifted my hips, sliding over her firm ass to show her how much I desired her.

Aria pressed her palms to my chest, still not moving. "I want you in control."

Fuck. "Don't say something like that to a man like me." I shoved down the need to claim her in one stroke. Instead, I shifted her body until my cock nudged her pussy lightly. Aria peered down with puckered brows. I slid my tip through her wetness, teasing her clit with it, trying to relax her. My free hand caressed her breast. Aria began to loosen up and I grabbed her hip to slowly lower her body. Her hand clung to my shoulders, and she sucked in a deep breath when I was more than halfway in. She slowly ran her hand down to my chest, her fingers twitching against my skin. I stroked and tugged at her nipples, before one of my hands found its way to her pink nub and I slid my thumb over it. Aria moaned, and I used the moment to fill her completely, groaning at the delicious sensation of her pussy pressing down on my pelvis, on how deeply my cock was buried in her.

Aria tensed with a cry.

I stilled, my gaze flitting to her eyes, trying to see if I'd hurt her. "Aria," I murmured.

A hesitant smile pulled at her lips and the fist around my heart loosened. "Give me a moment."

I stroked my thumbs over her hipbones and higher, then back down, never taking my eyes off my wife's face as she took a few deep breaths. She exhaled and moved her hips. Her moves were unpracticed, and it was obvious that they didn't bring her much pleasure yet, but I held back, waiting for her to get used to the position even when I wanted to show her how amazing it could be.

Aria's eyes met mine. "Help me?"

My chest constricted. I held onto her waist, my big hands touching her firm ass. I helped her rotate her hips as I made small upwards thrusts. I watched her closely to see the angle she liked best as I shifted my hips with each push.

Aria was gorgeous, and I loved how she trusted me to make this good for her, how she trusted me enough to ask me for help. She trusted me to hold back for her, and fuck I did. It wasn't the best sex I'd ever had, if you counted only the physical aspect, but by god it beat everything else anyway, because by taking care of Aria, by shoving down my own needs, I felt a different kind of satisfaction I'd never felt before. It would have been easy to seek the ultimate pleasure with Aria, to take more than her body was capable of giving just yet. Aria might have denied me in our wedding night but, deep down, I knew that something had changed, that she'd yield to my demands now, no matter what I asked, and that was exactly why I would be twice as careful to honor her own needs.

And when Aria finally came on top of me, her body loose with pleasure, her blond strands trailing like silk down her back, and my own body tightened with release, I wondered how I'd ever enjoyed the senseless fucking, the uncaring pleasure-seeking of the past.

Aria fell forward, kissed my lips then clung to my neck and I held her tightly, feeling my heart speed up for no good reason at all, and overcome with something I could only describe as...fear. An emotion I'd rarely felt since becoming a Made Man and even less in recent years.

"I won't lose you," I rasped, confused by the chaos churning my insides.

"You won't."

Aria didn't understand in how much danger she was. "The Bratva is closing in. How can I protect you?" The Bratva would target my weakest point, and every day it became more apparent that Aria was that weakness because I cared for her when I'd never cared for anything but the Famiglia. Protecting her would be difficult.

"You will find a way," Aria said firmly. Again that unfailing trust in me. A trust I was bound to break at some point.

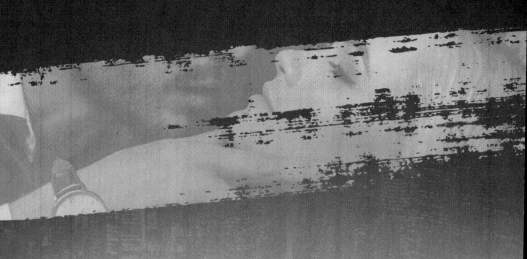

CHAPTER 22

My days in the next two weeks were filled with countless discussions with my father about possible ways to make the Bratva pay. We targeted another of their drug labs and killed a few of their dealers because Father was convinced that losing money would hurt them the most. The only light in my day was when I returned to my wife, saw her beautiful smile and worshipped her body.

Today, it became clear the moment I entered the penthouse that I wouldn't be on the receiving end of her smile.

Aria's face was a mask of fury when she rushed inside from the roof terrace.

She didn't slow down until she was right in front of me and hit my chest with her fists, catching me off-guard. What the hell had gotten into her? I snatched up her wrists, holding her tightly. "Aria, what—"

Aria jerked her knee upwards, but I managed to evade a direct hit by jumping back.

"Get out," I growled at Romero, who disappeared in the elevator at once. Aria glared up at me and actually tried to ram her knee into my balls again. Anger surged through me and I shoved her down on the sofa before I held her down with my body. "For god's sake, Aria. What's gotten into you?"

"I know about Gianna and Matteo," she hissed, and then the anger slipped off and she began crying.

I let go of her and stopped holding her down. "That's what this is about?" I couldn't believe she was losing her mind about something like that. Her sister would have to marry anyway. I'd have thought she'd be happy to have her in New York.

"Of course you don't understand, because you never loved anyone more than your own life. You can't possibly understand how it is to feel your own heart breaking at the thought of the person you love getting hurt. I would die for the people I love."

I'd give my fucking life for Aria, wouldn't even hesitate to do it, but she didn't know that. I got to my feet. "You're right. I don't understand."

Aria pushed up from the sofa as well. "Why didn't you tell me? You've known for weeks."

"Because I knew you wouldn't like it."

"You knew I'd be mad at you, and you didn't want to ruin your chances of fucking me."

Fuck her? She thought I had only *fucked* her? "Of course I wanted to fuck you. But I got the impression you enjoyed our *fucking* sessions."

Aria's face twisted with anger. "And you worried I wasn't a good enough actress to fool everyone after our little trick on our wedding night. But it turns out, I even fooled you. I made you believe I actually enjoyed it."

Some wives pretended they enjoyed their husband's touch and his company—

like Nina, because it was the only way to survive a marriage to a man like my father.

I'd tried not to be that kind of man with Aria, and yet she made me feel like I was. I smiled cruelly. "Don't lie to me. I've fucked enough whores to know an orgasm when I see one."

Aria flinched, eyes growing wide. "Some women even experience an orgasm when they're being raped. It's not because they're enjoying it. It's their body's way of coping."

She didn't have to tell me anything about rape. I'd seen what it did to women, what it had done to Mother and still did to Nina. Fury slithered under my skin, wanting to be unleashed, but I shoved it down.

"Your sister should be happy that Matteo wants her. Few men can stand her gab," I said coldly.

Aria shook her head with a look of disgust as she peered up at me. "God, that's the reason, isn't it? It's because she told him that he'd never get her hot body that day in the hotel. He didn't like it. He couldn't bear that she was immune to his creepy charm."

"She shouldn't have challenged him. Matteo is a determined hunter. He gets what he wants."

"He gets what he wants? It's not hunting if he forces her into marriage by asking my father for her hand. That is cowardice."

"It doesn't matter. They're getting married." I began to turn, tired of this discussion.

From the corner of my eye, I saw Aria dash toward the elevator, and my first instinct was that she was trying to run away. "Aria, what the fuck are you doing?"

I was too slow to reach her in time. The elevator doors closed in my face and it went down one floor. Tension flooded my body when I realized she was confronting Matteo. Fuck it. I hammered against the elevator button until it came back up. Matteo wouldn't hurt Aria. He wouldn't because she was mine.

When I stepped out, Matteo had Aria pressed against the wall, holding her wrists up above her head. My fingers twitched, a fierce wave of protectiveness rushing through me.

"Let her go," I demanded. Matteo didn't hesitate releasing Aria and bringing space between them, but I could tell he was majorly pissed at her. The way his cheek turned red, I had a feeling I knew why.

I moved toward them, checking Aria for any signs that Matteo had hurt her even when I knew that it would take more than a slap to make him hurt a woman, especially *my* woman.

"You won't do that again," I told my brother, glaring at him.

Matteo gave me a hard look. "Then teach her manners. I won't let her hit me again."

I got right into his face. "You won't touch my wife again, Matteo. You are my brother and I'd take a bullet for you, but if you do that again, you'll have to live with the consequences." Challenge shone in Matteo's eyes. He wasn't used to anything or anyone coming between us.

"I won't hit you again, Matteo. I shouldn't have done it," Aria said, surprising me.

Aria looked between Matteo and me. "I'm sorry if I hurt or scared you," Matteo said. I could still see his anger, but I wasn't sure if it was still directed at Aria or at me for siding with her.

"You didn't," Aria lied. Matteo would be able to see through it like I did. I walked toward her and wrapped an arm around her waist. She looked up to me, her eyes filled with disappointment. Was she still pissed because of Gianna? For god's sake, her sister would have to marry anyway and Matteo was definitely not the worst choice. He wouldn't abuse Gianna, no matter how much of a bitch she was.

Aria faced Matteo once more. "Don't marry Gianna." I squeezed her waist in warning, but Aria continued. "She doesn't want to marry you."

"You didn't want to marry Luca either, yet here you are," Matteo said, nodding toward us. It was true, but he wasn't taking Gianna's character into consideration. She wouldn't be as sensible as Aria.

"Gianna isn't like me. She won't come to terms with an arranged marriage."

I regarded Aria, wondering if this was only accepting the unavoidable, or if this marriage was really more to her, if her words about love could really be true and not her way to make this easier for her. But more than that, I wondered why the hell I cared.

"She will become my wife the moment she turns eighteen. No power in this universe will stop me from making her mine," Matteo said.

Aria shook her head. "You disgust me. You all do."

She walked past me, but I didn't follow her, not even when she took the elevator back up to our apartment.

"And you say Gianna is trouble," Matteo muttered, rubbing his cheek. "Your wife is quite a handful."

I made a noncommittal noise. Aria was growing more confident, and even though part of me was annoyed by her outburst, I couldn't help but be relieved that she wasn't so painfully submissive around me anymore. I loved her fiery side as much as the rest of her.

I loved every little thing about her, even her frustrating emotionality.

Love.

I loved Aria.

"You look as if you had a stroke," Matteo said.

Love was a risk. A weakness. Something I shouldn't entertain.

"Luca?"

I shook my head at him, and at myself. I wasn't capable of love.

CHAPTER 23

I avoided Aria over the next three days, hoping that my feelings would wane if I kept my distance, but they didn't. It was torture, lying beside her at night without kissing and touching her, but even worse was not seeing her smile.

I spent even more time in the Sphere, determined to drive Aria out of my system with sheer work overload, but even that wasn't working. Matteo and I were on our way back home when Cesare called. I knew at once that something was wrong. I'd seen him only two hours ago for a quick fight workout. If there was something he had to say, he could have done it then.

I picked up.

"The Bratva shot your father," Cesare grunted, sounding out of breath.

For a moment, I was sure I hadn't heard him right. Only Matteo's wide-eyed stare confirmed the words.

"What?"

"He was out with his mistress and was hit by several bullets. I'm on my way there. It's in his favorite restaurant. He's still alive. The Doc will be there in a few minutes. Should I call an ambulance?"

"No ambulance. You know the rules," I said then hung up. I jerked the steering wheel around and did a U-turn before hitting the gas and speeding toward the restaurant.

"Fuck," Matteo breathed. "Maybe that's it. Maybe someone took him off our hands."

"He's not dead yet," I gritted out. "And the Bratva are the last people I want involved in his death. They'll get overconfident."

We arrived at the restaurant within five minutes. I jumped out of the car. A few men were gathered inside and outside the restaurant, most of them soldiers who lived close by. The police hadn't arrived yet. Everyone in this area knew what kind of restaurant this was. Calling the police was out of the question. I jogged into the restaurant. The Famiglia soldiers had their guns pulled, and Cesare stood beside the Doc who was bent over Father. The ground was covered with broken glass and blood.

A young woman with a hole in her forehead was sprawled out beside an overturned chair.

Matteo and I headed for our father. The Doc was pressing down on a wound in Father's stomach while his assistant held up a transfusion bag. Father was clutching the Doc's arm in a desperate grip, sucking in one rattling breath after the other, and staring at us wide-eyed. For as long as I could remember, I'd wondered how it would feel to see my father like this, to watch him taking his last breaths. Occasionally I'd feared I'd feel regret or sadness, but there was nothing. Only relief.

I knelt beside him and Matteo on his other side.

"I can't help him. If we call an ambulance, he might survive," Doc said, his weathered wrinkly face solemn.

Father grasped my hand, bulging eyes on me, begging me. Didn't he remember how he'd beaten and cut any hint of compassion out of me? He was trying to say something. I leaned down. "H-hospital…take me…take me hospital."

I met his gaze and gave a nod, then I turned to the Doc, motioning for him to stand. He staggered to his feet and so did his assistant.

"Leave and tell the others," I told them. "Father doesn't want his men to witness his last moments. He wants to be remembered as the strong Capo that he was."

Doc and his assistant headed toward the front of the restaurant. From the corner of my eye, I caught Matteo pressing down on a wound in Father's side to stop the words he wanted to say and turn them into a pained gurgle. He wouldn't be saved tonight.

The remaining men left with bowed heads until only Matteo and I remained with our father. I got down on my knees beside them again.

Father gasped in a ragged breath, growing paler and paler. "You…you traitorous…."

Matteo ripped the transfusion needle out and we both bent over our father. The man who'd tortured us and his wives, who'd driven our mother into suicide, he'd finally disappear.

"We would have killed you with poison soon. It would have been painless," Matteo murmured, then paused with a twisted grin as he regarded the bullet wound in Father's stomach. "I prefer it like this. With your last moments filled with agony."

Father sucked in a rattling breath. He tried to move, to look for help, but Matteo and I barred everyone's view, and I doubted anyone was even watching. They were giving us time to say goodbye. "That whore set you up to this…"

For a moment I thought he meant Nina, but then it dawned on me whom he was talking about: Aria.

"Lead you around by your dick," he spat in disgust. "Wish…wish I'd fucked her before you."

I leaned even closer to him and shoved one of my fingers into the wound in his stomach as fury consumed my veins in a raging fire. Matteo pressed a palm over his mouth to stifle the screams.

"You won't ever touch my wife, Father. Aria's a queen, and I'll treat her like one. I won't be like you. Your legacy dies today. Matteo and I will make sure of it."

Father's chest heaved more and more, and blood trickled out between Matteo's fingers still pressed against Father's mouth.

"I'll tell Nina you suffered through your last minutes. She'll be ecstatic to hear it. Maybe Matteo and I will toast your death with her with your favorite bottle of wine," I growled. Father's eyes bulged and he convulsed and then went still. I pulled my finger out of his wound and Matteo released his mouth, and for a moment everything was silent.

Matteo's and my eyes met, our hands covered with our father's blood. Matteo gripped my shoulder. "He's gone."

Gone. Finally gone from our lives.

My eyes took in the mess in the restaurant. Bullets from Russian guns littered the ground. "A traitor must have told the Bratva where to find him. Very few people knew."

"Probably one of our uncles."

"Probably. The question is how many men were involved beside them, and how to prove it."

"We—"

"Down!" Cesare screamed. Shots rang out. Matteo and I dropped to the ground as bullets barreled through the restaurant. I pulled my gun as I crawled toward the bar. Matteo was close beside me. Outside, my men were shouting and firing.

Peering out behind the bar, I tried to make out our attackers. They must have been waiting for our arrival on nearby rooftops, or someone had alerted them that Matteo and I had come to see our father. A fucking traitor in our ranks. I started firing bullet after bullet in the direction of the shooters, letting my fury consume me, letting it guide my actions. Eventually the flashing lights of the police filled the dark. I shoved my gun into my pants before I walked out of the restaurant with raised arms, my pulse pounding in my temples. Cesare was trying to talk with the police, but they had their guns drawn. He pointed toward me. One of the police officers approached me while his colleagues aimed their guns at my men and me. "You're in charge?"

For a moment I only stared at the man before reality sank in. Everyone was watching me as I stood covered in blood amidst broken glass. This mess was my responsibility now. My men expected me to find the people responsible, to dish out revenge, to keep the Famiglia together. "I'm Capo of the Famiglia."

I barely listened to the officer. This was none of their business. It was mine, and I'd handle it. I'd find the men who'd worked with the Bratva to kill my father and tried killing Matteo and me—again.

My anger spiraled higher and higher. Soon the area was swarming with Famiglia soldiers and police. My father's Consigliere Bardoni arrived not long after. "Where's our Capo?"

I glared down at him. My father's man through and through. "He stands in front of you."

Bardoni's eyes widened, then he plastered that slimy smile on his face. "My condolences. I'm sure you and your brother need time to grieve. I can take over business until you feel ready."

I gave him my coldest smile. Did he really think I'd allow him to take control? I didn't trust him one bit, but whom could I really trust at this point? My eyes took in the men around me. Matteo always. Cesare maybe. But everyone else could be a traitor. "I don't need time. I will rule over the Famiglia, and Matteo will be my Consigliere from this day on."

Bardoni took a step back, anger flashing across his face. "But—"

I gripped his collar, jerking him closer. "I'm your Capo. I don't tolerate words of objection. You'd do well to remember that I'm my father's son. Cruelty runs in my veins, and right now I want nothing more than to spill blood."

"I apologize, Capo," Bardoni sputtered, and I released him.

Two hours later, I was finally on my way home. My anger had only risen higher. I wasn't even sure why. I felt such a myriad of emotions but anger was the most familiar option. For years I'd dreamed of getting rid of my father, of becoming Capo, and today my wish had finally been fulfilled. But it had come through betrayal. The traitors were still among us, waiting for their next chance to remove Matteo and me as well.

Someone had betrayed us again. Fucking again. Whom could I trust?

Fury turned my vision into a red haze. Violence burnt in my veins, pounded in my temples, wanting to be unleashed.

I staggered out of the elevator. Romero stood from the couch. "I heard what happened."

Did he now? I stalked toward him. How could I be sure he was trustworthy? Few people knew what my father did. I shoved Romero against the wall. "Who told you?" I growled.

"Matteo," he bit out.

"So you didn't know before?"

Romero tried to unlock my hold on his throat but I pressed harder into him, so fucking desperate to rip something to shreds.

"I would never betray the Famiglia," Romero choked out, then coughed. "I'm loyal. I'd die for you. If I were a traitor, Aria wouldn't be here, safe and unscathed. She'd be in the hands of the Bratva."

I released him and he dropped to the ground, sputtering. Aria came down the stairs in a little nothing.

Romero looked her way and I lost it. "Out, now," I ordered, the rushing in my ears growing in crescendo. I gripped Romero, my body shaking with hardly suppressed rage. I threw him into the elevator then hit the button. The doors closed and I locked this floor so nobody would be able to come up.

Who knew if the murderer of my father was out for Aria as well.

Aria.

My body throbbed with a dark hunger, a ferocious burning. Everything around me was utter darkness, except for her.

"Are you okay?" Aria asked.

I turned my head toward her as she approached me slowly. My eyes took in her nipples straining against her nightgown. My need for bloodspill battled with lust in my body.

Aria took another step closer and I snapped, letting my hunger take control. My thoughts turned to static, my body driven by instinct. I grabbed Aria, feeling her heat, smelling her divine scent. Mine. Always mine.

I needed her, every inch of her. I jerked her forcefully against me and silenced her with a harsh kiss.

I turned, discomfort dragging me from sleep. My brain was foggy, my muscles tense and sore as if I'd worked out for hours. Groaning, I peered up at the ceiling before I realized I wasn't in the bedroom. I jerked, fumbling for my gun, which wasn't there, and sat up. Early morning light streamed into the living room. I was on the floor, completely naked. Images from last night, small glimpses as if taken through a foggy lens, materialized before my inner eye. Father being shot. Me returning home in a rage, attacking Romero and...Aria.

My chest constricted. I looked around and then my eyes landed on my wife, lying on her side on the wooden floor. She was curled into herself, her body covered in goose bumps. Slowly I got on to my knees and moved closer. Bruises bloomed on her lower back where she must have rubbed over the floor. Bile traveled up my throat at the sight. A sight I remembered from my childhood when Father had violated mother.

What had I done? Fuck, what the hell had I done?

I pushed to my feet, staring down at Aria. With shaking hands I lifted her and found more bruises on her hips, finger shaped bruises. For a moment, I was sure I'd throw up. I hadn't thrown up in a decade, not even when I had been surrounded by my enemies' blood, bowels, shit, vomit and piss. I carried Aria into our bedroom and gently lowered her to the bed. Aria didn't stir, deep asleep. And then a new worry shot through me. I carefully felt the back of her head for bumps, but there were none. She let out a small sigh. I sank down on the edge of the bed, feeling drained.

My eyes were frozen on my battered wife. All my life I'd sworn I'd never become my father, not in that regard at least. I curled my hands to fists, despair and guilt battling a furious war in my chest. I considered calling Matteo but shame stopped me. He and I had hated our father fiercely for how he treated his women. How could I admit that I was as bad as him?

Aria's lids fluttered and I tensed, dreading the look in her eyes when she saw me. Would she hate me? Fear me?

How could I ever make it up to her? Ever apologize if I'd hurt her like I thought I had? There was no apologizing for something like that. It was unforgivable.

Aria looked at me with a small frown.

"What did I do?" I rasped, torn between not wanting to know and desperately needing to.

Aria peered down her body. I didn't understand her reaction. Was she in shock? How badly had I fucked up? She brushed her fingers over her throat and I winced at the bite marks I'd left on her unblemished skin. I was a monster. I should have never been given someone like Aria.

Aria pushed into a sitting position and grimaced, pain flashing across her face. A new wave of self-hatred slashed through me sharper than any knife ever could.

"Aria, please tell me. Did I...?" I couldn't even say the fucking word. What kind of man could perform the deed but not say the word?

Aria's brows drew together as she looked at me as if she didn't understand a word I was saying. "You don't remember?"

"I remember bits and pieces. I remember holding you down." That was the worst memory of all. Aria bent over the couch, me on top of her.

"You didn't hurt me," Aria said softly.

Her body spoke a different language. Why was she trying to protect me? "Don't lie to me."

Aria crawled over to me. I regarded her without moving. "You were a bit rougher than usual, but I wanted it. I enjoyed it."

I had trouble believing it, considering how my rougher side was. "No, really, Luca," Aria murmured, kissing my cheek. She didn't look scared or broken. "I came at least four times. I don't exactly remember everything. I passed out from sensory overload."

I closed my eyes a moment. Fuck. Not like my father.

"I don't understand what got into you. You even attacked Romero."

I put my hand on Aria's knee, savoring the feel of her soft skin, glad that she didn't flinch. "My father is dead."

Aria's eyes widened. "What? How?"

"Last night. He was having dinner at a small restaurant in Brooklyn when a sniper put a bullet into his head." Aria didn't need to know the entire truth. It wouldn't serve any purpose. The less she knew in this regard, the safer she'd be.

"What about your stepmother?"

"She wasn't there. He was with his mistress. She was shot too, probably because the Bratva thought she was his wife. Someone must have told them where to find him. Very few people knew he went there. He was in disguise. Nobody could have recognized him. There has to be a traitor among us."

Nina was probably slurping champagne and dancing on the tables as we spoke. I needed to go see her with Matteo later today. Part of me wondered if maybe she'd been involved in his death. I needed to find out so I could figure out if there was a traitor among our men. I had my suspicions, of course.

"How do you feel?" She touched my chest as if I needed consoling. I hadn't felt an ounce of sadness over my father's death. Seeing him lying in his own blood with open, empty eyes, I hadn't felt a sliver of the emotions the sight of Aria's bruises had evoked in me. I stroked Aria's upper arm, then lightly traced the bite marks on her throat. "Relief."

Aria tilted her head. "Because you're finally Capo?"

Because Father could never hurt Aria, because I wouldn't have to kill the man myself to protect her. He was finally gone, and I would rebuild the Famiglia to something stronger and better.

"Yes," I said. I leaned forward and kissed her forehead. "I really didn't hurt you?"

Aria kissed me. "You needed me and I needed you, Luca." The look in Aria's eyes tore at my last wall. I quickly got up. "I need to handle the situation.

The Famiglia needs me to take control and uncover the traitors."

Aria smiled. "You're going to be a great Capo." I didn't say anything, only regarded my wife's kind face. She slid out of bed. "Can I help you with anything? Should I keep Nina company?"

I shook my head. "Take a bath and relax. I'll handle everything."

Aria nodded, but I could tell that she was disappointed but I didn't want her involved in this mess as long as I didn't know exactly what had happened, and Nina didn't need consolation any more than I did. After a last kiss, I went into the shower. When I was done getting ready, I found her downstairs in a satin bathrobe, sipping coffee. "Shouldn't Romero be here by now?"

"Fuck," I breathed. Searching the mess of my bloody clothes on the floor, I finally found my cell. I picked it up. I'd turned it to silent and I'd ten missed calls and countless messages from Romero and Matteo, as well as Dante and Scuderi. I called Matteo as I unlocked the elevator. Matteo picked up after the second ring. "Have you lost your fucking mind? I've been trying to call you for hours. What's your fucking problem?"

"Did something happen?"

"I should ask you that," Matteo said carefully. The elevator began moving up from his floor. "Romero is here. Where's Aria?"

Matteo sounded worried.

I glanced at my wife who held her cup against her lips, watching me worriedly. I gave her a tight smile, which she returned at once.

"Luca?"

The elevator doors slid open and Matteo and Romero got out, both moving carefully as if they expected the worst.

Their eyes found me then moved behind me. Disapproval flashed across Romero's face and his mouth tightened but he didn't say anything. I could imagine what he thought, seeing the marks on Aria's throat. A bruise circled his own throat where I'd held him in a chokehold.

"That shouldn't have happened," I said, trying to ignore the way Matteo was x-raying me with his gaze.

Romero's angry eyes hit me. "*I* can handle it."

I straightened. I'd have despised myself forever if I'd hurt Aria the way I'd first thought but Romero had no right to criticize me, not now, not ever. "I am your Capo," I said in a low voice, and those words filled me with a new purpose, a strange sense of arriving. "If there's something you want to say to me, then do it."

Romero looked away eventually, but I could tell that he was still pissed on Aria's behalf.

"Would you like a coffee?" Aria piped up, as usual saving the day.

"Yes," Romero said without hesitation and walked over to her. I narrowed my eyes at his antics, even if I had to admit that his protectiveness over Aria was a good thing.

Aria hopped off the bar stool and headed for the coffee maker. "What about you, Matteo?"

My brother shook his head, his eyes still focused on me.

Aria prepared coffee as Romero stood close beside her, his eyes lingering on the bruises. Aria gave him a smile and said something I didn't catch, and he relaxed.

"What happened?" Matteo asked as he stepped close to me. "Is Aria all right?"

"What do you think?" I muttered.

He searched my eyes. "I think that even in a blind rage, you wouldn't hurt your wife."

I gave a terse nod. "We should head out to Nina and set up a meeting with the Underbosses and Captains as soon as possible. And someone needs to organize the funeral."

"It won't be me. For all I care we can dump the body in the Hudson."

"We'll give the task to Nina. She'll make a spectacle out of it for appearance's sake," I said. Then I remembered something. "Did you tell Dante or Scuderi about our father's death?"

Matteo shook his head. "You're Capo. It's your job."

We stepped into the elevator and I showed Matteo my list of missed calls. "I have a feeling someone else told them."

"Then we should find out who it was and have a long talk with them." His lips twitched.

I gave a nod. The weight that had been lifted when my father died was replaced by a new weight of responsibility. The Famiglia needed a strong Capo.

"You'll be a better Capo than our father," Matteo said.

Matteo and I stepped into the Vitiello townhouse. It was oddly quiet. I'd have thought Nina was dancing on the tables by now. Matteo sent me a questioning look.

"Nina?" I called.

No reply. We pulled our guns and slowly made our way upstairs.

"Where are the guards?" Matteo muttered.

That was what I'd asked myself as well. Nina could still be the target of possible attacks unless she was involved in Father's death.

We didn't find her in her bedroom when a choked laugh came from down the corridor. Matteo and I followed the sound toward Father's bedroom and found Nina on the ground amidst shredded clothes. In one hand she was clutching scissors and, in the other, an almost empty bottle of Father's most expensive scotch. Her flimsy nightgown was splattered with blood from wounds in her hands and forearms. She must have cut herself in her drunken stupor while destroying Father's suits and dress shirts.

She peered up at us with teary unfocused eyes. "He's dead?"

"He died in agony," I told her.

Nina threw her head back and let out another choked laugh that turned into a sob. She lifted the hand with the scissors to wipe a strand of hair from her forehead. I quickly grabbed her wrist and pried the scissors from her fingers before she lost an eye by accident. She clutched at my shirt when I helped her to her feet. "What happens to me now?" she slurred.

"What do you mean?" I asked, trying to loosen her grip without breaking her fingers, but it became clear pretty quickly that she couldn't stand on her own.

"I have nothing...nothing. Your father disinherited me. He didn't want me to be happy when he was dead."

He didn't want anyone to be happy. Matteo gave me a look. I'd suspected that Father would find a way to make Nina's life hell even after his death.

"Take a shower, Nina," I ordered. "We'll talk when you're sober."

I led her into the bathroom, turned the shower on cold and sat her down beneath it. She gasped sharply.

"We'll be waiting downstairs. Hurry. We've got a lot to discuss," I said then turned and left with Matteo at my side.

Nina's family consisted of low soldiers. Father had chosen her for that very reason because it guaranteed he could torture her without an influential family getting in the way. Nina had nothing. "What are you going to do? I assume you won't marry her off again?"

"No," I said immediately. "Call Cesare and tell him to send over a couple of trustworthy men to become Nina's new guards. I don't want Father's men around her."

We headed into the kitchen, which was also deserted. Had everyone left

LUCA VITIELLO

the moment they'd found out about Father's death? I turned on the coffee maker as I called Bardoni. He picked up immediately. "Luca, what a pleasure."

I grimaced. "Why's Nina all alone in the house?"

"Your father gave me orders in case of his death. The personnel weren't supposed to work for Nina, and she's supposed to move out of the house."

"My father is dead. I'm Capo now. Everything belongs to me, and I decide what happens. You won't ever give a single order without consulting with me first, understood?" I hung up, seething.

Matteo leaned beside me. "Cesare sent two men."

I prepared coffee, trying to control my anger. Steps rang out and Nina walked in. She was pale and didn't wear make-up. She looked younger than thirty-three in that moment, reminding me of the girl at my father's mercy many years ago. She'd gone through hell with him, which was why I didn't hate her as much as I should for how she'd treated us when we were only boys.

She wore a black sleeveless dress that revealed the bruises on her wrists and forearms and her ankles. She regarded Matteo and me as she often had my father then wrapped her arms around her middle. "You'll throw me on the street, won't you?"

I filled a cup with coffee and walked over to her. "Drink."

She took it with shaking hands, regarding me like a beaten dog waiting for his master to punish him. Fuck. I preferred Nina's bitchiness to this. She swallowed then looked at Matteo. "I could...maybe you...I..."

Matteo grimaced. She was offering herself to him for whatever she thought he might want with her.

"Nina," I said firmly, and her eyes darted up to me. Father had done a marvelous job breaking her. "I'll give you this house. Do with it whatever you want. Sell it or burn it, I don't give a fuck."

Her eyes grew wide. The house had a market worth of around fifteen

319

million dollars.

"I chose two new bodyguards for you. They'll guard you from now on. As the stepmother of the new Capo, you need protection."

She didn't say anything, only stared at me.

"Keep your credit card. I'll give you ten thousand dollars per month so you can live comfortably. You are free to live your life within the confines of our rules."

She set the cup down on the counter and took a step toward me then stopped. "What do you want in return?"

"The truth about my father's death and for you to tell me if someone tries to conspire behind my back."

She raised her chin. "I don't know who killed Salvatore, but I wish I could thank them."

I nodded. "And?"

"You know your uncles want you and your brother gone, but I don't know anything. They don't talk to me. I'm only a woman."

"One last thing," I said. Nina tensed, but her face wasn't as submissive anymore. "Organize a splendid funeral. We want everyone to believe we're inconsolable about Father's demise. Spend as much money as you need."

With that I left. There was no sense in pretending we were a family or cared about each other. I'd done what honor dictated, and now Nina wasn't my problem anymore.

I had more than enough to do, most importantly talk to Fiore Cavallaro and make it clear that my father's death didn't weaken the Famiglia. I'd make sure the Famiglia got through this and emerged stronger.

CHAPTER 24

Nina had outdone herself. My father was buried in the most expensive mahogany casket money could buy. Everyone who mattered from the Famiglia and the Chicago Outfit gathered at the cemetery, as well as many high-ranking politicians.

They had all sought me out in the last few days, wanting to make sure the Famiglia would keep paying for their campaigns now that I was in power. The same could be said for the Captains and Underbosses, even my uncles—they'd all come to me to offer their condolences and confirm their positions. This morning I'd officially taken over as Capo, had spoken the oath in front of the Captains and Underbosses, but I knew that didn't mean they'd all accept me without reservations.

None of them were sad my father was gone, except for Bardoni, and that was only because he'd lost his position as Consigliere. Every pair of eyes rested on me and Matteo, considering us, looking for a flicker of weakness. We were both young, and many would try to weaken us. I doubted they'd wait until the first official meeting of the Famiglia with me as Capo to do so. My uncles had probably already started behind my back.

I peered down to Aria when I felt her eyes on me. She regarded me with a hint of worry as she'd often done these last few days. I resisted the urge to grab her hand or kiss her and kept my expression cold and hard. She dropped her gaze back down to the casket that was lowered into the ground by six Made Men. Aria thought that, deep down, part of me felt saddened by my father's death. She didn't know I'd planned on killing him myself to protect her, and she never would. He was dead now. That was all that mattered.

My uncles kept giving me fake empathetic smiles as if any of us would miss him.

Afterwards, everyone came to Matteo, me and Nina to offer their condolences and congratulate me on becoming Capo. Nina had perfected her fake tears as she clung to Aunt Criminella. I tried to keep an eye on the area despite the many guards surrounding the perimeter. I had a feeling the Bratva would try to eliminate Matteo and me again soon. Today was the perfect opportunity to get rid of many important members of the Italian mafia.

I pulled Romero aside during the wake. "Take Aria and her siblings to the Hamptons. I don't want them in New York for the meeting tonight."

Romero nodded. "I assume Umberto will be coming with us."

"Yes, and Cesare as well," I said. Scuderi wanted his own bodyguards around when his children were in my mansion, and I didn't mind the additional protection.

Several hours later, the Cavallaros as well as Scuderi had gathered around the meeting table in the Sphere with Matteo and me to discuss the rising Russian threat but, as usual, they weren't very forthcoming with information about the

Bratva in their territory. From the start of our cooperation, we'd always only exchanged the bare minimum of information. After a tense dinner together, Matteo and I were on our way to my car to head home when Cesare called.

A feeling of dread settled in my stomach. "Cesare?"

Gunfire sounded in the background. "We're under attack. The Bratva's trying to enter the premises."

"Take Aria to the panic room. Don't let the Russians get her! We'll take the helicopter!" I shouted, already running toward the car.

"What's the matter?" Matteo asked as he flung himself into the seat beside me.

"The Bratva attacks the mansion," I got out past my tight throat then called our pilot to get the helicopter ready. Matteo was on the phone with our Captains to organize reinforcement.

The second we were in the helicopter, I called Aria's cell. It took almost a minute before she finally picked up, moments that felt like eternity. "Aria? Are you safe?"

"They killed Umberto," Aria whispered.

I didn't give a fuck who died as long as Aria was safe. I'd kill them all with my own hands if that meant she'd return to me. "Where are you?"

Aria's breathing was quick. "Searching for Gianna."

My stomach hollowed out. "Aria, where's Romero? Why isn't he taking you to the panic room?"

"I have to find Gianna."

"Aria, the Bratva wants you. Get into the panic room. I'm taking the helicopter. I'll be there in twenty minutes. I'm already on the way." There could be only one reason why the Bratva attacked the mansion when every member of the mob was in New York. They wanted Aria because they'd figured out she was the only way to get to me.

"I can't talk anymore," Aria said.

"Aria—" I didn't get further before the call was cut off. For a second, I could do nothing but stare at my phone.

"Luca? What did she say? Is Gianna with her?" Matteo asked, but I ignored him. If we'd been alone, maybe I would have talked to him, but as it was there were three more men in the helicopter and I didn't want them to realize how worried I was about my wife. I'd never felt this helpless. I reached for my gun and began checking it to make sure everything was working. I couldn't allow myself to consider what might happen in case the Bratva got their hands on Aria. I'd be there in time.

Our pilot brought down the helicopter on the lawn behind the mansion. The second we jumped out of it, bullets soared through the air toward us. We ducked behind one of the Italian marble statues decorating the garden and began firing.

Soon, we'd shot our way closer to the house. I motioned for Matteo and my other men to have my back. Then I stormed the house. I shot the first Russian in the head, the second in the throat.

"We have your wife, Vitiello. If you want to see her in one piece, you'd better stop fighting and drop your weapons," Vitali shouted.

"Nobody acts until I give an order. Got it?" I snarled, fixing my gaze on Matteo. He gave a nod, but I wasn't sure how much it was worth—after all, Gianna was in there as well.

Trying to keep my face calm was a losing battle. I could feel fury simmering under my skin, and worse: fear. I focused on the former. Showing fear for Aria's life in front of my enemies would have been the ultimate mistake.

Slowly, I walked into the living area of the mansion, guns clutched in my hands. My eyes registered Cesare lying in his own blood on the ground, eyes wide as his chest heaved with every rattling breath. I lifted my gaze. He was lost. Matteo was close behind me, but my eyes focused on Vitali and Aria. He held her against his body, his knife pressed against her throat. I'd dismember him in the cruelest way possible.

"So this is your wife, Vitiello?" Vitali asked with a dirty grin. He pressed his blade against Aria's skin and blood trickled down. My heart sped up, fear spiking hard and fast. One slice of his knife could kill her, could ruin everything.

"Let her go, Vitali," I growled, furious and terrified. I didn't remember the last time I'd been scared during a confrontation. I didn't fear death, but losing Aria...the thought tore a gaping hole in my chest.

Vitali grabbed Aria's throat. Her terrified eyes met mine. "I don't think so," he said. "You took something that belongs to us, Vitiello, and now I have something that belongs to you." Vitali ran his hand along Aria's cheek, and I almost lost it. If his goddamn head hadn't been so close to Aria's, I would have put a hole in his fucking forehead. "I want to know where it is."

I rocked forward, wanting to rip him to shreds, but Vitali raised his knife again. "Put your guns down or I'll cut her throat."

Aria closed her eyes for a moment, resigning herself to her fate. Did she think I'd refuse Vitali's order because I didn't want to lose face? That I'd give her up to appear strong in front of the Russian asshole?

I released my guns. I'd put my life down for Aria. I'd do anything for her. Matteo looked at me as if I'd lost my mind, but I narrowed my eyes until he, too, dropped his weapons.

Vitali leered as he licked Aria's face again. "Your wife tastes delicious. I wonder if she tastes this delicious everywhere." He forced Aria's face around to him. She looked like she was going to cry when he brought his face closer, and all I could think about was how I could protect her, how I could kill the bastard to keep my wife safe.

Aria tried to move back, her expression desperate, and I glanced down at my guns.

Vitali licked Aria's chin and I began shaking with so much rage, I was sure it would consume me any second. And then everything happened very quickly. Aria pulled a knife from her back pocket and shoved it into his thigh. He screamed in pain, releasing her. I pulled my own knife from my back holster, barreled toward them, pulled Aria to my side, and slid Vitali's throat open. Blood shot out of his gaping wound and onto my clothes.

Shots and screams rang out. I pressed Aria against my body, grabbed guns from the ground and began firing. Aria bent down and picked up a gun for herself. I aimed at another Russian fucker and split his skull. Dragging Aria toward the asshole, I reached for his gun because one of mine was out of bullets. "Luca!" Aria screamed. My gaze shot up as another attacker aimed his gun at me. Fuck. Aria jumped in front of me and fired at the same time as the Russian pulled the trigger. The shot rang in my ears and Aria jerked.

Her eyes grew wide, lips parting in an agonized cry, and my entire world seemed to stand still. I wrenched Aria against me once more but her legs gave away, and that's when I saw the blood soaking her shirt. My heart rate tripled as cold fear speared my insides. I lowered her to the ground, holding her in my arms, but she lay completely unmoving. For a second I was sure she was dead, that I'd lost the one person I loved more than my own life. I'd never known love meant being scared all the time, scared of losing someone you couldn't live without.

"Aria," I rasped, my eyes burning in a way they hadn't in almost fifteen years. My fingers brushed her throat, feeling her erratic pulse. Alive. Pure relief burst through me. I pressed down on her wound to stop the bleeding, causing Aria to let out a low moan.

She had thrown herself in front of me, had caught a bullet for me.

I swallowed, stroked her hair from her forehead. "Aria, love, wake up," I murmured, bending low over her pale face.

Everything was quiet around us.

"Luca?"

I peered at my brother, who held on to Gianna. The look in his eyes was one of blatant worry, as if he waited for me to lose my shit.

Aria whimpered and I quickly looked down to her. Due to the pressure I applied to her wound, she'd stopped bleeding, but she was ashen. And then her eyes fluttered open and those blue eyes that had held power over me from the very first moment met mine.

I loved this woman. The words lingered on my tongue, but everyone was watching and I couldn't say them, not now.

"You okay?" Aria asked in a whisper.

She asked me if I was okay? I was the one who'd failed protecting her. I'd have never forgiven myself if Aria had died today. "Yes," I pressed out through my tight throat. "But you aren't."

Aria's expression twisted with pain, but I couldn't loosen my hold on her wound.

"What about Gianna, Lily and Fabi?"

"Fine," Gianna shouted, still pressed up to my brother. Aria's eyes went unfocused once more. She needed treatment. Now.

I let go of Aria's wound and carefully lifted her into my arms. Her pained cry made me tense, but worse were the tears trailing down her pale cheeks. I carried her into the entrance hall, which was by now crowded with my soldiers. Most of the attackers were dead, and those who weren't would soon wish for death.

"I'll take you to the hospital," I said.

Matteo appeared in front of me. "Luca, let the Doc handle it. He's been taking care of our business for years."

I scowled at my brother. If I wasn't carrying Aria, I would have shoved him out of the way. "No," I growled. "Aria needs proper care. She's lost too much blood."

"I can do a blood transfusion," said Doc as he entered the mansion.

I narrowed my eyes at him. Aria touched my arm. "It's okay, Luca. Let him take care of me. I don't want you to take me to a hospital. It's too dangerous."

I searched Aria's face. She was begging me to agree. Aria was too selfless, too good. I nodded slowly, realizing why she did it. She wanted me to appear strong. Aria wasn't a weakness. I tore my eyes away and jerked my head toward the Doc. "Follow me!"

Aria went slack in my hold again.

"I have to get everything I need from the car," Doc said.

"Hurry," I growled as I carried Aria up the stairs and into a bedroom. I put her down on the mattress gently then stroked her cheek. "I love you, Aria," I said quietly. Admitting it aloud, even when no one could hear me, felt like a huge step. I bent down and kissed her forehead but straightened when I heard steps.

Doc limped inside with his female assistant. He sometimes worked with a guy as well, but he probably knew I wouldn't have let a young man anywhere near my wife.

"I need to take a look at her injury," Doc said carefully.

I took a step back so he could pass but stayed close. I wouldn't leave Aria alone with anyone in her state. Doc eyed me briefly before he bent over her. He felt her pulse then lifted one eyelid to check her eyes before he continued with more examinations.

"Will she be okay?" I asked tightly.

Doc glanced up, his brows crinkling. "Of course. But she needs a blood transfusion. B-positive."

"I'm O-positive," I said immediately. "Take my blood. Don't waste time."

Doc didn't argue with me. I held out my arm as he prepared everything for the direct transfusion.

I glanced back down at my wife, lying helplessly in front of me. "Can you remove her shirt?" Doc asked me respectfully.

I hesitated, but then I took my knife and cut open Aria's t-shirt. Her white bra was covered in blood, but I left it on.

Doc checked her wound while his assistant shoved the needle into my arm then into Aria's. When my blood finally entered Aria's veins, I relaxed. I kept a close eye on the Doc as he removed the bullet from Aria's wound and stitched it up. Guilt cut me deeply at the sight. It would always serve as my reminder to protect her.

My gaze returned to Aria's pale face. It was difficult to stay put and not to kiss her forehead and hold her as close as possible. Eventually the transfusion was done and the Doc and his assistant left. I was alone with Aria for the first time. I stretched out beside her and carefully cradled her in my arm, burying my nose in her hair. Closing my eyes, I tried to calm my still racing pulse. Aria would be fine. Only a small scar, nothing else, but I doubted I could ever forget the moment I thought I'd lost her. "I won't ever lose you, *principessa*," I murmured against her temple.

Matteo stepped in without knocking. His eyes took in the sight of me holding Aria against me and, for once, I didn't give a fuck. I trusted my brother, even with this truth.

"How is she?" he asked quietly as he walked closer.

"Still knocked out from the pain meds the Doc gave her. She won't wake for a few more hours."

"The Doc will stay in one of the guestrooms in case we need him."

"Good," I said, peering down at Aria's face once more.

"We're going to start interrogating the Russian bastards. I assume you want to be part of it."

I wanted to tear into them, but the idea of leaving Aria right now made my pulse speed up. "I'll join you later."

Surprise crossed Matteo's face. "I can't promise there'll be much left for you then."

"Focus on one of the fuckers and leave the others for me," I pressed out, meeting my brother's stare. He searched my eyes then nodded slowly before he walked out.

I must have fallen asleep because I jerked awake when an earsplitting scream rang out in the house. Aria was still knocked out beside me. I carefully slid my arm out from under her, grabbed my gun and rushed out of the room. I listened for a possible attack, but it was quiet in the house except for the wail.

It took me a moment to realize it was Liliana who made the sound. Locking Aria's door, I stormed downstairs then followed the screaming into the basement, finding Gianna and Liliana down there. The sight of the tortured Russian must have made Liliana snap. I didn't give a fuck. All that mattered was that Aria didn't wake. She'd be upset.

It took Matteo, Romero and me almost fifteen minutes to silence Liliana and take her up to her room and Gianna back into her bedroom under loud protests.

"Damn it," I growled when I was alone with Matteo.

He was covered in blood and had an excited gleam in his eyes. "Are you going to help us now?"

My eyes darted to the master bedroom. "I want the Doc to check on Aria again, then I'll join you."

"I've never seen you like this," Matteo said.

I didn't comment. "Send the Doc."

After the Doc had checked on Aria, I finally allowed Gianna to visit her sister and I joined my brother down in the basement.

The second I entered, my men stepped back from our captives. Romero gave me a tight smile. Matteo motioned at the left fucker. He wasn't as bad off as the guy on the right. That was the bastard Matteo seemed to have a particular interest in.

I rolled up my sleeves as I approached my target. "So Vitali wanted to get his dirty hands on my wife?"

I stared down at the bastard who gave me a bloody smile. "We would have fucked the slut. Every single hole. That's what three-hole-sluts are for."

My smile widened as I brought my face close to his. "Let's see how many of your holes I get to fuck with my blade before you apologize for calling my wife a slut."

He spat against my chest. "I won't apologize to an Italian whore."

I straightened and held out my hand toward Matteo, who handed me one of his knives. "Before your death, you will call her queen."

———————————>———————————

I was covered in blood from head to toe as I knelt beside the whimpering Russian bastard and leaned down to his ear. "Tell me again who's my wife?"

I held the blood-covered blade in front of the eye he still had. He whimpered.

"I can prolong this for at least another hour, maybe more," I said with a smile.

"She's..she's a queen," he choked out.

"That's right." I rammed my blade into his eye, ending his miserable existence.

———————✕———————

I stepped out of the shower in the guest bedroom when I heard knocking. I quickly wrapped a towel around my waist and hurried toward the door, ripping it open and staring at the redhead.

She frowned. "Trying to wash off the blood?"

"What do you want?" I growled. I was still on edge from the day's events and had no patience for her snark.

"I thought you'd like to know that Aria is awake."

I returned into the bedroom and got dressed quickly, then stormed toward the master bedroom barefoot.

The second I saw Aria, my heart thudded wildly in my chest. Dark shadows spread out under her gorgeous blue eyes and she gave me a small smile.

My legs carried me toward her and I kissed her forehead. To my surprise, Gianna left without hesitation.

"Do you need morphine?" I asked.

"Yeah."

I injected Aria with the morphine then held her hand in mine, needing to touch her.

"Did we lose someone?" she asked.

"A few. Cesare and a couple of soldiers," I said before I added, "and Umberto."

Sadness flashed in Aria's eyes. "I know. I saw him get shot."

I couldn't feel sad over the men we'd lost because Aria was here.

Aria swallowed. "What did that guy Vitali mean when he said you had something that belonged to him?"

"We intercepted one of their drug deliveries. But that's not important now." The only thing that mattered was keeping Aria safe.

"What is important then?" she whispered.

"That I almost lost you. That I saw you get shot," I got out, remembering that moment. I'd never felt this way, like a part of me was ripped out because of another person. "You're lucky the bullet only hit your shoulder. The Doc says it'll heal completely and you'll be able to use your arm like before."

Aria blinked slowly and the corners of her mouth twitched up briefly. The meds were dragging her down again.

I moved my face close to hers. "Don't do that ever again," I rasped.

She tilted her head as if she didn't know what I meant. "What?"

"Taking a bullet for me."

Aria squeezed my hand lightly, her eyelids dropping. "I'll always take a bullet for you." She fell asleep before I could say another word.

I kissed her lips lightly. "I won't allow it. Never again."

CHAPTER 25

A ria slept through most of the day, only waking a few times to talk to her siblings. I tried to visit her as often as possible, but I had to talk to my Captains and Dante on the phone. I wouldn't go to New York for a meeting until I could take Aria with me into the city, and she was still too shaky.

Things began to calm down a bit when her family left for Chicago, and I'd ordered my Captains to wait with attacks on the Bratva until we had the perfect target. I didn't want to lose more men with attacks in blind rage. We needed to hit them where it hurt.

After my last call, I made my way back to the master bedroom. Water was running in the bathroom so I sat down on the bed, waiting for Aria. When she finally emerged, she was fumbling with her nightgown, trying to slip the second strap on her shoulder, but with her injury it was impossible.

"Done with business?" she asked with a soft smile as I walked over to her. I led her toward the bed and gently pushed her down. Her eyes were clear and kind, not pain-filled and drug-hazed. My Aria.

"I'm fine," Aria said firmly.

All the worry and fear I'd been feeling crashed down on me. I knelt before her and pressed my face into her stomach. "I could have lost you two days ago."

Aria trembled. "But you didn't."

I met her soft gaze.

"Why did you do this? Why did you take a bullet for me?" If she'd died because of me, if I'd lost her, I'd have lost my mind. Even just thinking about it, reliving that moment when I thought she was dead, it ripped a huge black hole into my chest.

Aria's eyes became even softer. "Do you really not know why?"

Her expression told me why. Everything seemed to stand still. I knew what I felt for the woman in front of me, had known it with absolute certainty the second I almost lost her, but even before then I'd known the nature of my feelings but had clung to my doubts. I loved Aria. And how could I not? She was lovable. She was kind and gracious and forgiving. She was pure light. She was someone who deserved to be loved.

I didn't.

I knew what I was.

"I love you, Luca."

I cupped her face, bringing our faces close but never close enough. I searched her eyes, trying to understand how she could love me, how she found something in me that deserved to be loved. "You love me," I repeated. No one had ever said those words to me. No one should. "You shouldn't love me, Aria. I'm not someone who should be loved. People fear me, they hate me, they respect me, they admire me, but they don't love me. I'm a killer. I'm good

335

at killing. Better probably than at anything else, and I don't regret it. Fuck, sometimes I even enjoy it. That's a man you want to love?"

Aria gave me that smile; the smile that burst like a ray of sunshine through my darkness, that warmed even my cold heart.

"It's not a matter of want, Luca. It's not like I could choose to stop loving you," she whispered.

Few things in her life had been her choice. It was only fitting that even her feelings for me weren't. She was as trapped in her love for me as she was trapped in this marriage. "And you hate that you love me. I remember you saying it before."

Aria shook her head. "No. Not anymore. I know you aren't a good man. I've always known it, and I don't care. I know I should. I know I should lie awake at night hating myself for being okay with my husband being the boss of one of the most brutal and deadliest crime organizations in the States. But I don't. What does that make me?" Aria shifted her head in my hold, glancing down at her hands in her lap with a small frown. "And I killed a man and I don't feel sorry. Not one bit. I would do it again." She met my gaze and her eyes were full of love. No hate, no regret, nothing but love. "What does that make me, Luca? I'm a killer like you."

"You did what you had to. He deserved to die." I wished I could have killed him, not just because I wanted each and every single Bratva fucker to suffer as much as possible but also because I didn't want Aria to be burdened with death.

"There's not one of us who doesn't deserve death. We probably deserve it more than most," Aria whispered.

"You are good, Aria. You are innocent. I forced you into this." How could she compare herself to me? She didn't know what I'd done, what I enjoyed doing. She had killed to protect someone she loved. I killed for many reasons, few of them noble or altruistic.

"You didn't, Luca. I was born into this world. I chose to stay in this world. Being born into our world means being born with blood on your hands. With every breath we take, sin is engraved deeper into our skin."

"You don't have a choice. There's no way to escape our world. You didn't have a choice in marrying me either. If you'd let that bullet kill me, you would have at least escaped our marriage."

She wouldn't have been free because freedom didn't exist in our world, but Matteo wouldn't have forced her to marry again.

"There are few good things in our world, Luca, and if you find one, you cling to it with all your might. You are one of those good things in my life."

My chest swelled with love. "I'm not good."

"You're not a good man, no. But you are good for me. I feel safe in your arms. I don't know why, I don't even know why I love you, but I do, and that won't change."

I had to close my eyes against the fierce emotion in her expression. "Love is a risk in our world, and a weakness a Capo can't afford." I'd believed in those words all my life. I should still believe in them if I wanted to be an invincible Capo.

"I know," Aria whispered miserably.

I looked at her. Didn't she know? Couldn't she see? "But I don't care, because loving you is the only pure thing in my life."

Aria's eyes filled with tears and incredulity. "You love me?"

"Yes, even if I shouldn't. If my enemies knew how much you meant to me, they'd do anything to get their hands on you, to hurt me through you, to control me by threatening you. The Bratva will try again, and others will too. When I became a Made Man, I swore to put the Famiglia first, and I reinforced that same oath when I became a Capo dei Capi even though I knew I was lying. My first choice should always be the Famiglia."

Aria watched me with parted lips as if she didn't trust her ears.

"But you are my first choice, Aria. I'll burn down the world if I have to. I'll kill and maim and blackmail. I'll do anything for you." She couldn't possibly fathom what I'd do for her, the length I'd go to protect her. The Russian fucker today had gotten a taste and anyone else who dared to insult or hurt her would end the same way. "Maybe love is a risk, but it's a risk I'm willing to take and, as you said, it's not a choice. I never thought I would, never thought I *could* love someone like that, but I fell in love with you. I fought it. It's the first battle I didn't mind losing."

Aria wrapped her arms around me, her tears falling onto my neck. She twitched with a whimper when her shoulder bumped against me. I withdrew slowly, worried about hurting her. "You need to rest. Your body needs to heal."

I gently pushed her down until she lay back, but she dug her fingers into my biceps. She peered up at me through her lashes. "I don't want to rest. I want to make love to you."

My eyes darted down to her beautiful legs then back to her pleading face. I wanted nothing more than to be as close to Aria as possible, but she was injured. "I'm going to hurt you. Your stitches could rip open."

Aria caressed my chest then my stomach until her fingers reached the growing bulge in my pants. I stifled a groan when she began rubbing me lightly.

Her expression turned teasing. "He agrees with me."

"He always does, but he's not the voice of reason, believe me," I muttered.

Aria laughed only to flinch a moment later.

She was in pain. "That's what I mean."

"Please. I want to make love to you. I've wanted this for a long time." Her begging broke down my resolve piece by piece.

"I've always made love to you, Aria," I admitted. The feelings I hadn't understood in the beginning and fought later, they had been there when I'd

338

taken Aria's virginity. It was the first time I'd made love, and Aria would always be the only woman I'd make love to.

Aria rubbed me harder. "Don't you want this?"

I almost laughed. "Of course I want it. We almost lost each other. I want nothing more than to be as close to you as possible."

"Then make love to me. Slow and gentle."

And my last wall crumbled as it always did with Aria. "Slow and gentle," I agreed.

I knelt at the end of the bed and massaged Aria's feet and calves, enjoying the feel of her soft skin. Aria parted her legs and my eyes took her up on the invitation. My cock jerked at the sight of her soaked panties. Groaning, I pressed a kiss to her ankle.

I trailed my fingers up her leg until I brushed over her crotch. She was so wet and hot. "You make slow and gentle really hard on me. If you weren't hurt, I'd bury myself in you and make you scream my name."

"If I wasn't hurt, I'd want you to do it."

I suckled Aria's ankle. "Mine." I kissed her calf. "Mine." Then her knee. "Mine." Her thigh. "Mine." Until I finally reached her pussy. I dragged her panties down before I wedged myself between her thighs. I planted a kiss on her folds. "Mine."

Aria moaned then whimpered in pain because she'd moved.

"I want you to relax completely. No tensing your muscles, or your shoulder will hurt," I ordered as I brushed my lips along her crease.

"I always tense up when I come. And I really, really want to come."

I'd make her come as often as she wanted, not just today but for the rest of our lives. "You will, but no tensing."

Aria gave me a look that made it clear that wouldn't work.

I began pleasuring her with my lips and tongue, keeping my ministrations light and gentle, guiding her slowly toward her release. Aria's breathless moans and her body's arousal spurred me on until it took everything not to dry hump the edge of the mattress. When Aria finally came, her body seemed to go even softer, her legs falling open as she surrendered to pleasure.

I got out of my clothes and positioned myself between Aria's legs. I entered her slowly, watching her face as she moaned low and sweet.

"Mine," I said when I was buried all the way inside her.

Aria held my gaze as I made love to her gently.

"Yours," she whispered, her expression the greatest declaration of love I could imagine.

All my life I'd thought becoming Capo would be the biggest triumph of my life. Not the happiest day, because I hadn't known true happiness. But now, as I met Aria's loving gaze, I knew that she was my greatest victory. Only she brought happiness into days of blood and violence, only she could fill my dark world with light.

She was my light, my love…my life.

With the smile that always got me, she pressed her palm against my Famiglia tattoo, right over my heart. A cruel heart that only beat for her.

"Mine," she said without doubt.

I held her gaze. "Always."

BOOKS BY
CORA REILLY

BORN IN BLOOD MAFIA CHRONICLES

Bound by Honor

(Aria & Luca)

Bound by Duty

(Valentina & Dante)

Bound by Hatred

(Gianna & Matteo)

Bound By Temptation

(Liliana & Romero)

Bound By Vengeance

(Growl & Cara)

Bound By Love

(Luca & Aria)

COMING SOON:

Bound by the Past

(Dante & Valentina)

THE CAMORRA CHRONICLES:

Twisted Loyalties

(Fabiano)

Twisted Emotions

(Nino)

Twisted Pride

(Remo)

ABOUT THE AUTHOR

Cora Reilly is the author of the Born in Blood Mafia Series, the Camorra Chronicles and many other books, most of them featuring dangerously sexy bad boys. Before she found her passion in romance books, she was a traditionally published author of young adult literature.

Cora lives in Germany with a cute but crazy Bearded Collie, as well as the cute but crazy man at her side. When she doesn't spend her days dreaming up sexy books, she plans her next travel adventure or cooks too spicy dishes from all over the world.

Despite her law degree, Cora prefers to talk books to laws any day.

Made in the USA
Monee, IL
01 October 2023

43806006R00203